Other Books by Lynn Bohart

NOVELS
Giorgio Salvatori Mysteries
Mass Murder
Murder In The Past Tense

Old Maids of Mercer Island Mysteries
Inn Keeping With Murder
A Candidate For Murder
A History of Murder
All Roads Lead to Murder

Stand Alone
Grave Doubts

SHORT STORY BOOKS
Your Worst Nightmare
Something Wicked

THE ESSENCE OF MURDER
A Detective Giorgio Salvatori Mystery

By
Lynn Bohart

Cover Art by
Mina Smith

ACKNOWLEDGEMENTS
There are so many people I rely on to bring these books to you. They include the writing group I belong who reads the books two chapters at a time over a period of 8–10 months, helping me to clarify the story and the characters and eliminating things that just don't work: Tim McDaniel, Michael Manzer, Gary Larson, Irma Fritz, and Jenae Cartwright. I also rely on a group of "beta" readers who read the final draft from cover-to-cover. My thanks go to Karen Gilb and my daughter, Jaynee Bohart. I would be lost without my friend and colleague, Liz Stewart, who not only serves as my editor but listens to my endless ramblings as I work out the plot. My deepest thanks go to Dr. Katherine Taylor, forensic anthropologist and King County Medical Examiner who helped with some of the forensics information. Additional thanks go to Carl Ueland, retired police officer, who vetted the book from a law enforcement angle. I'd also like to thank Dr. Richard Wall, a pulmonologist in Renton, WA, who gave me the idea to use GHB and Dr. Alana Curatola, my ophthalmologist, who gave me advice on cataract examinations.

Thanks also to my friend, Mina Smith, my cover designer who is a wonderful artist who sells her work on Etsy. Thanks, too, to my close friend Dakoda Mondragon. An artist in his own right who not only 'nudged' me to finally finish the book but manipulated the cover for the paperback version. And a big shoutout to my daughter, Jaynee, for just being my biggest supporter. I rely on her balanced advice and creative abilities to brainstorm story details with me.

Disclaimer: This book is a work of fiction and while many of the businesses, locations, and organizations referenced in the book are real, they are used in a way that is purely fictional.

Dedicated to the many friends who have followed me on this writing journey and whose endless support and love continues to nourish my creative soul.
You know who you are.

CHAPTER ONE

She had read once that Xanax was the brake pedal needed to slow a speeding car fueled by anxiety. The drug was that good. And, God knows, she needed it.

After all, her anxieties had sabotaged her life at every turn. The large dose she had taken of Xanax just an hour earlier had begun to work like a tranquilizer on her neurotransmitters, neutralizing the fears that threatened to turn the upcoming ceremony into a disaster.

But there was something else. She could feel it.

Another 'something' pulsed through her veins. It was a different feeling all together and left her with a mind-bending sense of euphoria. In fact, it was a different drug. She knew it. Coupled with the Xanax, her claustrophobic anxieties were not just being numbed—they were being stripped away one by one.

But where had this other drug come from? And what was it?

She lay on what the group referred to as the altar, bare except for a light, cotton sheath covering her naked body. When someone came close and touched her skin, she flinched despite the drugs, sparking a fear that registered somewhere deep within her brain.

It was her fear of needles.

She knew this ceremony included being pierced by the essence device. It was the main reason she had taken the Xanax. Now, memories surfaced of epic struggles at the doctor's or dentist's office when she was young. In those days, she would be reduced to episodes of primeval crying, screaming, and lashing out. Once, when a dental assistant had attempted to inject her with Novocain, she'd jerked, and her arm slammed into the poor woman's nose, nearly breaking it.

Now, as her ears sought out the muffled voices of the people nearby, she contemplated the biofeedback class her sister had suggested the year before. She had gone to it reluctantly. But it had done wonders, giving her the courage to take control of her life.

She had conquered her fear of heights by forcing herself to learn rock-climbing. She'd even grown to like it. To overcome her dread of public speaking, she'd joined Toast Masters and found that once she got past the fact she was facing a room full of people, she was good at waxing poetic on random topics.

And then, a few weeks ago, a friend had encouraged her to join The Essence of Life Society.

"It's a group of people who practice vampirism," her friend had whispered conspiratorially over lunch. *"It's very exciting."*

She had scoffed at the idea. No respectable person would join a group like that. But her friend wasn't eccentric. She held down a perfectly normal job and even went to church on Sundays. And her friend named other professional people who belonged to the group. A teacher. A marketing consultant. Even a lawyer.

Upon further reflection, the idea had begun to intrigue her, even titillate her. She wanted to know more. Especially when her friend showed her a picture of the leader of the group, a man referred to as The Maestro. His sex appeal almost jumped off the page, leaving her breathless.

In the end, she had decided to attend a meeting.

The moment she'd made the decision, she was rewarded with a rush of adrenalin which had left her giddy. After all, she would be entering a world filled with shadows and secrets; it was a world purposely hidden from the public and shunned by most of cultured society.

The thought of moving so far from the norm was exhilarating to someone who had lived a sheltered life. Now, even though she was naked under the sheer fabric of her initiation gown while a group of society members looked on, she was barely aware of any sense of impropriety. The drugs were working their magic. She felt as weightless as a leaf bobbing along with the current of a river.

She *was* aware of him, though—The Maestro. He was there. And he was close. His musky aftershave intoxicated her, and the anticipation of his touch was overpowering. She didn't care if she lived or died. There was no reality anymore, only a peaceful haze of recognition; she was about to be initiated into an exclusive club. She would become one with The Maestro and enter a world previously anathema to her.

She felt a movement next to her. He was there.

As he pressed against her, a cool breeze raised goosebumps along her arms and legs, and her nipples grew hard. Her breath came in short, spasmodic gasps. His hand skimmed across her breasts as he reached for her chin, and her skin reacted with small electrical pulses that scattered down her midriff and into her groin.

Her body was on fire, and she moaned with anticipated pleasure.

Something cold flicked against her neck. The essence device. It was the one thing she feared. But the image was lost in the shadows of her mind.

He placed the device onto her neck and settled his teeth into the prongs. She felt the sharp tips prick the flesh, causing short spasms of pain as it opened the vein.

It should have hurt. But it didn't. Not really. The pain was too fleeting. It registered dimly in the cortex of her brain as if that part of her body had gone to sleep.

As he brought her into a tight embrace and began to draw her blood into his mouth, the last thing she felt was his hand drifting beneath the hem of her gown and up her leg.

CHAPTER TWO

Detective Giorgio Salvatori sat at his desk drumming his fingers and gazing out the window at a crow that had landed on a telephone wire across the street. It was a late Monday afternoon in late February, and he was bored because there were no major cases on deck.

He slouched back in his chair and shifted his gaze to the empty Styrofoam coffee cup that sat on his desk bouncing to the rhythm of his drumming fingers. With a sigh, he stopped and allowed his gaze to take in the rest of the room, including the bank of four dented gray file cabinets that sat against the wall, piled high with file folders and loose papers. He knew he needed to get some filing done but cringed at the thought.

His eyes came back to his own wood grain desktop that had been marred by years' worth of cigarette burn marks, scratches, and coffee stains. He swept his fingers across the dented surface and stopped at a coffee stain shaped like a question mark.

The story this desk could tell, he thought. *Arguments. Promotions. Demotions. Firings. Murders.*

Murder.

He didn't wish for a murder. Who would? In fact, his stomach grew queasy at the memory of the case they had just finished—the investigation of seven young women who had been tortured and buried decades earlier on the grounds of an historical bed and breakfast.

No, he didn't wish for a murder case.

But he would take a simple carjacking or store break-in. Even a drug bust. Instead, he'd been relegated to a cold case that was so cold it was frozen. Literally. A refrigeration repair man had disappeared while on the road in 1990. There were no leads. And no one left to talk to.

The man's wife had died in early 2012, and the couple had no children. Most of the man's friends had moved, and the company he'd worked for had gone out of business. But the mayor was related to the victim, and so the case was front and center again.

As lead detective for the Sierra Madre Police Department, Giorgio oversaw major crimes. The problem was there weren't any right now. So, he began to drum his fingers again, pondering what his wife, Angie, might be cooking for dinner.

The phone rang, making him pause mid-drumroll. The sixth sense he'd relied on his entire life activated the acid in his stomach. He reached out and grabbed the receiver.

"Salvatori," he said.

"Joe, this is Simmons on dispatch. You've got a call. Should I put it through?"

"Do you know what it's about?"

"Pretty sure it's a kid. He sounds scared. Said his dad told him to call you."

"Okay, I'll talk to him." He heard a clicking sound and then, "Hello?"

"This is Detective Salvatori. Who am I talking to?"

"My name's Shorty Daniels. There's…there's a dead body," the boy said in a faltering voice.

"Hold on," Giorgio replied, sitting forward in his chair. "Where are you?"

"Me and my friends…we're up…up…in…in Bailey Canyon. There's a body in the stream. My dad told me to call you."

The boy's voice wavered as he sucked in air.

"Who's your dad?"

"Larry Daniels. He works for search and rescue."

"Sure. I know your dad. Okay, tell me exactly where you are." Giorgio grabbed a notepad and pencil.

"At the trailhead. We came back here to make the call. It's a woman."

"And you're sure she's dead?"

"Yeah. My dad taught me how to take a pulse. She's dead, all right."

"Any sign of how she died?"

"No," the boy said in a soft voice. "But she's not wearing much."
    "What do you mean?"

"Like no shoes. No socks. No…you know…underwear. Just a dress."

"Okay, wait there," Giorgio ordered. "Don't move, and don't touch anything."

"Okay," the kid said. "But you're coming?"

"I'll be there as soon as I can." He hung up and swung into action.

Dead bodies were not common in a town of 18,000, and yet they'd had two cases within the last few months that had involved multiple murders. And each case had turned the department upside down.

Giorgio was accustomed to investigating murder cases, having served as a New York City police detective for several years. But the truth was that murder cases were unpredictable. So, as much as he wanted to leave the refrigerator repairman case behind, Giorgio silently hoped the body in Bailey Canyon was just the result of an accident or a heart attack.

He got up and leaned around the doorjamb. "Hey, McCready, call my brother. He's out interviewing that old lady whose mail was stolen. Tell him to meet us up at the trailhead to Bailey Canyon. We have a body."

The young officer's blue eyes lit up. "Really? Want me to go with you?"

"Yeah. Swan's not back until later this week. Call Rocky and then get Mulhaney. I'm calling a homicide protocol. This death is suspicious if nothing else, so we'll get the M.E. and the forensics team out there. I'll let the captain know. Meet you out back."

÷

Ten minutes later, he and McCready were headed north on Baldwin Avenue with Francis Mulhaney, the department's photographer, in the back seat. Giorgio drove, while McCready toyed with his iPad, and Mulhaney changed the batteries in his camera.

Sierra Madre was a small, bedroom community to Los Angeles and sat at the foot of the San Gabriel Mountains. Most officers in the department did double duty. Mulhaney and McCready were no exceptions. Mulhaney helped manage the evidence room, search case files, and document crime scenes. McCready conducted most of the cell phone and bank account searches. Since the town was flanked on three sides by larger cities, they often borrowed resources, such as the medical examiner and forensics team. Lately, Giorgio felt like he had them all on speed dial.

Despite the layer of leaden clouds overhead, Giorgio realized his mood had lifted. He had a case.

Bailey Canyon was a popular hiking destination on the northeast side of town. It was named after R. J. Bailey, who had homesteaded the area in 1875. Giorgio had never explored the area, but his son Tony had hiked into the canyon with his Cub Scout troop the year before.

They pulled into the canyon parking lot a little after three o'clock. Late afternoon shadows were already beginning to blanket the hillsides, spilling onto the edges of the park entrance. Three young boys huddled together next to a sign that posted park hours. Giorgio glanced into the rearview mirror as he pulled into a parking spot. Their faces were drawn and pale. Most likely, they'd never seen a corpse up close before.

Giorgio glanced around the nearly empty lot as he exited the sedan, his cop's brain taking over. The parking lot was at the north end of Grove Street, surrounded by scrub oaks and smooth, red-barked manzanita trees. The park bathrooms sat across from where the boys stood, along with three trash cans, each chained to a picnic table. There were only two cars in the lot. One was an old beater pickup truck. The other was a city maintenance vehicle parked next to the restrooms.

As his gaze roamed the lot for other signs of life, he inhaled the woody aroma of the manzanita and felt his chest expand with the fresh air of the outdoors. When he turned back, a tall, thin boy stepped forward.

Shorty had a rash of black hair and a splatter of freckles across an angular nose. Inwardly, Giorgio smiled at the contrast between the boy's nickname and his height. He'd once had a friend in New York whose nickname was Sugar, and yet had the nastiest personality of anyone he'd ever met.

"Are you Shorty?" Giorgio asked him.

"Yeah," the boy replied.

"Where's your dad?" Giorgio asked him.

"He's working in Pomona."

"Why'd you call your dad first?"

"We didn't know what to do," the boy said with a shrug.

Giorgio's eyes flitted to the boys on either side of Shorty. One was ten to fifteen pounds overweight, while the other, an Asian kid, was almost tiny in stature with delicate facial features. They hung back, letting Shorty take the lead.

"You're that cop who solved all those monastery murders," the overweight kid blurted. His small brown eyes had come alive with excitement. "My mom thinks you're hot."

Short chuckles from McCready and Mulhaney made Giorgio turn to them with a stern look. Their smiles evaporated, replaced quickly by vain attempts to appear serious.

Giorgio turned back to the boys. "Okay, let's have your names." He pulled out a notebook.

"I'm Shorty…uh, Robert Daniels. This is Jason McKay." He pointed to the overweight boy.

"And I'm Steve Liu," the third boy said with a slight raise of his hand. "We were following the creek up past the switchbacks."

"Why were you up there?" Giorgio asked.

"We have a fort just off the Canyon View Trail," Steve said. "We come up on the weekends and after school to hang out when the weather's nice."

"We're not in any trouble, are we?" Jason asked.

Sweat glistened on the bridge of his nose, and he kept opening and closing his fingers into a fist.

"No. Not yet, anyway," Giorgio replied.

The boy's nervousness reminded Giorgio of when he and his best friend, Jake, had commandeered an old building in their Queens neighborhood when he was young. The building had been a women's lingerie company until it had gone out of business and been abandoned. The two boys had found a way into the building through an air vent and set up shop with some other friends, calling themselves the *Corner Street Club*. They had spent hours there reading comic books, talking about girls, and playing hooky. Unfortunately, Officer Ricci, a local beat cop, had followed them one day and confronted them as they were leaving. The first thing Giorgio asked was, *"We're not in any trouble, are we?"*

Giorgio turned to McCready and Mulhaney. "One of you go see if you can find that city worker and ask him if he knows anything. The other can get the license plate off that pickup truck and run the numbers." After the two officers left, he turned back to the boys. "And you're sure this woman is dead?"

"Yes, sir," Shorty said. "I took her pulse, and her eyes are open and glassed over."

"Did you see anyone else on the trail?"

"No. Well, just Mr. Phillips," Jason replied.

"We didn't actually see him on the trail," Shorty corrected him. "He was just leaving the parking lot when we got here."

"Who's Mr. Phillips?" Giorgio asked.

Eyewitness statements were notoriously unreliable, but it was still better to glean as much information from them while facts were fresh and before they had time to doubt their memories.

At Giorgio's question, the boys glanced at each other as though they had gotten someone they knew in trouble. Finally, it seemed like a silent message passed between them, and Steve Liu turned to Giorgio.

"He's a teacher at Bethany Christian."

"The elementary school?"

"Yeah. We see him up here a lot. I think he just comes here to jog or exercise or something."

"Have you ever actually seen him jogging?" Giorgio asked, looking up along the trail. "Seems pretty rocky for jogging."

"Um…well, no," Steve admitted, throwing a nervous glance at Shorty.

"We've seen him on the trail, though," Shorty added.

"What kind of car does he drive?"

"An old Range Rover," Shorty replied. "Hey, listen, I…I don't think he had anything to do with this. I mean…he's a nice guy. He was my sister's fourth-grade teacher." The boy's voice cracked.

"Okay, we need to see the body," Giorgio said.

Mulhaney appeared at Giorgio's side. "I spoke to the park guy. He just got here and went straight into the john to clean it. He didn't see anything."

"And I got the license plate from the truck," McCready said, appearing behind Mulhaney. He was staring at the tablet in his hands. "The truck belongs to a Robert Cincera. He's a 24-year old who lives here in Sierra Madre."

"What do we know about the body?" Mulhaney asked.

Giorgio turned to the boys. It was Steve Liu who spoke up.

"She's just lying there, half in and half out of the water," he said. He shifted his weight from one foot to the other like he had to pee. "She's not wearing much. You know? You can see…well…you can see her…" He stopped and looked at the ground in embarrassment.

"Okay, we've got to get going." He turned to McCready. "You wait for the M.E."

Just then, the sound of tires on gravel made everyone turn as a mortuary vehicle pulled into the parking lot. Two men in blue coveralls climbed out and opened the back to pull out a gurney. Giorgio walked over and stopped them with a raised hand.

"Looks like we're hiking in," he said. "Better bring the stretcher."

Giorgio turned to McCready. "Can you make sure to record everyone's name? Also, the time and temperature."

McCready nodded. "Way ahead of you," he said, holding up his notebook.

As the mortuary technicians unloaded the stretcher, McCready moved over to get their names. As they closed the rear doors, a large, black SUV pulled up with the words *L.A. County Medical Examiner* stenciled on the door. A tall, lanky man dressed in a black suit and tie emerged holding a medical bag. He nodded at Giorgio as a woman in her fifties climbed out of the passenger side door.

"Dr. Pearce," Giorgio said, greeting him.

"We're seeing too much of each other these days, Detective."

"Agreed," Giorgio replied.

"You were lucky. We were just finishing up a meeting in Arcadia. This is Kate Colburn. She's a forensics pathologist."

"Nice to meet you," Giorgio said to the woman.

Her brown eyes flicked towards him, and she nodded.

"Well, let's hope this situation is simpler than the last one," he said to Dr. Pearce.

"Amen to that," he said. "Let's get this over with."

Giorgio nodded and turned to the boys. "Okay, we'll follow you."

CHAPTER THREE

The group of six men and one woman set off, trailing behind the boys. As they passed an informational kiosk that listed the flora and fauna native to the area, McCready asked Giorgio, "Ever been up here?"

"No. But Tony has. He earned some sort of merit badge by studying the kinds of plants that grow up here."

The group entered the canyon by a narrow path and crossed a short, wooden bridge that spanned Bailey Canyon Creek. They moved onto an unpaved road and continued until they found a marker for *Canyon View Nature Trail.*

They were just about to veer off, when a young man and woman appeared along an intersecting trail about fifty yards to their left. The man was dressed in faded jeans and a long-sleeved t-shirt and had longish brown hair. The woman wore jeans and a t-shirt with a denim jacket. They casually chatted as they approached until the man finally looked up and stopped short, surprised by the group on the trail in front of him. Giorgio gestured to McCready to join him, and the two officers approached the couple.

"I'm Detective Salvatori," he said, showing his badge. "This is Officer McCready. We're with the Sierra Madre police. Are you Robert Cincera?"

The young man nodded, his eyes darting back and forth between the two officers.

"We believe there may have been an accident," Giorgio said.

Cincera inhaled at the news, and the woman reached for his hand.

"Where?" Cincera asked.

"On the Canyon View Trail. We need to ask…did you see anything? Anyone else on the trail or in the parking lot?"

The couple glanced at each other with furrowed brows and then both shook their heads.

"We got here about two hours ago," Cincera said. "There was a guy just getting out of his car, but we never saw him again. I just assumed he used the other trail." He gestured toward the Canyon View Trail.

"Did he get out of a Range Rover?" McCready asked.

"Yeah. An old one," Cincera replied.

"And you never saw him again?"

"No," he said with a shrug.

"What'd he look like?"

The man looked at his companion, who shrugged.

"Sorry, um…I didn't pay attention."

"Did you hear anything while you were up there? Voices. Shouts. Anything?"

"No, sorry. The trails split off from one another. We were by ourselves the entire time."

"And that's your old truck over there?" Giorgio turned and pointed to the old truck in the parking lot.

"Yeah."

"Okay, just in case, we'll need your names and contact information." Giorgio gestured to McCready. "And please give me a call if you think of anything." He handed the man his card, while McCready stepped forward, ready to write.

McCready took down the couple's information, while the rest of the group moved off onto the Canyon View Trail. As the couple left, McCready caught up to the others.

The canyon was filled with dense chaparral, large evergreen bushes, and tall sycamores, and huge pine trees dotted the upper reaches of the canyon. The path was a few feet wide and weaved around rocks and woody shrubs as it followed along the west side of the gurgling stream.

They hadn't gone a hundred yards before Giorgio heard his name called and turned to find his brother, Rocky, jogging up behind them. Everyone stopped, allowing Rocky to come up next to Giorgio.

"What do we got?" he asked, stopping to catch his breath.

"Don't know yet," Giorgio said. "Just that it's the body of a woman lying in the creek. These kids found her," he said, gesturing to the three boys.

Four years separated the two brothers in age; Giorgio was 37, and Rocky was 33. Their dark, wavy hair, dark eyes, and olive skin marked them as siblings. But at six-foot three, Rocky towered over everyone but the medical examiner. While Giorgio was shorter and stockier, Rocky had the good looks that Giorgio always noted but never envied. After all, he considered himself to be the cleverer of the two, and his early success as a detective proved it. According to his old partner in New York, Giorgio had the 'touch,' meaning he was able to piece the puzzles together necessary to solve complex crimes.

They continued along the winding dirt path until the trail split off onto a smaller one. Bailey Canyon cut deep into the foothills that stood as a backdrop to the small town of Sierra Madre. Giorgio was familiar with the wildfires that had devastated the area more than once and he glanced around as they progressed, picturing flames roaring down the canyon to obliterate the beauty that surrounded them now.

Shorty stayed on the main trail as it opened along the stream, cutting in and out of the trees and bushes that grew right up to the banks. At this time of year, mountain run-off pushed the water to the upper edges of the creek bed. At certain places, the creek was over fifty feet wide and a foot or more deep. During the spring, it would be even worse. Old logs and a few boulders forced the water to twist and turn, creating small pools and eddies along the banks.

Giorgio glanced down at the swirling water, wondering what they would find at the end of their trek. The death of a young woman was tragic no matter what the circumstances.

"You know, there's two new housing developments just above us," Rocky said from behind him. "I wonder if she lived close by."

Rocky's comment drew Giorgio's attention back to the task at hand. "Dunno," he replied, side-stepping a large rock. "But those housing developments are disturbing the wildlife. I've seen two recent reports of mountain lions in someone's backyard."

"Yeah, and a guy at the top of Michillinda Avenue saw a bear last week," McCready called out from the back. "We should keep our eyes out."

"So, do we think this is a homicide?" Rocky asked from behind Giorgio.

"Don't know that either," Giorgio replied over his shoulder. "The kids just reported a half-naked dead body."

As Giorgio walked on, anticipating what they might find, his mind wandered back to the last few months. He and Rocky had almost died investigating the murder of a young woman who had attended a conference at the old Catholic Monastery, which sat on the other side of the hill from where they were now. On the heels of that, they had become embroiled in the investigation of the seven murdered women. Now, he was hiking into the canyon where the lifeless body of another woman had been found. Life–or death as it were–was beginning to weigh heavy on him. And yet, the adrenalin had begun to course through his veins as it did whenever he began a new case.

As Giorgio trudged along, a chill pushed its way along his neck and down his back, making the hair on his arms stand on end. The suddenness of it made him shift his eyes to the trees and bushes that grew along the streambed and then up to the looming rock walls that lined the canyon.

He was being watched; he could sense it. And he knew exactly who it was.

It had happened so many times before, he recognized it for was it was. It was the boy—Christian Maynard. As his gaze skimmed the terrain, looking for the ghost of the ten-year-old boy who liked to insert himself into Giorgio's investigations, his sixth sense told him Christian was about to do it again. The boy's father had been a police officer, just like Giorgio, a fact revealed by a local psychic they had used on their last case. The only questions now were when and how the boy would present himself?

"Just up ahead," Shorty called out.

Giorgio's head whipped around, short-circuiting his thoughts about the boy.

He was first in line behind Jason, the overweight kid who was laboring up the switchbacks that allowed them to climb a short, but steep, incline. The group scrambled to the top of the hill, ducked under some low-hanging Manzanita branches, and rounded a corner before Shorty finally stopped.

"She's right over there," he said, pointing across the creek.

Giorgio stepped forward and glanced across the fast-flowing water to where the afternoon sun had broken through the clouds, sending streaks of sunlight down to bathe the half-naked body of a woman sprawled in the creek bed.

The picture was striking in its simplicity and almost artistic. And yet, Giorgio felt a pang of remorse. Yes, the case had interrupted his boredom but at the cost of a woman's life. Now, their work would begin to determine how and why she died.

He heaved a deep sigh. "Okay, did you boys touch her?"

Shorty's eyes narrowed. "I did. But just to take her pulse."

"Okay, stay here."

He turned and nodded to the rest of his team.

Giorgio led them into the mid-calf deep water, pushing through the current and over moss-covered rocks until they made it to the other side. He glanced back at Dr. Colburn, wondering what she thought about possibly ruining her shoes, but since she was dressed in lightweight pants and tennis shoes, she didn't seem to care.

The group spread out around the body, as Mulhaney pulled the camera off his shoulder and began snapping pictures. Several footprints were pressed into the sandy dirt leading up to the water's edge, and McCready began placing evidence markers out. Three sets of prints were clearly those of the boys. They were small and rounded, like tennis shoes. One set of prints was different, however. These shoe prints stood side-by-side, right next to the body.

"Someone stood here," Giorgio said, careful not to disturb the prints. "Looks like maybe size 11 or 12. Probably not the kids. But it still looks like a pair of running shoes. Make sure you get a shot of all of these," he said to Mulhaney. "We'll have to eliminate the boys."

He studied the prints for another moment and then noticed something that made him lean in.

"Look at this," he said to the others. He was pointing at a toe scrape in the damp sand closest to the dead woman's shoulder. "It looks like whoever was standing here may have raised one foot to lift her or turn her over."

Rocky peered over his shoulder. "I bet she was face down before. Whoever this was used his foot to push her shoulder back to get a look at her."

They both glanced across the water at the boys.

"Could be Shorty," Rocky surmised. "His feet might be big enough. I'll go talk to him."

As Rocky returned to the boys, Giorgio turned to Mulhaney. "We need to get close-ups and measurements of these. Did you bring casting material?"

"Yeah," Mulhaney said, tapping a leather bag hanging off his shoulder.

"Okay. Good."

"This is a boot print," Mulhaney said, pointing to the ground nearest the woman's head.

They all turned. Giorgio moved over next to where Mulhaney pointed.

"Looks like a man's," he said. "It's much larger than the others."

The heel print of what looked like a man's boot was pressed into the wet sand only twelve inches or so from the woman's feet. It had a unique imprint, with three triangles in a row down the middle of the insole.

"Yeah, that's too big for any of the kids," Giorgio said. "Also, look at that mark on the left side. It looks like a small chunk was cut out of it. Get a good shot of it," he told Mulhaney. "We might be able to ID the brand."

"I wonder why there's only one boot print, though," Dr. Coburn wondered out loud.

Giorgio glanced at her. "Could be he stepped into the water, and it got washed away. This looks like the left foot, which means he might have stepped into the water with his right foot."

"Makes sense," she said. "Looks like there are dimmer impressions that lead up to the water."

Giorgio stepped back and glanced at the body, while the ME waited to one side.

The woman in the water was Caucasian and lying on her left side, her feet almost on dry land. She was dressed in a sheer, muslin smock smudged in places with dirt. It floated around her bare hips like gossamer wings, exposing a red heart tattoo on her left ankle. The heart was accented by two drops of blood.

"Get a good picture of that tattoo," Giorgio told Mulhaney.

Mulhaney nodded as he scribbled measurements and notes into a notebook. Then, he swung his camera off his shoulder and zeroed in on the tattoo.

As Giorgio scanned the body, he noted she wasn't wearing undergarments, shoes, or jewelry.

That was curious. *Was the smock her night dress? And, if so, had she wandered away from home in the middle of the night?*

He glanced around again, wondering how a half-naked woman without shoes would have been able to hike into this place alone. Straining his neck, he looked up to the top of the canyon on both sides to see if homes had encroached this far into the hills. All he saw were trees and shrubs.

"There are no cuts or bruises on the bottom of her feet," Dr. Colburn said.

Giorgio leaned down to look. "You're right. I wonder how she got here without shoes."

The dead woman's bloated face was half submerged in water. She had been scratched in several places, but the water had washed away any blood.

Giorgio surmised she was in her late twenties to early thirties. She had shoulder-length brownish-blond hair, was short in stature and maybe twenty pounds overweight, with full breasts and hips. A scar on her left knee suggested she'd had surgery at some point in her life.

"None of the boys touched her other than to take her pulse," Rocky said, coming up behind Giorgio. "No one pushed her over, either. They said she was just like this when they found her."

"That means someone else was here before they were," Giorgio surmised.

Giorgio's mind went immediately to the man the boys identified as Mr. Phillips, who they saw leaving when they arrived. Did the larger soft-soled shoe prints belong to him?

They continued to place evidence markers anywhere there were shoe prints and where the woman's feet touched dry land. When Mulhaney was finished snapping photos of the body and the immediate surrounding area, he began to make a sketch of the scene while the medical examiner and Dr. Colburn stepped in to begin an examination. McCready stood back and took notes.

Dr. Pearce scanned her body for obvious injuries and then attempted to extend an arm. "She's still in full rigor," he said.

"It's cooler up here than down below, and she's been submerged in cold water," Dr. Colburn said.

"Right, so there's no way we can determine when she died," Pearce said. "My guess is within the last 48 hours, though." He pulled the woman's head forward and did a cursory search of her scalp and then moved her arms and legs around to check for wounds. "I don't scc any obvious injuries that might have caused her death."

"Did she die here?" Giorgio asked.

"I doubt it. See here, around her cuticles?" he said, lifting her right hand. "They're filled with dirt. She also has dirt in the crevices of her ear, in her hair, and around her eyes."

"What does that mean?" Giorgio asked.

The doctor gave Giorgio a solemn look. "That she's been buried."

A jolt shot through Giorgio. "Buried? And then dug up? Shit. So, we are looking at murder."

"Maybe," the medical examiner said. "Which also makes it more difficult to determine the time of death. If she were buried for any length of time, that would slow rigor down." He leaned forward and checked her eyes. "But there isn't any trace of bug activity yet, either."

"Which means what?" Rocky asked.

"Probably that she hasn't been here that long," Dr. Coburn said. "Maybe only overnight."

"But that's not all," Dr. Pearce added.

"What do you mean?" Giorgio asked, stepping in closer.

The medical examiner released a deep sigh and turned the victim's chin, exposing the side of her face that had been hidden by the water. Everyone leaned in for a better look.

"This," he said, pointing to two jagged puncture wounds along the vein in her neck.

"Damn!" Rocky mumbled. "We're looking for a vampire?"

CHAPTER FOUR

It was dark by the time they finished processing the scene, and the body had been removed. The boys had been released earlier in the afternoon into the care of their parents with the request they all come back to the station the next day for formal statements.

The next morning, Giorgio launched a search through missing persons files for the entire Los Angeles basin to try and ID their victim. Rocky attempted to find Mr. Phillips, the teacher the boys had seen in the canyon parking lot. And McCready conducted an internet search into the heart tattoo and wannabe vampire groups, while Mulhaney interviewed the kids a second time.

"I called the school asking for Phillips," Rocky said after a brief phone conversation. "They said he didn't show up for work yesterday or today."

Giorgio looked up from his computer. "That doesn't sound good."

"Agreed," Rocky agreed. "Anyway, I'm going to find his wife."

"Yeah. Maybe he's just sick or something, but if so, it's a pretty big…"

"Coincidence," Rocky interrupted him. "Yeah, I know. And you don't believe in coincidences."

Giorgio grunted and went back to his computer. A few minutes later, Rocky interrupted him again.

"Phillips' wife works for Comcast. She was in a meeting, but I got a minute with her. She doesn't know where her husband is and hasn't seen him since Sunday."

Giorgio began to tap a pencil on his desk. "And she didn't seem worried about that?"

"No. She said they had an argument, and she didn't really care if he ever came back."

Giorgio's eyebrows shot up. "I think we need to talk to her."

÷

It was just after eleven o'clock when Giorgio and Rocky joined Mrs. Phillips in a small conference room at the Arcadia Comcast/Xfinity office. She was in her early forties with short brown hair, glasses, and an extra fifty pounds around her waist and hips. Her stiff posture indicated that whatever the argument had been about with her husband had kept her angry until now.

"What's this about?" she asked. "I told you Jessie and I had an argument. I don't know where he is, and I don't care."

"I'm sorry," Giorgio began, "but we need to ask you some questions. What was your argument about?"

"That's none of your business," she snapped, her brown eyes blazing.

"I'm afraid it is. We're investigating the suspicious death of a young woman up in Bailey Canyon."

Her body flinched, and she brought her hands together on the table. "A woman? What did she look like?"

"I'm not at liberty to say. We need to know what you and your husband argued about," Giorgio repeated. "And we need to find him."

She released a breath and glanced down at her hands. "He was seeing someone else. I confronted him about it after church on Sunday. He stormed out of the house, and I haven't seen him since." The last words caught in her throat, and she sucked in a deep breath to calm herself.

"Do you know who he was having an affair with?" Rocky asked.

She didn't look up but continued to stare at her hands. "No. I found a pack of condoms in the glove compartment of his car. And a hair tie; that's how I knew." She pressed her lips together, gritting her teeth. She finally looked up. "Can you believe it? He teaches at a Christian school, and he's banging another woman."

The woman's crass language didn't surprise Giorgio. It was amazing how people let their guard down when they had been betrayed.

"But he didn't say who it was?" Giorgio asked.

"No. He just blew up, as if I'd done something wrong. He told me that I was the one who was being cold and distant, and so why wouldn't he look for it somewhere else?" A sob escaped her lips, and she reached for a tissue.

"And then he left?" Rocky asked.

She nodded. "I assume he went to *her*," she replied, dropping her gaze again. "He must have come home yesterday when I was at work, though, because I noticed some of his clothes were gone."

"And you haven't heard from him?" Giorgio asked.

She shook her head and used the tissue to wipe her nose.

"Can you give us his cell phone number?"

She glanced up, her eyes dull with pain, and rattled off his phone number.

"Thanks. He was seen up in the canyon yesterday. Do you know why he would have been up there?" Giorgio prodded.

"He often goes up there," she said with a sniffle. "He says it helps clear his head."

"And there was no clue as to who the woman is?"

She sniffled and shook her head.

"What about women at the school?" Rocky asked. "Did he ever talk about someone too much? Have too many late afternoon meetings?"

Her head came up with a snap, and she stared at him for a moment. "Oh, my God! Yes. He has a teacher's assistant. Jennifer something-or-other. A young girl from one of the local colleges. Ohhh, shit," she cried out. She slumped back, deflated. "I assumed it was another woman. One of the teachers. Not a girl. But, yes," she said, tears forming again. "He talked about her a lot. How she came from a troubled home and was turning her life around. He offered to tutor her." Her eyes locked on Giorgio's. "That's not who you found up in the canyon, is it?"

"I don't think so. Listen, we really need to talk to him. He may have seen something. If you hear from him, please have him call us right away." He handed her his card. "He might know something that would help."

÷

By 12:30 pm, the brothers were back at the station getting ready to go to lunch when McCready appeared at the door with a stack of loose papers in his hands.

"I didn't find out much about the tattoo," he said. "But I did find a bunch of weird stuff on people who actually believe they're vampires." He dropped a few color photos on Giorgio's desk. "Some of the weirder ones have their teeth filed down to look like fangs," he said, pointing to an especially creepy picture of a man with his lips drawn back, exposing a set of pointed canine teeth. "And look at this one," he said, pulling one photo forward. "This guy had horns implanted into his forehead. There are also groups who drink blood as part of their rituals," he continued, curling a lip in disgust. "I even found a questionnaire people can take in case they suspect they're vampires."

Rocky erupted in a laugh. "You've got to be kidding? Did you take it?"

The young cop broke into a smile, crinkling the skin around his blue eyes. "Yeah. I scored high on two questions. Whether or not I had pale skin. What redhead doesn't? And whether people often tell me I look young for my age."

"How old are you?" Rocky asked.

"Twenty-nine."

"Damn. You don't look a day over twenty-two. How'd you do on the rest of the questions?"

"Not so good," he said with a sly grin. "I failed the question on whether I tend to get high when I drink human blood."

"Thank God," Giorgio said with a sigh.

"Wait a minute!" Rocky said, spinning around to look at his brother. "When we were kids you used to lick the blood out of a cut."

Giorgio's eyes narrowed. "All kids do stuff like that. You used to eat boogers."

McCready laughed. "I knew a kid who smelled his own farts."

"Whoa!" Giorgio said raising both hands. "How did we get from drinking blood to smelling farts?"

"Well, all of this stuff is weird," McCready said, dropping the rest of the photos on the desk. "Some of these people only drink blood from a cup. It's sort of a symbolic thing. But there are several groups that initiate members by drugging them and then using devices to puncture their veins. They pretend they're Dracula."

"Sounds like our vic," Giorgio said.

"Are these willing volunteers?" Rocky asked, thumbing through the pictures.

McCready shrugged. "I think so. It seems these people get caught up in this stuff. I'm not sure I would call them cults. I mean, they don't sign over all their worldly goods or anything. But they share some of the same characteristics. There is usually a charismatic leader, the members pledge confidentiality to the group, and some groups use sexual rituals as part of the initiation."

"So, if some of these wannabe vampires use drugs in their rituals," Rocky said. "Maybe our vic had a bad reaction to the drug."

"Or maybe they scared her to death when they tried to drain her life-giving essence," McCready said with a dramatic hand flourish.

Giorgio's head came up. "What?"

"I don't mean they actually drained her blood," McCready replied.

"No. What did you say before that?"

He shrugged. "Um…they drained her life-giving essence."

"Why did you describe it that way?"

"Several of the online sites define vampires as feeding on a victim's life-giving essence. In other words, blood."

"Shit!" Giorgio felt a rush of adrenalin flood his body.

The ghost of Christian Maynard *had* provided a clue but long before the young woman's body was found in the canyon. He opened a drawer in his desk and extracted a folded piece of paper that he flattened out and stared at for a moment. Then he pushed it across the desk to Rocky.

"I forgot all about this. I found it at the theater during *Arsenic and Old Lace* a few weeks ago."

That was a lie. Giorgio belonged to a local theater group and often played leading roles when his schedule permitted it. He hadn't just found the flyer. It had magically appeared in the pocket of the vest he'd worn as Teddy Roosevelt in *Arsenic and Old Lace*—a pocket that had been empty only moments before. As Giorgio waited to go onstage that night, he was thinking about Christian Maynard. A moment later, the boy's other-worldly image had appeared in the backstage shadows. At the same moment, Giorgio felt a tug on the pocket of his vest. When he reached inside, he had drawn out the flyer.

Rocky glanced at the creased piece of paper. "You gotta be kidding me."

"What is it?" McCready asked, stepping forward. "Wow," he murmured looking down.

They were staring at a promotional flyer with the image of a handsome man with thick, black hair swept back from his face. His head was tilted back, his sharpened fangs poised to bite the alabaster neck of a young woman. In the background was a snarling Rottweiler. Across the top, printed in crimson ink were the words *The Essence of Murder*.

"Why would this flyer be at the theater?" Rocky asked.

"It was in the pocket of my costume," Giorgio admitted. "Someone must have left it there."

"Okay, but what is it?" McCready asked. "A play or something?"

"None I ever heard of," Giorgio said, picking it up again.

"Didn't the theater do Dracula last year?" McCready asked. "Maybe this was a prop?"

"No," Rocky countered, pointing at the sheet. "Whatever this is, it has a time and location for this coming Friday night." Rocky turned to his brother. "I take it we'll be going."

Giorgio shrugged, staring at the sheet. "Only way we'll find out what it is."

"And you think it might have something to do with our dead woman?" McCready asked.

"I don't know. But again, it seems like too much of a coincidence."

Rocky chuckled. "I never thought I'd be glad you picked up theater again. If we're going to attend some sort of rave or whatever this is, I'll get to dress all in black, and you can apply some of your stage makeup again. You'll fit right in."

"Funny," Giorgio said with a grimace.

CHAPTER FIVE

The two brothers strolled across the street for lunch at Mama's Café. They entered the small restaurant and paused to read a large, rectangular chalkboard propped on an old whiskey barrel. It listed gluten-free spaghetti and meatballs, fried clams, and grilled ham & cheese sandwiches as the day's specials.

Rocky read it and said, "God, what happened to pizza and chili dogs? Who would eat gluten-free spaghetti?"

Giorgio laughed. "You just miss Rose and all the Elvis Presley memorabilia that used to be in here."

"No," Rocky snapped. "I don't miss Rose. Hopefully, she's snapping those false teeth of hers at the staff of some old folk's home. But I do miss the posters of Marilyn Monroe."

"You just miss looking at her legs."

The restaurant had changed hands recently. Besides losing some of their popular greasy-spoon food items, customers had lost Mom's iconic waitress, Rose Calhoun, who still shouldered food trays well into her seventies.

About two-thirds of the tables were taken, so the brothers took a booth along the front windows. A young brunette appeared to hand them menus and take their drink orders. When she left, Rocky turned to watch her shapely legs disappear into the kitchen.

"Stop leering," Giorgio said, opening the menu.

Rocky laughed. "I may miss the chili dogs, but the view in here has certainly improved." He turned back to Giorgio with a lingering grin. "What are you gonna get?"

"I don't know," Giorgio said in frustration. "I've lost fifteen pounds and want to keep it off. So, maybe just a chef's salad." He slapped the menu closed.

Rocky stared at him. "Seriously? Hell, maybe you could start a yoga class, and we could stop later and get you a yogurt smoothie."

Giorgio grimaced. "You realize that we've both almost been killed twice in the last few months. I'm just trying to get back in shape. Goes with the job."

Rocky's chuckles softened. "I get it. How's it going?"

Giorgio eyed his brother. He never knew if Rocky was just setting him up for another snide remark.

"I'm working out twice a week and started a class in Jiu Jitsu. And I've cut back on the beer and nachos on the weekends."

Rocky smiled. "But not on Angie's pasta."

Giorgio blew out a scoffing breath. "I'd never give up Angie's pasta. So, what do you think about this woman we found?"

Rocky shrugged his broad shoulders. "I'm surprised no one has reported her missing yet."

"Maybe she hasn't been gone long enough for someone to notice. She could live alone," Giorgio said.

"True. And it is only Tuesday," Rocky said, spinning the saltshaker in front of him. "Depending on where she worked, if she died Saturday or Sunday, an employer might not worry about her yet."

"If she even worked," Giorgio emphasized.

"Good point. What do you think about Phillips?" Rocky asked.

"The kids said they'd seen him up there before. And Cincera said he saw him getting out of the Land Rover, but never saw him on the trail. I think that means he probably took the Canyon View Trail. Even if he had nothing to do with her death, he should have seen the body."

Rocky nodded. "Yeah, but then why didn't he call it in?"

"Exactly."

"Think the woman we found is his mistress?"

Giorgio's eyebrows arched. "She looked too old to be a teacher's assistant. But maybe the wife is wrong on that. If our vic is his mistress, then he's on the run. We ought to talk to some of his colleagues and interview his TA. Someone might know who the mistress is if it's not her."

"I'll call the school when we get back and get the girl's info," Rocky said. "And we need to see if he has a sheet."

"Yeah. If he has a record, that gives him even more of a reason to run."

The waitress arrived with their drinks and asked for their food orders.

"I'll take the grilled ham and cheese," Rocky said. "But it's not some weird foreign cheese is it?"

"Uh, I…no," she stuttered. "Just…uh, cheddar."

"Okay, good."

"I'll take the chef salad," Giorgio said.

She wrote down the orders and turned to leave.

"Thanks, Maddie," Rocky said, eyeing her name tag. His dark eyes danced as he gave her one of his winning smiles. She faltered a moment at the obvious flirtation and then turned toward the kitchen. Rocky's eyes followed her again. When she disappeared, he turned back to his brother. "So, what do you know about subcultures?"

"You mean vampires?"

"Yeah. I had a roommate in college whose girlfriend was into that sort of stuff. Although, she would have been considered a Goth."

Giorgio's eyebrows arched. "I thought Goth stuff was dead."

"I don't think so. Anyway, I think there's a whole subculture that gets into body alteration. Like that picture McCready showed us of the guy with implants in his head. I saw a picture on Facebook once of a guy who had his tongue split to look like a snake."

Giorgio shook his head. "Christ. People are so weird."

Rocky shrugged. "Have you ever counted the number of piercings on Flame?"

Flame was the psychic who had aided them on their last investigation. She was an attractive young woman in her mid-twenties with multiple piercings and tattoos.

"I get the willies every time I look at stuff like that," Giorgio said. "I can't say I'm afraid of needles, but the whole idea of someone piercing the inside of my nose or my lip…ugh." He shuddered.

"Would you ever get a tattoo?"

"No," Giorgio snapped. "I'll get poked by a needle if I have to get a shot or give blood. That's it."

"So…no vampire society for you?" Rocky asked with a chuckle.

"God, no. I don't even like vampire movies."

"You wouldn't want to live forever?"

"The little bit I know about vampires is that they can't stand sunlight, need to drink blood each day, sleep in coffins, and have very few friends. So, no, I wouldn't want to live like that, no matter for how long." Giorgio took a long draw from his Coke, swallowed, and then said, "And besides, they can't stand garlic, so how the hell could I eat Angie's pasta?"

Giorgio's phone rang. He withdrew it from his pocket and answered it. It was Mulhaney.

"The M.E. called while you were out. He wants you to call him."

"Okay. Thanks. Also, have Drew check to see if Phillips has a sheet."

"Will do," Mulhaney replied.

Giorgio hung up and dialed the number. "Detective Salvatori for Dr. Pearce," he said when the call went through. He tapped his fingers while he waited.

"Thanks for calling, Detective," the doctor said. "I have some information. My best guess is that the young woman died sometime Saturday night or Sunday morning. But because she was buried and then spent time in the water, it's impossible to get closer than that."

"Cause of death?"

Giorgio heard a sigh on the other end of the phone. "I don't know yet. There were no signs of trauma. I peg her age between 28 and 31. She was in good health except for a surgery on her right knee to repair a tendon. Her fingerprints didn't show up in any database. But she's had breast implants. I'll have the serial number for you when I fax the preliminary report over," he said.

"Great," Giorgio said. "Back to the cause of death, though."

"Like I said, I don't know yet. There's no blunt force trauma, knife or gunshot wound. We did a basic toxicology screen. Her urine showed she had a trace amount of alcohol in her system and enough Xanax that I believe she took a pill only an hour or so before she died. The alcohol may have been consumed earlier, but her liver, heart and other organ function seemed fine. It's a bit of a mystery at this point. I…" The medical examiner stopped talking.

"What?" Giorgio asked.

"Nothing. I have a suspicion, but I want to get the full tox screen back first. I put a rush on it but won't get it back for another twenty-four hours."

"Odd that someone so young would just drop dead," Giorgio said.

"I agree. I wasn't wrong about her being buried and dug up, though. There was dirt in almost every crevice of her body. Even some in her mouth."

"She wasn't buried alive, was she?" Giorgio asked with a start.

"No. The dirt was just underneath her lips, which would happen as the dirt settled around her face. She didn't breathe any in, so she was dead when she was put in the ground. Sorry, I can't be more help right now."

"Thanks, doc." Giorgio hung up and relayed the news to his brother. "The M.E. says she had Xanax in her system," he said.

"That could have reacted badly with anything the vampires might have given her," Rocky said. "Maybe that's why they buried her. They were using illicit drugs and didn't want to get caught."

Giorgio sat back. "Maybe. He's guessing that she died Saturday night or sometime Sunday morning. We won't get the rest of the tox screen back until late tomorrow. And she had breast implants. I'll have McCready track those down as soon as we get the numbers."

"What are we going to do in the meantime?" Rocky asked.

"Go back up in the canyon," Giorgio said. "If she was buried and then dug up, we need to find out where. Let's take Grosvenor."

CHAPTER SIX

Giorgio had decided to get a dog in the middle of their investigation into Mallory Olsen's murder the year before. What prompted it was a fight with his wife. He couldn't stand having Angie mad at him. They had been together since they were teens, and he idolized her. When she had announced she was pregnant with their third child, he had lost his temper, fearful he couldn't afford a third child on a detective's salary.

Angie was more than heartbroken at his response; she was royally pissed. As the rift between them increased, he got the brainy idea to get a dog as a peace offering. It hadn't worked. She had seen the dog for the ruse it was—a juvenile attempt at taking the heat off him. But over time Grosvenor had worked his magic on Angie and was now a well-established member of the family.

He and Rocky swung by the house, and Giorgio went in and came back out with the black and brown spotted Basset hound. He helped the canine wiggle his way onto the back seat, as the dog slapped him with his tail, happy to be going for a ride.

"Hey buddy," Rocky said, reaching over the seat to scratch under the dog's long snout. Grosvenor responded by slobbering all over Rocky's hand. "You know, when you rescued Grosvenor, I never thought he'd make such a good detective," Rocky said. "Especially because he'd been abused."

"I know. Kills me to think someone treated him that way. What monster burns a dog with a cigarette?"

"Well, so far, he's two for two on finding dead bodies during our investigations," Rocky said, turning back around. "Is that why you're bringing him to the canyon?"

Giorgio glanced at his brother. "We need to find a grave. Not a dead body."

Rocky shrugged. "Kind of the same thing. What'd you bring to give him the scent?"

"The woman's smock."

They pulled into the parking lot at Bailey Canyon Park ten minutes later. The two men exited the car, got Grosvenor on a leash, and set off on the trail. They made better time without the entourage of kids and county personnel, and Giorgio could appreciate the sounds and smells of the canyon.

The creek gurgled along beside them, while birds flitted in and out of nearby trees. Across the stream, a doe turned to watch them and then darted off into the brush. When a rabbit scurried across Grosvenor's path, the dog yanked the leash out of Giorgio's hand and took off after it, releasing an anguished howl.

Grosvenor scrambled up a hill, his long ears flying, and then stopped when the rabbit disappeared into the underbrush. He circled halfway around the bushes in frustration, whining and pushing his nose under branches until Giorgio called him back.

"Too bad Uncle Joey isn't here with his 12-gauge to take out that rabbit," Rocky said, as the dog lumbered back down the hill, his long snout covered in dirt.

Giorgio laughed. "You know Uncle Joey wasn't that good with a gun. Hell, he probably would have taken out the rabbit, you, me, Grosvenor, and half of the surrounding vegetation."

When Grosvenor made it back to the trail, Giorgio leaned down, grabbed his leash, and gave him a pat. "Good try, Bud."

They left the rabbit on the upside of the hill twitching its nose at them and started off again.

"You have to admit Uncle Joey made a mean rabbit stew, though," Rocky said.

"Yes, but you do know that he never killed anything. He always bought his meat down at Frankie's Meat Market."

"No shit?" Rocky exclaimed. "But he had such great stories about hunting trips in upstate New York."

They came to a fallen log and stopped to help Grosvenor over it.

"All tall tales," Giorgio said, lifting the dog's hind end over the log. "Dad told me once that Uncle Joey couldn't stand the sight of blood."

"Where'd he go then when he was supposed to be hunting?" Rocky asked, stepping over the log.

"Fishing," Giorgio replied.

"Damn!" Rocky said, prompting a laugh from his brother.

Five minutes later, they scrambled up the steep hill and arrived across the creek from where they had found the body. The entire scene had already been processed, so there was no yellow tape or evidence markers left behind.

The brothers crossed the creek a second time, with Grosvenor wading through the water behind them. When they arrived at the spot where the young woman had lain, Giorgio pulled out the plastic evidence bag holding her smock. He allowed Grosvenor to smell it and then closed it up again.

He and Rocky stood back and watched.

It took the dog only a moment to push his nose into the dirt along the creek bed and begin to sniff the ground at the water's edge. Giorgio leaned down and removed his leash.

"Have you thought about getting him trained as a cadaver dog?" Rocky asked, watching Grosvenor.

Giorgio shook his head. "He's a family pet. I wanna keep him that way."

"And yet, here he is, working a crime scene again," Rocky replied, nodding toward the dog.

"True. But if I have him trained, then I'd start getting requests to send him out on other jobs. I don't want that." Giorgio glanced down to where Grosvenor had his nose pressed to the ground, sucking in the smells.

"He's good at it, though," Rocky said.

"He's good as a pet, too," Giorgio countered.

Grosvenor began to move away from the creek, nose to the ground.

"He's got something," Rocky said.

The canine followed the curve of the creek, north. The brothers hurried to catch up. He went fifty to sixty yards, his nose in the air now, as if sniffing the breeze. He suddenly turned and climbed a hill using a deer path. He followed the scent over the hill and through some thick vegetation, leaving the creek behind.

"Look over there," Giorgio said, stopping.

He pointed to an area off the trail where the long grass had been tamped down and a shelter had been carved out of the underbrush. Rocky stepped off the trail and used his foot to sift through nude magazines, empty cigarette packs, and Coke cans left behind.

"The kids' fort," Rocky surmised.

They continued to follow Grosvenor into a gulley. Halfway through the gulley, the canine stopped as if he had lost the trail. His head came up, and he whipped his head back and forth, his long ears slapping him in the face. He moved a few feet left and then a few feet right.

Finally, he started off on a wide path that led them through some trees and up another hill. Minutes later, the path opened onto a flat, grassy area surrounded on two sides by steep inclines. The fourth side dropped off a few feet to the creek.

"This is weird," Giorgio said, looking around.

Grosvenor had stopped at the center of the clearing and begun to nose around a group of eight, short tree stumps lined up in pairs. The stumps were around three feet tall and were set close enough to form a table of some sort. Cut logs formed a half circle in front of the stumps, almost like audience seating at an outdoor theater. In between the logs and the makeshift table were the remains of an open campfire.

"You think people are camping up here?" Rocky asked, kicking at the ashes.

"Maybe. Although I read that the fire service has labeled this area off limits because it's so close to homes," Giorgio replied. "I wonder if there's some sort of Boy Scout camp close by. Maybe they get special permission. With the makeshift seating and firepit, this looks like something straight out of a scout jamboree."

"Minus the Boy Scouts," Rocky quipped.

"Yeah, but they could pitch their tents all around this grassy area," Giorgio said, gesturing around them.

"Maybe. But I think this is something else. And, frankly, this place gives me the creeps. It's too quiet," he said, glancing around. "Have you noticed that? No birds."

"Yeah, it is quiet," Giorgio said, scanning the area.

A soft rustle made them spin toward the hill in front of them. Grosvenor also came to attention, emitting a low growl as the hair along his back stood on end.

"What the hell was that?" Rocky's hand was already on the butt of his weapon.

"I don't know," Giorgio said, staring up into the tree line. "Grosvenor stop it!" The dog had begun to move away, making Giorgio grab Grosvenor's collar and re-fasten the leash.

"Wait a minute. I think someone's up there," Rocky said. His deep brown eyes were focused like lasers on the crest of the hill. "Do you see anything?"

They were both fixated on the bluff. Grosvenor continued to yank and pull at his leash, barking at something hidden on the hillside.

"I don't see anything," Giorgio said, peering at the top of the hill.

"I thought I saw something move up there," his brother said.

"There!" Giorgio said, pointing to a fleeting image moving through the bushes.

"I don't think it's a person," Rocky said. He was leaning forward staring. "Some sort of animal."

The image disappeared, and Grosvenor grew quiet. Giorgio glanced down to where the leash had gone slack. The canine had stopped barking and whined in defeat.

"Whatever it was, it must be gone." Giorgio glanced one more time at the tree line and then relaxed. "Well, it looks like Grosvenor's trail ends here, so let's look around…see if we can find where they buried that woman."

Rocky moved off toward the cliff that overlooked the creek, searching through the long grass. Giorgio headed to the opposite side of the glen where there were several trees and large boulders. Grosvenor trailed beside him, tail wagging.

Giorgio scanned the ground as he went, crisscrossing the area, looking for any disturbance in the soil. At one point, Grosvenor stopped to study a spot between two trees. The area looked like it had been dug up and filled in again. After poking through the dirt with a stick and sniffing the air, Giorgio decided it had once served as a latrine.

"C'mon, boy," he said, moving away from the trees.

Giorgio went back to studying the ground, using the stick to part grasses and poke at bushes. Grosvenor began to pull at the leash again. When Giorgio ignored him, he whined and strained at the collar. Finally, Giorgio turned to his left and stopped cold.

Outlined in the shadow of a large pine tree was the boy Giorgio often saw, dressed in the same white shirt, dark knickers, and suspenders he had probably died in. The boy's hazy image flickered in the afternoon light.

Christian Maynard had attended the boys' school at the monastery in the 1940s and was part of a group of boys that had been abused by the priests. He had killed his main abuser, the abbot, and hung himself afterwards.

Christian had never appeared to Giorgio during the daytime, so the fact he was here now had to mean something. Giorgio stepped forward, feeling the adrenalin electrify his body as it did each time the boy appeared. As he stared, the boy raised his right arm and pointed to a group of boulders. Giorgio turned in that direction. As he did so, he relaxed his fingers, and Grosvenor pulled free, making a beeline for the three boulders about fifteen feet away.

"Grosvenor!" Giorgio yelled, striking out after him. "Come back here!"

He chased the dog, ignoring the ghost for the moment. As he rounded the first giant rock, he slid to a stop. Grosvenor was already in a hole, pawing through a pile of dirt as if searching for his favorite bone.

Rocky ran up behind him. "What's he doing?"

"I don't know."

Giorgio turned back, but the boy's image was gone. "Damn!" he murmured. A chill rippled

across his shoulder blades as he turned his attention back to the dog.

As the dog worked, Giorgio's gaze roamed across the broken soil. Then, he took a sudden breath. He was looking at the outlines of a long, rectangular hole, most of which had been filled in with dirt.

"This is a grave," he said quietly.

He moved in and grabbed Grosvenor's leash to pull the dog out.

"Wait a minute," Rocky said, coming around the other side.

Giorgio dragged Grosvenor back as Rocky squatted down and reached forward, tracing his index finger along a dark spot in the dirt.

"What is it?" Giorgio asked.

Rocky sat back on his heels, rubbed his fingers together and glanced up at his brother. "Blood."

CHAPTER SEVEN

They had found the grave. Now they needed to process it.

Giorgio pulled out his cell phone to call for a forensics team, but there was no connection.

"It's getting late. Can you go back to the car?" he asked his brother. "Call it in and see if you can get Fong out here. I'll continue searching the area."

Rocky nodded and headed back to the trailhead. Giorgio grabbed Grosvenor's leash to keep him out of the grave and began searching the area by the campfire. He even traced his fingers along the top of the tree stumps and noticed remnants of candle wax and blood.

As he wandered around, he found cigarette butts, a crumpled beer can, an abandoned half-chewed pack of gum, and a fake fingernail, painted black. He let go of Grosvenor's leash at one point to place all of these into separate plastic baggies he carried in his coat pocket.

Rocky had been gone about ten minutes when Giorgio heard a strange trill in the bushes at the top of the cliff. He glanced up, thinking it was a large bird but went back to searching, allowing Grosvenor to wander about thirty feet away. Giorgio had just zeroed in on a metallic glint of something caught in a bush when there was a heavy, crashing sound to his left.

He spun around and focused on a blur of movement streaming down from the top of the cliff. Before he could react, a tan projectile launched itself at Grosvenor with an ear-splitting yowl. The basset hound was suddenly enveloped in a writhing ball of dust, tail, and sinew.

It was a mountain lion, fighting to get hold of the dog's neck.

Grosvenor fought back, snapping desperately at the cat. The quiet glen filled with a cacophony of snarls, growls, and cries of pain as the intruder's teeth slashed the dog open. Giorgio pulled his gun but couldn't get a clear shot as the two animals whipped back and forth. He shot into the air, hoping to scare off the attacker, but the two animals were embroiled in a fight to the death.

The cat got Grosvenor on his back. Grosvenor fought for his life, his head thrashing from side to side as the mountain lion tore at the thick folds of his throat. Dust rose around them as grass and pebbles flew in all directions.

Giorgio got close enough to chance a shot, but his hands shook as the dog's painful cries electrified him. He put tension on the trigger, figuring even if he hit Grosvenor, it would be more humane then having him ripped apart.

He was about to pull the trigger, when a second animal exploded onto the scene, slamming into the big cat's shoulder at top speed. The cat was thrown sideways and forced into an awkward roll with its legs and tail flailing.

Giorgio stared in disbelief as a muscle-bound, gray pit bull slid to a stop in between Grosvenor and the mountain lion. He didn't know if this animal was friend or foe, but Grosvenor was now free, so he inched forward, gun still drawn.

The pit bull ignored him as it stood its ground, hunched over and growling, spittle flying as it challenged the cat to come back. The dog's thick muscles were tensed into knots across its broad shoulders, and its lips were drawn back as it snapped and growled at the cat.

Giorgio finally crouched next to Grosvenor's head. The cat had regained its footing and turned back toward the dog, hesitating, making Giorgio tense up again. But the cat was focused on the pit bull, perhaps calculating the danger.

As Giorgio's heart thudded in his chest, the cat yowled and shivered, its muscles flickering across its tawny coat. After one more plaintive cry, it turned and loped off into the trees in defeat.

Giorgio gasped for air, sitting back on his heels. He put his gun down and ripped off his jacket and then his shirt. Keeping one eye on the pit bull, which had taken a few steps in pursuit of the retreating cat, he carefully wrapped his shirt around Grosvenor's throat, which was bleeding freely. Giorgio tied off the shirt and then reached back for his gun, all the while watching the pit bull.

After all, he was alone with another potential killing machine. Giorgio knew that dogs are not born to be mean, but everything he had read or heard about pit bulls made him consider this dog with caution.

The pit bull turned towards him, kicking Giorgio's heartbeat into high gear. His hands shook as he laced his fingers around the butt of his gun, ready to fire. But the dog merely sat down, panting, all challenge gone.

Giorgio pulled back his gun and slipped his arms through his jacket, never taking his eyes off the gray dog. Finally, the pit bull rose and calmly walked over and lowered its nose and began to lick the blood from around Grosvenor's neck.

"What the…? Wait, stop that," Giorgio demanded.

The dog glanced at him and backed up, so Giorgio holstered his weapon.

"Stay!" he said, pointing a finger at the pit bull.

Faltering, because he didn't know what the pit bull might do, he leaned down and scooped Grosvenor into his arms. Grosvenor whimpered as his body was lifted off the ground.

"C'mon, boy," Giorgio said with a heavy heart. "You're going to be okay."

He eyed the other dog, but when it didn't move, Giorgio backed up a few feet, turned and started an awkward run back to the car.

It was difficult going, and he slipped going down the hill above the stream, sliding onto his hip and almost dropping Grosvenor. Carefully, he got up and made it back down to the creek, where he encountered Rocky coming the opposite way.

"What the hell happened?" Rocky called out, jogging up the trail. "I heard a gunshot." When he saw Grosvenor in Giorgio's arms, he whistled. "Sheesh, what *did* happen?"

"Stay behind me," Giorgio ordered, yanking his head over his shoulder. "There's a pit bull back there. We've got to get Grosvenor to a vet, or I'm going to lose him."

"Did the pit bull attack G?" Rocky asked, getting in behind his brother.

They splashed through the stream and began a fast descent down the switchbacks.

"No. It was a mountain lion," Giorgio replied, gulping air. "The pit bull chased the cat off."

"No shit," Rocky replied.

Giorgio labored down the trail, sweating and gasping for air.

"Joe, let me take him," Rocky said, grabbing his shoulder.

Giorgio was spent. He stopped and handed Grosvenor over to his brother. Rocky began to jog forward, cradling the dog in his long arms. Giorgio bent over, took a couple of deep breaths, and then followed.

By the time they made it to the car, the dog's eyes had closed, and his breathing was shallow. Giorgio threw open one of the back doors so that Rocky could place Grosvenor's limp body on the seat. Then he ran around to the other door to get in the back seat next to the dog.

"You drive!" Giorgio snapped, as he slid in.

Rocky began to close the door, but not before the pit pull appeared out of nowhere and jumped in.

"What?" Rocky exclaimed, stepping back in surprise.

Giorgio froze. He slowly reached into his jacket and pulled out his weapon. But the dog ignored him and began to lick around Grosvenor's head and neck again, as if grooming him or attempting to heal his wounds.

Giorgio looked up at Rocky with clenched brows. Rocky just stared at the dog with an open mouth.

"Let's go," Giorgio said. "I'll shoot the damn thing if I have to."

Rocky closed the car door and raced around to climb in behind the wheel. He started the engine and spun the tires as he rushed out of the parking lot.

"Where to?" he asked.

"It's close to five. Let's go to that emergency vet off Sierra Madre Boulevard. You know it?"

"Yeah. I've seen it." Rocky glanced into the rearview mirror at his brother. "He's going to be okay, Joe."

Giorgio just grimaced and gave him a short nod. He didn't dare reply. His throat had constricted, and his eyes had begun to water. He could not lose this dog. They had become best friends, and the kids loved him.

He focused for a moment on the pit bull, trying to control his emotions. Its head reminded him of a squared-off bowling ball. It had narrow, watery gray eyes on either side of a low, broad forehead. Small, spiked ears framed his skull, although one ear had a chunk taken out of it. A single white patch of fur extended across its broad chest.

It was the most intimidating animal he had ever been this close to. And yet, the dog that had moments before challenged a mountain lion now seemed as placid as the rabbit Grosvenor had chased earlier that afternoon.

As Giorgio contemplated where this dog had come from, it laid its head across Grosvenor's injured neck and expelled a heavy sigh.

They traveled like that for another few minutes until Rocky pulled into the parking lot at the veterinarian's office. Giorgio checked on Grosvenor and felt panic well in his chest. The dog was barely breathing, and the shirt around his neck was saturated with blood.

As Rocky killed the engine, Giorgio threw open his door, climbed out and rushed around to the other side of the car. He opened the door and paused as the pit bull turned towards him.

"C'mon, boy," he said, patting his leg to encourage the dog to come out. "I've got to get him out."

The pit bull glanced at Grosvenor and then jumped lightly out of the car. Giorgio reached in and lifted the dog and followed Rocky through the front door of the vet's office.

"Go back to the canyon to meet the forensics guys," Giorgio said to Rocky as they got inside. "I'll take care of things here."

"You sure?"

"Yeah. You'll need to lead them up there."

Rocky nodded. "Okay, good luck," he said, patting Giorgio's shoulder.

Rocky left, while Giorgio stepped up to the reception desk.

"My dog's been attacked," he said.

The girl took one look at Grosvenor and stood up. She hurried around the end of the counter. "Come with me."

She pushed open a door to her left and held it for Giorgio. He carried his bundle into the examining room, which was lined with counters, cupboards, and cages.

"Put him on the table," she said. "I'll be right back."

Giorgio laid Grosvenor onto a metal exam table and then stroked his head, his nose twitching at the smell of antiseptics. "C'mon buddy," he said. "Don't leave me now."

He choked up, but was saved when the girl returned, followed by a tall, dark-haired young woman.

"I'm Dr. Vincent," she said crisply. "What happened?"

She was already removing the stethoscope from around her neck and placed it on Grosvenor's chest.

"He was attacked by a mountain lion," Giorgio said, almost choking the words out. "About twenty minutes ago."

"Okay," she said, looking up at him. "Wait out front and give me some time with him."

He hesitated.

"Go," she said quietly. "You can't help him in here."

He squeezed Grosvenor's big paw and then turned on his heels and returned to the lobby, his heart thudding in his chest. As he came through the door, the receptionist stopped him.

"Excuse me, sir?" she said. "Your other dog has to be on a leash before I get your information."

He glanced at her, his mind struggling to concentrate. "Excuse me?"

She nodded toward the door. "Your other dog. It needs to be on a leash."

Giorgio turned and found the gray pit bull sitting just inside the front door. A woman with a cat carrier sat scrunched in the corner, staring at the pit bull.

"Uh…he's not mine," Giorgio said to the young woman.

"First of all, it's a female," she said.

"What?" Giorgio asked.

"The dog. It's a female."

He turned back to the dog, which lowered its head and came forward.

"Uh…okay," he replied. "But she's not mine. She saved my dog, though."

The receptionist turned to the wall behind her and pulled a leash off a hook. "Here," she said, dropping it onto the counter. "Loop this around her neck."

Giorgio glanced from the leash to the dog, wondering if this was a good idea. After all, a neighbor in New York had lost her poodle to a pit bull roaming the street unattended. But this dog sat at Giorgio's feet with no menace, just calm acceptance.

He reached out with a tentative hand and looped the leash around her neck, pulling it tight. She turned that rock-hard head and licked his hand. The shock made him jerk away.

"She seems like a nice dog," the receptionist said, leaning over the counter. "Pit bulls get a bad rap."

Giorgio gave her a brief smile. "She's just not mine."

"You can take her to the shelter," the girl said. "Although pit bulls don't do too well there. Especially one that's so scarred up." She nodded toward the dog's head.

Giorgio followed her gaze and for the first time realized how battered and beat-up this dog was. Besides the chewed off ear, multiple scars crisscrossed her head and trailed down her massive shoulders, like strings glued to her skin. Her left foreleg looked like it had been stitched back together just above her knee, pulling the skin over the bone.

"I didn't even notice," he admitted. "I was too upset about my own dog."

"She's a fighting dog," the young woman said. "Or, more likely a bait dog."

The bell over the door jingled, and an older woman came in with an old Labrador retriever. The receptionist turned to help her, and Giorgio took the pit bull and sat at the end of a line of empty chairs by the window. He leaned forward, his elbows on his knees, his mind replaying the moment the cougar had engaged with Grosvenor. The dog's sharp cry of pain reverberated in his mind, and he had to hold his breath a moment to calm his nerves.

The pit bull moved over to tuck herself in next to his leg, resting her head on his knee.

"Who are you?" he whispered to her. He reached out and stroked the dog's head, making her look up at him. "I guess it doesn't matter. You saved his life. Thank you."

She pushed harder against his leg. Giorgio marveled at her passive behavior. *Where was all the bravado she'd shown before?*

He pulled out his phone to call his wife. When she answered, he said, "Hey, Ange, I…I have some bad news."

CHAPTER EIGHT

Giorgio knew Grosvenor had lost a lot of blood, which made waiting for news about his injuries excruciating. He had warned Angie not to tell the kids yet. No need to worry them until necessary. His son, Tony, only eight, would take it the hardest if the dog didn't make it.

"Who am I kidding? I will take it the hardest," he thought.

A sob caught in his throat, and he took a deep breath to relax as he put his phone away. As much as he liked to tell himself he had gotten Grosvenor to appease his wife, he knew he had gone to the shelter that day to make himself happy.

He had lost another dog, Butch, several years earlier through a mistake of his own. He had thrown a ball too hard, and his small mixed terrier had chased it into the street where a truck hit him. Giorgio had never forgiven himself and vowed never to get another pet.

But he loved dogs, and now, once again, he was holding watch over a dog that had been injured due to his own poor choices. True, Grosvenor had likely found the place where their vic had been buried, but Giorgio could have found it on his own. He hadn't needed to take Grosvenor into the canyon. But he was proud of Grosvenor's ability to help with his investigations, and now he was paying the price.

Since he knew he was in for a long wait, he decided to take the opportunity to check in with Rocky. He pulled out his phone again.

"Hey," his brother said when he answered. "How's G?"

"I don't know yet. They still have him in the back. And I still have the pit bull. They made me put a leash on her."

"It's a she?"

"Yeah. Tough little dog," he said, leaning over to stroke the top of her head. "She looks pretty beat up," he said, studying the dog's badly scarred back. "Where are you?"

"We're just heading back up the creek bed," he replied, his breath coming hard. "I'm with Mulhaney and Fong."

"Okay. Do you have a camera?"

"Yeah. We'll shoot the entire area first. Don't worry. I'll be out of cell phone range for a while. We're also losing the light, so we need to hurry."

"Okay, we'll talk later."

Giorgio hung up and settled in to wait. Forty-five minutes later, the door to the surgery area opened, and the doctor stepped out. She gestured for him to follow her into the back. His throat tightened at the sight of Grosvenor stretched out on his side on the exam table. He wasn't moving.

"Is he…is he…"

"He's alive," she said, moving over to him. "Barely."

Grosvenor's neck was bandaged, and there was an IV tube hooked up to one of his front legs. He also had deep gashes in his side. The areas had been shaved and wounds stitched up.

"Is he going to make it?" Giorgio stepped closer and reached out to touch one long, silky ear.

"He's lost a lot of blood, so it will be touch and go for the next 12 hours or so. He'll need to stay here."

Something pulled at Giorgio's right hand. He looked down to see the pit bull rise and put her front paws on the edge of the metal table. She leaned in and nosed the back of Grosvenor's head, whining.

"She likes him," the doctor said, watching the pit bull. "They must be good friends."

"They don't even know each other. But when Grosvenor was attacked, this dog came out of nowhere and chased off the cat."

Her eyes opened in surprise. "Really?" She moved around the end of the exam table and came up to the pit bull. The dog dropped to the floor as the doctor crouched down to pet her.

"She's a nice dog." The doctor used her fingers to examine the dog's head. "Hold on. She's bleeding. No, sorry," she said, correcting herself. She probed the area in front of the dog's ear. "This blood came from somewhere else."

"Could be Grosvenor's," Giorgio said. "She laid her head across his neck when we were in the car."

The doctor examined the rest of the dog's head and neck. "I think she's been used as a bait dog."

"Your receptionist mentioned that."

She craned her neck to look up at Giorgio from where she crouched next to the pit bull. The dog had scooted in close to her to enjoy the attention.

"Dogfighting rings use bait dogs to train their fighting dogs. They are usually smaller and less aggressive. They sometimes breed dogs just for that purpose. Only the strongest survive. But they'll also steal dogs or troll Craigslist for dogs that someone is giving away for free."

"But she was out in the woods."

The doctor shrugged. "She might have gotten away. You say she chased off the cougar?"

"Yeah. Slammed into it at full speed and then stood guard in front of Grosvenor—almost like she was challenging the cat to come back. Brave little dog."

"She's been through hell. She has scars everywhere. And yet, she survived and escaped. I would say she's more than brave. She's smart."

He looked down at the gray dog that was built like a small Mack truck. The pit bull was staring up at Grosvenor again.

"She seems to have a thing for your dog. I wonder why," the doctor said.

He glanced over at his drugged companion. "I guess that's the sixty-four-thousand-dollar question."

The doctor stroked the dog's neck as two technicians came to move Grosvenor into one of the cages. The pit bull strained at the leash to go with him.

"Do you have a place to take her tonight?" she asked.

"No," he replied. "I don't know what I'll do with her."

"Listen," she said. "We have a couple of empty cages. Why don't you leave her with us for tonight? She can sleep right next to your dog. It might give him comfort if he wakes up."

Giorgio gave her a grateful look. "Thanks. I'll have a lot to deal with just telling my kids about Grosvenor when I get home."

"No problem. Give us a call tomorrow. Meanwhile, if his condition changes overnight, we'll call you."

"Thanks," he replied, giving the pit bull a tentative pat on the head.

Giorgio texted for an Uber and headed home. On the way, McCready called.

"Rocky is on his way back. He left an officer there, but they will have to return tomorrow. They lost the light."

"Okay. Did you get that teacher assistant's name?"

"Yeah. I talked with the principal. There were rumors about Phillips and a girl named Jennifer Menendez."

"Okay, if Phillips doesn't show up tomorrow, we need to go out to the school and talk to her. And if she isn't the mistress, we need to find out who is. What about Phillips' record? Does he have one?"

"Yeah. He's been arrested twice. Once when he was in his teens for selling weed and once in his twenties for male prostitution."

"How the hell did he get a job teaching at a Christian school?"

"His cousin is the principal."

Giorgio let out a low whistle. "Well, I guess we know now why he might not have reported the dead body."

"And might be on the run," McCready added.

CHAPTER NINE

Giorgio was parked in the driveway of his two-story Spanish-style home on Sunnyside Avenue, contemplating what he would say to his kids about Grosvenor. He thought about being brutally honest, but instead, decided to gloss over the gruesome details and be optimistic yet cautious. He climbed out of the car and up the brick steps to the arched wooden front door, dreading the conversation.

Inside, he stood in the entryway feeling comfort in familiar surroundings. His son's laughter floated into the hallway from the den, and the aroma of cheese wafted in from the kitchen. All that was missing was the clickety-clack of Grosvenor's nails on the hardwood floor coming to greet him.

He dropped his head, sighed, and then shut the door.

Optimism was not his normal mindset. Not that he was a pessimist. But after seeing as much trauma and tragedy as he had, he was a realist. And there was a real chance Grosvenor wouldn't make it.

He tossed his jacket onto the coat tree tucked in the corner of the entryway and patted Prince Albert, a suit of armor that stood guard at the foot of the stairs. He had rescued Prince Albert from the theater many years earlier and often talked to him as if the metal antique were a real person.

Today, however, he remained silent as he headed down the hallway to the kitchen. Angie was at the stove. He snuck up behind her and encircled her waist with his arms, resting his chin on her shoulder.

"Oh!" she cried, flinching, and laying one of her hands over his. "I didn't hear you come in. How's Grosvenor?"

He kissed the top of her head, released her, and then went to the refrigerator for a beer.

"He's alive—for now, at least." He pulled out a can and popped the top, took a big swig, and then slumped into a chair at the table. "God, Angie, it was awful. I didn't see the damned thing until it was on top of him. Poor little guy didn't have a chance."

She turned down the flame on the stove and joined him, placing her hand on his forearm. "He'll be okay, Joe. He has to be."

"I hope so. But he's weak. We were so far up in the canyon that he lost a lot of blood before we got him to the vet."

"And you said that another dog saved him."

"Yeah, a pit bull. Came out of nowhere and chased off the cat."

"Where's the pit bull now?"

"At the vet's office. They had an empty cage." He sat up straight. "You know the weird thing is that she loves Grosvenor."

"The pit bull is a she?"

"Yeah. And she not only saved him but kept licking the blood off his neck. Then, at the vet's office, she put her paws up on the exam table and whined at him. Like she knew him."

Angie smiled. "God has funny ways of bringing us together. There was a reason she was there just at the right time."

"I guess," he mumbled before taking another swig of beer. After he swallowed, a chuckle bubbled up from his throat. "Do you remember your reaction when I brought Grosvenor home that first night?" He raised his gaze to sneak a peek at her.

Her smile lit up her deep brown eyes. She had let her hair grow out and had it pulled back into a ponytail, with some wispy bangs framing her heart-shaped face.

"Yes," she replied. "I thought it was one of your many juvenile attempts to draw attention away from how mad I was at you about having another child. But he has been a wonderful addition to the family. I can't imagine life without him now." She swallowed and dropped her gaze.

He squeezed her hand, and she smiled through the tears that threatened to cloud her eyes.

"I love you, you know," he said.

"I know." She leaned forward and stroked his cheek. "He's going to be okay, Joe. I know it. Now, go talk to the kids and then tell them to wash up for dinner."

Giorgio kept the conversation with the kids brief. He described the incident as Grosvenor getting into a fight with a cougar and a second dog coming to the rescue. Now, they had to wait until the doctors did their magic and Grosvenor could come home.

His daughter, who was the spitting image of her mother, frowned before saying, "You're not telling us everything." Her eyes were narrowed in suspicion, and her pretty mouth twisted to one side.

"I don't think the details are necessary," he said. "The point is that Grosvenor is resting at the vet's and will hopefully be home soon."

"What happened to the cat?" Tony asked.

He was sitting on the sofa with a tablet in his lap, his legs sticking straight out over the edge of the couch.

"The other dog chased it off."

"Was it hurt at all? Grosvenor fought back, didn't he?"

"Yeah, he did," Giorgio replied. "He was really brave. I don't know if the cat was hurt."

"Someone will go after the cat, though, won't they?"

Giorgio had not even thought about that.

"I'll report it. I'm sure the park rangers will want to find it."

"Good. Because that cat could hurt somebody else," his son said.

Inwardly, Giorgio smiled at the fact that Tony thought of Grosvenor as a person. But then, so did he. Grosvenor was family, and his throat tightened again at the prospect that the dog might not make it.

"C'mon," he said, slapping his son's leg. "Mom says dinner is ready, and it smells really good. So, go wash your hands."

The family shared homemade minestrone soup and cheese toast and talked about how they would take care of Grosvenor when he got home. Angie promised to get him a new, cushy bed for the kitchen, while Tony promised to be the one to feed him if he needed help. Even Marie, who didn't like to get her hands dirty, said she would help in any way she could.

Both kids had become attached to the dog in the way only a child can. And as they related funny stories about Grosvenor, Giorgio faked a more positive attitude than he really had, telling them both to say a prayer that night for their friend.

÷

It was long after midnight, and the house was quiet except for an antique clock ticking quietly on the dresser. Giorgio lay in bed wide awake. Images of the encounter with the cougar kept invading his thoughts. His eyes had just begun to close when a noise startled him. Disoriented, he glanced over at his wife, but she slumbered peacefully.

He climbed out of bed and pulled the curtain aside to look out the window.

A floodlight above the garage bathed the driveway below in a golden glow. There was nothing there, but this had happened too many times before for him to ignore it.

He grabbed his robe, pushed his feet into slippers and moved into the hallway. The house was cloaked in darkness as he snuck a glance into each of the kids' rooms just to make sure all was well. A sliver of light from the window at the end of the landing afforded little light. He decided to check downstairs and made the turn at the head of the stairs, where he stopped cold.

Two images waited for him on the ground floor; Prince Albert and Christian Maynard, whose unearthly glow illuminated the darkened shadows in the entryway.

"Shit," Giorgio muttered, dropping onto the top step.

He began to shiver, but not from the cold morning air. The boy had never shown himself inside the house before. Things were changing. First, he had appeared during the daytime up in the canyon, and now this. *What did it mean?*

Giorgio had a talent for solving puzzles. As a kid, his mother often complained that it was too expensive to buy him jigsaw puzzles because he put them together too quickly. In response to her complaints, he would shrug his shoulders and say, "*I just see the patterns.*"

Then there was that sixth sense he had. His 'hunches' as Rocky called them. They had made him fodder for a lot of teasing in his New York precinct. Now, he had begun to wonder if they were the reason he could see the boy. Maybe he had some sort of connection to the other side, even though he wasn't sure he even believed in the other side. But during their last investigation, Rocky had admitted to seeing images of his fiancé after she'd been murdered in New York. Maybe it was something that ran in the family.

"What is it this time?" he whispered to the boy.

Christian just stared at Giorgio with big hollow eyes, dressed in the same dark knickers and white shirt. Even though the boy was only trying to help, Giorgio didn't feel particularly close to him. In fact, he was terrified by him. Christian just kept appearing and revealing clues that Giorgio had trouble deciphering.

As Giorgio fought to control his breathing, Christian raised an arm and flung something up the stairs. Giorgio ducked as it flew over his head and clanked against the wall behind him.

"This again?" he muttered.

The boy had done something similar during the Pinney House case. Giorgio had been watching Christian through the kitchen window to where he stood across the street. Christian had thrown something that magically landed at Giorgio's feet. It was a coin that would later prove to be an important piece to his then current investigation.

But now, the boy was in his house. That alone freaked him out, and his elevated heartbeat proved it. He took a deep breath to calm his nerves and turned to see what had hit the wall.

His eyes searched the shadows until he found a small piece of metal on the floor near the baseboard. Giorgio got to his feet and stepped back to pick it up. As he flipped it over in his hand, he realized it was an old dog tag with the word Sombra inscribed on it. A phone number had been scratched off.

Since he didn't believe in coincidences, he felt a short flutter of anxiety in the middle of his chest. *Why a dog tag?*

When he glanced back to the foot of the stairs, the boy was gone.

CHAPTER TEN

Giorgio didn't sleep much the rest of the night. Every noise made him flinch awake so that he crawled out of bed the next morning feeling groggy and completely drained.

He had just finished breakfast and was getting ready to leave the house when the phone rang. It was the receptionist at the veterinarian's office.

"Hi, Mr. Salvatori?"

"Yes," he replied.

"This is Rachel from Evergreen Vets."

"How's Grosvenor?"

"He's doing fine," she said. "But we'd like to keep him at least until tonight. However, we need you to pick up the pit bull. We've had another emergency and need the kennel."

"No problem. I'll be there in half an hour."

He relayed the news to Angie and left in a better mood. At least Grosvenor had made it through the night.

It was eight-thirty when he got to the emergency clinic. He looked in on Grosvenor before getting the pit bull. He was still asleep, but the doctor on duty said his vital signs were improving, and that he may be able to go home by the end of the day.

Giorgio took the pit bull back to the car. On a whim, he called out the name on the dog tag before letting her inside, but she didn't respond. He said Sombra again, but the dog waited patiently by the car door.

"So, maybe this isn't yours," he mumbled, fingering the dog tag in his pocket.

He returned to the station and stopped to see McCready, who eyed the dog warily from across the desk.

"This is the dog that saved Grosvenor. Can you watch her? I'll need to get back up into the canyon with the forensics people," Giorgio said.

"She's not going to rip my leg off, is she?"

"No. She seems very well-behaved." Giorgio leaned down to give the pit bull a pat. She shifted her scarred face in his direction, and he suddenly felt sorry for her. She had been mistreated and yet seemed grateful for the smallest bit of affection. "The vet said she was probably used as a bait dog for a dogfighting ring. But she hasn't shown any aggression since chasing off the cat." He handed the leash to McCready. "Take good care of her."

McCready took the leash as if he had just picked up a rattlesnake. When the dog stepped toward him, he moved back in his chair.

Giorgio chuckled. "Feed her some of those little fish crackers you keep in your desk, and I'm sure you'll be best friends."

"By the way," McCready began, still staring at the dog. "We got the preliminary medical examiner's report and we've ID'd the woman. Her name was Lindsey Nagel." He handed Giorgio a sheet of paper. "Thirty-two years old. According to her Facebook page, she was a bookkeeper."

"Okay, find out who the next-of-kin is and where she worked. And you might as well begin setting up the white board so we can begin tracking information."

Rocky appeared around the doorway to their office. "I see you brought the pit bull in. We're scheduled to meet Fong in fifteen minutes."

"Got it," Giorgio said.

A half hour later, Giorgio was wading through the creek bed for the third time, heading towards the area where Lindsey Nagel's body had lain. Behind him were his brother and two technicians carrying evidence cases. An angry crow chattered in a tree on the other side of the stream, its head jerking around to follow their movements. As Giorgio splashed out of the water, he spooked a squirrel, which scurried up the base of the tree, its tail flitting back and forth.

If only the local wildlife could talk, he thought, watching it disappear into the leafy branches.

Giorgio scanned the far rock wall that rose above the stream, wondering again how close homes had been built up there. *Could Nagel have lived in a neighborhood nearby or been at a party? And where was that mountain lion?*

The thought made him glance around his immediate area and listen for the trill that had signaled the cat's presence. He didn't think he'd ever forget that sound or the moment the cat had plummeted down the hillside to launch itself at Grosvenor.

He sucked in a deep breath and dropped his gaze back to the spot where Nagel had been found. He used the moment to study the area at his feet and suppress the memory of Grosvenor's painful cries. With a sigh, he looked up toward the trail Grosvenor had taken to the glen. It appeared that Nagel had been buried up there. *So, why would someone dig her up and carry her all the way down here?* As he scanned the hilly terrain, he remembered how difficult it had been to carry Grosvenor back to the car. Although Nagel probably didn't weigh more than 135 pounds, carrying that much dead weight over this terrain would've been tough for anyone but Arnold Schwarzenegger in his prime.

"C'mon, Jo Jo," Rocky said.

The group was clustered a few feet ahead of him, ready to move on.

"Sorry…just thinking. Let's go. But keep your eyes open," he said to the group. "I have a feeling something bigger is going on here. And someone had to have carried her down to the stream."

"That had to be a chore," Fong said. He followed right behind Rocky, who was in the lead. "Why would someone do that?"

"Don't know. Maybe just to make sure she was found."

The group climbed the trail, studying the ground and the surrounding vegetation as they went. Giorgio kicked rocks and pushed aside sage brush and ivy as he passed. Rocky was in front and studied the branches above his head as he passed. Halfway back to the clearing, he pushed a branch aside and stopped short.

"Look at that," he said, pointing at the branch he had just passed under.

They all paused, following Rocky's gaze. Giorgio stepped past Fong and the second technician and peered up into the leaves.

"It's a tuft of hair," he said.

Rocky was a good four inches taller than his older brother. He snapped on a rubber glove and reached out to retrieve the hair.

"Wait. Let me get a picture first," Giorgio said, grabbing his cell phone. He took a quick picture. "Okay, let's bag it."

"Here, use these," Fong said, handing him a pair of tweezers.

Rocky pulled the hair away from the clutches of the branches and dropped it into a small paper coin envelope that Fong held out for him.

"It's not the victim's hair," Fong said, studying it. "This is dark, almost black."

"Which means, if it belongs to whoever was carrying her, he was at least your height or taller," Giorgio said to Rocky, calculating the height of the branch.

"Makes sense," Rocky said.

"Carrying her down this trail would have been difficult," Fong said. "My guess is whoever carried her was also pretty muscular."

"You could've carried her," Giorgio said to his brother.

"Not easily. This trail is steep in places. It's slippery and narrow. And she would've been dead weight."

"So, we're looking for a big guy. Maybe muscle-bound," Giorgio said.

"At least physically fit. Yeah," Rocky agreed.

They reached the glen about five minutes later, and Rocky showed Fong the grave.

"We'll also need you to check those stumps," Giorgio said, pointing to the altar. "This area may have been used for rituals of some kind."

Fong walked over and ran his fingers across the top of one. "We won't be able to get fingerprints. Too rough and too porous." He leaned down to stare closely at the top of one of the stumps. "This looks like it could be blood though," he said, pointing.

"That's what I thought. This could be where she died. If so, could you get other bodily fluids?"

Fong shrugged. "Possibly. But we'll need to get the stumps into the lab, the sooner the better."

"Shit," Giorgio said. "Okay, see what you can get today, and then we'll have to see who can carry them out." He looked above him. "A helicopter might be able to get in here."

"That's gonna cost," Rocky said.

"We could seal the tops to protect evidence and then have someone saw them off," Fong suggested.

"Good idea," Giorgio said. "And a lot less expensive."

While the technicians got down to business taking samples of dirt from the grave, Rocky and Giorgio measured everything, noting the measurements in a small notebook. Then, Rocky did a cursory sketch of the area, while Giorgio did another sweep, bagging anything he found, including a few gum wrappers, more cigarette butts, and an empty Sprite can that had been crushed and stuffed into a bush. Even though most of the trash he found had probably been there a while, there was a small chance they could get fingerprints.

When they were ready to leave, Giorgio stuffed his hands into his pockets and looked at Fong. He was slender, in his mid-thirties, and rarely smiled or cracked a joke. Perhaps because his job was to gather the most gruesome evidence at crime scenes.

"Can you definitely say she was buried in that hole?"

Fong managed a shrug. "Something was buried there. We found blood and took samples from several other locations," he said, pointing to the logs. "The blood on the table was probably human, but we won't know if it matches what we found in the hole until we do some tests. But we'll get on it right away."

Giorgio thanked them, and the two technicians left.

When Giorgio didn't follow, Rocky asked, "We're not leaving?"

Giorgio glanced around again at the thickets of trees and bushes that hugged the rocky slopes. "Something's going on up here, and I wanna know what. You up for a little more hiking?"

Rocky rolled back on his heels. "Sure. I won't have to work out for a while."

"Okay, so this is where she died," Giorgio said, gesturing to the fake altar. "Most likely right on those logs."

"And they buried her over there," Rocky said, pointing to the boulders. "But we've been over this area with a fine-tooth comb. What do you think you'll find?"

"A way in and a way out," Giorgio said, studying the bluff. "If a group of people come here on a regular basis, there has to be an easier way to get here. I just don't see them tromping up that trail."

"Good point," Rocky said. "If there were ten or twenty people up here very often, I'd think the grass would be squashed, too."

"What if they only come up once a month, or even once a quarter?" Giorgio said.

Rocky shrugged. "Like on the night of a full moon."

"Exactly."

"Makes sense. And if these people work, they probably wouldn't come during the week, either. Okay, so, we're looking for a trail out of here?"

"Yeah, but keep your eyes out for the mountain lion," Giorgio warned.

"Speaking of…," Rocky said. "Do you think the blood in that hole attracted the cat?"

"Maybe," Giorgio said, glancing to the top of the rise again. "And remind me to report that cat to the park rangers."

"I wish we could find footprints, but there's too much grass," Rocky said, kicking at the ground.

"No footprints over by the grave?"

"Yeah, they found another boot print."

"Did it have those triangles?" Giorgio asked.

"Yeah. If we can ID the boot, we might be able to ID whoever dug her up."

"Well, that's something. Okay, let's see if there's a trail from the top of that bluff down here," Giorgio said, pointing to the top of the hill.

They moved to the southern end of the glen, away from the cliff overlooking the stream, and split up. They searched the underbrush and behind boulders and rocks looking for a break in the foliage.

As Rocky pushed brush aside with his hand, he called out, "Are there rattlesnakes up here?"

Giorgio stopped. "Shit. I hope not. Keep your hands out of small, dark spaces."

He passed the grave and moved toward the spot where he had seen the image of Christian Maynard the day before. He rounded a couple of big bushes and smiled.

"Shit," he muttered to himself. *Maybe this was what the boy was trying to show me and not the grave.* "Here!" he shouted to his brother.

Rocky jogged over to where Giorgio was standing beside two boulders set off by two narrow pine trees.

"What d'ya got?"

"This," Giorgio said pointing to a well-worn dirt path tucked behind a large bush. The path wound its way into the trees, turned left and continued at an angle up the hill. "Let's go," Giorgio said.

They followed the path up the incline. It wasn't as steep as the hill behind the glen, but they had to circumvent trees and rocks as they made their way to the top of the bluff. At the top, they stopped to gaze down on the glen and the grave.

"Okay, we know how they get to the glen," Giorgio said. "But they have to park somewhere." He looked behind him. "Let's keep going."

"Hold it," his brother said. Rocky moved off towards the cliff that overlooked the stream. "Back there," he said, pointing. "There's a building."

Sure enough. Out of view from the glen stood a sagging wooden structure surrounded by trees. They trudged through the brush to the back of the building.

"It's an old house," Giorgio said. He circled around to where a front porch faced the canyon and stream below. "This thing has probably been here a hundred years," he said, studying the rotting wood and splintered steps. He tested the first couple of steps and climbed to the porch.

"Be careful," Rocky warned. "You don't know what's in there."

"I don't think anyone lives here."

Giorgio yanked open the screen door and turned the dented metal doorknob. The door squeaked open to reveal a dark interior filled with old furniture and frayed curtains. Giorgio stepped inside.

"Hello?" he called.

When no one answered, he moved further into the room. "There's nothing here," he said.

Rocky came in behind him. "Somebody's been in here, though. It's too clean." He moved into the small kitchen and opened some cupboards. "There's no food, and the refrigerator is empty," he said, opening and closing an ancient refrigerator door.

Rocky went into one of the bedrooms. He took a quick look and came back out.

"There's some evidence in there that maybe kids have used this place to hook up. There's an old mattress and some blankets."

The two brothers stood in the main room glancing around.

"I don't think there's anything to see here," Giorgio said. "Let's keep going."

"Wait," Rocky said, peeking out a side window.

He left through the front door again and strode off to the side of the building.

"What's up?" Giorgio said, following him.

They walked all the way around to the north side, where Rocky stopped.

"This," he said, pointing ahead of him.

Giorgio followed his gesture and froze. "Shit. No wonder our vampire group chose this area for their rituals."

Extending before them was a small graveyard. Four gravestones rose out of the ground, two leaning to one side, and a fifth stone lying flat. They stepped forward to gaze down on the headstones.

"The family's name is Suzchek," Rocky said, reading a couple of them. "Looks like a family plot."

"Yeah," Giorgio said, roaming around. "A couple of children are buried here. Creepy."

"I wonder why they didn't bury Nagel up here," Rocky said.

"Well, they would have had to carry her up here," Giorgio said. "And we already speculated how hard that would be." Giorgio kicked his foot at a headstone. "I think they decided to bury her quickly, without much thought. Then, someone carried her down to the stream later, so that her body would be found."

"Which means that whoever dug her up had to have been here when she died," Rocky said.

"Or have been told about it later. I'm beginning to think her death was unexpected. And the group panicked. They buried her and left. Otherwise, they might have buried her up here."

"No one would have ever looked for her here," Rocky said.

They wandered around for another minute just to see what else they might find and then returned to the main path and followed it west, away from the glen and the canyon. Dense forest surrounded them as the ground flattened out. When a small rodent scurried across their path, Giorgio flinched and reached for his gun thinking it was the mountain lion.

"Easy, pardner," Rocky said.

"Sorry," Giorgio said. "But that cat is still up here somewhere."

"I get it. But we both have guns."

Giorgio grimaced. "Right."

They trudged on, kicking up dust and rocks as they went. The air was cool, but with all the exertion, Giorgio felt sweat gather across his back. When they came to a fork in the trail, they stopped.

"Which one?" Rocky asked.

Both paths were well-worn, but one looked like it hadn't been used recently. Branches and shrubs had begun to advance into the pathway.

"Let's take this one," Giorgio said, starting off on the one that remained clear.

Rocky followed as they struck out on what soon became a wide and well-worn path through a waning forest.

As the trees and heavy brush thinned, Rocky said, "Look at all this trash." He pointed to a treasure trove of abandoned soda cans, cigarette cartons, and Styrofoam cups.

"Interesting that whoever uses this place is careful to clean up the ritual site, but not out here," Giorgio murmured glancing down.

The path continued for another eighth of a mile over relatively flat ground. Within a few minutes, they came out into another clearing surrounded by hills, trees, and powerlines. Here, the grass had been obliterated, leaving only hardpacked dirt behind.

Giorgio studied the area. "Cars have been parked here," he said, pointing to tire tracks and oil spills. "There's room for at least fifteen, maybe twenty cars."

They crossed through the makeshift parking lot to the far side and found a one-lane dirt road that descended the hill to the left.

Giorgio stopped. "Let's get a forestry map and see if we can find out where this road goes."

"It's not big enough to be public," Rocky said. "I bet it's a maintenance road."

Giorgio took pictures of the area with his cell phone before they began the long trek back to their cars. When they reached the fork in the trail, Giorgio stopped.

"What?" Rocky said with a smirk.

Giorgio stared at the narrow path they had bypassed earlier as it wound through a stand of dense trees and disappeared into some bushes.

"C'mon."

He pushed aside branches and started off on yet another search. As he went, he continued to scan the trail and the surrounding area.

"Hold on, Joe," Rocky yelled.

"What is it?" Giorgio said, stopping.

Rocky left the trail and waded through the dense vegetation. Twenty or thirty feet off the trail, he bent over and reached into a laurel bush. He yanked something away from the clutches of the branches and held up a thick, leather dog collar attached to a short chain.

"Think this belongs to the pit bull?" Rocky climbed out of the undergrowth and handed the collar to his brother. "There's blood on it," he said, pointing to a streak of dried blood along the inside.

"It's been broken," Giorgio said, gesturing to where the collar had snapped apart at the buckle. "And the chain looks like it's been snapped off, too."

"It could belong to the pit bull. Maybe that's why she was wandering around up here."

Giorgio stared at a bent ring that had once held a dog tag. He reached into his pocket and fingered the old dog tag Christian Maynard had thrown at him the night before.

"Maybe," he said. He wadded the chain up and put the collar and short chain into his pocket. "C'mon."

He moved off with more purpose, his heart racing at the thought they might be close to answering questions about the pit bull. They weaved in and out of a copse of trees until they broke into another, smaller clearing.

"What the…" Rocky began, staring at a line of six weathered wooden doghouses. In front of each was a metal stake. A few were still driven into the ground and had thick chains attached. One stake had been pulled free and another was listing to one side. Two battered metal dog bowls lay close by.

They moved into the clearing and up to the kennels. Each one was empty.

"You think this is where she was kept?" Rocky asked.

"Don't know."

"Look at this," Rocky said, kicking at something in the dirt.

He had moved away and was pointing to something in the ground.

"What is it?" Giorgio said, coming up to Rocky's side.

"A series of holes." Rocky pointed at the hole and then to another one a couple of feet in front of him.

They followed the line of demarcations in a large circle. Giorgio stopped, his eyes roving around the rest of the circle.

"It's a dogfighting ring," he declared. "The vet said she thought the pit bull had been a bait dog."

"But where are they now? And why out here in the wilderness?" Rocky asked. He kicked at a metal stake that had been left in the grass.

"It's private. They could train the dogs here unobserved and then, with relative privacy, invite people in for a match."

Giorgio twisted his shoulders to survey the surrounding area. When he spied a small patch of raised dirt under some trees, he started off at a jog in that direction.

"What's up?" Rocky called after him.

"Not sure," he yelled over his shoulder.

When he got to the bare ground, he studied the area in front of him. Something caught his eye, and he stepped forward and dug his toe into the loose dirt.

"Shit," he said. He crouched down and used his fingers to pull away loose dirt until he felt something smooth and hard. He glanced up at his brother with a grim expression.

"What is it?" Rocky asked, towering over him.

Giorgio brushed more dirt away, exposing the emaciated head of a black dog. Its eyes were gone, eaten by bugs. But it hadn't been in the ground more than a few weeks, so much of the fur and skin remained.

"Shit," Rocky murmured. He crouched down next to his brother and began clearing away more dirt.

They worked for several minutes. Before long, they had uncovered the bodies of several dogs, all in varying states of decay, along with a skull that had been separated from the body and cleaned of any flesh. Giorgio pulled it from the ground and held it up. He let out a defeated sigh.

"This one's been here a long time."

"Dogs that didn't make it," Rocky said. "This is a killing field, but of a different sort."

"No kidding. The question now is," Giorgio began. "Does this dogfighting ring have anything to do with Lindsey Nagel's death?"

CHAPTER ELEVEN

It was early afternoon when they made it back to the cars. They passed two young adults starting off on the trail and saw the same city maintenance truck next to the restrooms. They let the hikers go, but Giorgio walked over to the truck. The maintenance worker was just coming out of the women's restroom with a full bag of trash.

"Excuse me," Giorgio said, showing his badge. "I'm Detective Salvatori with the Sierra Madre Police."

"Okay," the man said and kept moving. He was in his late thirties and already almost bald. He shuffled a little as he walked, as if he had had an injury to one of his legs.

Giorgio followed him to the truck. "We're investigating the body that was found up here a few days ago. Were you the one who took care of the restrooms and trash cans on Monday?"

The man threw the bag of trash into the back of the truck and then turned to Giorgio, wiping his hands on his pants. He crossed his arms over his chest and leaned back against the truck bed. "Yeah. Sure. That was me. You think I had something to do with that body?"

"What? No."

Giorgio zeroed in on his defensive posture. Sometimes people automatically assumed they were suspected of something when the police approached them. But sometimes they had a record. Giorgio suspected the latter, especially when he noticed the tattoo on the back of the guy's hand. It was a simple tattoo: five dots in between his thumb and forefinger shaped like the five on a pair of dice. It was a common prison tattoo that indicated he had been incarcerated for several years.

"What's your name?"

The man swayed backwards, watching Giorgio. "Rick Toreno."

"Okay, Rick. I was wondering if you happened to find any clothes that day in any of the trash cans?"

"Clothes?" Toreno's small brown eyes shifted to Rocky, who stood next to the car watching them. "I heard about that body," he said, turning back to Giorgio. "I read about it in the paper. It was a woman, wasn't it?"

"That's right."

He smiled for no apparent reason. "Too bad. A young woman dying like that." The smile disappeared. "So, you're looking for women's clothes."

"Yes. See anything like that?"

"No," he said shaking his head. "I didn't find no clothes."

Giorgio was watching him closely, wondering if this guy knew anything. "Did you see anything unusual that day?"

"Like what?"

"Anything out of the ordinary."

The man dropped his head and laughed and then looked back up at Giorgio. "You kidding? Normal day for me is cleaning toilets and picking up other people's shit."

Giorgio pulled out a copy of Lindsey Nagel's autopsy photo. "Ever see her before? Up here in the canyon?"

He glanced down and studied the photo. His eyes narrowed, but there was no sign of recognition. "No. Never saw her before. I have to get back to work." He pushed off the truck and walked past Giorgio, heading back to the restrooms.

"Wait!" Giorgio said. He caught up to him as the man turned back. "What about large groups of people. Have you ever known any groups to come up here for, I don't know, events or rituals or anything?"

The man's beady eyes narrowed to almost nothing. "What the fuck you talking about? There ain't no rituals up here. Just a bunch of stupid kids gettin' high or gettin' a blow job. Now I need to get back to work." He spun on his heel and disappeared into the men's room.

Giorgio returned to the car.

"Anything?" Rocky asked.

"Naw. He didn't see anything. He's got a record, so we should run his sheet just in case. His name is Rick Toreno."

"I'll do it when we get back."

Giorgio pulled out his phone and called McCready. "Have you found an address for Nagel yet?"

"Yeah. She lived on Cora Street right here in town." He rattled off the address and Giorgio programmed it into his phone.

"Okay, put a rush on a search warrant. Email it to me. We're going to head over there now. And then find me a forestry map. One that shows the maintenance roads behind the canyon. Also, I need some research on dogfighting rings in the area."

"Dogfighting rings? Why?"

"Because we think we found one up here. Or, what's left of it. The dogs are gone, and it doesn't look like anyone has been here in a while, but I want to see if we can find out who ran it."

"You think that's where the pit bull came from?"

"Maybe."

"Okay. Will do."

"And McCready, did you find the next-of-kin?"

"Yeah. Her mother."

"Okay, she needs to be told. You up for the notification?"

"Um…I…yeah, I guess so."

Giorgio smiled. "You'll do fine. Tell her the truth. That her daughter's body was found up in the canyon, but that we don't know yet how she died."

"And the holes in her neck?"

"Don't mention it. But find out where Nagle worked and then check with the M.E. and see if you can get the mother down there for a positive ID. Tell her I'll come talk with her tomorrow."

"Okay," the young cop said with a distinct lack of confidence.

They stopped for a quick burger at McDonald's and were just about to leave when McCready sent over the search warrant. They arrived at Nagel's apartment just shy of 2:00 p.m. She lived on a short, dead-end street in a smart-looking red brick apartment building. It was flanked by small ranch-style homes with immaculate front lawns, curved driveways, and large, shady oak trees.

"Not a bad area for a thirty-something single woman," Rocky said, eying the neighboring homes.

Giorgio checked his notes. "Yeah. She lived in 212."

They parked behind a newer model Honda Civic and entered the building through double glass doors, heading straight for the manager's office. After they presented the search warrant and had a short discussion with a woman who looked right out of the seventies, complete with long, braided hair and a tie-dyed skirt and blouse, they took the elevators to the second floor with an extra key to number 212.

They found the door ajar.

Giorgio held up a hand as they reached for their weapons. "Police!" he announced, pushing open the door.

They stepped into what was once a small but neat combo living room and dining room separated from the kitchen by an open bar and bar stools. It now looked like a tornado had gone through it.

"Shit," Giorgio murmured.

All the furniture had been turned over and pillows tossed onto the floor. The flat screen TV had been ripped off its wall mount above a gas fireplace and thrown to the floor. Books had been pulled off the shelves of an IKEA-style bookcase and the bookcase tipped over. Tiny glass figurines from a curio cabinet lay strewn across the carpet, many smashed underfoot.

"Check the bedroom," Giorgio told Rocky.

Rocky entered the bedroom through a short hallway. "Police!" he called out.

Meanwhile, Giorgio checked the bathroom, where the medicine cabinet and all the drawers in the sink area had been opened. Pill bottles and tubes of ointment filled the sink. Even the top to the toilet tank had been taken off.

Giorgio returned to the living room. A moment later, Rocky emerged from the bedroom.

"It looks the same in there," Rocky said, holstering his weapon.

"Bathroom, too," Giorgio added. "Clearly someone was looking for something."

He pulled on a pair of rubber gloves. "Call Fong. Be careful. We might be able to lift some prints."

"Okay," Rocky said, reaching for his phone. "I'll start in here."

Rocky called for a forensics team and then donned rubber gloves. "No one from forensics can get here for a couple of hours," he told his brother a minute later.

"Okay. Take pictures of everything first."

"Got it."

Rocky began to shoot pictures with his cell phone, starting in the bedroom and then moving to the bathroom. Giorgio took photos in the living room, careful not to move major pieces of furniture. When he finished, he began to search.

He found two large, framed prints on the floor that had hung on the wall above the sofa. The frames had been broken and glass shattered; their backing had also been ripped off. The only other picture he found was a framed photo of Lindsey Nagel at the beach. She was with another woman who shared similar facial features. He set that one aside.

"Interesting," Giorgio said over his shoulder to Rocky. "Found two boilerplate posters and one personal photo. That's all."

"Who's in the photo with her?" Rocky asked from the kitchen.

"A woman. Maybe a sibling. We'll take it."

Giorgio had moved to a small desk in the corner by the front door. The lamp was on the floor, and all the drawers had been emptied out. But a single book still sat on top. He picked it up and fingered through a few pages.

"She was reading Bram Stoker's *Dracula*."

"Wonder if it was required reading," Rocky said with a chuckle. He was opening and closing cupboards in the small kitchen.

Giorgio put the book down next to the framed photo and sorted through other things from the desk that had been scattered across the floor: some unopened mail, a letter from someone in Pennsylvania, a basket once filled with desk supplies, a map of the Los Angeles basin, and an instructional manual for an iPad. He looked around but didn't see the iPad.

"Hey, Rocky, let me know if you find an iPad."

"Okay." Rocky leaned over the kitchen bar. "You know, we never found her purse or her cell phone up in the canyon, either."

"Yeah," Giorgio said. "Good point. I don't see them here, though," he said glancing around. "So, whoever has them must have carried them out, or she left them somewhere beforehand."

"She could have changed somewhere else. You know, like McCready said. She was the willing volunteer that night."

"So, you're thinking she met these people somewhere and changed into the smock. Then, she went with them, leaving all of her belongings behind?"

"Makes sense," Rocky said with a shrug.

"So, we need to find where that was." Giorgio glanced down to the floor. "I wonder what all of this stuff is." He was staring at about fifty sheets of copy paper scattered across the floor, all filled with text. He picked one up and began to read out loud. "*She reached for the closest drawer and withdrew a sharp knife. Lacing her fingers around the hilt, she dropped her hand by her side and turned to face the door.*" Giorgio picked up another sheet, skimming the text. "She was writing a book. By the looks of it, a murder mystery."

"Look at this," Rocky said, coming to the door of the kitchen. He held up a flyer. "I found this in a drawer."

Giorgio glanced over. "The *Essence of Murder*," he murmured. "Shit. Let's get it fingerprinted."

Rocky left it on the counter and turned to open a cupboard that held several bottles of pills. He pulled one out. "Xanax," he said.

Giorgio turned towards him. "Take all the pills."

Rocky nodded and put the bottles of pills next to the flyer. Giorgio began picking up the numbered pages off the floor. He set the small oval dining table back on its feet and began to put the pages in order. He leaned down and picked up a box that at one time had held a ream of paper. The lid had been nestled into the bottom of the box, and the last few pages of the manuscript were still inside. He finished organizing the pages and dropped them in with the others and then set the box on the table.

Over the next forty minutes, the two detectives did a thorough search of the apartment, going through her bedroom and bathroom and even attempting to get into her computer. By the time they were ready to leave, Rocky carried a trash bag filled with the Bram Stoker book, the map, her address book, iPad, the photo, pills, mail, flyer, and laptop.

Giorgio had ripped off his gloves and was stuffing them into his pocket. "We need to talk with the manager again on our way out. Find out what kind of car she drove. And we need to get McCready to go through her computer and emails."

"Let's also see if the manager knows where her car might be," Rocky said.

"Good idea."

Rocky opened the door and came face-to-face with a disheveled young man, his hand raised and ready to knock.

"Oh," the young man said in surprise. "Who are you?"

"Sierra Madre police," Rocky said, lifting the badge hanging around his

neck.

"Uh, okay, but where's Lindsey?"

"What's your name, son?" Giorgio asked, stepping forward.

The man wasn't much over twenty-five and slight in stature. His dark eyes flashed when Giorgio asked his name.

"Uh…Dave. Dave Baker. What's going on?" He tried to glance past them into the apartment. "Is Lindsey here?"

"How do you know Lindsey?" Giorgio asked.

Baker shifted from one foot to the other. He was medium height and dressed in baggy jeans, a loose-fitting black t-shirt with the name H.I.M. splashed across the red image of a butterfly. Silver crosses dangled from each ear, a silver stud decorated one nostril, and several heavy, silver necklaces hung from around his neck. It was the black eye makeup and the tattoo of a red heart with a teardrop on his forearm though, that stood out most to Giorgio. The heart matched the one on Nagel's hip.

"She's a friend," Baker replied.

Giorgio glanced at Rocky and nodded toward the apartment.

Rocky reached out and pushed the door open wide. "Why don't you come inside, Mr. Baker."

Rocky and Giorgio parted, allowing Baker full view of the destruction behind them.

"Uh…I really have…Jesus, what happened?" His eyes grew wide as he stared at Lindsey Nagel's apartment.

"We could use your help," Giorgio said. "It will just take a minute."

He reached out and guided the young man inside, while Rocky closed the door. Rocky put the bag down and stood in front of the door, blocking the young man's exit.

"I don't get it," Baker said, looking around. "What happened in here? And where's Lindsey?"

"We need some information first," Giorgio said. "How do you know Lindsey?"

Baker stood in front of the overturned sofa, twisting a large peace symbol at the end of one of the chains around his neck. "We took a writing class together."

"When was that?"

Baker's eyes roamed the apartment. "About six months ago. We decided to become writing buddies and met once a week to write at a Starbuck's. Why? What the heck is going on? Has something happened to her?"

"When was the last time you saw her?" Giorgio asked.

The boy's eyebrows clenched. "Uh…Friday night. We…uh, had dinner together."

"Where"? Rocky asked, taking notes.

The boy shifted his eyes back and forth between the brothers. "At the Cave. It's a small place in Arcadia."

"And where did you go after that?" Giorgio asked.

Baker licked his lips. "Um…out with some friends."

"Did Lindsey go with you?"

"Um…no."

"What time did you get home that night?"

"C'mon. What's going on?" he asked in frustration.

"What did she do after you left?"

"I, uh, don't know. What's happened?"

"Did you leave the restaurant together?" Rocky asked.

He paused. "No. She stayed behind."

"Why?"

He paused again, shifting his feet. "I think she was going to meet someone else. She didn't really say. What the heck happened to her?"

"We'll ask the questions," Giorgio said. "What time did you get home Friday night?"

He began to tap his right heel against the floor. "It was late. Maybe two."

"Did Lindsey meet you at the restaurant?"

"Yeah. We were supposed to meet at 6:30."

"And she drove her own car?"

Baker hesitated, took a breath and then said, "Yeah. I mean, I guess. I met her inside."

"And you say you left first?" Rocky asked.

His eyes darted toward Rocky. "Yeah. It was my mother's birthday."

"You said you went out with friends."

He paused and then swallowed. "Um…yeah, I did. But I had to stop by my mom's too."

"If I were you, Dave, I wouldn't lie," Rocky said.

"I'm not. You can call my mom."

"We will. Once again, was Lindsey alone when you left?" Rocky pushed him.

He let a breath out in defeat. "No."

"Who was she with?" Giorgio prodded.

The young man stared at Giorgio as a bead of sweat broke out on his brow. He swallowed, cleared his throat, and said, "Just a guy."

"What guy?"

"A mutual friend, that's all."

"That's fine," Giorgio placated him. "What's his name?"

Baker erupted in a dry laugh. "I don't know his real name. He's known as The Maestro."

Giorgio shared a look with his brother. "Odd name. Or title. What does it mean?"

"I don't know, really. It's just what everyone calls him. Look, I need to get to work, but I want to know what happened to Lindsey."

Giorgio paused, deciding whether to tell him. In the end, it didn't matter. He'd know soon enough.

"I'm sorry, but Ms. Nagel was found dead yesterday up in Bailey Canyon. We believe she died sometime Sunday morning. Do you know any reason why she would have been up there?"

Baker's face went pale. "Oh my God," he whimpered, dropping his chin.

Rocky stepped forward and righted a chair, allowing Baker to fall onto it. He was silent for a moment.

"Mr. Baker?" Giorgio prompted him.

He looked up with a haunted expression. "Uh…no, I don't know why she would have been up there. What happened? Did she fall or something? She was very afraid of heights."

Giorgio noted the change in his demeanor.

"The circumstances of her death are still unclear. Do you know if she liked to hike? Or, if she had friends who lived up there?"

"No. I didn't really know her that well."

"You just said you met once a week to write together," Rocky interjected.

He glanced up at Rocky and swallowed. "Yes, well, we did. But we talked about writing. I mean, we didn't talk all that much about our personal lives."

"And yet, here you are at her apartment," Giorgio said. "Why are you here?"

Baker sucked in a small pocket of air. "Um...uh...I just wanted to stop by and see...if..."

He paused again, his foot tapping against the floor.

"What, Mr. Baker? You stopped by to see if...what?"

He stared hard at Giorgio. Giorgio had interviewed hundreds of people and knew the telltale signs when they were lying. This kid was lying out his ass.

"I wanted to know if she would sign up for a webinar on writing with me."

He seemed relieved by his answer because it was a plausible lie. His leg relaxed.

"What did she like to write?" Giorgio asked.

"Murder mysteries," Baker said. "She was working on a novel. It would probably be on her laptop."

"Any chance you know her password?" Rocky asked.

"No. I don't."

"Would you say she lived in a fantasy world?" Giorgio asked.

"Uh, no, not really. I mean, no more than any of the rest of us."

Giorgio allowed his eyes to take in Baker's appearance again. "What about you? What sort of fantasies do you dabble in?"

"Look, I need to get going," he said, standing up. "I'm supposed to be at work in a few minutes."

"This late in the day?" Giorgio said, glancing at his watch.

"Yeah, I'm subbing for a friend today," the boy said, moving toward the door.

"Just a minute," Giorgio said. "We'll need to know how to get hold of you in case we have any more questions."

Baker bit his bottom lip and then pulled out his driver's license and handed it to Giorgio. "I work at the Radio Shack on Foothill Boulevard in Arcadia," he said.

"Cell phone and your mother's name," Giorgio said.

The kid looked stricken at having to give them his mother's name. But he rattled off his cell phone number and his mother's name and address.

"Sorry, but I really do have to go now."

Giorgio handed back the ID, and the kid turned and started for the door.

"Wait a minute," Giorgio said, stopping him. "Here's my card. Please let us know if you think of anything. Also, did Ms. Nagel have a cell phone?"

"Yeah."

"What's her number."

He hesitated. "What? Why?"

"Just give us her number."

Baker pulled out his own cell phone and read off Lindsey's number. Rocky wrote it down.

"Thanks," Giorgio said.

Without a word, Baker disappeared out the door and down the hallway.

"Well, that was interesting," Giorgio said. "What the heck do you think he was hiding?"

"Dunno," Rocky replied. "But maybe we need to read that novel of hers," he said, nodding toward the box sitting on the desk.

"I agree. But first, dial her cell phone. Just in case."

Rocky pulled out his phone and dialed the number. It rang until an automated message on the other end said, "Hi, leave your number, and I'll get back to you. Happy day!"

Rocky looked up at his brother with a somber expression. "Well, the phone isn't here," he said.

C'mon," Giorgio said, moving toward the door. "I want to talk to the manager. We need to find her car. We also need to send someone down to talk to the neighbors," he said. "And then we need to find out more about that tattoo. Clearly, more than one person has it."

Rocky smiled. "Sounds like a trip to see our resident psychic, Flame."

"Wait, let me get the book," Giorgio said, reaching for the box. He pulled the top of the box away from the bottom to replace the lid and three sheets of paper fluttered out.

"What are those?" Rocky asked.

"Don't know." Giorgio scooped them up and glanced at them. "These aren't pages from the book. They look like some sort of medical bills."

He handed the papers to his brother. Rocky skimmed them. "No, these are insurance forms. All for the same person."

"But why the hell would Lindsey have them?"

Rocky shrugged. "And why would she have hidden them in the top of that box?"

Giorgio leveled a grim stare at his brother. "Maybe we just found what the intruders were looking for."

CHAPTER TWELVE

The manager didn't have much to add other than Nagel had been a quiet resident and rarely entertained. The woman didn't seem to know anything about Baker or why the apartment had been ransacked.

"There was a plumbing van outside yesterday, though," she said. "No one complained about a clogged toilet, so I don't know whether the plumbers came inside or not."

"Do you remember the name of the company?"

She blinked once and stared at him. "Naw. It was dark gray, though. And Lindsey drives a blue Chevy Malibu. Slot #14. Don't know whether it's there or not."

"Thanks. We'll check."

They left the building by the side entrance that led to the resident parking lot. Slot number 14 was empty.

"Shit," Giorgio said, exhaling. "Let's go."

They circled the building and met the forensics people coming up the front walkway. Rocky took them to see the manager and then to Nagel's apartment, while Giorgio called McCready.

"How'd it go with Nagel's mother?" he asked when McCready came on the line.

McCready sighed. "She was devastated but somehow not surprised. She said Lindsey had been taking some unnecessary risks lately, but she didn't say what. Anyway, she met me at the medical examiner's office and made a positive ID. I told her you'd stop by tomorrow."

"Actually, we're done here. Give her a call and see if we can see her now. We also need an officer down here right away to tape off the apartment and guard it. It was broken into and forensics just arrived. They'll be here for a while. Ask the captain if he can send a couple of officers down to talk to the neighbors, too. We need to know if they heard or saw anything unusual."

"Okay. I'll text you the mother's address, and I'll let her know you're on your way.

"Thanks. And, by the way, good job."

When McCready sent the mother's address, Giorgio took the 210 Freeway past businesses and residential neighborhoods to Hawthorne, a community of 28,000 located about twenty miles from the ocean on the west side of the Los Angeles basin. Hawthorne was a non-descript town whose major claim to fame was that it was home to the Beach Boys.

They pulled into the driveway of a tidy home on Rohler Street. Nagel's mother, a woman in her late fifties, answered the door. Her grayish-blond, shoulder length hair framed a round face, but her eyes were rimmed in red from crying. She wore a blue apron tied around a bulging midriff, and the smell of cookies wafted in the air behind her.

Giorgio and Rocky introduced themselves and showed their badges.

"Please, come in," she said in a shaky voice.

She drew them into a small living room. "Officer McCready said you were on your way, so I made some cookies," she said, wringing her hands together. "Please, have a seat. I'll be right back."

The brothers shared a curious look before sitting down.

Victim's families responded to their loss in different ways, Giorgio thought to himself. But often women who have lost a child automatically fall into their role as mother and consoler-in-chief, repeating things they had done so often for their children. Hence the cookies. Men were more likely to focus on something manly, like fixing a lawn mower or cleaning the garage. Anything to distract them from reality.

Giorgio glanced around the small living room as Ms. Nagel busied herself in the kitchen. It was a near duplicate of Lindsey Nagel's apartment, minus the mess. Worn but comfortable light brown furniture filled the room, along with a glass curio cabinet that held shelf after shelf of small figurines. A white brick fireplace stood at the far end, and a small entertainment center sat off to one side holding a flat screen T.V.

The big difference between the two homes was that framed prints of birds and flowers covered the walls here, and the fireplace mantle was littered with family photos. Lindsey had shown no personality in her decorating, while Mrs. Nagel not only displayed splashes of color and a fondness for the outdoors, but her family as well.

Giorgio perused the pictures that lined the mantle.

All the photos were of the Nagel family. Lindsey was pictured in three of them from the approximate ages of 7 to 20. Mr. Nagel had been a small man with olive skin and brown hair and eyes. Lindsey apparently also had an older sister, who shared her facial features. She was the woman in the photo Giorgio had taken from Nagel's apartment.

"Here we go," a voice said from behind him.

Giorgio spun around as Mrs. Nagel came back into the room carrying a tray with a plate of cookies and two cans of beer. He raised his eyebrows at the alcohol.

"Please, help yourself," she said, putting the tray on the coffee table. "I know how you men like your beer."

Her voice caught, and she had to swallow as she sank into a nearby chair. Rocky shot a plaintive look at his brother.

"Thank you, Mrs. Nagel, but we're on duty," he said.

She pulled a tissue from the pocket of her apron and began wringing her hands again. "Of course. How silly of me." She began to rise. "I'll get some lemonade."

"No," Giorgio said with a raised hand. "Please. The cookies will be fine. Don't trouble yourself."

She resumed her seat, wiped her eyes, and blew her nose. Rocky took one of the cookies and began to nibble on it.

"Chocolate chip. My favorite," he said, swallowing. "Thank you."

Giorgio watched the woman, contemplating her obvious obsession to please.

"Thank you for seeing us," he said, sitting down.

"Janet. Please call me Janet," she said, staring at her hands.

"Janet," he said. "We're very sorry for your loss, but we need to ask a few questions about your daughter."

Her eyes began to tear up again, and she dabbed at them with the tissue. "Of course, anything."

"Do you know why she would have been up in Bailey Canyon?"

She gave an almost imperceptible shake of her head. "No. In fact, I was shocked to hear that's where she was found."

"Why do you say that?" Giorgio asked.

Her head came up and her pale blue, watery eyes held his. "Because since Lindsey was a little girl she was afraid of heights."

Giorgio was reminded of what young Dave Baker, her Goth-looking friend, had said.

"What do you mean?" Rocky asked.

"Lindsey was what they call polyphobic. She was afraid of everything," she said with a throwaway chuckle. "She had a list of phobias as long as your arm."

"Phobias?" Giorgio asked. "What kind of phobias?"

"Oh, dear. Where to start," she said. "She was afraid of crowds. We found that out when she was only two, and we took her to the zoo. At first, we thought she was afraid of the animals, but realized it was the crowds. She became hysterical when people would bump up against her. After that, we couldn't take her anywhere where there was a congestion of people. She would throw a fit and disrupt everything."

Giorgio had a notepad out and was taking notes. "What else?"

"She had an irrational fear of heights. She could just barely climb stairs or use an elevator, and only then if she couldn't see how high she was going. But if she had a view of the ground, she'd become paralyzed." She sighed deeply. "Then, there were sharp objects. Needles terrorized her. Taking her to the dentist was traumatic for both the staff and me because she would cry until snot came out her nose. Doctors would have to hold her down to give her shots. And forget drawing blood. When she was thirteen, she had to get a blood test because the doctor thought she was anemic. She hyperventilated until she actually passed out in the chair."

"And yet your daughter had breast implants. That's how we identified her," Giorgio said.

She swallowed a gulp of air and paused to steady herself. "Her husband talked her into those. But, of course, she was unconscious for the surgery, and they gave her some medication before they put the IV in her arm."

Giorgio was leaning forward, his elbows resting on his knees, but his mind was whirring. *How could a woman so afraid of sharp objects allow her neck to be punctured?*

"Mrs. Nagel…"

"Janet," she corrected him.

"Janet…when we found your daughter, she had two puncture wounds in her neck." The woman flinched. "Do you have any idea how that could have happened?"

"Nooo," she said plaintively. "What do you mean?"

"Just what I said. She had two holes in her neck, over a vein," he said.

Her face contorted. "I can't even imagine what that's about. I do know she was working hard to overcome some of her phobias. After all, they had nearly ruined her life."

"How so?" Rocky asked.

"She'd lost jobs and relationships because of them."

"But she was married," Rocky said.

"Well, yes, but it didn't last long. And he was an awful man."

"What's his name?" Giorgio asked.

"Craig Velchy. She took back her maiden name as soon as she got divorced. Lindsey liked familiar things."

Bingo! Giorgio thought. Now he knew why Lindsey Nagel's living room looked so much like her mother's.

"Where does Mr. Velchy live now?" he asked her.

"I think he still lives in Arcadia. He works for the UPS store on Live Oak Street there."

"Why do you say he was awful?"

She paused and shifted her weight in the chair. "He was a controlling son-of-a-bitch…excuse my French."

Both men smiled.

"He wanted to know where she was twenty-four hours a day. That's why she divorced him. That and the fact that he hit her."

"He abused her?" Giorgio said, his antenna going up.

"Yes, at least once that I know of."

"Did she report it to the police?" Rocky asked.

"Oh, no, I doubt it," she said, shaking her head. "Lindsey was a very private person. I only know about it because I stopped by the day after it happened and saw the bruise on her face and asked her about it. I had to drag it out of her. I think Craig rather liked the fact that Lindsey was so timid. He could control her. Then, she began taking bio-feedback classes. I don't really understand it, but she said it was helping. Craig didn't like it, though."

"And you think they divorced because he didn't like that she was beginning to shed her phobias?" Giorgio asked.

"Yes. Like I said, he was very controlling. When she began to make her own decisions, they started to argue. That's when he hit her. And she told me he threatened her after that. He said he could make her disappear and no one would ever know. Eventually, she got up the courage to leave him."

"How long ago was that?"

She paused to consider the question. "Like I said, maybe a year ago. She moved in briefly with her sister, Carey."

"And Carey doesn't suffer from any phobias?"

"No," she said, shaking her head and looking at the floor. "She has her own problems, but not phobias."

"What kind of problems?"

She shrugged. "Just lifestyle choices. Nothing more."

"Were the two sisters close?" Giorgio asked.

"Yes, I think so," she said. "Carey is older by two years and works in Hollywood for Premier Films."

"How'd she take her sister's death?" Rocky asked, reaching for a second cookie.

Mrs. Nagel dropped her head again, using the tissue to wipe her nose. "I'm not sure."

Giorgio and Rocky shared a guarded look.

"What do you mean? Have you talked with her?" Giorgio asked.

She heaved a sigh. "I called her as soon as I was told. Carey has always been Lindsey's opposite. She's self-assured and assertive. I'd even describe her as opinionated. Compare that to Lindsey who was such a mouse." She paused, as if hesitant to say anything further. "Carey said to me once that it would be better if Lindsey just killed herself."

Giorgio perked up. "Why would she say that?"

"Because Lindsey's phobias were so debilitating." She looked at Giorgio with sad eyes. "The phobias dictated everything we did as a family. I'm sure Carey resented that. But I also think Carey thought life wouldn't be worth living if you had that many fears. When I called her this afternoon to tell her about Lindsey, she just said, 'Maybe it's for the best, Mom.'"

A sob bubbled up in her throat, and she pressed the tissue to her lips to control it. Giorgio gave her time to recover.

"You know, I saw Lindsey just a week ago," she continued. "She said that she'd made real progress on her fears. She was doing rock-climbing and had joined Toastmasters. Said she enjoyed it. Maybe that's why she was in the canyon."

"What do you mean?"

"Well, maybe it was some sort of rock-climbing challenge." Her voice caught, and she clamped her lips tight to stop herself from crying.

"But she did live on her own," Rocky said.

She nodded. "Oh, yes. When she left her husband, she moved in with Carey but just for a few months. Then, she got an apartment."

"Mrs. Nagel, did Lindsey belong to any groups that you know of?" Giorgio asked.

She took a deep breath and shook her head. "No. But Carey said something today that surprised me."

"What's that?"

"She said that after living a life filled with debilitating fears, it was finally the sex appeal of one man that probably got Lindsey killed."

CHAPTER THIRTEEN

The two brothers left Mrs. Nagel and her plate of cookies and returned to the station. McCready had set up the case board. So far, he had filled it with photos of Nagel's body in the creek bed along with several pictures of the shoe prints, the sketches of the area, a close-up view of the two holes in her neck highlighted by question marks, a photo of the tattoo, and a couple pictures of the canyon and one of the log platform in the glen.

Giorgio studied it for a moment and then turned to Rocky.

"When you get a chance, add pictures of the grave site. I'm going to go check on Grosvenor."

"No problem. I'll write up notes from today and check Toreno's record."

"Thanks."

Giorgio picked up the pit bull from McCready and made it to the vet a few minutes before six. He took the pit bull inside with him and found Grosvenor still lying in the cage, his eyes closed, an IV taped to his right back leg.

"Let me get the doctor for you," the young technician said, disappearing through the door.

Giorgio watched Grosvenor until he sensed someone at his shoulder.

"He's resting," a male voice said.

Giorgio turned to find a short, dark-haired man.

"I'm Dr. Stevens," the man said, holding out his hand.

"How's he doing? I thought I was going to take him home," Giorgio said, shaking the doctor's hand.

"He's still very weak. I would like to keep him one more night. You can check with us tomorrow." He glanced down at the pit bull standing with her nose pressed against Grosvenor's cage door. "She seems to have bonded with your dog."

"Yeah, but I don't know why. She came out of nowhere up in the hills to save his life."

"Dr. Vincent mentioned her to me," the doctor said, crouching down to run his hand over her back. "I agree she looks like she's been a fighting dog."

"We think we found where she may have been kept," Giorgio said.

His head came up. "Really? Any chance you'll get to shut them down?"

"The area's been abandoned. It's hard to tell how long ago." He reached into his jacket and pulled out the broken collar and chain. "We found this, though. It might have been hers."

The doctor stood up and fingered the collar. "Looks like the right size." He leaned down and searched the dog's neck. "Yes, her neck has been rubbed raw here," he said, pointing to a spot behind her ear. "I bet she pulled against it hard enough that the collar finally broke." He straightened up. "I'm glad she escaped. It would've been only a matter of time before she'd died there."

"We found several dogs buried up there. That would have been her future, I suppose. Any chance I could leave her here overnight again?"

"I'm sorry. We have an accident coming in," he said. "We'll be full. But I wouldn't worry about it. She is a nice dog. Take her home tonight, and if you have to, you can drop her off at the shelter tomorrow."

Giorgio glanced down at the dog. "I don't know…I have kids."

The doctor stuck his hands into the pockets of his lab coat. "I understand. People are afraid of pit bulls. It's too bad. They're only as mean as their owners. Let me warn you that if you take her to the shelter, they're not usually adopted. Especially one that looks like her. She'll most likely be put down."

Giorgio's jaw clenched. "That wouldn't be right. She saved Grosvenor's life."

The doctor shrugged. "Won't mean anything to people looking for a pet. They'll just see a pit bull that's been in a lot of dog fights and assume she's aggressive."

"But she hasn't shown any aggression." He paused. "I'll find her a home."

The doctor smiled. "Sounds good. Besides, in the meantime, she'll be good company for Grosvenor while he's recovering."

When Giorgio returned home, the front door opened before he could even turn the handle, bringing him face to face with his wife.

"How is he?" she asked, her soft brown eyes pinched with concern.

"For now, okay," Giorgio replied. He stepped into the foyer, bringing the pit bull with him. "But they want to keep him until tomorrow."

Angie closed the door behind him. When his wife didn't say anything, he turned and found her staring wide-eyed at the pit bull.

"Why is that dog here?"

Giorgio paused, unsure of what to say. When he had brought Grosvenor home from the shelter the year before, Angie had reacted in an equally negative way. But soon, the entire family had grown to love him. He wasn't so sure about the pit bull. Not only because of the breed's reputation, but this one was too battle-scarred to look friendly.

"Um…I brought her home because, well, the only alternative was to take her to the shelter."

"What was wrong with that idea?"

"C'mon, Angie. The vet said pit bulls aren't usually adopted. Especially ones that have been part of a dogfighting operation. She'd be euthanized."

"Dogfighting?" Angie's voice rose in pitch, and she stepped back from the dog.

"Only as a bait dog. She wasn't the aggressor," he said, hoping to placate her.

"But…"

"Angie," he said, placing his hand on her shoulder. "She saved Grosvenor's life. He would have been ripped apart. And she was a perfect lady at the department today."

Giorgio knew he was pleading, but sometimes it worked. He had known Angie since he was twelve. At her core, she was a softy. But she was also a mama bear when it came to her family. He held his breath, because right now the liquid brown eyes that could seduce him in a heartbeat had grown anxious as she stared at the dog.

"Okay," she said with a reserved sigh. "But you keep it on a leash or in the kennel at all times. Understood?"

He nodded. "Okay, but she's a nice dog."

"She chased off a mountain lion, Joe," she replied with steel in her voice. "I'm not taking any chances. Dinner will be ready in a half hour." She turned on her heel and disappeared into the kitchen.

"Dad!" a voice screamed. Tony ran out of the den in his stocking feet, coming to a sliding halt on the hardwood floor as he stared at the pit bull. "Where'd this dog come from?"

Giorgio swallowed as the dog pulled at the leash, edging toward Tony. "She's the dog that saved Grosvenor. She has no place to go." Giorgio kneeled and held the dog back as Tony's face disintegrated into a frown.

The pit bull had reached the boy's hand and licked it. Tony's dark eyes searched the dog's face. He reached out slowly, and the dog leaned forward and licked his hand again.

Tony grinned. "She's cool, Dad. But why does she have so many scars?"

Giorgio didn't like to lie to his kids, but he didn't think his son was ready for the harsh truth about how some people made money off the suffering of animals.

"Um…we were up in the canyon, remember. The mountain lion attacked Grosvenor, and this dog ran it off. I think she's been up there for a while and probably had run-ins with the lion before."

Tony's eyes grew wide. "Wow, she's one tough dog. How's Grosvenor?"

"He's resting at the vet. You'll get to see him tomorrow. Meanwhile, we need to figure out what to call *this* dog."

The distraction worked. His son stroked the dog's head. He scrunched up his young face and studied the animal. "Well…" he began. "She's all gray, and she even has gray eyes." The dog had moved in close to Tony and sat down, leaning into his leg. "I think she likes me," he said with a smile. "Why don't we call her… Shadow?"

Giorgio chuckled. "I think that's a great name. Shadow it is."

The dog reacted by once again licking Tony's hand.

Giorgio reached down and stroked the dog's head. "Okay, Mom says dinner will be ready soon. So, finish up your homework, and then you and I can take her for a walk later."

"Okay," he said, his eyes alight with enthusiasm. "Can we take her over to Stewie's house?"

"Sure," Giorgio said.

Tony returned to the den, and Giorgio joined his wife in the kitchen, where she was chopping up a cucumber for a salad.

"She seems well-behaved," Angie said, watching the dog cautiously. "Did you talk to Tony?"

"Yeah. He named her Shadow."

Angie turned to him with an arched brow. "Shadow?"

He smiled. "Yeah. Cuz she's all gray."

"Joe, do you think that's a good idea? Naming her? We can't keep her."

"I know. I just didn't know how to talk to him about her past." He chuckled. "Kind of weird, don't you think? When you wanted to start a day care, the state turned us down because of Grosvenor's past abuse. They thought he was too unpredictable. I wonder what they'd think of Shadow?" He gave his wife a weak smile.

Her eyes narrowed. "So, instead of taking care of kids, we've become a doggy daycare."

Giorgio knew when he was skating on thin ice. "Right. Listen, I'm going to take her out in the backyard. I'll be back in a minute."

He took the dog through the back door and into the yard, closed the gate, and removed her leash. As he watched the dog sniff her way around the small space, he stuffed his hands into his jacket pockets. Shadow poked her head under bushes and finally squatted in the grass.

Giorgio's mind had wandered back to the kitchen and the aroma of onions and peppers. He was contemplating what Angie was making for dinner when something caught his eye. A glimmer. A flicker off to his left. He turned to the big oak tree in the corner by the garage and flinched.

It was the boy again. According to an article Giorgio and Rocky had found in a time capsule buried at the monastery, Christian had been ten years old when he killed the Abbot who had sexually abused him and then hung himself by tying a bedsheet around his neck and jumping out a second floor window. Giorgio couldn't help but think of that every time he saw the boy's ghost. What a sad way to end such a short life.

As the boy hovered by the tree, Giorgio fingered the old dog tag in his pocket, thinking he needed to find a better way to interpret the boy's intentions. It was clear he wanted to help with investigations because that's the only time Giorgio saw him. He never turned up when things were quiet. *But how did he know when things changed? And how did he find clues regarding crimes he had nothing to do with? At least the clues he had provided during the monastery investigation made sense since he had lived there before killing himself.*

These were all questions Giorgio hoped to answer someday. But right now, watching the dog and eying the glimmering image by the tree, he wanted to know what Shadow had to do with his current case.

He turned to the dog and called, "Sombra!" again.

The dog ignored him and continued to wander past two rhododendron bushes and over to the oak tree.

He called out again, "Sombra!" And still, she ignored him. When she neared the boy however, her nose came up, and she stared into the darkness right where the boy's image floated above her. Giorgio's heart rate accelerated.

Did she see him?

The boy's gossamer arm rose like the wing of a butterfly and pointed directly at the dog. A heartbeat later, his image faded and was gone. Only the soft evening light remained.

Giorgio's skin grew cold and goosebumps rose on his arms as he stared at the place where Christian Maynard had been seconds before.

Giorgio shifted his attention to the dog, still fingering the dog tag in his pocket. *Did the pit bull carry some sort of clue?* It seemed unlikely, but the boy had been spot-on before. And if the dog tag was hers, *why didn't she answer to her name?*

Shadow returned to finding new smells in the yard, and once again, Giorgio felt a heavy stone of anxiety settle into his gut. It happened every time he saw the ghost. Clearly, Shadow was meant to play a role in this case and to stay close to the family for some reason. But would Angie let him keep her that long?

His daughter, Marie, was at a friend's house, so it was just the three of them for dinner. Giorgio kept Shadow on a leash, but she kept scooting under the table to sit near Tony. After dinner, he and Tony took her for a walk as promised. Though Stewie's parents were less than enthusiastic about welcoming the dog into their home, they allowed it while they stood guard.

Shadow was a perfect lady, showering everyone with friendly licks and wagging her tail. She even rolled over so Stewie could rub her belly, prompting giggles from the two boys.

On the way home, Tony said, "I wonder where she came from, Dad. She's such a good dog. Do you think someone's looking for her?"

Giorgio tensed. The only people looking for her were probably the guys who had abused her. Not some loving family.

"I don't know."

"Maybe we should put an ad in the paper," Tony suggested.

"No," he said quickly. "I mean, not yet. She is part of an investigation right now. Besides, she has a thing for Grosvenor. I'm hoping when he comes home, she'll help him heal."

He released a sigh, knowing Shadow's fate would become an issue with his wife. *But if he put out an ad with Shadow's photo, who could come calling?*

Once they returned home, Marie was back, and the kids became engrossed in a TV program. Meanwhile, Giorgio pulled out the old dog tag. Perhaps the tag didn't have anything to do with the pit bull. Why would a dogfighting ring have dog tags for their dogs anyway? They weren't pets. But he was sure the tag had something to do with Lindsey Nagel's death. Otherwise, why would Christian Maynard have given it to him?

On a hunch, he pulled out his phone and Googled one of the translator sites. He typed in the word sombra, assuming it was Spanish, and asked for the English translation.

What appeared on the small screen gave him a jolt.

The translation for sombra was—*shadow.*

CHAPTER FOURTEEN

The next morning, Angie refused to let Shadow stay at the house unattended, so Giorgio took her to work again. Images of the boy and the pit bull had scrolled through his head all night, once again keeping him awake. *Was there some sort of pattern he was missing?*

Christian had so far helped to find Nagel's grave and the trail the vampire group most likely took to the glen. Since then, he had also offered up the dog tag and seemed to know the dog.

The problem for Giorgio was that he just didn't know how to interpret the boy's appearances or the connection to the dog. He wasn't even sure whether Shadow had already played her role by saving Grosvenor.

These questions were tumbling around inside his brain as he rounded the reception counter at the police department and approached McCready's desk. Every head turned to watch as he led the pit bull down the hallway. When he got to McCready's desk, he stopped. McCready was on the phone.

"What d'ya mean eye surgery?" the young cop said to whomever he was talking to.

Giorgio leaned over the desk and whispered. "Everything okay?"

McCready glanced up with the phone cradled against his ear. He put up a hand as he listened to the response on the other end of the phone.

"What's the prognosis?" he asked. "Okay. I'll drop down to see her this weekend. Thanks." He hung up the phone and stared at it for a moment.

"Bad news?" Giorgio asked.

McCready's head came up. "It's my grandma." He sighed. "She suffers from dementia. She's been in a care facility in Arcadia for the past year. Anyway, they take their clients to get regular checkups, and I guess they found she has cataracts. They want to have them removed."

"That's a pretty common surgery, isn't it?"

"Yeah. I just never heard her complain about her eyesight. In fact, she's a voracious reader and doesn't even wear glasses." He sat back, thoughtful.

"Does she still remember who you are?" Giorgio asked.

McCready attempted a smile. "Most of the time. Although sometimes she gets me mixed up with my dad."

"Well, if you need some time off, just let me know."

"That won't be necessary. The care facility has scheduled her for surgery on Friday. I'll go see her on Sunday."

"Okay. Listen, will you be able to get into Nagel's laptop?"

"Yeah, unless it's encrypted for some reason."

"You're sure? We won't have to send it to someone else?"

McCready rolled his eyes. "No. All I have to do is…"

"Wait. I don't need to know how. I just need you to find out if she used social media and if there's anything we can use in her emails. And see if her book is on the computer. I think what we have is just part of it." He held out the pit bull's leash. "And…I also need you to look after Shadow again."

"You named her?"

"Tony did. Can you watch her today?"

"Sure. By the way, I've already checked out Lindsey's social media, and frankly, there isn't any," McCready said.

Giorgio's eyebrows lifted. "None?"

"Nope. She's a bit of a ghost. Her sister has a Facebook page, but Lindsey only shows up there once. It's a picture taken of her last year at Christmas. That's all I could find." McCready leaned down and stroked Shadow's head. "Hey, girl. She really is a nice dog, you know?"

"I think so, too. Angie, not so much."

"I get it," McCready said with a smile.

"Thanks. I need to do some more interviews. Did you find where Nagel works?"

"Yeah," McCready said. He dropped the dog's leash and rifled through some papers on his desk. "Here it is. Southwest Financial Services, which is owned by a Dr. Edward Cook. His office is at Southwest Surgical Clinics." He handed the sticky note to Giorgio.

"Thanks. First up, we are going to go see Lindsey's sister. Apparently, she made a comment to her mother about Lindsey's death that needs attention. Then, we'll stop by the clinic. And I need the address of the UPS store in Arcadia where her ex-husband, Craig Velchy, works."

Giorgio left the young officer looking up the address and went to his desk. He nodded to Rocky, who was on the phone, and then called Lindsey's sister to make an appointment. She said they could come out right away. When Rocky hung up, he said, "C'mon, we're going to Sherman Oaks."

Rocky paused, his hand halfway to picking up the last half of a fast-food breakfast sandwich that sat on his desk. "Um…okay," he said with a mouthful of food. He grabbed the sandwich and then his jacket off the back of the chair and joined Giorgio in the hallway. "By the way," Rocky said swallowing. "I was just checking in with forensics. They dusted Nagel's apartment last night. They not only got a ton of prints, they got DNA."

"No shit?" Giorgio said with appreciation. "How?"

"On a piece of glass from the curio cabinet. Whoever smashed everything cut themselves."

In the car, Rocky strapped himself in and finished off his sandwich, filling the car with the greasy smell of fried food.

"Don't you ever cook for yourself?" Giorgio asked him, pulling out of the parking lot.

"Sometimes," Rocky mumbled with his mouth full. He swallowed. "But this stuff is so cheap." He balled up the sandwich wrapper and tossed it into the backseat. "And I don't have Angie at home to give me home-cooked meals every day."

"Touché," Giorgio said with a smile. "You'll pick that up when we leave the car, though, right?"

Rocky rolled his eyes and let out a low grunt. "Listen. Turns out that Rick Toreno, the city maintenance worker, has a sheet. He was in the joint for three years for embezzlement. He used to work construction and found a way to steal from his employer."

"Okay. Not surprising. I don't think he's on our radar though. Thanks."

Sherman Oaks was an upper-middle class community on the other side of the Hollywood Hills. They parked two blocks down the street from a two-story building on Ventura Boulevard marked as Premier Films. As they walked back to the building, they passed an Alpha Romeo, a Mercedes, and a BMW all parked along the street.

Rocky eyed them and said, "Must be nice."

"It's another world up here," Giorgio said.

They climbed a few steps to a glass door and pushed their way through to a small lobby. The back wall of the room was glass, exposing an atrium filled with leafy, green plants and a water fountain. A cherrywood desk sat to their left, where a good-looking young man sat in front of a flat screen monitor dressed in a crème-colored polo shirt and gold chain around his neck. He looked up when they stepped up to the desk.

"Good morning. May I help you?"

His hazel eyes locked on Rocky. Even though Rocky was wearing grey slacks and a loose-fitting black sweater, you couldn't hide the physique underneath. The man's gaze roamed across Rocky's frame, lingering on his hips.

"We have an appointment with Carey Nagel," Giorgio said, showing his badge.

The young man reluctantly shifted his gaze. His eyes opened wide at sight of the badge. "Of course. Just a moment." He picked up a phone, punched in a number and said, "There's a couple of police officers here to see Carey. Yes, thanks." He hung up. "If you'll just have a seat, her assistant will be down in a moment."

"Thanks," Giorgio said. "What does Ms. Nagel do for Premier Films?"

"She's the site coordinator. Once a script has been accepted for production, she's in charge of researching appropriate locations for filming."

"What kinds of films does Premier Films make?" Rocky asked, glancing around at the bare, wood-grained walls.

A smile played across the young man's face. "We're an adult entertainment company," he said. "If you're interested, I can give you an application."

Giorgio chuckled, while Rocky's lips compressed into a straight line. "Thanks, but I prefer my sex sans audience."

The ding of an elevator drew their attention across the room. A short, stocky woman dressed in tailored gray pants and a tucked shirt emerged.

"Detectives. I'm Ursula Gray, Carey's assistant," she said, approaching them. "Please, follow me. I'll take you to a private conference room where Carey will join you."

The brothers followed her back to the elevator. A moment later, they stepped out onto the second floor and turned right down a long hallway.

"In here," Ms. Gray said, opening a door and gesturing inside.

They stepped into a small room that held a six-foot conference table and several chairs. The walls were graced with framed posters from several of Premier's films. Rocky's gaze swept across the lurid pictures as the assistant left and the door closed.

"Interesting," he said, taking a seat. "One sister is timid as a mouse, and the other works for the porn industry. Mrs. Nagel wasn't kidding when she said they were opposites."

"Well, siblings aren't always cookie cutouts of each other. Look at us," Giorgio said, taking a seat.

Rocky's head swiveled to face his brother. "What do you mean?"

A broad grin spread across Giorgio's face. "Everybody knows you're the good-looking one in the family, and I'm the smart one."

The door opened, cutting off the response poised on Rocky's lips.

A woman with brown hair and brown eyes entered. Unlike her assistant, she was slender and dressed in jeans and a royal blue tunic top that accentuated a generous bust.

"Detectives," she said. "I'm Carey Nagel. How can I help you?"

Giorgio was struck by the lack of emotion in her voice. Just the fact she was at work on the same day she had heard her sister had died was a statement all its own.

She pulled out the chair at the end of the table and sat down. Rocky took a seat across from his brother. She folded her hands and rested them in front of her as if this were just any normal business meeting, but Giorgio noticed she had begun to press her left thumb into the soft tissue of her right hand.

"We're sorry for your loss," Giorgio said.

She nodded her confirmation.

"We wanted to talk to you about your sister," he said. "We're trying to clarify some of the circumstances surrounding her death."

"Do you know yet *how* she died?" she asked. "When my mother called, she said it was unclear."

"No, not yet. Although there were no overt signs of foul play. Do you know if she had any health issues?"

She shrugged her shoulders. "No. She had a lot of other issues, but she was physically healthy."

"Did she take any medication?"

Giorgio knew the answer was yes but wanted to hear it from people who knew her best.

"Oh, yes. She was under a psychiatrist's care. A doctor, um…" she said, pausing. Her eyes fluttered as she tried to remember. "Um…Sandford. That's it. I don't know his first name."

"Do you know where his office is?" Giorgio asked, taking notes.

"Arcadia, I think," she said. "I don't understand, though. I assumed she had some sort of accident if she was found in a canyon."

A strained pause stretched between them. Finally, Giorgio said, "She was found in Bailey Canyon dressed only in a light smock. No shoes. No undergarments. And no one seems to know why she would have been up there."

Carey stared at him for a moment and then broke the stare with a deep sigh. "You've been to see my mother, so I'm sure she told you about the myriad of phobias Lindsey suffered from." When Giorgio nodded, she continued. "They were extensive. I loved my sister, but her illness was frustrating to say the least. She had been seeing a psychiatrist for years and was on medication to control her anxieties. At my urging, she began bio-feedback classes at the local community college about a year and a half ago. I saw a change in her immediately. So did her husband."

"Craig?" Giorgio asked.

"Yes. What a piece of work. He didn't like it that Lindsey was becoming stronger and more independent. He not only threatened her, he threatened me."

"Tell us about that," Giorgio said.

She sat back in her chair and began to fidget with a pearl ring on her right hand. "It was New Year's Eve a year ago. We were at a local restaurant. Just Craig, Lindsey, my girlfriend, and me. Lindsey announced that she had signed up for a rock-climbing class. That shocked all of us. This was a woman who was terrified of heights. But she said that through the bio-feedback she was learning to confront her fears."

"And Craig didn't like that," Rocky said.

"Oh, no," she said. "He didn't react well at all. But he took it out on me since I'd been the one to talk her into the classes in the first place."

"What did he say?" Giorgio asked.

She paused for a long moment. "I'm gay. I've been out for a long time. But Craig lashed out at me when Lindsey went to the ladies' room. He said that just because I was a freak, I shouldn't try to influence Lindsey into doing weird stuff."

"He thought rock climbing was weird?" Rocky asked.

"It wasn't just that. It was the whole bio-feedback thing. Lindsey had begun to meditate and attend yoga classes. She was learning to relax and enjoy her life. He saw it all as trendy, mind-controlling stuff. He told me that if I didn't leave her alone, I'd regret it."

"Do you have any idea what he meant by that?" Giorgio asked.

She shook her head. "No. I knew that he'd hit her once and blackened her eye. She also told me that he locked her in the bathroom for two hours one day because she wanted to attend a Toastmaster's class. It was another indication he was losing her."

"Did he ever follow up on his threat to you?" Rocky asked.

She inhaled and held it for a moment. When she exhaled, she said, "I saw his car outside my house once in late January last year. He was just sitting there. I think he was trying to scare me."

"Did he?"

"Yes. He knew I'd seen him. I think it's what he wanted. I also saw his car a week later when I was shopping on Hollywood Boulevard. He's not the type to hang out on Hollywood Boulevard. Nothing else ever happened."

"Did Lindsey ever complain that her husband was following her or that she feared him in any way?"

"Yeah. When she left him, she moved in with me for a couple of months. She said she kept seeing him in the lobby of the building where she worked. She finally got a restraining order against him. So, then he left her alone. Several months ago, she got her own place. She called me last week and mentioned that she'd seen Craig three different times and thought he was checking up on her. She wanted my opinion on whether she should report him to the police."

"And you said…"

"Yes. I said yes. But you need to understand that when she asked for a divorce, he accused her of cheating on him. Then, he joked that he might kill her *and* her lover."

Rocky's eyebrows arched. "Was she cheating on him?"

"Not that I know of. That doesn't mean she wasn't attracted to other men. But Craig is one of those guys who thinks he is the be-all and end-all to women. He couldn't imagine Lindsey would be attracted to anyone else."

A long silence ensued between them. Finally, Giorgio asked. "And she divorced him."

"She filed the papers while she stayed with me. I'm not sure the divorce has gone through, though."

"Can you give us the name of her attorney?" Giorgio asked her.

She sat up straight. "Sure. He is my attorney as well. Gerald Pepper. His office is here in Sherman Oaks."

"What about life insurance? Do you know if she had any?" Rocky asked.

Carey thought a moment and then shook her head. "I assume she did, but she never mentioned it."

"We found her apartment trashed yesterday," Giorgio said. "Do you know why anyone might do that?"

Her eyes opened wide. "No. Other than if someone knew she was dead, maybe they were stealing stuff. I don't know."

"Your mother said you thought her death had something to do with the sex appeal of a man."

She gave a brief smile. "I was being flippant. When Lindsey and I spoke last week, she said she was on her way to meet the *man of her dreams*. That's how I ended up learning that Craig was following her. She was afraid he would follow her when she met this guy."

"Did she say what this man's name was?"

"No. Just that he was sexy and dangerous and very popular." Her eyes flitted over to one of the posters on the wall. "Don't they say women go for the bad boys? I never thought Lindsey would, but that's what it sounded like."

"Wasn't her husband dangerous enough?" Rocky asked.

Her eyes shifted to his. "Not in the same way. He's just a brute."

"And you don't know who she was going to meet?" Giorgio asked.

"No."

"Did she say where she was going to meet him?"

"Some restaurant in Arcadia."

"Was it The Cave?" Rocky asked.

Her eyebrows lifted in recognition. "That sounds familiar."

Giorgio and Rocky shared a quick glance. That was the restaurant mentioned by young Dave Baker, Lindsey's writing pal.

"She was a bookkeeper? Is that right?" Giorgio said.

"Yes. She worked for Southwest Eye Clinics. Had for a couple of years."

"Did she have any close friends at work that you know of?"

Carey glanced at the table for a moment, thinking. "She mentioned a nurse she had dinner with occasionally. A Mimi something." She looked up again. "I got the feeling it was this Mimi who was introducing her to the man of her dreams. She also mentioned a couple of people in her writing class. Some guy named Dave. The woman's name sounded Middle Eastern. Sorry, that's all I know."

"Are you aware of any group she might have joined recently?"

She looked confused. "What kind of group?"

Giorgio paused before responding. "She was found with two holes in her neck."

"You mean…like a vampire?"

"We don't know. But there are groups that like that sort of thing."

She relaxed back against the chair. "Jesus. That makes more sense."

"What do you mean?" Rocky asked.

"When we talked, she mentioned she'd just come from the library. She had gotten Bram Stoker's *Dracula*. I thought it had something to do with her writing class."

"Not something she'd normally read?" Rocky pressed her.

"No. She mostly read romance or mystery novels. That's why the comment about the man of her dreams didn't surprise me. When she mentioned him, I pictured one of those guys on the cover of a cheap paperback novel." She sighed before continuing. "Listen, I work in the porn industry and, frankly, some of the films we do involve a lot of weird fantasies. So, I wasn't judging her."

"Where was she taking the writing class?" Rocky inquired.

"Pasadena City College, I think."

"What about social media," Giorgio asked. "We couldn't find any."

"I asked her about having a Facebook page once. She said, 'Absolutely not.' She thought it would be like having an entire crowd of people around her all the time. She was a very private person."

"Why did you think a sexy man had been the cause of her death, though?" Giorgio asked.

She shrugged. "When I heard she'd been found up in a canyon…I guess I just leapt to the conclusion that she was living out some sort of fantasy by meeting this guy up there."

"Does your film company do any filming up in that area?" Rocky asked.

She turned in his direction with a cold look. "I had nothing to do with her death, if that's what you're thinking."

Rocky shrugged. "I wasn't implying anything. But we must ask. Just like we have to ask where you were Saturday night."

Her hackles were raised. "Home with my girlfriend. And, no, to my knowledge Premier has never filmed up in Bailey Canyon." She stood. "I have to get back to work. Let me know if you need anything else."

Both men rose, and Giorgio slipped his card across the table to her.

"Thank you, Miss Nagel. We'll be in touch."

She took the card and then glanced at Rocky. "In case you're interested, I'm sure our casting director would love to talk to you."

CHAPTER FIFTEEN

Back on the street, Giorgio turned to his brother. "Well, you clearly have a backup career at Premier films in case this detective gig doesn't work out," he said with a grin.

"Like I said, I'm not into voyeur sex," Rocky said with a stormy expression.

"Well," Giorgio began. "Speaking of sex, I haven't heard you mention any lately. Seeing anyone?"

Rocky exhaled an exasperated sigh. "No one special if that's what you mean. But, no, I'm not horny. All good on that score. Now, back to the case. Do you believe her?"

"Carey?"

"Yeah."

"About what? That she influenced her sister into taking bio-feedback classes? Yes. That Craig Velchy threatened her? Yes. That she doesn't know anything about her sister's death? I'm not sure." Giorgio drew his keys out of his pocket as he walked. "She just found out today that her sister died two days ago, and yet she showed almost no emotion."

"She could be one of those self-absorbed people who needs to be in control all the time. Like you." Rocky stopped at the passenger side door to their car and glanced over the top towards his brother.

Giorgio paused before opening his door. "What the hell's that supposed to mean?"

A mocking smile spread across Rocky's face. "Don't pretend not to understand. You have always had a control issue. It's your thing."

Giorgio grimaced as he clicked the key fob and unlocked the doors. "No, it's not. I am just older. Wiser. And I have better taste." He climbed into the car hoping to end the conversation.

"Seriously?" Rocky said, getting in. "That's the best you've got?"

"You're exaggerating," Giorgio said, starting the car. "I just like…to…"

"What?" Rocky asked, interrupting him. "Just like to what?"

Giorgio sighed, glanced in the sideview mirror, and pulled away from the curb. "Let's drop it. We have work to do. Call McCready and tell him to find Nagel's psychiatrist."

Rocky clicked his seatbelt into place. "You're changing the subject. Let's face it…you just feel more comfortable when you are in control. I get it. I've lived with it for thirty-four years."

"You do realize you're not the easiest person to live with either," Giorgio retorted.

Rocky chuckled. "God, don't I know it. ADHD will do that to you."

His brother grew quiet, and Giorgio snuck a glance in his direction. Rocky had always been 'hyper' as his mother used to call it. He couldn't sit still and had trouble concentrating. But she had never had him formally diagnosed or put on medication and, somehow, he had made it through school with a C average. So, Giorgio was surprised at the sudden admission.

"You're not necessarily ADHD," he said. "You've never been tested."

"I'm on the lower end of the spectrum. I was kicked out of more classes than I could count and would have been kicked out of school if it hadn't been for dad."

"What d'you mean?"

Rocky turned to Giorgio with a somber expression. "Dad was well-known as a local cop. You know that. Mom told me a few years ago that when they wanted to have me transferred to an alternative high school, he went in to talk to the principal. The nuns were not trained to deal with someone like me. I was all over the place. Got into arguments and fights. And kept gazing out the window. So, they wanted to get rid of me. Instead, he volunteered to start a self-defense club there if they gave me another chance."

Giorgio's head swiveled to face his brother. "That's why he started that club?" He turned back to the road. "I'll be damned. You kicked ass in that club."

"I know. It was the one thing that focused my attention, used up a lot of energy, and calmed me down. It's also what made me want to be a cop."

They drove in silence until Giorgio heaved a sigh and said, "Okay, you're right. I do like to be in control. Shit. I watched you struggle your whole life. You were always fidgeting or moving around the room. It used to drive me nuts. It scared me. Then, Mom told me once that we were two sides of the same coin."

"What'd she mean by that?"

"She said that while I was quieter and more focused, you had the flair and personality of the gods."

"She said that?"

Giorgio smiled. "Yeah. She did. She told me not to belittle you, that one day I'd come to appreciate everything you had to offer, including your inability to sit still."

"I'm not sure how that will ever help anyone."

"I don't know," Giorgio said with a shake of his head. "But you're a black belt in something or other and could probably take my head off with a well-placed kick."

"It's called Krav Maga. And I started that when I met Rebecca. Is that why you started Jiu-Jitsu?"

"Maybe. I have always been more of a street fighter. I thought I could use better training. I'll never reach your level though."

Rocky let out a sigh. "It's how I spend my free time now because it was something Rebecca liked. It uses up my excess energy, and it makes me think of her. And it helps me to focus on things other than finding the son-of-a-bitch who killed her."

Giorgio snuck a glance at his brother. "They'll find him."

"I don't know," Rocky said. "I checked in with Romano a few weeks ago, and the leads have dried up."

Romano was the lead detective in New York working on Rebecca's case. Giorgio was not fond of him as a person, but he was a good cop.

"Well, you'll be ready when they do."

Giorgio punched the button in the car that would activate the phone and called McCready. When the young cop answered, he said, "Hey, Drew, two more things. We need to find the contact info for a Dr. Sandford. He was Nagel's psychiatrist. Also, we're going to want to talk to her lawyer, a Gerald Pepper. And…she took a writing class at Pasadena City College. See if you can find out who her instructor was."

"Will do," McCready said.

÷

Southwest Eye Clinics sat at the back of a large parking lot, flanked by an industrial park on one side and a strip mall on the other. As the two officers entered the two-story building through large electric doors, they passed a reader board that listed the names of multiple optometrists, ophthalmologists, and eye surgeons. Dr. Edward Cook's practice was on the second floor.

They took the elevator to a large waiting room where some fifteen people sat in comfortable chairs, waiting to be seen. Three women in blue smocks sat at a curved desk taking insurance information from people in line.

Rocky circled around to the far end of the counter where a fourth woman flipped through a stack of file folders. "Excuse me," he said, pulling out his ID. "We're with the Sierra Madre Police Department. We need to speak with Dr. Cook."

She studied his badge for a moment and then said, "Yes, of course. Just a moment." She picked up a phone and spoke softly to someone on the other end. When she hung up, she said, "He's with a patient right now. But if you would like to wait, I can show you in when he's free."

"Thanks. We'll wait."

She retreated down a hallway, while the brothers pulled back to stand in the corner. They were ignored by people who chatted or read magazines. A good ten minutes passed before the woman reappeared through a side door.

"Dr. Cook can see you now," she said, waving a finger at them.

They followed her through the door and down a hallway, past an open work area where several nurses and technicians were busy at computers or shuffling papers.

"He's in here," the woman said. She gestured into a large office with Dr. Cook's name on the door.

Giorgio stepped through the door just as a tall man in a lab coat rose from behind a desk. He looked to be in his late fifties, with a shock of white hair, tanned features, and glasses.

"I have just a few minutes, I'm afraid," he said in a voice as smooth as a cello. "We're very busy today. But, please, sit down." He gestured toward two armchairs in front of the desk. "Thanks, Jenny," he said to the woman, who stepped back and closed the door.

Giorgio introduced himself and his brother before launching into why they were there.

"We're investigating the suspicious death of one of your employees. Lindsey Nagel," he said, pausing.

"I'm sorry, but I don't know that name," the doctor replied, his face a blank mask.

"Really? That's surprising. I believe she's worked here for several years."

Dr. Cook leaned back in his chair. The branches of a large tree rustled against the window behind him. "I'm sorry, Detective. But there are almost two hundred people working in this building, and most of them work for other doctors."

"She was one of your bookkeepers," Rocky said.

His eyebrows arched, and he sat forward again. "Oh, then you'll need to talk to Mrs. Simpson. She's our Finance Director. But you said a suspicious death?"

"Yes. We found her body in Bailey Canyon."

He took a quick intake of breath. "Oh, dear. I didn't know Ms. Nagel, but we'll help in any way we can."

"Perhaps you can help us understand how you're organized," Rocky spoke up. "We noticed there are a multitude of different specialists in the building. Do they all work for you?"

Dr. Cook rewarded his question with a patronizing chuckle. "No. Of course not. Dr. Morro and I own the building and this clinic. We also own Southwest Financial Services. That's who Ms. Nagel must have worked for. We contract financial services to many of the other doctors in the building. But they are all separately incorporated."

"So, Lindsey could have done the books for any of the doctors under contract with you?" Rocky asked.

"Yes. But again, you will have to talk with Mrs. Simpson. Her daughter had a baby over the weekend, and so she is out of the office until tomorrow. I could ask my clinic administrator to come in. He might have known Ms. Nagel." He reached for his phone.

"That's okay," Giorgio said, stopping him. "If you could mention us to Mrs. Simpson, we'll stop by tomorrow."

Dr. Cook stood up. "I'll send her a quick email and let her know. I'm sure she will be devastated to hear about this. Mrs. Simpson works very closely with her staff."

As Giorgio stood, he asked, "Dr. Cook, where were you Saturday night?"

The man's gray eyes flared. "You don't think I…"

"Please," Giorgio said with a raised hand. "It's routine."

He barely relaxed. "I was…let me see. Saturday. Oh, of course, my wife and I were out with friends. Didn't get home until eleven or so and then went to bed."

"Your wife and friends can verify that?"

He paused ever so briefly. "Yes, of course."

Giorgio pulled out his notebook. "Names?"

"Is this really necessary?"

When Giorgio didn't respond, he said, "Gabe and Jenny Sanders. They live in Pasadena."

"Thank you," Giorgio said.

As Giorgio started for the door, the doctor asked, "You said she was found in Bailey Canyon. Do you know why she was up there?"

Giorgio turned back. The man was framed by the glow from the window. "No. Why do you ask?"

"No reason," he said, reaching out for a pen on his desk. He began to roll it back and forth between his fingers. "I just wondered. Seems an odd place for a young woman to be so late at night."

"We didn't say anything about her age or the time."

He stopped rolling the pen.

"Are you familiar with Bailey Canyon?" Giorgio asked.

"Um…yes. I've done some hiking up there. It's rough terrain. I imagine she fell."

There was a touch of hope in his voice.

"We don't know yet how she died," Rocky said.

The door opened behind them. A voice said, "Hey, Dad…"

Giorgio and Rocky turned to see a tall, dark-haired man in his early thirties with brilliant blue eyes standing in the doorway, one hand on the doorknob and the other on the doorjamb. Giorgio eyed a familiar tattoo on the back of the man's hand and felt a familiar prickle run the length of his spine.

"I'll be with you in a minute, son," Dr. Cook said. "These officers are just leaving."

The young man glanced at Giorgio and at the badge attached to his belt. His features hardened.

"Got it," he said and disappeared into the hallway.

Giorgio swiveled to Dr. Cook. "Thank you. We'll show ourselves out." Giorgio followed Cook's son out the door just in time to see the man vanish around a corner. "C'mon," he said to his brother.

They hurried to a set of waiting elevators but missed getting in with the doctor's son. They took the stairs and stepped out at the first floor just in time to see the young man climb into a red Camaro that had pulled up to the front curb. It drew away and bounced over a speedbump as it exited the parking lot.

"What's wrong?" Rocky asked.

Giorgio continued to watch the Camaro until it evaporated into traffic. "Did you see the back of his hand?"

"No."

"He had that same damned heart tattoo."

"Well, dear ole dad referred to Lindsey as a 'young' woman and that she was in the canyon late at night. We don't even know when she was there."

Giorgio looked at his brother with appreciation. "My thoughts exactly." Giorgio exited through the sliding doors. "Listen, neither one of us knows much about tattoos, but we know someone who does."

Rocky's face lit up. "Flame."

"Yeah. Why don't we see if she has an opinion on that tattoo?"

They headed for their car. Once inside the sedan, Rocky asked, "Think she'll help us again? I don't think she was too happy with us last time."

Rocky was right. The young psychic had helped them find the remains of the seven young women who had been tortured and murdered decades earlier. While only the women's bones remained, with her psychic abilities, Flame had been able to 'see' the women's bodies and the terrible wounds inflicted upon them.

Giorgio shrugged. "All we can do is ask. Did you bring the picture of the tat?"

Rocky tapped his jacket pocket. "It's on my phone."

Giorgio took a side street off Colorado Boulevard and pulled up to a small white bungalow. A sign in the window read 'Psychic, Madame Mirabelle.' It was embellished with an open hand holding a purple crystal ball.

"She doesn't use a crystal ball, does she?" Rocky asked as they strolled up the walkway.

"No," Giorgio replied with a scoffing laugh.

He opened the door into what had once been the home's living room. It now served as a waiting area, filled with the gurgling sounds of a table fountain sitting in the corner. A stick of incense filled the air with a suffocating floral scent.

At the sound of the bell above the door, a slender woman with shoulder length, curly dark hair appeared. She was attractive, with high cheek bones and deep green eyes. Probably in her mid-forties, she was dressed in loose-fitting pants and a long, colorful muslin top.

"May I help you?"

"We were hoping to see Flame," Giorgio said.

She smiled. "Police," she said.

Giorgio snuck a glance at Rocky. "Yes, ma'am. I'm Detective Salvatori. We worked on a case with Flame."

"Yes. I know. Please, make yourselves comfortable," she said, gesturing to an overstuffed sofa draped with soft throws. "You're brothers, right?"

"Yes, ma'am," Rocky said.

"Flame is in the kitchen. We're in between clients. By the way, I'm Cora, her aunt. I'll get her."

"The sign says Madame Mirabelle," Giorgio said, stopping her.

She chuckled lightly. "Well, let's just say that Mirabelle is my alter ego. Sounds more ethereal than Cora, don't you think? Let me get my niece."

The two men nodded as she swept out of the room.

"How'd she know we were cops?" Rocky asked.

"I've been told more than once that I look like a cop," Giorgio replied. "Something to do with my demeanor."

"Yeah, you're all uptight and crabby," Rocky said with a smile.

"Funny," Giorgio replied with a grimace.

The water feature filled the silence as they waited. A moment later, a young woman in her mid-twenties appeared. She had large, deep brown eyes, short, dark hair with a red streak flowing from front to back along one side. Tattered jeans torn off at the ankles hugged her slim figure and the sleeveless, embroidered top she wore was short enough to show her midriff and pierced navel.

"Detectives," she said. "I hoped it would be a long time before I saw you again. What can I do for you?"

She stood with her hands clasped in front of her. Although she gave them a brief smile, Giorgio thought her expression was guarded. Perhaps Rocky was right, and she wouldn't want to help them again.

"We just have a question," Rocky said, stepping forward. "We were wondering if you might know who could have done this tattoo." He held out his phone with the close-up picture of the heart.

Giorgio couldn't help but glance at the tattoos that covered Flame's arms when she took the phone. Another tat peeked out from underneath the bottom of her short blouse. Her nose was pierced, along with each eyebrow and the corner of one lip. And multiple earrings ran up the side of each ear. He wondered why she thought so much embellishment was necessary when she was already so pretty.

She took the phone and glanced down, studying the photo. "No," she said after a moment. "It's just a heart. Pretty basic. Any tattoo artist could have done that. What part of the woman's body is it on?"

"How did you know it was a woman?" Giorgio asked.

She chuckled. "First of all, I had a fifty-fifty chance of getting it right. But I thought you trusted me more than that by now."

"I do. That's why we're here. You know this world better than we do."

Her full lips curled into a sneer, and her dark eyes narrowed. "You mean the world of freaks."

He frowned. "No, not at all. I thought you knew *me* better than that. I just don't know anything about tattoos. But I am smart enough to know that tattoo artists are just that, artists. And with any art, artists have distinctive styles. Anyway, the tattoo was on the woman's ankle."

She studied the photo. "You're right. Although simple, this has some advanced shading. Also, the color is different than most reds I've seen."

"What do you mean?" Rocky asked. "Isn't a red a red?"

She laughed derisively. "No. The spectrum of reds is endless. First, there are different types of tattoo ink, and the color changes with the type of ink. The guy I go to uses vegan and organic inks. Some inks have a higher pigment, so the colors are bolder. Some come in pre-mixed colors. But the more experienced artists will mix their own. This looks like one of those to me."

"A specially mixed ink," Giorgio said.

"Yes," she said. "It's not meant to look like the red of a Valentine heart, but…" She paused, staring at the photo.

"What?" Rocky asked.

She glanced up at him. "Blood."

A pause stretched between them.

"Do you know anything about the vampire subculture?" Giorgio finally asked.

Her dark eyes flared. "This has to do with vampires?"

"We don't know for sure. But she was found in…"

"A creek bed," she said, glancing back at the photo and rubbing her thumb across the screen. "She wasn't scared when she died, though." She looked up at Giorgio.

Giorgio's initial response caught in his throat. "I…I thought you had to have a piece of her clothing or something."

A brief smile flickered across her rouged lips. "Not always." She turned to Rocky. "You touched her?"

Rocky shifted his weight uncomfortably. "Um…yeah. I helped get her out of the creek bed."

"Well, then you've been in contact with her and with the phone…sometimes, that's enough."

"What else can you tell us?" Giorgio asked.

Her thumb played across the small phone screen again, as if stroking it. Her eyes closed halfway. "I don't get much from this. The contact is too weak. I just feel a tranquility. No rage. No fear. Not even sadness." Her eyes popped open. "But I hear music. Classical music."

She handed the phone back.

"Classical music? That's interesting. Do you recognize it?"

"No," she replied. "It's some piano concerto or something."

"Thanks. I see your aunt is back," Giorgio said, changing the subject. His eyes shifted toward the kitchen.

"Yes," she said with a smile. "I decided to stay a while. We've gotten more clients, and she needs the help. Listen, let me think some more about the tattoo artists I'm familiar with. I'll make up a list for you."

Giorgio nodded. "I'd appreciate that."

They started for the door when she stopped them. "She was married, right? The woman you found."

"Yes," Giorgio replied.

"Okay, good. I thought so. Because he was there when she died."

CHAPTER SIXTEEN

Back in the car, Rocky said, "I guess it's time to see the husband."

Giorgio was staring out the window tapping his fingers on the steering wheel.

"What are you thinking?" Rocky asked him.

Giorgio snapped out of his thoughts. "We have two holes in our victim's neck. A heart meant to look like real blood. Some guy called The Maestro, who may or may not be the man of her dreams, and an event flyer for *The Essence of Murder* that has a vampire and snarling dog on it."

"You're thinking that could be the dogfighting ring?" Rocky said.

Giorgio turned to look at him. "Maybe. And now we suspect that her controlling husband, who joked about killing her, was there the night she died."

"I wonder how this all ties back to that *Essence of Murder* thing, though," Rocky said. "There wasn't a heart like this anywhere on that flyer. But you know that Baker also had the same tat."

"Along with Dr. Cook's son," Giorgio said, starting the car. "The circle is already getting larger. Let's tackle the ex-husband first."

Twenty minutes later they were in Arcadia, parking in front of the UPS store.

"How do you want to handle this?" Rocky asked.

"Let's assume he doesn't know yet about Lindsey. All they've reported on the news so far is a body found in the canyon, and I doubt the mother or sister would have called him."

"But what if he was there, like Flame said?"

"Well, let's play it as though we don't know that, either."

Rocky nodded. They left the car and entered the store. A woman in a brown UPS uniform stood at the register helping a customer. Two packages sat on the stationary conveyor belt that ran behind the counter.

Giorgio and Rocky waited behind a short, heavy set man who was signing his name on an electronic box. When he finished, he spun around to leave, almost bumping into Giorgio. Giorgio sidestepped him and moved up to the counter to show his badge.

"We're with the Sierra Madre Police. We'd like to talk with Craig Velchy."

"Yes, of course," she said. "Hold on."

She pushed her way through a swinging door behind her. A moment later, a tall, muscular man appeared. His eyes scanned the two men before he asked, "What do you want?"

His voice was gruff, which matched his overall demeanor. He had unruly black hair and brows, dark, penetrating eyes, and a recent scratch across the bridge of his nose.

"We need to speak to you alone," Giorgio said. "Can we step outside?"

The man pushed past them and led them through the front door and over to the side of the building. He leaned up against the wall, one leg bent with his boot placed on the plastered surface behind him. Giorgio noticed that his right hand played with something in his pocket.

"What's this about?"

"Your wife," Giorgio replied. "Lindsey. We were wondering if you'd spoken to her recently."

His eyes shifted to Rocky, a sure tell he was contemplating a response. "I…uh, saw her a few days ago. Why?"

"Where did you see her?" Rocky asked.

"Outside the Starbucks on Grand. Why?"

"Did you talk to her?" Giorgio asked.

He stared hard at Giorgio. The two men held their gaze for a full five seconds before Velchy broke. "Yeah. I talked to her. I said hello, and she threatened to call the police."

"Why would she do that?"

"Cuz the bitch is crazy."

He stopped jangling whatever he had in his pocket and pulled his hand out. In it, was a small coin he began rotating back and forth between his fingers.

"You're talking about your ex-wife," Rocky said.

He paused and seemed to think better of his attitude and heaved a big sigh.

"Right. I know. I know. I loved Lindsey."

"Loved?" Giorgio asked.

He jerked his head in Giorgio's direction. "I just meant that I didn't want the divorce…she did."

"So, you're officially divorced?"

"Yeah. As of about six days ago. She's on her own now. I guess that's what she wanted. She can have sex with whoever she wants." He suddenly launched the coin into the air.

Giorgio noted the trajectory of the coin and then turned back to Velchy. "I take it you don't approve."

"Would you? She was *my* wife," he said, jabbing a finger into his chest.

"Do you know for a fact that she had been dating anyone?" Rocky asked.

Velchy clamped his jaw tight, and his face turned red, making it look as if he were beginning to boil from the inside out. Both Rocky and Giorgio waited. He finally responded.

"How would I know?" he said through clenched teeth. "I'm not her babysitter."

Inwardly, Giorgio smiled. Velchy was not good at lying.

"Why are you asking me all of these questions? Did she file a complaint against me?"

"Why would she do that?" Rocky asked.

Velchy clamped his mouth shut and just stared into the parking lot.

"Listen, Mr. Velchy, we need to know where you were Saturday afternoon and Saturday night," Giorgio said.

His left eye twitched, leading Giorgio to believe the next thing out of his mouth would be a lie.

"During the day I was home most of the day."

"Doing what?"

"Laundry and stuff. I don't know. Why?"

"And Saturday night?"

"What's this about?"

"Where were you Saturday night?" Giorgio stressed.

He paused, rapping his fingers against the wall. Finally, he said, "Out with a friend."

"How late?"

"Um…maybe, I don't know, ten o'clock. Why?"

"Where did you go with this friend?"

"Why are you asking me all of these questions? I haven't done anything wrong. What did Lindsey tell you?"

"Please just answer the question," Giorgio insisted.

"Just out for drinks."

"Where?"

He pursed his lips before answering. "It's called the Hot Spot. In Arcadia."

"And after that?"

"I went home."

"Alone?" Rocky asked.

"Yes. Why?"

"We'll need the name of your friend."

A look of panic swept across his face. "Why the hell are you badgering me? What's going on?"

Giorgio had questioned too many relatives before he revealed that the person he was asking about had died. Inevitably, realization that something was wrong with their loved one would dawn on them like a slow burn. And each time, there would be a moment when full realization hit, and their body would shut down. Just for a second. A pause when their body became still because they realized that the person they loved was dead.

Velchy was doing the opposite. His nervousness was ratcheting up.

"Look, I have a right to know. What has she charged me with?"

Giorgio took his time. "I'm sorry to inform you, Mr. Velchy, but we found your wife's body

up in Bailey Canyon Sunday afternoon. She wasn't identified until late yesterday."

Velchy's expression froze for a moment. Then, he burst out in anger. "What the fuck? And you're just telling me now?"

"I'm sorry. But she died under suspicious circumstances. We've been trying to learn as much as we can about the days leading up to the time she died."

Velchy broke away from the wall and strode to the corner of the building. Giorgio couldn't tell if he was letting off steam or stalling for time.

"Mr. Velchy, we still need to know if anyone can confirm where you were Saturday night," Rocky said.

The man turned with a haunted expression. "Okay, I didn't go out with anyone. I just drove around for a while."

"All alone?" Giorgio asked.

"Yeah. I…followed Lindsey. I figured she was seeing someone."

"Followed her where?" Rocky asked.

"To this restaurant called The Cave. It's here in Arcadia. She met up with a guy, some little wimp of a thing. They had dinner, and then he left. But she stayed. I waited, thinking she was going to meet someone else."

"When you followed your wife that night, was she driving her own car?"

"Yeah, why?"

"And did she meet up with someone else?"

"Yeah, another woman. A short blond."

"And then what?" Giorgio prodded him.

He stared at the ground, thinking.

"Mr. Velchy. What did you do then?"

His head came up. He just stared at Giorgio a moment, then he took a breath before answering. "I waited a little bit, and then I left. I just went home." His eyes narrowed. "How did she die? Did she drown?"

"Why would you ask that?" Rocky asked.

His head jerked towards Rocky. "There's a stream up there. I just thought…"

"So, you've been up in Bailey Canyon," Giorgio said pointedly.

"No," he replied. "I've just heard about it. A friend likes to hike up there."

"Who's the friend?" Giorgio asked.

Velchy froze. "I…I don't remember. Just one of the guys."

"How'd you get the scratch on your face?" Rocky asked.

Velchy's hand flew to his nose. "What?"

"The scratch. Where'd you get it?"

"None of your business."

"I'm afraid it is," Giorgio said in a low voice. "This could be a murder investigation. Answer the question."

He swallowed. "Murder?" he said, stretching out the word. "Shit. Uh…a delivery," he stammered. "I…uh, a box fell…in the truck. It skimmed across my face and scratched it. That's all. No big deal."

An awkward pause stretched between the three men. Velchy's anxiety seemed to dissipate as he contemplated something.

"Is there anything else you'd like to tell us, Mr. Velchy?"

His head came up with a jerk. "No," he snapped.

"We have a witness that says you were in the canyon Saturday night."

Velchy grew quiet and stared at Giorgio as if looking straight through him. Finally, he came to attention.

"I don't know what you're talking about. It wasn't me. I went home. Like I said."

Giorgio watched him another moment, contemplating how much they could get out of him. They didn't really have a witness. Not one they could call to the stand anyway. So, they couldn't prove anything.

"Okay, we'll be in touch, so don't go anywhere. And we're sorry for your loss."

Velchy pushed past them and went back inside, allowing them to return to their car.

"He was lying through his teeth," Rocky said.

"Yeah. I'd bet my signed Derek Jeter baseball mitt he was in the canyon that night."

Rocky swung his head toward his brother in surprise. "Seriously? You must be positive. You love that mitt."

"Bingo."

Giorgio was just about to start the car when his phone pinged.

"Salvatori," he said, answering it. "What? Yes. Okay, great. Thanks." He hung up and looked across the seat at his brother. "That was Flame. She's already put together a list of a few tattoo artists we can talk to. She emailed it to me." He started the engine. "Let's head back to the office for now. I need to check on Grosvenor and see what McCready has found out about the writing instructor and psychiatrist. You can begin checking Flame's list. And we need to find a way to learn more about Velchy and his movements on Saturday night. We don't have enough to get a search warrant yet, but I'd sure like to know if the boot print we pulled from the creek matches those boots he was wearing today."

CHAPTER SEVENTEEN

Giorgio dropped his brother off at the station and pulled into the emergency vets again with Shadow in the front seat. He left her in the car and entered the waiting room.

"I'm here to check on Grosvenor," he said to the young woman at the desk.

She smiled. "Of course. He's ready to go home."

"Really?" Giorgio felt a flood of relief sweep through his body. "What do I owe?"

"Why don't you talk to the doctor while I get your bill ready."

Giorgio reached into his pocket and extracted his wallet. He handed over his credit card. "Here, I don't care what the bill is."

"Mr. Salvatori?"

He turned to find Dr. Vincent in the doorway. "Come on back."

He followed her into the back room, where Grosvenor lay on the exam table. When Giorgio appeared, the dog's tail began thumping on the metal surface.

"How's he doing?" Giorgio asked, reaching out to stroke the dog's front leg.

"Good. He lost a lot of blood in the attack, so he's still weak. But his vital signs are strong. He'll be unsteady on his feet. We'll have to carry him to the car." She glanced at her assistant standing behind her. "Sally, can you bring the medication? I'll help Mr. Salvatori take Grosvenor." She turned to Giorgio. "Keep him quiet for a few days. The cone on his head is to keep him from licking his wounds. Do you have kids?"

"Yes."

Grosvenor leaned his head back and flashed mournful eyes at his owner. A small whine escaped, prompting Giorgio to reach out and stroke his nose.

"Instruct the kids not to rile him up. He needs to rest. If you carry him outside tonight, he should be able to relieve himself, and then he might be able to walk out on his own tomorrow. I have given him pain medication, so he will mostly sleep tonight, and we have some antibiotics and pain meds to send home with you. He'll need to come back in three days to change the dressing."

Giorgio nodded. He stepped forward to give Grosvenor's front paw a squeeze. "Hey, bud."

"Here. Put your hands under the center of his body." The doctor demonstrated. "Keep your right hand under his neck." She turned to Sally. "Go ahead, Sally. I'll get the door."

Sally left the room, and the doctor caught and held the door open. Giorgio gently lifted Grosvenor, careful to support his head as instructed. He stepped past the doctor and moved toward the front door. The doctor scooted ahead of him to open it and then followed him out.

"Which car is yours?" she asked.

"The sedan," Giorgio said, nodding toward his car.

Sally quickly stepped over and opened the back door, allowing Giorgio to slide Grosvenor onto the back seat. Shadow whined from where she sat in the front. Grosvenor lifted his head and whimpered back.

"It's okay, boy. We're going home," Giorgio whispered.

He straightened up just as the receptionist appeared with a copy of the bill, his credit card and a bag filled with two bottles of medication.

"Thank you," he said. He felt himself choke up. "I…uh…" He cleared his throat.

The doctor put a hand on his shoulder. "We were happy to help. We're open 24 hours, so don't hesitate to bring him back if something happens. Watch the dressing for bleed through."

Giorgio nodded and climbed behind the wheel.

He called ahead to alert Angie. When he pulled into the driveway, she came out with the kids. Tony took Shadow, and Angie helped get Grosvenor out of the car and safely into Giorgio's arms, while Marie ran ahead to open the door.

"Bring him into the kitchen," Angie said.

She led the way down the hall and into their square kitchen. Angie had bought a new foam dog bed and had placed it in the corner on the black and white tiled floor. She directed Giorgio to lay him down.

After Giorgio made Grosvenor comfortable, he sat at the kitchen table and relayed the doctor's instructions. Both the kids nodded in agreement.

"Is he going to be okay though, Dad?" Marie asked, her brown eyes scrunched with concern.

Giorgio put his arm around her narrow shoulders. "Yes. We just need to give him time to heal."

"I'll sleep down here," Tony offered. "I can bring my sleeping bag down."

"No, Tony," his mother said. "You have your bed, and Grosvenor has his."

"But, Mom," Tony protested.

"Tony…" Giorgio began.

"Dad, look," Marie said. She pointed to Grosvenor.

The basset lay on his side facing them. His eyes were closed, but Shadow had moved behind him and laid her head across his back. She cast those gray eyes at them and repositioned herself, so she could be even closer to the basset hound.

Angie shook her head. "They're like best friends."

"She's been like that ever since she saved him," Giorgio said. "I don't get it. But…"

"What?" she asked.

"Nothing," he said, shaking his head.

In his mind, Giorgio remembered how Christian Maynard had pointed at Shadow in the backyard. Giorgio was beginning to think of the pit bull as a ghost dog, or at least a dog that was meant to be with them for some ghostly reason.

Tony walked over and laid down facing Grosvenor and patted his tummy. The basset opened bleary eyes, and Tony reached inside the cone and stroked his silky ears. A moment later, Tony stroked Shadow's head. She nuzzled his hand.

Angie rolled her eyes at the tableau and kicked Giorgio, giving him a knowing look. He relented.

"Okay, how about a slumber party?"

Tony jumped to his feet. "Really, Dad?"

"I'll bring some blankets down for you," Angie said to Giorgio with a smile. She turned to her daughter. "What about you?"

Marie scrunched up her face. "I'm not sleeping on the floor."

"Okay," Giorgio said. "Looks like it's boys' night out. Get your pillow, Buddy."

His son was out the door in an instant. As he thundered up the stairs, Angie chuckled.

"We can bring in the cushions from the sofa later. With your old bones, you're going to need them."

÷

After dinner, the family retired to the den. Marie sat on the sofa playing games on her tablet. Angie sat behind a desk in the corner to pay bills. Tony stayed in the kitchen with the dogs, while Giorgio fidgeted with the remote control, flipping through TV programs.

Giorgio had just skipped over a commercial when Rocky called.

"How's G?" Rocky asked.

"Doing good," Giorgio said. "What's up?"

"I made some preliminary calls on Flame's list of tattoo parlors. No one I talked to remembered Lindsey. But we may have identified the artist. It's a guy named Jaimie Haru. He's a Japanese American who works at Ink Art in Pasadena."

"Did you get to talk to him?" Giorgio asked.

"No. He works a couple days a week."

"Why do you think it's him?"

"We showed the picture of the heart tattoo around to a few of the other artists. Remember what Flame said about colors? Well, Haru mixes his own inks and is known for his reds. We were told he caters to the Goth crowd and can give you oxygenated or deoxygenated blood color, whichever you prefer. Weird," Rocky said with a laugh. "Anyway, one woman told us he has it down to a science. I guess he has a degree in art."

"Okay, when's the guy due back?"

"Not 'til Wednesday. But…he plays in a band four nights a week at a local club."

Giorgio put the remote down. "Why do I get the feeling we're going clubbing tonight?"

Rocky laughed. "Just try not to look so much like a cop. I'll pick you up in half an hour."

Giorgio hung up and snuck a glance at his wife. Her eyes shifted in his direction.

"You're going out," she said without trying to hide the reproach in her voice.

"A guy we want to talk to plays in a band. We're going to try and connect with him tonight. I shouldn't be late."

Marie looked up from the game she was playing. "That's what you always say, Dad."

So much like her mother, he thought. Giorgio heaved himself out of his recliner.

"I'll be back in time for the slumber party. I'll go tell Tony and take Grosvenor out before I go."

He disappeared upstairs to change into something he thought might pass for club-wear. In other words, a pair of jeans, cowboy boots, a long-sleeved open-collared dark shirt, and his New York Yankees baseball jacket. As an afterthought, he took his jacket off and slipped on his gun and holster, just in case.

Downstairs again, he went into the kitchen. Shadow looked up from where she still lay next to Grosvenor.

"You guys want to go out?"

Shadow stood up and wagged her tail. Grosvenor struggled to rise, but Giorgio leaned in to scoop him up. "Hold it, buddy. Let me help you." He lifted the dog awkwardly. "Can you grab the door?" he asked his son.

Tony opened the kitchen door. Giorgio carried the dog out, while Shadow followed. Once on the lawn, he set Grosvenor down. The canine teetered and almost fell over but got his bearings and then squatted to pee.

"He doesn't look too steady," Tony said.

"He's still on a lot of medication," Giorgio said, resting his hand on his son's shoulder. "The doctor said that by tomorrow he should be much better."

After relieving himself, the Bassett took a few faltering steps in the direction of the oak tree and then abruptly sat down. Shadow came back and touched noses with him.

"They sure like each other," Tony observed.

"Yeah," Giorgio agreed.

"Can we keep Shadow?" Tony asked.

The hope in Tony's voice cut to Giorgio's core. "I don't think so. We ought to find her a good home."

"We're a good home," Tony argued, looking up at his dad.

"Yeah, but I think one dog is enough for your mom." He smiled and ruffled Tony's hair again. "Listen, I have to go out tonight. But I'll be back for the slumber party."

÷

Fifteen minutes later, Giorgio emerged through the front door to find Rocky's small pickup idling next to the curb.

Rocky eyed his brother as he climbed in. "Seriously? That's your club look?"

Giorgio turned to find his brother in sharp black slacks, a soft-gray crew neck sweater and a black leather jacket. Giorgio fingered the zipper on his baseball jacket.

"I didn't realize I was supposed to dress like Matthew McConaughey."

Rocky laughed. "You need to get out more."

He started the engine and pulled away from the curb.

"What else do you know about this guy?" Giorgio asked as they drove.

"Not too much, other than he keeps to himself and takes a lot of pride in his work. But he's developed an entire line of ink colors he hopes to sell to a production company."

"And he plays in a band at night," Giorgio said, as if that was an odd juxtaposition.

"He's the drummer. Like I said, he has a degree in art. And guess what? The club he plays at is the same place both Baker and Velchy mentioned."

"The Cave?"

"Yep."

Twenty minutes later, the brothers pulled up in front of The Cave, a small restaurant and club in South Pasadena.

"Jeez, this place is packed," Giorgio said, scanning the parking lot.

Rocky found a place to park near the street. As they exited the car, two women dressed in black tights, short skirts and black, lace jackets hurried past them chatting. Rocky's gaze followed them.

"I have a feeling neither one of us is dressed appropriately for this place."

As the two women entered the club, another couple exited. The woman coming out wore a long black coat dress with black lace at the collar. Her inky-black hair was pulled up in a Victorian bun with bright red streaks of hair pulled out on either side of her crown. The man had dyed black hair and wore heavy, black eye makeup and a thick, studded dog collar around his neck.

"Let me correct my last statement," Rocky said, passing the couple. "I think we may be *under*dressed."

"Do you know what this drummer looks like?" Giorgio asked, catching holding the door open.

"Just that he's Asian."

They entered a room filled with heavy-metal type music and a sea of people dressed in black, accented with flashes of red, maroon and an abundance of silver jewelry.

"I sense a theme here," Rocky said surveying the crowd.

"At least you got the color right," Giorgio agreed. "I probably look like the guy who should be delivering the beer."

They shouldered their way through the crowd and found a table against the wall just as a couple got up and left. A waitress in thigh high black boots approached to take their drink orders.

When she left, Rocky's gaze followed her. "This is like living in an alternative universe."

"Or maybe an early Halloween party," Giorgio replied.

While they waited for their drinks, they focused their attention on the band. The drummer was a thirty-something Asian man dressed in black slacks and a long-sleeved black t-shirt with the sleeves pushed up to his elbows. Besides the tattoos running up each forearm, he wore a dangling earring in his left ear and had black hair, shaved short on the sides but long on the top.

"That must be Haru," Giorgio said, nodding toward him. "We'll have to wait until the band takes a break."

"Hey, isn't that Baker?" Rocky asked. He nodded across the room to a young man standing at the bar talking with a woman whose face was as pale as moonlight.

"Yeah, that's him," Giorgio agreed. "He said he brought Nagel here. It doesn't seem to fit her MO, though."

Rocky stood up. "Let's ask him."

He pushed his way through the crowded room to approach Baker. The young man looked up in surprise when the tall police officer put his hand on his shoulder.

Giorgio watched as Rocky leaned down to whisper something in his ear. Baker looked across the room, and Giorgio raised a couple of fingers in a wave. Baker turned back to the woman and said something. Then he allowed Rocky to guide him back to their table.

"Have a seat," Rocky said, gesturing to the inside chair against the wall.

The young man looked back and forth between the two detectives and then awkwardly moved into the seat. Rocky sat next to him, blocking his exit.

Rocky turned to face Baker, allowing his height and proximity to intimidate him. "How're you doing, Dave?"

"Um…fine."

"So, does Radio Shack approve of this sort of attire?" Rocky asked, gesturing to Baker's black waistcoat, slacks, and pointed black boots.

Baker shrugged. "I work in the supply room. I take in deliveries and do inventory," he said with a shrug.

Giorgio's antenna went up. "Who makes deliveries there?"

"What do you mean?"

"What companies?"

"Uh…FedEx and UPS. Several of the vendors."

"Same delivery guys most of the time?"

"Yeah. Why?"

"Craig Velchy one of your UPS delivery guys?" Giorgio asked.

"Um…yeah?" he said, thoughtfully. "I think so. A big guy? Kind of mean? Why?"

"That's Lindsey Nagel's ex-husband," Giorgio said. "She never mentioned him?"

He shook his head. "No. I mean, she said she'd been married before, and that he was pretty controlling. But I didn't know who she was talking about. And I didn't know Craig's last name."

"That's a big coincidence, don't you think? That her ex-husband would be your delivery guy?"

"No, I mean…I don't know. Why would it be?"

"Do you come here often?" Rocky asked, glancing around the room.

"Yeah. Sometimes. It's a popular hangout."

"Did you ever bring Nagel here?"

"Um…no. No."

"Careful, Dave. Tell the truth," Rocky cautioned him.

Baker paused. "I…um…oh, yeah. I brought her here once, but we didn't stay. She was uncomfortable and wanted to leave."

"Because she didn't fit in?" Giorgio asked.

"No. The crowd bothered her. She began to hyperventilate."

Rocky leaned in real close. "Dave, you're lying. You told us earlier that you brought Nagel here for dinner. Now, why would you lie about that?"

Sweat began to glisten on Baker's brow. "I…uh…sorry, that's right. I did bring her here for dinner. We sat over there," he said, nodding to a table at the very front of the room, near the door. "It was the only way she could handle the crowd."

"When was that?" Giorgio asked, already knowing the answer.

Baker paused, as if contemplating what to say. "Last week," the boy replied. "Friday."

"Did you meet anyone else here? Anyone join you for dinner?"

Baker seemed to stop breathing. His eyes roamed the room, as if afraid someone might be watching. His eyes flared, and he froze.

Giorgio followed his gaze.

Baker had caught the attention of a tall European-looking man at the bar surrounded by three fawning women. The man had dark, brooding eyes and long, white hair pulled into a ponytail. He stood erect, holding a gold-headed walking stick in his left hand. He was posturing, while the women giggled and fluttered around him like birds. He ignored the women, staring instead at Baker. A black double-breasted, tight-fitting coat with a high collar accentuated his broad shoulders, while the dark eye makeup, pale skin and hollowed-out cheeks made him appear other-worldly, which Giorgio assumed was the point.

The man seemed to give a quick shake of his head to Baker and then shifted his gaze to Giorgio. The two men locked eyes, as the man took a slow drink, showing off the black ruffles that dressed the sleeve of his shirt.

One of the fluttering birds moved in front of him when the waitress returned to deliver drinks, cutting off Giorgio's view. Rocky paid her, and she moved away. By then, the man at the bar was gone.

Baker took the opportunity to stand. "Listen, I have to go. I'm supposed to meet a friend."

It was at that moment the lead singer announced the band would be taking a break. Before Rocky could stop him, Baker had squeezed out from in between the chairs and disappeared into the crowd.

"Damn!" Rocky said. "I wasn't done with him."

"That's okay. We can follow up later," Giorgio said. "Let's see if we can get Haru over here. I'll be right back."

Giorgio made his way to the bar where Haru had gone for a drink. "Mr. Haru?" Giorgio asked, coming up next to him.

The man turned. "Who are you?"

Giorgio pulled his coat aside to show his badge. "I'm with the Sierra Madre police. I was wondering if we could talk."

"I only have ten minutes."

"We just have a few questions," Giorgio said. "If you could join us."

The two men made their way back to Rocky, where Giorgio introduced him to Haru. Rocky switched to the inside chair, and the drummer sat down.

"What's this about?" He took a sip of his drink.

Rocky pulled out his phone and the picture of the heart tattoo. "Is this your work?"

He took the phone and studied it. "No. That's not mine. Amateur shading and the shape of the heart is too whimsical." He tossed the phone onto the table with an arrogant twist of his chin. "If I do heart graphics, I make them look real." He took another sip of his drink.

"Meaning what?" Giorgio asked. "You would only draw a real heart with veins and ventricles?"

"No. Although I've done a few of those. I just meant that mine would look three dimensional. That looks like my ink, though. If it is, then I know who did it. He works at Ink World in Monrovia."

"How can you tell?" Rocky asked, studying the photo again.

"We all have signature styles," he said. "And I sold him the ink. Besides, that design belongs to a group of vampire enthusiasts. I'm not into that. He is."

"Vampire enthusiasts?" Giorgio asked.

"Yeah. People who pretend they're vampires."

Giorgio looked around the room. "Any of them here tonight?"

"Like I said, I'm not part of that scene. I just play in a band. And this month we're playing here." He stood up to leave. "Sorry, but I have to get back."

"Do you have a name for that artist?" Giorgio asked.

"Sure. Derek Grueger."

"Okay, thanks for your time."

Haru left and went back to the stage area.

"What d'you think?" Rocky asked.

"Well, we know Nagel got caught up in this vampire stuff, and it looks like the connection might be Baker. Let's follow up with him tomorrow. Maybe we can also touch base with Velchy again, just in case."

"And the tattoo?"

"Swan's back tomorrow. Why don't I take him with me to see Baker, and you see if you can find this Grueger guy?"

CHAPTER EIGHTEEN

Outside in the truck, Rocky was just about to start the engine when he pointed to the corner of the building. "That's Baker."

Baker had just left the restaurant and was crossing in front of the club, heading towards the side parking lot.

"Let's follow him," Giorgio said.

Rocky backed out of the slot and pulled past a long line of cars. He then turned away from the street and drove toward the front of the building.

"There," Giorgio said. He gestured to the side parking lot that bordered a closed real estate office.

Rocky pulled over and stopped. Baker had opened the back of a small truck and was sliding out a dog kennel. Inside were flashes of white, which Giorgio assumed belonged to a dog. They watched as Baker handed off the kennel to a heavyset man dressed all in black.

"What the heck is he doing?" Giorgio murmured.

"Giving someone a dog?" Rocky answered.

"I see that, but why?"

The man took the kennel and shoved it into the back of a dirty white van. Then he turned and handed something to Baker. Baker opened the palm of his hand and appeared to flip through whatever it was.

"He just got paid for that dog," Giorgio said.

Baker stuffed the bills into his coat and returned to the bar, while the other man climbed into his van and backed out of the parking slot.

"Let's follow this guy," Giorgio said.

"Why? Where do you think he's going?"

Giorgio sat back in his seat, his eyes watching the van as it drove toward the back exit.

"Remember what the vet said about the pit bull? She was used as a bait dog. I was also told they're taken off Craigslist when people offer them for free and sold to dogfighting rings."

"That sucks."

Rocky shifted the pickup into drive and followed the van. They turned onto a darkened street, with the van about half a block in front of him.

"So, you think the little dog in that kennel might have just been sold as a bait dog?"

"Yeah," Giorgio said.

"He'd be killed in an instant. What's the point?"

Giorgio turned and gave a knowing look to his brother. "I assume they want the fighting dogs to get a taste for blood."

"We're not going to try and save that dog, are we?"

"No. I just want to see where they go."

"You realize if we find this guy is somehow connected to a dogfighting ring, we now have a connection between Nagel and dogfighting. And Baker is the connection."

"I understand perfectly," Giorgio replied.

They followed the van through two intersections until it reached Allen Street and turned right. Rocky hung back as the van traveled south for another mile or so and then turned into a parking lot behind an auto parts store.

"What should we do?" Rocky whispered, watching the van park next to a large black SUV. "Bust them?"

"For what?" Giorgio replied. "They could just say they're a rescue group."

A tall, well-built man dressed in jeans and a leather jacket got out of the SUV and opened the back. The two men transferred the dog kennel into the SUV, and then the van left. The man in the leather jacket entered the store through the back door.

"Now what?"

"We wait," Giorgio replied.

It was a few minutes before the tall man remerged accompanied by a shorter man with a shiny bald head. The two got into the SUV and pulled out of the parking lot. Rocky followed them north to the 210 freeway.

"Did you get a good look at either one of those guys?" Giorgio asked.

"No. Too dark. Where do you think they're going?" Rocky asked as he turned onto the freeway onramp.

"Dunno," Giorgio replied. "But hopefully to wherever they moved their dogfighting operations."

"Did you bring your weapon?"

Giorgio turned to him in the shadowed cab. "Yeah. You?"

"Yeah. It's in the glove compartment."

"Can you see the license plate number?" Giorgio asked.

"No. But there's a pair of small binoculars in there." He pointed to the glove compartment.

Giorgio extracted an opera-sized pair of binoculars and focused on the SUV's license.

"Got it," he announced, writing the license plate number into his notebook.

The two grew quiet as Rocky merged with traffic and followed the SUV west, past Sierra Madre to the turnoff for La Canada Flintridge. Meanwhile, Giorgio called McCready and asked him to run the license plate.

A few minutes later, Rocky left the freeway and followed the SUV until it reached the Angeles Crest Highway.

"This road goes to the Mt. Wilson Observatory," Rocky said.

The observatory sat high above Pasadena in the San Gabriel Mountains, making the domed astronomical building visible from much of the Los Angeles basin. But it was late, and with the observatory closed, the only cars on the road would be those traveling back and forth to a town called Palmdale on the other side of the mountains.

"The observatory won't be open. I wonder if they'll turn off onto a side road," Giorgio said.

Sure enough, a mile past the turnoff for the city of Palmdale, the SUV swung off the paved highway onto a dirt road that angled sharply down the hill to the right. The SUV's taillights disappeared into a cloud of dust and shadows.

"Wait," Giorgio warned as Rocky was about to take the turn.

"Don't you want to follow?" he said, pulling the truck to the side of the road.

Giorgio pointed to a small sign. "That's a U.S. Forest Service road. Which means it will be narrow and one-way."

"So?" his brother challenged him.

"We'd be sitting ducks. It would be like every bad cop show I have ever seen. One way in and one way out, and yet they go in anyway. If we get caught down there, we have zero explanation as to why we're there."

"What do you want to do?"

Giorgio glanced around them. "Turn around and park on the upside of the road and kill the engine. We'll follow them when they come out."

Rocky did as he was told, pulling the small pickup under some low hanging branches fifty feet uphill of the turnoff.

"They'll probably turn downhill when they come back out," Giorgio said. "Then we can hike in tomorrow in daylight."

They only had to wait forty-five minutes before the SUV appeared again in a cloud of dust and turned downhill. Rocky waited a minute before flicking on his headlights to follow.

The return trip was uneventful. The SUV went back to the auto parts store, where the bald man got out and climbed into a parked red Camaro. The SUV drove off.

A virtual chorus of bells went off in Giorgio's head at the sight of the Camaro. "It's the Camaro from the clinic," he said. "Let's see where it goes."

Five minutes later, they were across the street from a mission-style house in South Arcadia. The bald man had pulled into the driveway and gone inside. Giorgio pulled out his notebook and jotted down the address and the Camaro's license.

"If this is the same red Camaro we saw yesterday at the clinic, my bet is the guy who owns the SUV is Dr. Cook's son."

"The plot thickens, as they say," Rocky said.

CHAPTER NINETEEN

Giorgio woke the next morning with a sore back and a stiff neck after sleeping on the floor with Tony.

"You look like hell," his wife said when she found him struggling to get off the floor. "Where's Tony?"

Giorgio glanced over to a jumbled pile of blankets. Both Tony and the dogs were gone.

"He must've taken the dogs out. That's good. That means Grosvenor can walk on his own."

The kitchen door opened, and the three of them came back inside. Shadow hurried over to Giorgio, wiggling up next to him to get attention. Grosvenor waddled over, and Giorgio brought him in for a hug.

"How're you doing, big guy?"

"Is he gonna be able to eat with that thing on his head?" Tony asked his mom.

She smiled. "We can take it off while he eats. Why don't you fill their bowls?"

Tony grabbed the two bowls on the floor and raced over to a plastic bin in the corner, while Angie unfastened the cone around Grosvenor's head.

"Did you learn what you wanted last night?" she asked Giorgio. She placed the plastic cone on the counter and then went to a cupboard to grab a box of cereal.

Giorgio hoisted himself off the floor with a groan and dropped into one of the kitchen chairs. "Maybe." He yawned. "Remind me to get one of those blow-up mattresses next time we go camping."

Angie laughed and put the cereal box on the table. "You okay with cereal, or do you want something hot?"

"Cereal is fine. Let me grab a shower first, though."

He started to leave, but Angie stopped him. "Hon, a woman called for you last night. She didn't say who she was, but said it was important that she talk to you soon."

"Did you get a number?"

"Yes. On a sticky note next to the phone."

He climbed the stairs and took the next twenty minutes to shower, shave, and get dressed. On the way back to the kitchen, he stopped in the hallway and picked up the note.

"Joe," Angie said, coming around the end of the stairs. "Can you take Shadow with you? The kids will be at school and I…I…"

"I'll be out most of the day doing interviews. She should be fine here."

Angie looked unconvinced. "Okay. I'm just a little nervous…you know."

"She hasn't shown any aggression. She saved Grosvenor, Angie," he said, stepping forward and putting his arms around her waist.

"I know," she said, relenting. She lifted her arms and encircled his neck. "I'm glad Grosvenor is going to be okay, Joe. I know I didn't want him when you first brought him home, but now I can't imagine life without him." She kissed Giorgio lightly on the lips. "We'll take good care of him today." Her lips parted in a brilliant smile. "Me and Shadow." She kissed him again and went back to the kitchen.

÷

Giorgio walked into the station at 8:10. McCready looked up when he passed his desk.

"How's Grosvenor?"

Giorgio stopped and smiled. "Good. He's got one of those giant cones around his neck. And he has to stay quiet."

"And the pit bull?"

"She hasn't left his side." He shrugged. "I don't get it. But I don't care. As long as he gets better. Have we found that Phillips guy, yet?"

"No one has seen him since Sunday."

"It's time to put out an APB on him as a person of interest," he said as he approached his office door. "And we need to get up to the school to talk to the teacher's assistant."

"Got it. By the way, the red Camaro is owned by a guy named Arthur Cordova. He owns an auto parts store in Arcadia."

"And the SUV is owned by Dr. Cook's son," Giorgio said.

"Right. How'd you know?"

"Just a hunch. Did you find Dr. Sandford?"

"Yeah. He has an office on Adams in Arcadia."

"Okay. See if Mulhaney can go talk to him. I want to know how much Xanax she took and how often. And I want to know if he knows anything that would help this investigation. Get a subpoena if you have to."

"Got it," McCready said.

"I heard you've got a case," a familiar voice said.

Giorgio turned to find Detective Chuck Swan, his partner, sitting at his desk.

"Hey, welcome back," Giorgio said. "How's your aunt?"

Swan was built like a linebacker and shrugged his massive shoulders. "She's okay. We got her moved into a care facility. She did not go quietly, but my cousin was at his wit's end. Feels good to be back. I can take only so much of my extended family."

"Did McCready bring you up-to-speed?"

"Yeah. And I've been studying the board," he said, pointing to the white board. It was now filled with pictures and notes from the case, along with several sketches of where the body had been found and a sketch of the glen and the grave.

"Well, we have a couple of things to add."

Giorgio went to the board and wrote "Dr. Cook's son" and "bald guy and red Camaro."

"What's that mean?" McCready asked from the doorway.

"Rocky and I went to a club last night to track down the tattoo artist who gave Lindsey Nagel that heart tattoo," he said, pointing to the photo of the tattoo. "He turned out to be the guy whose ink was used, and he gave us the name of Derek Grueger as the possible artist." Giorgio wrote this name on the board as he talked. "Rocky's going to check him out today. But we also watched Dave Baker," he said, pointing to Baker's photo, "hand off a dog to some fat guy who then met up with a bald guy. That's Arthur Cordova. The two of them drove the dog up into the Angeles Crest Forest."

"For what purpose?" Swan asked,

"We think for a dogfighting ring."

"What does dogfighting have to do with Nagel's death?" Swan asked.

"We don't know yet. But we believe there may have been a dogfighting operation up in Bailey Canyon, not too far from where Nagel died. And the pit bull that saved Grosvenor's life may have escaped from there."

Swan leaned back in his chair. "Jesus, I've missed a lot. What can I do?"

Rocky sauntered in with a Starbuck's cup in hand. "Morning. Hey, Chuck, good to see you."

Swan nodded to Rocky. "Thanks. I was just getting caught up. By the way, I heard about Grosvenor," he said to Giorgio. "He's okay?"

Giorgio went to his desk and dropped into his chair with a heavy sigh. "I think he's going to make it. Not sure I will, though."

"Why the groan?" Rocky asked, sitting in his own chair.

"Tony insisted on sleeping on the floor next to the dogs all night." He dug his fist into the small of his back and twisted to one side.

Rocky laughed. "I assume it didn't go so well."

"Let's just say that old kitchen floor is harder than my back."

Swan leaned forward in his chair and flexed his two hands together. "Want me to do some of that magic again?"

Giorgio's hand came up in an instant. "No! I don't need any of that reflexology shit."

Swan laughed. "You're such a baby," he chastised him.

"What's that about?" Rocky asked, dropping into his chair.

"Swan offered to relax the muscles in my back a while ago by kneading the palm of my hand," Giorgio said. "It's called reflexology. The pain nearly brought me out of my chair."

"Like I said, baby," Swan said, chuckling. "So, what's the order of the day?"

"Rocky is going to talk to this tattoo artist, Grueger. We need to talk to this kid again who was friends with Nagel. Dave Baker. If there is a connection between the dogfighting operation and Nagel's death, he's it. We've talked to Nagel's ex-husband, but you and I are going to talk to him again, too. But let's go see Baker before we see the ex-husband."

"Anything's better than arguing with an eighty-year old woman who still thinks her dead husband is alive and having an affair."

Giorgio and Swan headed to the car. On the way, Giorgio tried Baker's cell phone but got no answer.

"Let's see if he's at work," he said, climbing behind the wheel of the sedan.

They drove to the Radio Shack that Baker had said was his place of employment and strolled in a little after nine o'clock. A young woman was just finishing up with a customer.

"Excuse me," Giorgio said when the customer left.

The young blond looked up with an expectant smile. "Yes. May I help you?"

"We were hoping to speak to Dave Baker. Is he working today?"

Her pretty face scrunched with disappointment. "He's supposed to be here, but he hasn't shown up yet."

Giorgio showed his badge. Her pale blue eyes opened wide.

"Has he done something wrong?"

"He may have some information we need. Can we get his address?"

"Um…sure. He lives on North Hermosa Avenue in Sierra Madre. He has an apartment there." She went to a computer and pulled up a file. "Here you go," she said, jotting down the address. "If you find him, tell him to call me. Roger is going to be pissed."

"Roger?"

"The boss," she replied.

Baker lived in an old shingle apartment building at the end of a dreary street lined with what looked like low-rent single family homes. They approached the double doors by a wide paved entrance that led to a set of chipped concrete steps.

"Hey, look at this," Swan said, stopping Giorgio. "Is this blood?" Swan leaned down to peer at a red splotch on the edge of the top step.

"Looks like it," Giorgio said, following his gaze. "And it looks fresh. Shit! C'mon." He swung open the door and stepped through.

They took the stairs two at a time to the second floor. Giorgio was about to knock on number 217 when a squat little woman in her fifties came down the hallway carrying a laundry basket.

"He's not there," she said, short of breath.

She had curly gray hair, glasses, and carried an extra forty-plus pounds around her middle.

"How do you know?" Giorgio asked.

"I knocked myself a little while ago and didn't get an answer."

Giorgio pulled his jacket aside to show his badge. "If you don't mind, we just wanted to ask him a few questions about an investigation we're conducting. Do you know where he might be?"

"Probably at work."

"We stopped there first."

"Why did you knock earlier?" Swan asked.

"I heard banging. Sounded like things were hitting the wall. I got concerned. But then it all quieted down."

The two officers shared a glance. "Would you happen to have a key?" Giorgio asked.

Her eyes popped opened. "Yes. I do. I feed his bird when he's gone. Hold on a minute."

She disappeared into her own apartment and emerged a moment later with a key in her hand and a purse hanging off her shoulder. "Here you go. I have a hair appointment, but you can just slip it under the door when you leave."

They thanked her, and she bustled down the hallway. Giorgio glanced at his partner, nodded, and both men drew their weapons. Giorgio used the key to open the door.

"Police!" he called out. "Mr. Baker, are you home?"

The apartment was quiet. But as the door swung open, it was clear something was wrong. They were in a small, ordinary living room. Worn sofa on the right. Entertainment center and bookcase on the left. Moon chair and end table in front of the window. But that's where the normalcy ended. The lamp from the end table was on the floor, along with most of the books from the bookcase. A standing lamp had been thrown up against the window, and the cheap coffee table had been upended.

"Mr. Baker, are you here?" Giorgio called out. He broke to the left into the galley-style kitchen.

Swan broke right into the bedroom.

Giorgio scanned the small kitchen and yelled, "Clear."

"Clear," Swan called out from the bedroom.

Giorgio lowered his weapon and glanced around. A dirty plate with crusted cheese and a few remaining tortilla chip crumbs rested in the sink. The counters, however, were bare of clutter, and the stove top was clean.

In the corner of the kitchen was a hanging bird cage. Inside was a small canary hopping back and forth on its perch.

The rest of the kitchen was a mess. Giorgio kicked food cans and boxes aside to make his way to the small kitchen table where another *Essence of Murder* flyer sat. Giorgio fingered it thinking, once again, there was that event promotion.

The sound of shattering glass brought him into the living room, just in time to slam into a man wearing a dark hoodie. Giorgio was thrown backwards against the wall, as the man rocketed out the door.

Giorgio righted himself and ran to the bedroom door, where he found Swan leaning against the dresser, blood running down the side of his face, a smashed mirror behind him.

"I'm fine. Go!" Swan yelled, wincing.

Giorgio turned and rushed into the hallway as the door at the far end of the dim corridor closed. He gave chase, emerging cautiously into a stairwell.

He heard someone's feet pounding down the last few stairs and leaned over the railing as the sound of another door opening and closing reverberated within the enclosed space. Giorgio flew down two flights of stairs and crashed through the first-floor door into an alley.

As he came out into the sunlight with his weapon drawn, he caught the fleeting image of a dark figure disappearing around the end of a dividing fence between two homes fifty yards in front of him. He broke into a sprint, passing trash cans and discarded wooden pallets in the alleyway.

He reached the dividing fence and swung around the fence post just as a bullet splintered the wood next to his head, making him duck and shield his eyes. When he looked up, he was in the space between two small stucco homes. A quick movement at the far corner made him sprint forward.

It took him only a few seconds to make it to the front corner of the home. He pressed his shoulder against the brown plastered wall and rolled to his right, both hands grasping his weapon and holding it at arm's length.

Several cars were parked along the street, but there was no traffic. The sound of a car door opening half a block up the sidewalk made him turn in that direction.

The hooded stranger had just opened the passenger door of a blue Chevy Malibu parked at the curb. He was maybe 5' 11" and medium weight. The man jumped into the passenger seat, and the car screeched away from the curb and disappeared up the street.

Giorgio lowered his gun and let out a frustrated sigh.

Shit! he thought. *That was Lindsey Nagel's car. But who the hell was driving it?*

Giorgio rubbed his shoulder remembering what it felt like when the guy slammed into him. The man was solidly built and young. He wore jeans, a dark hoodie, and tennis shoes.

But there had also been a sound. What was it?

He turned back up the green corridor between the two homes, wondering about the sound. He stopped to inspect the place where the bullet had clipped the fence.

"Have to get forensics out here," he mumbled to himself.

The back door of the house to his right opened, and a young girl poked her head out.

"You okay, mister?"

"Yes. I'm a police officer. Did you see a man run past here?"

She shook her head. "No. I just heard a bang and saw you run by."

"Is anyone else home?"

"No."

"Okay. Thank you. You should go back inside."

He waved her away and turned into the alley. When he approached the door to the apartment building, he kicked a trash can to vent his frustration, knocking the lid off onto the pavement. The metal lid rattled and banged until it lay quiet.

His antenna went up, and he stopped, staring at the lid, thinking again about the sound he had heard inside Baker's apartment.

"No," he murmured. "Not a rattle."

His brain strained to remember. *It was more like a jangle. The sound a chain makes.* Giorgio smiled. The man who had hit him had been wearing a chain necklace. Like so many of the ones he had seen people wearing at The Cave.

He climbed the stairs and returned to find Swan sitting on the arm of the living room sofa with a wet towel pressed against his forehead.

"I lost him," Giorgio admitted.

"I heard a shot," Swan said.

"Yeah. He missed. How are you feeling?"

"He used a baseball bat," he told Giorgio. "He missed a direct hit, fortunately. It's on the floor in the bedroom. I never saw it coming."

"Where was he hiding?"

"The shower. The curtain was open halfway. I glanced into the tub, but too quickly. He was tucked behind the curtain. I'm an idiot, I know."

"Should we get you checked out?"

"I have a raging headache, but I'll live." The pain in his face was evident.

Giorgio pulled out his cell phone. Swan held up his hand.

"I've already called it in," he said.

Giorgio glanced past Swan to the messy floor behind him. "Well, you sit tight. I'll look around." Giorgio reached into his coat pocket and pulled out some nitrile gloves. "I'll start in the bathroom, since he apparently didn't find what he was looking for out here. Why don't you get some ice?"

Swan nodded and lifted off the sofa and headed for the kitchen. Giorgio went into the bathroom.

The sink and medicine cabinet were separated from the toilet and bathtub by a door. He stepped past the door and glanced into the tub. Pulling the curtain back, he spied the blurry image of a wet shoeprint right by the drain. He pulled out his phone and snapped a picture of it.

Going back to the sink, the intruder had succeeded in emptying the medicine cabinet and had even opened and emptied several pill bottles. Small pink capsules and tiny white pills lay strewn across the counter and in the sink.

Giorgio fingered through the drugs and then searched the drawers underneath the counter. He found nothing but tubes of Neosporin and hair gel, Band-Aids, cotton balls, an old electric toothbrush, condoms, and cough drops.

Something on the floor behind the toilet caught his attention. It was the heavy chain necklace Baker was wearing the day they met him. The clasp had been broken, and there was blood on the peace symbol. He slipped it into a plastic bag.

The sound of sirens brought him back to the living room, where he met Swan coming out of the kitchen holding a towel filled with ice.

"There's a footprint in the shower," Giorgio said. "I got a picture of it."

"What do you suppose this is?" Swan said, holding up a flash drive.

Giorgio frowned. "Where did you find that?"

"Let's say that Baker had more than ice in his freezer."

"Let's take it."

The pounding of feet made them both turn towards the door as two officers in uniform showed up, hands on their weapons.

Giorgio flashed his badge. "We're good."

"We got a 10-31. What happened?"

Giorgio knew Officer Booth, a short stocky man in his thirties. The other officer was a young African American woman, Kacie Renfrew. She was small and compact and had the highest shooting range scores in the department.

"We came to talk with the young man who lives here," Giorgio began. "His neighbor let us in. Said she'd heard strange noises earlier and came to check on him, but he didn't answer. When we came in, we found it like this." He turned and gestured to the disarray behind him.

They were both staring at Swan.

"Somebody hit me with a baseball bat," he said. "T guy took off, and Joe went after him."

"I chased him down the alley," Giorgio said. "He took a shot at me, then got away in a waiting blue Malibu on the next street over."

"Did you return fire?" Renfrew asked.

"No. I was half a block behind him."

"Okay, do you want us to get forensics out here?"

"Yeah. Have them check this out," he said, handing them the bagged necklace. "We'll also need you to talk to the neighbors and I'll show you where the bullet hit. I spoke to a young girl in one of the houses along the alley, but she only heard the shot. Someone else may have seen the guy."

"Will do," Booth said. "Do you know what the guy was looking for?" He glanced around at the mess.

"No. We found a flash drive, but we don't know what's on it."

"I doubt it's a coincidence," Renfrew said.

Giorgio just smiled.

CHAPTER TWENTY

It was almost one o'clock by the time the detectives and the forensics team had finished at Baker's apartment and the patrol officers had interviewed the neighbors. There was still no sign of Baker, but one of the officers reported that an older gentleman who lived at the end of the hall remembered seeing Baker heading into the stairwell with a tall, dark-haired man who held him by the arm.

"We'll go see the landlord and see if they have any security cameras," Renfrew said.

"Okay, I also want the crime scene guys to check out some blood outside on the front steps before they go. We'll head back to the station and see what McCready and Rocky have learned." He turned to Swan. "But first we ought to stop at the ER."

Swan's eye had blackened, and he had a lump on the side of his forehead the size of a small egg.

"I'm good."

"Dude, he hit you with a baseball bat," Giorgio said as they sauntered toward the door. "You've got one hard head."

"Where have I heard that before?" Swan said with a smile.

On the way back to the station, they called McCready to report in. When they returned to the station, a voice stopped them on the way down the hallway toward their office.

"Joe! Got a minute?"

They both turned to find Captain Ramos poking his head out his door. Ramos was a handsome man in his mid-fifties, with dark hair graying at the temples. He took one look at Swan and said, "McCready filled me in. Clinic or the ER…your choice."

"Yes, Cap'n." Swan rolled his eyes.

"Get Mulhaney to drive you," the Captain said.

Swan nodded and turned on his heel, heading for the back office where Mulhaney hung out.

"Was that it?" Giorgio asked his boss.

"No. Step in here a minute."

Giorgio followed him into the office and closed the door behind him. Captain Ramos was normally a cool, collected sort of guy. But right now, Giorgio could sense his anxiety.

"What's up?"

Ramos stepped behind his desk and began to play with a small clay dish his daughter had made for him when she was in high school. Everyone in the station knew its sentimental value. The captain stared at the dish a moment before speaking.

Finally, he looked up, his dark eyes cautious. "Joe, we need to be careful. We're a small police department. We've already been involved in a mob-type murder and a brutal serial killer case. All in less than a year."

"Yes, sir. And we solved both of those cases."

"You've done a fine job. But vampirism—well, that's an entirely different matter."

"I'm not sure what you mean."

Giorgio watched his boss fidget with different objects on his desk. He was uncomfortable with the subject. Perhaps it was his Catholic background. Like Giorgio, Ramos had grown up in the church. Unlike Giorgio, though, he was still a devout Catholic.

"I've already started getting calls from the media," he said. "Finding a dead woman with two holes in her neck was bound to leak out."

Giorgio's heart fell. He had hoped to gather more information before they had to go public with that.

"What did you say?"

"The standard. We are in the middle of an investigation and will release information when we have it. But that won't last long. They'll start digging on their own and very quickly we'll have parallel investigations going on, so…"

"So, hurry up," Giorgio said, finishing his thought.

"Just recognize that now you have an audience."

Giorgio gave him a short nod. "Got it."

"And it's time to do a press conference. Release the woman's name."

Giorgio nodded. "Okay."

"Keep me informed," Ramos said. "I want whatever you have, as soon as you have it."

"Copy that."

Giorgio left the office and headed toward the squad room, passing McCready's desk.

"Any news?" he asked.

The young cop looked up. "We have an APB out on Phillips. I called the school, but the TA hasn't been in, either. I have been researching Nagel's financial records and so far, zilch. I also searched her phone records, and the only call out of the ordinary was one to San Diego. And she has no social media. This woman lived a boring life."

"Do we know who she called in San Diego?"

"Not yet. But I'm on it."

"Okay, call her mom and see if she knows. Anything on Baker?"

"We tracked down his parents. They live in Hawaii. I haven't talked to them yet, since we don't really know if he's missing."

Giorgio nodded. "Good call. We'll put a rush on the DNA match from the blood on the apartment steps, but I doubt we'll hear before late tomorrow. And the guy who hit Swan got in a car with someone driving a blue Chevy Malibu. I just got the first letter on the plate – V. See if it matches Nagel's."

Giorgio's fingers played with a small piece of paper in his coat pocket. He pulled it out. It was the sticky note from the night before.

"I have to make a phone call," he said.

He went to his desk and dialed the number on the sticky note. A woman answered.

"This is Detective Salvatori. Someone from this number called me last night."

"Um…yes, that was me." Her voice faltered as if she were nervous.

"What can I do for you?"

There was a pause. "You're investigating the death of Lindsey Nagel."

"That's right. Do you have information for me?"

"You need to check into Southwest Eye Clinics. Specifically, look at Dr. Cook's and Dr. Morro's practices."

"Why?"

"Because Lindsey worked there."

"Right. She was their bookkeeper."

"Yes, and you need to check them out."

"You mean the company itself?"

"Yes."

"Miss, uh…"

"Just check them out. And don't try to call me back. This is a burner phone. I'm getting rid of it as soon as I hang up."

"Wait! What am I looking for?"

"Lindsey found something in their billing department and told the wrong people. It got her killed."

"Do you have any proof…"

"Listen. Her death was not an accident. She was murdered."

The line went dead.

CHAPTER TWENTY-ONE

Giorgio hung up, feeling a heaviness settle in his gut.

Murdered.

The moment they realized Nagel had been buried and then dug up he had suspected murder. The surprise was that this woman sounded so certain and as if there was evidence out there to prove it.

He poked his head back out his door, catching McCready returning to his desk with a can of pop in his hand. Other officers and a few members of the public mingled in the reception area down the hall.

"Hey, any chance we can trace a burner phone?" Giorgio asked.

McCready's brows furrowed. "Not unless we know who made the call."

Giorgio blew out a frustrated breath. "Okay. Listen, find out everything you can on the Southwest Eye clinics and Southwest Financial Services."

"What am I looking for?"

"I just got a call from a woman who knew Nagel. She says Nagel found something in the billing department. The two companies are owned by Dr. Edward Cook and Dr. Oliver Morro, and this anonymous source thinks they had something to do with her death."

"No indication who the caller was?"

"No. Other than she had a Middle Eastern accent."

As soon as he said the words, something clicked. *Nagel's sister had said one of the victim's friends might have been Middle Eastern.*

"Also, we need to find that writing instructor."

"Okay. By the way, I talked with Lindsey's mother. She said that Lindsey got her degree in finance from the University of California in San Diego, and that she remained close to one of her professors down there."

"Maybe that's who she called," Giorgio mused. "Did you get a name?"

McCready glanced down at a notepad. "Dr. Zak Adams."

"Okay, see if you can find out why she called him. It might be nothing, but now that we know she found something odd about the books at the clinic, I'm sure the timing of the call isn't a coincidence. See if Mulhaney can help you with some of this stuff. By the way, Swan is getting his head checked out, and Rocky should be back soon."

As if on cue, Rocky appeared around the corner of the reception desk with a McDonald's bag in his hand. He joked with another officer as he passed and then sauntered in their direction. When he saw his brother staring at him, he said, "What's up?"

"Learn anything from Grueger?" Giorgio asked.

Rocky grinned. "Yep. All about vampires."

McCready perked up. "Seriously?"

Giorgio winced and grabbed him by the elbow, steering him out of the public area. "Keep your voice down," he snapped, eying a woman standing with her daughter at the end of the hall.

"Why?" Rocky asked.

"The captain is worried about public perception. C'mon. Let's talk in private."

The three of them went into Giorgio's office. Giorgio perched on the corner of his desk, while Rocky dropped into the chair behind his own desk and opened the McDonald's bag. McCready remained at the door.

"So?" Giorgio asked with a snappy tone.

Rocky unwrapped his burger, took a giant bite and chewed for a moment. Meanwhile, Giorgio waited, drumming his fingers on his leg.

"C'mon, what'd Grueger say?"

"Hey, I'm starving," Rocky mumbled with a full mouth. "Only had a breakfast bar this morning." He swallowed and then wiped his mouth with a napkin. "Okay. Here's what I know." He guzzled some Coke and swallowed. "Derek Grueger recognized the tattoo. In fact, he remembered Nagel."

Giorgio straightened up. "Go on."

Rocky loved having an audience. He threw a couple of fries in his mouth, while Giorgio banged his heel against the leg of his desk chair.

"Okay. Grueger is this wiry little guy with long hair and more of a grunge look than goth."

"Who cares what he looks like?" Giorgio snapped.

Rocky rolled his eyes. "I just meant he's not part of the vampire scene."

"So, no eye makeup or fangs," Giorgio said. "Got it."

"Right. He just does their tattoos. And like Haru, he considers himself an artist."

"And he remembered Lindsey?" McCready asked.

"Yeah. He said she was unforgettable because she was so tense. She admitted taking Xanax before she got there, wore headphones to listen to music, put a rubber bar between her teeth and had a friend with her to hold her hand. Like I said…tense."

"That would fit the phobia part of her. I'm surprised she did it at all."

"She told him it was a challenge she had to overcome."

"So, who was with her?" McCready asked.

"A skinny woman in her thirties with stringy blonde hair. He said Lindsey called her Mimi."

"Bingo," Giorgio said, turning to a file on his desk. He opened it and took out a sheet of paper, skimming it. "Remember? Her sister mentioned a technician at the clinic named Mimi. And Velchy said she had dinner at The Cave with a blond woman."

"What does this guy know about the tattoo itself?" McCready asked.

Rocky popped another fry in his mouth. "He said he's the go-to guy for one of the local vampire groups. He called it a vampire cult."

"A cult?" Giorgio asked. "Like Waco?"

"No. But the way he described it, the group has a charismatic leader who sucks the life out of them—literally," he said with a chuckle. "People don't sign over all worldly goods or get cut off from their family, but there is good money involved. You have to pay to play."

"How much?" McCready asked.

"A thousand bucks. I guess it pays for their rituals and upkeep on 'the Fortress,'" Rocky said with air quotes.

Giorgio scoffed. "Fortress? What's that supposed to mean? Do they think they're going to war?"

"In all the stories, the vampires are at war with somebody," McCready interjected. "Werewolves. Other vampires. Or humans."

Giorgio turned toward the young cop. "In your research, did any of these groups have a conflict with someone? I mean, we're not looking at gang warfare of some sort, are we?"

"I doubt it. I think most of these people are living out a fantasy," he said.

"Except they actually suck blood out of people's necks," Giorgio said.

McCready shrugged. "Yes. But I'm sure this fortress will be a little like Disneyland. Made to look like what they perceive a vampiric stronghold would look like. Big candlestick holders, draped fabric—your basic Christopher Lee movie set."

Giorgio tapped the end of a pencil on his desk. "I want to see what this place looks like. But how do we find it?"

"Looks like we're going to have to go to that *Essence of Murder* thing tomorrow night," Rocky said. "Got your fake fangs ready?"

"I think we ought to see if Flame will go with us," Giorgio said. "She looks more like one of them, so people would be more likely to talk with her."

His brother shrugged. "Not sure she'll be willing to go."

"But she gave us the list of tattoo artists," Giorgio countered. "Why don't you give her a call?"

Rocky nodded and wiped his hands on a napkin before grabbing the desk phone. Giorgio got up and wandered over to the white board and focused on a photo of Nagel lying in the streambed. He leaned in, studying her hair.

"Hey, McCready," he said, turning. "I saw Officer Renfrew when I came in. She's back from Baker's apartment. Can you ask her to come in?"

"Sure," he said, turning to leave.

McCready disappeared down the hallway. A few minutes later, Officer Renfrew came into the room. She was one of only two female officers in the department.

"McCready said you needed me. I was just about to leave on patrol."

Giorgio slid the photo across his desk. "Take a look at this."

Renfrew was a compact 5' 5" and had once told Giorgio that her goal was to become a detective. She was known in the department for not pulling punches, which made people take her seriously. She drew the photo toward her.

"This was the body found up in the canyon," she said.

"Yeah. What do you see?"

She glanced at Giorgio, her espresso eyes curious as she lifted the photo and looked at it more closely. "I'm…uh, not sure what you mean."

"I want your opinion."

She looked again at the photo. "She's obviously dead. I heard she had two holes in her neck, but you can't see those in this photo. I don't see any other damage to the body. I…"

"What about her hair?"

Officer Renfrew raised an eyebrow as she snuck a glance at Giorgio. "Her hair?" She glanced back at the photo. "It's medium length. Brownish blonde. Wet."

"Is it dyed?"

She laughed. "You're kidding, right? You think just because I'm a woman, I know about hair dyes?" She gestured to her close-cropped Afro cut. "Clearly, my hair is natural."

"Sorry. I just thought you might know more than any of us."

She sighed and glanced back at the photo. "If I had to guess, I'd say yes. She colored her hair." She pointed to the photo. "I have a friend whose hair is about this color. She gets what they call highlights."

"What does that mean?" McCready asked, coming up behind her.

She glanced at the young cop. "This woman's natural color is brown. But if you look closely, you can see blond highlights." She pointed to Nagel's hair floating in the water. "See here? There are distinct lighter blond strands."

"How often do women get this done?" McCready asked.

She hunched her shoulders. "Again, I'm no expert." She pointed at the picture. "But she doesn't have any grow-out, so my guess is that she had it colored recently."

"Okay. Thanks. You've been extremely helpful."

Officer Renfrew gave a curt nod and left.

"Flame said she'll come with us to the *Essence* thing," Rocky said, putting his phone down. "Why was Renfrew here?"

"I wanna find the person who did Nagel's hair."

"Why?"

"Because we can't find Phillips or his girlfriend right now. So, if Nagel has been going to the same hair stylist for a long time, she'd be likely to share things she might not share with others."

"Kind of like a bartender," Rocky said.

"Exactly. Angie's been going to the same stylist for years. I shudder to think what that woman knows about me."

Rocky erupted in a laugh. "Now I know where to go to dig up dirt on you when I need it."

"Let's find Nagel's hairdresser," he said.

"How do we do that?"

"I'll call her mother. You call the sister. One of them is bound to know. Otherwise, we'll access her bank account." He turned to McCready. "Listen, we need to prioritize. Why don't you call the clinic's financial services group and find out if a Mrs. Simpson is back yet? She was Nagel's boss. We need to see her today. Then track down the writing instructor so I can get a bead on that woman who called me. Get Mulhaney to talk with Nagel's professor in San Diego. Let's see if we can nail down why Lindsey might have called him. Then someone needs to interview Phillips' boss at Bethany Christian school. Find out what they know about Phillips' absence and see if the TA has shown up."

McCready rolled his eyes. "Yes, sir. On it."

"What did Flame say?" Giorgio asked Rocky, as McCready left the room.

"Like I said, she's in. I told her we would pick her up around six-thirty tomorrow night. But you realize the flyer says it costs two hundred and fifty bucks to get in."

"Yeah. I'll talk to the captain."

÷

Rocky and Giorgio headed into Monrovia to find the Pixie Salon. On the way, Giorgio filled Rocky in on the anonymous caller and why Drs. Cook and Morro were now on their suspect list. They located the salon in a strip mall in between a sandwich shop and a laundromat and parked in front.

A bell jingled when they entered, prompting four sets of eyes to glance up. Giorgio cringed under the scrutiny of the women who waited in upholstered chairs, holding magazines in their hands. To his right were five large mirrors and five individual hair stations set against the wall. Each was sectioned off from one another by a black shelf unit holding hair products. In front of each mirror was a swivel chair, flanked by a hair stylist.

Giorgio showed his badge to the receptionist who sat behind a tall counter. "We're looking for Meghan Lent."

The young woman's eyes grew wide as she pointed to the first station. The men circled the counter and approached a medium-height woman with short, spiky blond hair.

"Meghan Lent?" Giorgio asked.

The woman glanced up eyeballing Giorgio's badge attached to his belt.

"Just a minute," she said.

She shifted her large brown eyes back to an older woman in the chair whose head was covered in strips of tin foil, making the octogenarian look like something out of a B sci-fi movie. Once Lent had finished folding a piece of foil back, she glanced sideways at Giorgio.

"What can I do for you?"

"You know Lindsey Nagel?"

"Yes, I do her hair."

"We were wondering if we could talk to you for a minute. Alone." Giorgio said, eyeing the older woman who was listening.

"Sorry, but I'm in the middle of this color. I can't stop. We either talk here, or you'll have to wait until I'm done."

She turned back to the woman and used a rat-tailed comb to separate out a thin line of hair.

"How long?" Giorgio asked in a curt tone.

"About fifteen minutes," she said, saturating the strands of hair with white goop. "I have a short break while the color sets. I can meet you next door at the sandwich shop." With deft fingers, she folded the strip of foil over the now goopy clump of hair.

"Okay. Thanks."

The two men left her and went next door to the sandwich shop.

"Do you want anything?" Rocky asked, stepping over to the counter. "I'm starving."

"You just had a hamburger!"

"I know, but now it's lunch time."

Giorgio sighed. "Grab me a Coke and some chips. I'll get a table."

Rocky nodded and turned to a young man who stood ready to take his order. Giorgio went to a small table in the corner and called Swan.

"How's your head?"

"They think I may have a concussion, so I'm home for twenty-four hours."

"Too bad. Just when you thought you were back at work. How do you feel?"

"Fine. Just catching up on the news."

"Listen, did you have a chance to check that flash drive into evidence?"

"Oh, shit no, I forgot. Sorry. I still have it."

"Okay, if it doesn't give you a headache, take a look at it and let me know what's on it."

"Will do. Any word on Baker?"

"Not yet. I'll check in with you later." Giorgio hung up and called McCready. "Is Nagel's boss back yet?"

"Yeah, she's at work today."

"Good. Find out anything useful on the clinic?"

"Just that Morro originally owned the clinic by himself, but it went belly-up six years ago. That's when Cook swooped in. He bought in and became half-owner, started the financial services group, and now they're all flush with cash."

"Interesting. Anything else?"

"One more thing. I was lucky and got a chatty secretary who works in the clinic. I guess they get audited every three years by something called the Joint Commission on Accreditation. It measures their standard of care and qualifies them to bill Medicare and Medicaid. Both times they were called into noncompliance, which warranted a second review."

"Do we know what for?"

"No. We'd need a subpoena for that."

"Okay. That's good for now," Giorgio murmured. "Thanks. Can you call this Mrs. Simpson and see if we can meet with her in about forty minutes?"

"Sure. Still want me to talk with the writing instructor?"

"Yeah. I'm trying to find out the names of the people who teamed up with Lindsey Nagel."

"Okay. I think I've ID'd who the instructor was, and I've been trying to get hold of the psychiatrist who prescribed for her."

"Great. What about Phillips' boss at the elementary school?"

"I sent Renfrew and her partner out to talk to the principal."

"Good call. I'll check in with you later."

Rocky was halfway through a meatball sandwich when the hairdresser pushed through the shop door. She stepped over to their table.

"Let me grab something to drink," she said. She went to the counter and came back with an iced tea. "So, what can I do for you? Is Lindsey in trouble?" She opened two packets of sweetener and dumped them into the tea.

"We just have a few questions. Did she come to see you recently?" Giorgio asked.

"Yes, just last week. She gets her hair cut every four weeks and colored every few months. Why?" A note of concern had seeped into her voice.

Giorgio snuck a glance at his brother. "I'm afraid she's dead. Her body was found up in Bailey Canyon."

The young woman flinched. "Dead? Wow. I can't believe it."

"Do you know of any reason why she would have been up in the canyon?" Giorgio asked.

"Um, no. She was afraid of everything. I can't imagine she would go hiking alone. Jeez," she said, expelling a breath and dropping her gaze.

"Miss Lent, we were wondering if she'd ever mentioned anything to you that might have raised questions in your mind."

"Like…what?"

"Work? Boyfriends? Anybody she was having trouble with."

"You think someone killed her?" Her voice now exhibited real concern. "Not Lindsey. She was a little bird. Why would someone hurt her?"

"We're not sure what happened," Rocky said. "The cause of her death is inconclusive right now. We're trying to figure out why she was up in the canyon all alone, perhaps at night. Would the little bird you knew do that?"

"Absolutely not." She sighed before taking a sip of her drink. "I've been cutting Lindsey's hair for, I don't know, six or seven years. She talked about her husband and a few guys she had dated briefly since then, but to my knowledge she didn't have a boyfriend. Her husband sounded like a piece of work, though, and had inserted himself into her life again a couple of months ago because he wanted money. She got the house in the divorce and was going to sell it. He wanted a piece of it."

"Did he threaten her?"

"I don't know. But I know he hit her once. I saw the bruise. He was very controlling. She used to check her watch all the time when she was here to make sure she would be home on time. Once she left him, that all changed. She seemed, I don't know, liberated."

"What about work?" Rocky asked.

She shrugged. "She seemed to like her job. She was a bookkeeper. But she mentioned last week that she might be leaving."

"Leaving? Why?" Giorgio asked.

"Lindsey loved numbers. Loved figuring things out. She even helped her mom do her taxes each year. Anyway, I guess she found something at work that concerned her. I don't know what it was, but she asked me if I'd ever been a whistleblower."

"A whistleblower?"

"Yeah. I laughed. I mean who would I blow the whistle on in a hair salon? Anyway, last week when she was here, she nearly fell asleep in the chair while I was coloring her hair. When I asked her why she was so tired, she said she'd been taking work home and staying up late doing research on something."

"And you don't know what she was referring to?"

"No. I cut hair. I wouldn't know a debit from a credit."

Giorgio smiled. "I think you know more than you realize. Anything else you can think of?"

She sucked on her straw a moment, contemplating. "I assume you know about her phobias?"

Giorgio nodded.

"She talked a lot about how hard she was working to overcome her fears. They had ruined her life. She was so proud that she had overcome her fear of heights. That's the only reason I can think of as to why she might have been in the canyon. You know, testing her limits. But not at night."

"What if she'd joined some sort of a group?" Rocky asked.

Lent shifted her gaze to the handsome cop. "She wasn't much of a joiner, either. Although she mentioned that a friend had talked her into trying something kind of risqué."

"Risqué?" Rocky echoed.

"Yeah. She didn't tell me what it was, but she joked that she hoped I wouldn't think less of her. And that she was about to meet 'the sexiest man alive.' That's why she wanted to get her hair done. To look good." Lent shrugged. "She didn't tell me who the guy was. But she did say she was going to meet him last weekend. Is that when she died?"

"I'm afraid so," Giorgio confirmed.

She shook her head. "Poor Lindsey." She glanced at her watch. "Listen, I need to get back."

Giorgio reached into his pocket and handed over his card. "Thanks for your time. If you can think of anything else, please give us a call."

After the young woman left, Rocky asked, "So, what now? Should we head to the clinic?"

"Yeah. Lent is the second person to tell us something was wrong where Lindsey worked."

Rocky wiped grease off his chin and rolled up his trash, tossing it all into a nearby can. "Okay, then, let's go."

As Giorgio pushed his chair back and stood, Meghan Lent walked back in and over to their table.

"Detectives, I remembered something. When I'm doing someone's hair, I kind of get into a zone, you know? I listen to them when they talk, but frankly, sometimes not too closely. Anyway, last week when Lindsey was talking about work, I made a bad joke." She rolled her eyes. "God, I can't believe I did this. Anyway, when she said she was looking for discrepancies at work, I said I hoped that the people she worked for weren't crooks, and I wouldn't hear that she had disappeared or something. She didn't laugh. She looked at me and said, 'Well, if I end up dead in a ditch somewhere, tell the police to find my book.'"

"Find her book?" Giorgio asked.

"Yeah. She was writing a novel. I'm not much of a reader, so I never asked to read any of it. But she said she was about halfway through it."

Giorgio thought about the loose sheets of paper they had found nestled in the box holding Nagel's manuscript. But he also wondered about the entire book that was on her computer.

"Okay, thanks, Ms. Lent—that's helpful."

The brothers followed the stylist out the door. As they climbed into the car, Giorgio pulled out his cell phone and dialed McCready.

"McCready here," the young cop said when he answered.

"What about Nagel's boss?"

"She's expecting you."

"Great. By the way, I need you to go to the evidence locker and pull out the box with Nagel's manuscript in it? There are three sheets of paper on top that look like insurance forms. Check them out. Also, have you been through Nagel's computer yet? We think the complete book should be there."

"Yeah. The book is there. It's called *Small Town Murder*. I haven't read any of it yet. I had Mulhaney go through her emails, though. She did email that Dave Baker a few times about the book, but nothing to raise alarms. Her ex sent her some threatening messages though."

"Threatening in what way?"

"Well, he didn't threaten to kill her. But he did say he deserved half the money she made on the sale of the house, since he had bought it. He even threatened to take her back to court if she didn't give it to him. Then there's an email from someone called Mimi about the event Saturday night. They were to meet at The Cave at six o'clock. Then this Mimi texted, 'The Maestro will be so glad to bring you into the fold. It will be the most special night of your life.' Sounds like Mimi might have been one of their willing volunteers."

"Okay, thanks. Listen, Swan is stuck at home, so email the book file to him, and ask him to read it if he feels up to it. I don't know exactly what he should look for, but her hairdresser said that Lindsey told her if she was ever found dead to have the police check the book. And we think it might have something to do with her work. The hairdresser also said Lindsey was researching something at the clinic. By the way, what happened up at the school?"

"Renfrew just called and said they talked with the administrator. She said that Jennifer, the TA, quit on Monday. There was no reason given, but that everyone suspected the TA and Phillips were involved. They were just about to question Phillips yesterday about the rumored affair when she got an email from him that he quit, too. The girl is nineteen, so it's legal, but against policy."

"Did we get Jennifer's info?"

"Yes. I've called her cell phone, but she's not answering. She lives with her parents. I sent Officer Renfrew over to her home, but no one was there."

"Okay, what did Mulhaney find out from the professor in San Diego?"

"Hold on. He's standing right here."

There was a pause as McCready handed the phone to Mulhaney.

"He wants to know what you found out from that professor," Giorgio heard McCready say.

"Joe?" Mulhaney asked. "The guy teaches healthcare law. She called him last week, asking about medical fraud and whistleblower laws."

"Did she tell him why she was asking?"

"Only that she suspected someone at work might be ordering unnecessary procedures paid for by Medicare and Medicaid. But she wasn't sure how to prove it."

"What'd he tell her?"

"That she'd need to obtain copies of the suspicious bills the clinic had submitted to Medicare and then see if Medicare would launch an investigation."

"Shit," Giorgio said with a defeated exhale.

"But that's not all," Mulhaney said. "I talked with her psychiatrist. She saw him just last week. He said that in no way was she suicidal in case we were wondering. In fact, she had confided in him that she was feeling exhilarated. Apparently, not only was she joining this wannabe vampire group, but she told him she was investigating something illegal at work. She was pleased with the progress she was making. The doctor said that even six months ago, she wouldn't have done either one of those things."

"Too bad," Giorgio lamented. "I think that progress might be exactly what got her killed."

CHAPTER TWENTY-TWO

They pulled into the parking lot at the clinic just after one-thirty. Once again, the lot was full.

"They certainly are busy," Rocky said.

"Yeah. McCready said that before Dr. Cook bought into the business, it was going belly-up. I wonder now how that might play into this investigation."

"Because you think Cook is committing fraud?"

"Well, the woman on the phone suggested it. The hairdresser said something about it. And now the professor in San Diego seems to confirm that Nagel was interested in something like that." He glanced around the parking lot once more as they pushed through glass doors. "So, yeah. I suppose defrauding the federal government would be one way to get you out of the red."

Southwest Financial Services was in the basement, so they grabbed the elevator. The ride was short, and the heavy steel doors slid open onto a reception area without windows. A pretty redhead sat at a desk with several modular walls creating small office cubicles behind her.

"May I help you?" she purred.

"We're here to see Mrs. Simpson," Giorgio said, producing his badge.

"Yes. I believe she's expecting you." She picked up a phone, turned away from the men and said something in a low voice. When she finished, she turned back around.

"She'll be right with you."

A few minutes later, an efficient looking woman in her fifties appeared through a side door. She wore a crisp blue pantsuit with the jacket buttoned up over a white silk blouse. She approached them with her hand out.

"I'm Carla Simpson. Why don't you come with me?"

After shaking hands, she led them back through the door to a tidy office halfway down the corridor. She closed the door and then took her place behind an oak desk. Giorgio and Rocky sat in two armless chairs facing her, staring at a series of framed beach photographs on the wall behind her.

"I'm the Business Manager and Lindsey reported to me. I was so sorry to hear about her death. Everyone liked her. But how can I help you?"

"Right now, we just have some questions," Giorgio said.

She relaxed back in her chair. "That's good, because you'd need a subpoena if you expect me to access any personnel files."

"That won't be necessary yet," Giorgio said. "Besides, it seems like you run a tight ship here."

She nodded. "I do. We do the books for eight different clinics."

"I can appreciate that. Mistakes can be costly."

She bristled. "Has someone suggested we make mistakes?"

"I believe the company's reputation is stellar. But *your* oversight is important. To maintain a reputation like that, you must have eyes in the back of your head." He managed a quick smile to cement the compliment.

She laughed, which brought color to her cheeks. "I'm sure some of the staff think I do." She leaned forward. "Just the other day, I noticed that one of the receptionists had logged in a full eight hours on a day when she had taken an extra half hour for lunch." She sat back with a self-satisfied smile.

"Exactly," Giorgio said. "Then you would have noticed if Ms. Nagel seemed distracted lately."

"Distracted," she repeated. "Actually, I'd have to say that Lindsey did seem distracted the last time I saw her."

"When was that?"

"Friday morning. She was a few minutes late. Unusual for Lindsey. She was never late. When I asked her about it, she almost stuttered her reply. She said she had had trouble sleeping the night before and didn't hear the alarm. Then she just walked away like she was in a daze."

"Did that concern you?"

"To be honest, it did. Lindsey was very sharp. Shy and kind of an introvert. But she was overly respectful. To walk away like that without a word, well, it was almost, I don't know, rude."

"And you hadn't seen anything like that before?"

"No. Not even when she was going through her divorce. Which had to be a difficult time for her. That husband of hers came to the office once and confronted her. It upset everyone. But this was different."

"She was one of your bookkeepers, is that right?" Rocky asked.

"That's right. We have three."

"What was the scope of her work?"

She paused, as if not certain releasing this information would be appropriate. But an inhale of breath confirmed she had decided to share.

"Lindsey handled all invoicing and payments. But she took over billing for the insurance companies when the young man who had been doing that for the past several years suddenly moved back to Michigan."

"Why do you say suddenly?" Rocky asked.

"One day he was here, and the next day he was gone. We were told he left to help out his parents." She rolled her eyes. "He didn't even have the decency to tell me directly. They ought to teach employment etiquette in school these days."

"What was his name?" Giorgio asked.

"I don't think I should divulge that without the proper authority."

"I understand. I take it Lindsey would never have done something like that."

"No. I had a lot of respect for Lindsey. And she took the position only until I could replace Kent. Now I'll have to replace them both. People don't realize how much time it takes to hire and train someone."

Inwardly, Giorgio smiled at the release of the man's first name.

"I get it," Giorgio said. "We go through that in the police department. These young kids come in with ideas that it's going to be like Hawaii 5 0. When they realize it's a lot of grunt work, they leave."

"Well, Lindsey will be hard to replace. She was a nice young woman and worked hard. She caught more mistakes than anyone and saved us a ton of money."

"What kind of mistakes?"

Mrs. Simpson reacted as if she had just swallowed a fly. Her eyes got big and her throat muscles contracted.

"Oh, just normal calculation mistakes," she finally replied.

But her demeanor told him she wasn't telling the complete truth. She had become agitated and was shifting her weight in the chair.

"I thought perhaps Kent had made some billing mistakes, and Lindsey caught them."

"Um…no…well, maybe a few. I…uh…"

"Maybe you could explain the billing process to us," Rocky interjected.

The interruption worked, and she refocused on Rocky.

"Oh, well, certainly. Each procedure, each medication, each supply has a billing code. Those are inserted into a form that includes the date of service and the provider, along with the diagnosis. The forms are sent to the insurance companies and Medicare for payment."

"So, it's the code that verifies what's been done and how much you'll get paid?" Rocky asked.

"Right. Every insurance company is different. So, authorization for the procedure must be obtained in advance."

"And you're authorized to bill Medicare and Medicaid?" Giorgio asked.

"That's right."

He looked down at his notes. "And a group called the Joint Commission on Accreditation reviews you on a regular basis."

She shifted again in her chair. "Yes. Why is that important?"

"I understand there were some problems with the last couple of reviews."

She straightened her shoulders. "That had nothing to do with us. From what I understand, there were problems with wait times and prep work up in the clinic. Not billing."

"I see," he said. "Who assigns the billing codes?"

"The physician does that when he or she makes the diagnosis. The billing coder can change it if it is wrong, but it's really up to the doctor."

"Do the physicians often make mistakes?"

"Oh, sometimes. There are some nuances to the billing code, and of course, we want to get reimbursed as much as possible. So, the more accurate the code the better."

"Did Lindsey find mistakes Kent might have made?" Giorgio asked again.

Again, she paused before saying, "I'm sorry, but what does this have to do with Lindsey's death?"

"We're just trying to learn as much as we can about her," Giorgio said. "She died under suspicious circumstances. For instance, would you say she was dedicated?"

"Yes. Very."

"Was she the kind that worked a lot of overtime, just to get the job done?"

Mrs. Simpson's eyes grew large. "It's like you knew her. Yes. She was often here after five o'clock, long after her co-workers had gone home. Especially when I gave her this new job. I live not far from here, and I saw her car here late three days just last week."

"We understand she might have taken work home last week. Would that be usual?"

"No. I can't imagine why she would do that. It would be uncalled for, not to mention against company policy." Mrs. Simpson's alarm bells had gone off, and her entire body stiffened. "Who told you that? And what work did she take home?"

"We were hoping you could tell us. Apparently, she was upset by something she found and wanted to study it further," Giorgio said, eyeing her.

"I…uh, I have no idea what that would be." She stood up. "I'm sorry, but I have some phone calls to make. You'll have to excuse me."

As she circled the desk, Giorgio stood and said, "We'll need to see Lindsey's workspace."

"Don't you need a search warrant for that?" she said, bristling.

"We can get one. But, as I said, we are just trying to get to know her better. You know she was found up in Bailey Canyon. We need to find out why she might have been up there, possibly late at night. Maybe she left a note or something. Dr. Cook told us you work closely with your staff. I was hoping you would want to help us find out what happened to her. You're welcome to stay with us."

The woman seemed to consider this and gave a quick nod. "Come with me."

They followed her across the hall into a tiny office. "This was Lindsey's office. As you can see, she was very neat and orderly."

Giorgio and Rocky split up. Giorgio went to her desk, while Rocky sifted through some paperwork behind her desk.

"Be careful," she admonished Rocky. "I'm sure all of that belongs to the clinic."

Rocky acknowledged her warning. "Just getting a quick lay of the land," he said.

Giorgio was searching through some papers on her desk. "Where would she have kept her appointments? In a book or on the computer?"

"We all use Outlook for that," she said. "I'm afraid you would need authorization to access it."

Giorgio opened and closed desk drawers, looking for anything personal. He also checked a credenza behind her desk. After a few minutes, he straightened up with a single key in his hand.

"There's nothing personal here," Giorgio said. "Do you provide lockers or locked drawers for staff somewhere?" He showed her the key.

Her eyebrows arched. "Well, yes. We have a few lockers. They're in the lunchroom."

She bustled out of the office and down the corridor to a room the size of a large bedroom. In it were two round tables, a countertop and sink, microwave, and cupboards. Along one wall was a bank of five old lockers.

There was no one in the room, so Giorgio stepped over to the lockers. "Do you know which one belonged to Lindsey?"

"I'm sorry, I don't."

He took the key and tried it on each padlock. On the third attempt, he was successful. With a clank of metal, the lock popped open, and he pulled the locker door wide.

Inside was a maroon sweater hanging on a hook, a zippered pouch that contained toiletries, including hand lotion, mouthwash, aspirin, and a packet of Xanax. Tucked in the back was her iPad.

"We'll need to take all of this," he said to Lindsey's boss. "If you need us to sign it out, we can."

She hesitated, confused as to the proper procedure. Then, she sighed. "No. I think that's fine. These are her personal belongings. They have nothing to do with the office."

She gave them a plastic bag, and they dumped everything into it.

"Now, I'm sorry, but I really do have to go."

"Thank you. We can find our way out."

She gave them a half smile and returned to her office, while they ambled down the hallway toward the elevator.

As Giorgio reached out to punch the button, Rocky said, "Didn't you say you had to use the head?" He nodded toward two women standing at a small, built-in coffee bar nearby.

Giorgio followed his gaze and caught his intent. He and Rocky had run this ruse several times to find out more information. Rocky would extract what he could from the women, while Giorgio pretended to look for the men's restroom.

"Right. I'll be back in a minute." Giorgio stepped over to the women and interrupted them. "Can you direct me to the restrooms?"

A tall brunette turned. "Sure. Just keep going. They're at the end of the hall."

"I'll be right back," Giorgio said to Rocky.

"I'll wait here," his brother responded.

The brunette ran her gaze up and down Rocky, and a brief smile flickered across her face.

Rocky turned on his typical charm offensive. "So, what do attractive women do around here after working with a bunch of stuffy doctors all day?"

Giorgio left the woman giggling and went in search of the restrooms or anything else of interest he could find.

He passed several offices and one small conference room. All doors were closed and no one else was about, so he made the turn into the men's room. One man was washing his hands as Giorgio entered, but turned and left. One stall door was closed, so Giorgio made a play at using the urinal.

He was just ready to zip up when the toilet flushed, and the stall door opened. A young man with a rash of dark hair came out. He was dressed in a suit that looked a size too large for him, and Giorgio thought he couldn't be more than twenty-two. They ended up at the sinks at the same time. Giorgio eyed him in the mirror.

"You look too young to be a doctor, unless you're like Doogie Howser or something."

The young man looked up. "Who's Doogie Howser?"

"Sorry. Showing my age. It's an old TV show where a teenage genius kid becomes a doctor."

The two men reached for paper towels.

"Naw, that's not me. I'm just the IT guy. I keep all their computers running and phone systems operating."

"That's not too shabby. I bet they're lucky to have you. By the way, did you know Lindsey Nagel?" He stopped to throw his paper towel away.

"I knew who she was. She seemed nice. I heard she died. Are you a family member?"

Giorgio showed him his badge. "We're looking into her death. We're not sure yet how she died. Do you know who she might have been friends with here? Who she might have confided in? It would really help."

"Adira Karim," he said without hesitation. "They used to have lunch together and hang out in the break room all the time."

An alarm bell rang in Giorgio's head upon hearing the name. *Was this the woman with the Middle Eastern accent who had called him?*

"Do you know where I might find her?"

"She's one of the nurses at the Kensington Clinic up on the second floor. But she's not in today. I heard a couple of the women talking. She's pretty torn up about Lindsey and is taking some time off."

Giorgio looked disappointed. "Too bad. We need to give Lindsey's mom some closure. Do you know where she lives?"

"I do, actually. We live in the same apartment building. It's behind the Safeway store on Canaway Street."

"Thanks. By the way, we could use someone like you at the police department. We like sharp young minds."

The young man's eyes lit up. "Thanks. It'd be more fun than working here."

"What's your name? You know, just in case."

"Ted Freemont." His eyes shone with enthusiasm. He whipped out his wallet and handed over his card.

"Thanks. Do you know someone named Kent who worked here?"

"That would probably be Kent Bledsoe. He was in the billing department. He left a few weeks ago."

"Okay, thanks for your help," Giorgio said. "I'll keep you in mind."

They left the restroom coming face-to-face with Mrs. Simpson as she left the women's restroom right across the hall. Her eyes opened wide at seeing Giorgio with an employee.

"What are you doing, detective? You have no right to be interviewing staff."

Before young Ted could respond, Giorgio spoke up. "No problem, Mrs. Simpson. We were just discussing old TV shows." He gave Ted an encouraging look. The kid picked up without a pause.

"Yeah. Have you ever heard of Doogie Howser, Mrs. Simpson? He thinks I look like him. Can you imagine me diagnosing anything but a computer malware?"

Young Mr. Fremont walked away shaking his head and laughing to himself. Giorgio watched him leave thinking he would make a good cop.

"Again, thanks for your time, Mrs. Simpson. Have a nice day."

Giorgio strode away, meeting Rocky at the elevator. The two men rode to the first floor without a word and exited the building. In the parking lot, Giorgio said, "That was fruitful."

"No kidding."

They approached the car, and Giorgio used his key fob to unlock it. "What did you learn?"

"The brunette works right behind the front desk. She was pretty chatty. I asked about the clientele since the clinic is in a high-end district."

"And?"

"She rolled her eyes and said that Thursdays are reserved for the dregs of society."

"She actually said that?"

"Yeah. I guess the clinic works a lot with local psychiatric facilities and homeless shelters. Those clients come in on Thursdays."

"Every week?"

"Like clockwork."

"The same people every week?"

"No. But she said a lot of the same people are billed every month or so."

Giorgio slipped in behind the wheel and turned to his brother as he closed his door. "That seems odd. I realize that psychiatric patients might have more physical ailments than the normal person, but not something that would require a monthly appointment. Especially at an eye clinic. How many people are we talking about?"

"I don't know, but I have her number," he said with a big smile. He brandished a slip of paper in his hand. "I plan to take her out for a drink tonight."

"Good. I'd like to know more about that." Giorgio started the engine and pulled out of the parking space. "I'll get McCready to do some research. And I want to find out what he learned about those billing forms we found."

On the way back to the department, Giorgio shared with Rocky what he had learned in the bathroom.

"Now we know the billing guy's name. Kent Bledsoe. Didn't Mrs. Simpson say his parents lived in Michigan?" Rocky asked.

"Yeah."

"Okay, so what now?"

Giorgio's phone jingled. It was McCready. Giorgio put it on speaker.

"Hey, I found Nagel's writing instructor. She teaches at Pasadena City College. I was able to talk to her by phone. She remembered both Nagel and Dave Baker. It was a semester-long class on writing fiction, and she divided the class into working groups."

"And?" Giorgio prodded him.

"They were in groups of three."

"So, Nagel and Baker. Who's the third person?"

"Thought you'd never ask. A young woman named Adira Karim. I've got her street address."

"Damn! Great job. Thanks."

McCready read off the address, and Rocky wrote it down. When Giorgio hung up, Rocky said, "That's the same person Freemont told you about, right? And didn't you say the woman who called you had an accent?"

"Yeah. That's what I was thinking. It could be her. If so, maybe they got to know each other in the class and became closer at work."

Giorgio made a beeline for the woman's apartment complex behind a Safeway in South Pasadena. The brothers went to the manager's office. A middle-aged black woman stood up from her desk behind the counter when they walked in. She had shoulder-length hair curled into ringlets and was dressed all in turquoise.

"Can I help you?"

They showed their badges. "We need to talk to Adira Karim. Can you let us know what apartment she's in?"

"Sure, but she's not there. I saw here leave this morning in a hurry. She didn't look happy, and she was carrying a suitcase."

"How do you know she hasn't been back?"

"Because she left the bathtub water running and flooded the apartment. I called her work number, but they said she didn't come in today. And frankly, now she may not want to come back here because I'll slap her ass with a major repair bill."

"What kind of car does she drive?"

"A Ford Escape," the manager said, her eyes ablaze. "Green. Hold on, I have the license plate number." She went into her computer, wrote a number on a sticky note, and gave it to Giorgio. "You find her, tell her I'm lookin' for her."

"We will. But we need to see her apartment first," he said.

Giorgio never knew who would demand a search warrant when he was out gathering information. But this woman didn't seem to care.

"Humph. No skin off my nose. But we've got fans blowing up there to dry it out." She reached behind her to grab a large ring of keys off her desk. "Follow me," she said with a deep sigh.

They followed her to the elevator and up to number 303. She unlocked the door and stood back.

"Just lock the door when you leave." She turned and retreated down the hallway.

They pushed open the door and were met with the musty smell of damp carpet. The room was chilly, and two industrial fans had been turned on full speed to blow air around in the living room and out the open windows.

"What d'ya think?" Rocky said. "We don't have a search warrant."

"No, but the landlady let us in, and Adira clearly left in a hurry. So, I'll take my chances."

Both men donned gloves and split up. Rocky started toward the bedroom, while Giorgio began to rummage around in the living room.

"Be careful little brother," Giorgio yelled. "It was a situation like this that got Swan clubbed with a baseball bat."

"Got it," Rocky called back.

Giorgio rifled through the young woman's books, drawers, and kitchen. Five minutes later, Rocky came back into the living room and handed his brother an old envelope. On it was written a phone number.

"Recognize this?"

Giorgio glanced at it. "Shit! That's my number. So, she *was* the one who called me."

"Yeah, but now, where the heck is she?" Rocky glanced around the apartment. "Cuz she sure ain't here. And she didn't go into work. So far, we're missing Adira Karim, Dave Baker, Phillips, and the TA."

"Yeah," Giorgio said. "None of this is looking good."

CHAPTER TWENTY-THREE

It was almost four o'clock when Giorgio and Rocky returned to the station. The final medical examiner's report was on Giorgio's desk, and he was reading it when he felt a new presence in the room. He looked up to find Flame standing in the doorway. Besides the multiple piercings, tattoos and red streak accenting her hair, she wore baggy jeans ripped open at the knees, military boots, and a tie-dyed t-shirt.

Rocky was out of his chair before Giorgio could even acknowledge her.

"Hey, Flame, come in," Rocky said.

He held out his hand and ushered her to a chair across from Giorgio. Then, he threw one long leg over the corner of the desk to perch there. Giorgio could see multiple officers lined up down the hallway all staring in their direction, and McCready was ogling them through the window.

Giorgio got up and closed the blinds.

"Do you have new information on the tattoo artist?" Giorgio asked her, coming back to sit down.

"No. Not that," she replied, settling into the chair. "Maybe something better. I asked around about vamp groups—people who dabble in that sort of thing," she said with a shrug. "Turns out there are several groups in the area. I thought you might like to know about them."

"We do, thanks."

She took out a single piece of paper. "Okay. One is called the Blood Cult and meets in South Pasadena. But to be honest, I understand they're more of a book club. They're a bunch of older women who are big fans of Anne Rice's books."

"Isn't she dead?" Rocky asked.

Flame swiveled to look up at him. "You must be thinking of Ann Rule. She wrote true crime books. Anyway, the women in the Blood Cult worship Lestat, Anne Rice's main character."

"So, probably not our group," Giorgio said.

"No. But there are several other groups," she said, referring to her notes. "The first is called The Darkened Souls. They operate in Hollywood and are quite large. Apparently, a few celebrity types belong. They're referred to as psychic vampires, or psi-vamps." A half-hearted laugh from Rocky stopped her. She looked at him again. "I know it sounds ridiculous, but these people believe it."

"Or wanna believe it," he retorted.

She gave him an arched brow. "What's the difference in the end?" She turned back to Giorgio. "There's a couple of role-playing vampire groups, too. These people have dress-up parties, sleep in coffins, and even decorate their homes to look like the vampire culture. But they know they're play acting."

"I have a feeling you're saving the best for last," he told her.

She gave him a half smile. "Two groups actually drink blood. One is called Clan of the Undead. Their home base is somewhere in Los Angeles, and they are led by someone they call their Sire."

"Weird," Rocky said with a modicum of disgust.

Flame didn't take the bait this time. "The last group is the one I think you want. It's local. Arcadia in fact."

Giorgio sat up straighter. "Really?"

"Yes. It's called the Essence of Life Society; the essence of life being blood."

"Bingo," Giorgio mumbled. "What else?"

"It's a very secretive group. You must be invited by a member to join. You also have to pay a hefty price to belong."

"That's sounding more like a regular cult," Rocky said.

"It feels more like a cult to me," she responded. "You go through an initiation where you pledge fealty to the leader, someone they call The Maestro. You also have to go through a ritual where you act as a donor—someone willing to donate their blood to the group."

"Shit," Rocky said. "I don't understand why people would do that."

She gave him a patronizing look. "Not everyone is as confident as you are, Detective. Some people need the acceptance of others."

"Which is what Lindsey Nagel was looking for," Giorgio said. "She was a prime target. And it was The Maestro she was supposed to meet last weekend. So, now we know which group she was joining. But how do they get the blood out of their volunteers?"

"Well, I had to read up on that. Some groups don't use human blood. They use animal blood. Others do it just like you were donating at the blood bank. And yet, others have devices that are designed to pierce the vein in your neck while the vampire sucks it out."

"Jesus," Rocky said with a shake of his head. "This is just too weird."

"But that wouldn't kill someone, would it?" Giorgio asked.

"I don't think so," she replied. "In fact, from what I read, since donors are hard to find, they're treated very well. Pampered, even. Do you know yet how this woman died?"

Giorgio grabbed the ME's report. "She had both Xanax and a hefty dose of GHB in her system. The medical examiner said she died from acute respiratory depression cardiac arrest brought on by the combination."

"That's heavy," Flame said under her breath. "Why would she have taken both?"

"We don't know. She suffered from a number of phobias and used Xanax for that. I assume the GHB was given to her as part of the ritual. After all, it's a date rape drug. It would reduce her inhibitions and make her feel euphoric. Probably just what they'd want."

"Maybe your victim didn't know she was given GHB," Flame said. "I had a friend back east who OD'd on it." She dropped her chin and toyed with the strap of her shoulder bag.

"I'm sorry," Giorgio said.

She looked up, tears in her eyes. "It's why I don't do drugs—of *any* kind. My aunt thinks I'm nuts because I don't even take aspirin."

"How'd you find all of this out?" he asked. "I mean about the vampire groups."

"I have a friend who belongs to one of the psychic groups. She tried to recruit me a few years ago."

"And you weren't interested?" Rocky asked.

"It's not for me. I have too many other weird things going on in my head. I don't need fantasies about blood-drinking guys with sharp teeth."

Giorgio smiled. "We learned that our victim was scheduled to go to an event last Saturday night. Her friend, someone named Mimi, said it would the most special night of her life. She was supposed to meet this Maestro guy there."

Flame sighed. "Sounds to me like she was being initiated. You should also know this group is into voyeur sex. Once she had given up her blood, the man they call The Maestro, or his Lieutenant, would have had sex with her on the sacrificial pedestal."

"Jesus," Rocky murmured again.

They were all silent a moment.

"I think we just figured out who the man of her dreams was," Giorgio said. "Now, we just need to find him."

CHAPTER TWENTY-FOUR

Giorgio glanced at the old black-and-white clock on the wall. It was almost six o'clock, and he was exhausted. Flame was gone, as well as McCready and Mulhaney. He stretched his arms over his head and yawned.

"I'm heading home," he told his brother. "Want me to check with Angie to see what's for dinner?"

Rocky grinned. "Anything she makes would be better than what I would pick up." He closed a folder and shoved it into a drawer.

"Thought you were going out with the brunette from the clinic tonight."

"Just for drinks. I'll text her later."

"Okay, let's go have some home cookin'."

Giorgio's cell phone rang. It was Angie.

He clicked the phone on. "Hey, Ange…"

"Joe! Someone broke into the house! I was…I was just leaving to pick up the kids. I…I heard something in the hallway and found a man standing there."

She was choking on tears, her breathing heavy and sporadic.

Giorgio was already out of his chair. "Are you hurt?"

"No. He's gone now."

"Okay, lock yourself in the bathroom and don't come out until I get there."

"Okay," she whimpered. "But Joe…Shadow chased him off. I think she took a chunk out of his leg."

"Just get to a safe place. I'll be right there." He hung up.

"What's wrong?" Rocky asked.

Giorgio grabbed his coat. "Someone broke into the house. Report it. I'm on my way home."

Rocky reached for his phone. "I'm right behind you."

Rocky picked up the receiver to call dispatch as Giorgio ran to the car and sped home. With his emergency lights flashing, he made it home in record time. Rushing through the front door, he called out Angie's name and was rewarded with a weak reply from the kitchen. She was huddled on the floor by the dogs, fear reflected in those deep brown eyes.

At the sight of him, she flew into his arms, her entire body shaking.

"Hey, it's okay," he said, holding her close. "I'm here."

He squeezed her and then released her, guiding her into one of the kitchen chairs. He pulled a second chair over and sat down, brushing back loose strands of hair from her face.

"Everything's okay, Ange. Tell me what happened."

She took a cleansing breath before beginning again. "I…I was about to leave to pick up the kids. They both stayed after school for their clubs. Anyway, I was going to run upstairs and get my jacket when Shadow got off the floor and growled. Her fur was standing on end, Joe. Then, I heard a noise by the front door." She glanced back at Shadow, who sat at attention next to Grosvenor. "I didn't trust her today, so I tied her to the cupboard door. Otherwise, I think she would have run out ahead of me."

Giorgio glanced to the cupboards and saw that one of the doors was missing. It lay on the floor attached to a rope, which was attached to the dog.

"She broke the cupboard," Angie said with a weak smile.

"She could have leveled the entire house if it meant saving you. Keep going." Sirens in the distance made them pause. "Ignore them. Just tell me what else happened."

"I went into the hallway, and there was a man in a dark hoodie standing there. He had something in his hand. I couldn't tell what it was. I was so surprised, Joe, I screamed. He grabbed me and put his hand over my mouth. But suddenly, there was a loud bang, and Shadow was lunging for him with that damn cupboard door banging around behind her. The man jerked back and turned to run, but she got his leg before he got the front door open."

"Jo?" Rocky called out from the front of the house.

"In the kitchen," he yelled back. He focused again on his wife. "Do you know how he got in?"

Rocky appeared at the kitchen door just as she said, "Through a window, I guess."

Giorgio looked at his brother. Rocky took the hint. "I'm on it. There are drops of blood in the entryway. I put a chair over it."

"Thanks," Giorgio said.

Rocky left and Giorgio turned back to Angie. "Okay, the uniforms will be here soon. You'll need to go with them to the station to make a full report. Do you want me to get Mrs. Greenspan from next door to go with you?"

"No. I'll be fine. But someone has to pick up the kids."

He could feel the stress emanating from her body like heat from an oven.

"Maybe I'll have Mrs. Greenspan do that."

No sooner had he said that than the sirens announced the arrival of the squad cars. Moments later, they heard heavy foot falls as three officers converged on them in the kitchen.

Giorgio explained to them what had happened and asked them to call for a forensics team. He also told two officers to check every nook and cranny in the house to make sure all was well. As two officers left, the third pulled out his phone and drifted into the hallway to call forensics. Rocky appeared again to report that the den window had been forced open.

"Okay. Officer Jantzen just went into the hallway to call forensics. Tell him to tape off the area outside that window," Giorgio said. "We'll let forensics do their work. Angie is going to go to the station."

"I'll go with her. Let me go give patrol directions. I'll be right back," Rocky said.

Giorgio gave him a look of relief. "Thanks." He pulled his wife up from the chair and enveloped her in a second hug. "Rocky will take you to the station. You'll be fine. I'll take care of things here. Do you think you could ID the guy?"

"It all happened so fast, and he had the hood up. All I saw was a scraggly beard and dark eyes. But he wore a big chain necklace around his neck."

Rocky came back just as she said this, and Giorgio shared a look with his brother. "That's good," Giorgio said to her. "Anything like that you can remember is helpful. Wait in the hall for an officer and then go upstairs and get your jacket."

When she had left, he turned to his brother. "This had to have something to do with this case."

"You think it's the same guy that attacked Swan?" Rocky said.

"I'd bet on it. Question is…what was his intent? Tell the Captain I need 24-hour surveillance on the house."

Rocky nodded. "Got it."

The brothers left the kitchen and met Angie coming down the stairs with a patrol officer. Giorgio drew her in for one more hug, kissed the top of her head and then leaned in close to her ear.

"I'll catch the son-of-a-bitch, Ange. You can count on it."

She raised her eyes to his, a plaintive look seated deep within their depths. "I know you will, Joe. But what if the kids had been home?"

"I know. I know." He kissed her forehead this time. "Go with Rocky. Let us do our work."

Angie and Rocky left, and Giorgio called Mrs. Greenspan to ask her to pick up the kids. She was all aflutter on the phone because she had heard the sirens, but Giorgio assured her everything was okay. He just needed his kids home.

He returned to the kitchen, where Grosvenor had gotten to a sitting position. Shadow sat right next to him, ears up. Giorgio moved over and knelt in front of them. Shadow pushed her head under his arm. He stopped her, lifted her head, and studied her jaw. Sure enough, there was blood along her lower teeth.

"Good dog, Shadow. I guess Christian was right--you were meant to be with us."

Hoping to preserve the blood before she swallowed it, he went to the bathroom and pulled out two Q-tips, which he used to collect blood samples from her jaw. He dropped them into a clean baggie and then enveloped both dogs in a hug.

"Damn! You are both good dogs. And with your help, Shadow," he said, scratching her under her chin, "maybe we can find out who this guy is and put his ass in jail."

Two of Fong's assistants arrived to process the window and take the blood samples into custody. There were footprints outside the window, and so they also made plaster casts of those.

Once the window had been nailed shut, Giorgio returned to the station, where Angie had just finished her statement and was working with a sketch artist to attempt a likeness of the intruder.

When she was done, Rocky offered to bring Chinese food home for everyone. Thirty minutes later, he arrived with an array of small containers of rice and chicken dishes. The mood at dinner was somber as everyone, including the kids, processed their thoughts about the danger posed by the man in the hoodie.

"Are you okay, Mom?" Marie asked.

Angie lifted her eyes from where she had been moving the fried rice around with her fork.

"Yes, I'm okay, sweetheart. No one was hurt."

"Your mom is pretty tough," Rocky said.

Giorgio snuck a glance at his wife. She was staring at her plate again. "She also had the dogs with her," he said.

"Shadow's a hero, isn't she, Dad?" Tony asked with pride.

Giorgio watched as Shadow nudged his son's arm, looking for attention. "Yes. She is. I think both dogs are exceptional."

"Can she sleep with me tonight?" Tony asked, his eyes pleading for permission.

"I'm not sure she'll leave Grosvenor yet. But maybe tomorrow night."

He glanced at Angie, expecting a fierce look of disapproval. Instead, she smiled sweetly, as if it was the most charming of ideas.

Rocky got up to leave right after dinner for his date with the brunette. Giorgio walked him to the front door.

"What do you suppose that guy had in his hand?" Rocky asked.

"I have no idea," Giorgio replied. "But let's face it…it had to be either a weapon or something he used to break into the house."

"Which could have been used as a weapon."

"Right," Giorgio agreed.

Rocky shook his head in dismay. "We need to find out who these guys are."

"I agree. We need to get into that canyon to find out if the dogfighting ring is there. And let me know if you learn anything else from the brunette tonight."

"Will do."

Everyone turned in early that night. Giorgio lay next to Angie as she tossed and turned, finally reaching over to wrap one arm around her. After a few minutes, she relaxed, and he turned away. The anger that welled inside him was enough to fend off his own sleep until the early hours of the morning. So, when his phone rang at six-fifteen, he answered with a grumble.

"Salvatori," he barked.

"Joe, they found Dave Baker."

CHAPTER TWENTY-FIVE

Thirty minutes later, he picked up Rocky and headed up into the mountains on the east side of Sierra Madre. Santa Anita Avenue turned into Santa Anita Canyon Road and wound upwards through a wide ravine. As they traveled, Giorgio glanced off to where the road dropped off into a deep canyon.

"I wonder if he went off the road up here somewhere," he said.

From the passenger seat, Rocky twisted his head to glance to the right. "But why was he up here?"

"Good question."

They followed the winding road into the Angeles National Forest and finally happened upon a wide dirt turnoff filled with emergency vehicles.

"I guess this is it," Giorgio mumbled.

He pulled off and stopped behind a county sheriff's SUV. The brothers exited the sedan and moved past two black and white patrol cars, a county fire department vehicle, and an ambulance. They joined multiple emergency personnel who lingered at the edge of the ravine.

About a hundred feet down, past the chaparral and sage bushes, a car lay on its roof, lodged against a large boulder. Giorgio's gut clenched; it was the blue Chevy Malibu.

"That's not Baker's car," he said to an officer standing next to him.

A big man in a sheriff's uniform turned. "Are you Salvatori?"

Giorgio turned and squinted up at the man. "Yeah. I was told to ask for Sheriff Peters?"

A large, meaty hand appeared. "That would be me. Glad to meet you."

The two officers shook hands and then turned to watch the activity below. Two men were attaching a large metal hook to the bumper of the car.

"We know it's not Baker's, but he's behind the wheel. The registration says it belongs to a Lindsey Nagel. When we ran her name, her recent death popped up. That's how we knew to call you. And there was an APB out on him."

"Was anyone else in the car?"

"No, just Baker. He's pretty banged up though."

"Dead, I presume."

"Yeah. We were able to get an EMT down there, but it's dangerous. That's why we're bringing the body up inside the car."

"Any chance he wasn't killed in the crash?"

The sheriff shrugged. "Don't know. We'll know more after the postmortem."

"Detective Giorgio Salvatori?" a deep voice boomed.

Both men turned to find a man in a dark suit and tie standing behind them. Giorgio thought, *this guy has Fed written all over him.*

"I'm Detective Salvatori."

"I'm Agent Stuart Robertson. FBI." He proffered his identification, but no handshake. He returned his ID to the inside of his coat. "Can we talk?"

The sheriff tipped his hat and stepped away. Robertson eyed Rocky.

"This is my brother," Giorgio said. "Also, with the Sierra Madre PD. He can hear anything meant for me."

Robertson acknowledged Rocky with a brief nod.

"What does the FBI have to do with this?" Giorgio asked.

"Let's talk privately."

He led them back a few feet, away from the emergency personnel working to bring the car up from the ravine.

"Baker was working for us," he said in a quiet voice.

Giorgio's face registered his surprise. "He was undercover? For what?"

Robertson glanced at the tow truck that had backed up to the edge of the cliff. The truck driver was getting ready to start the big winch hooked to the back.

"We're tracking a dogfighting operation. He was our man on the inside."

"We know about the dogfighting ring. We saw him pass off a dog to one of their guys the other night."

Robertson's heavy eyebrows arched in surprise. He was bland, in the way you think of most FBI agents. Short brown hair. Brown eyes. Square jaw and broad shoulders. Add to that his less than sparkling personality, and he could have been right out of central casting.

"We need you to eliminate him from your investigation," he said.

"Why? We're investigating the murder of a young woman. And he's our connection to a wannabe vampire group. A group that our vic joined and one that may have been responsible for her death."

"I understand. But I don't want Baker's undercover work to be compromised."

"He's dead. I think it's already been compromised," Rocky said.

Robertson gave Rocky an appraising glance. "Yes, but a critical piece of evidence is still out there. We need to find it before they do."

"What is it?" Rocky asked.

Robertson paused, as if deciding whether to tell them. "A memory stick. He was documenting the operation and its ringleaders."

The tow truck cranked up the winch with a loud whine, and the heavy-duty cable began to roll back, bringing up the Malibu.

"Why would the FBI be so concerned with a single dogfighting ring?" Rocky asked.

Robertson rocked back on his heels and stuffed his hands into his pants pockets. "We don't care much about the dogfighting ring. It's pretty small, in comparison."

"To what?" Giorgio asked.

"Drugs. The same guys who run the dogfighting, run a phony canine rescue group. They not only use some of the dogs as bait dogs but bring rescue dogs in from other countries."

A surge of recognition flooded Giorgio. "And smuggle the drugs in with the dogs."

"They stuff bags of the stuff down the dog's throats, and then cut them out once they're in the country. Brutal stuff."

"Christ," Rocky murmured.

"And you know who they are?" Giorgio asked.

"We know who's running the dogfighting. But he's not the kingpin for the drugs. That's what Baker was trying to find out."

"Let me guess. Dr. Jackson Cook is the guy running the dogfighting ring."

It was Robertson's turn to look surprised. "How do you know that?"

"Because that's who took possession of the dog Baker supplied the other night."

"Follow me," Robertson said.

Robertson led them back to his car and pulled out a file. When he opened it, he handed a photo to Giorgio.

"Is this your Jackson Cook?"

"Yes. He's an ophthalmologist at Southwest Eye Clinics. He runs with a guy named Arthur Cordova. Look, Jackson Cook's father, Dr. Edward Cook, owns the surgical clinic our vic worked for. A couple of nights ago, we saw your guy, Baker, pass off a dog to some guy in a van. The dog was passed off again to a waiting SUV that belongs to Cook."

"Okay, so you're knee-deep into this. But, like I said, I need you to back off any more research into Baker. You could spook Cook, and more importantly, whoever he's working for."

"I assume you know Baker's apartment was ransacked. And since I'm sure it wasn't you guys who did the ransacking, it must have been one of Cook's minions looking for your memory stick," Rocky said.

"Yes. We went to the apartment not long after you were there. Listen, I'll help you in any way I can, but leave Baker alone until I give you the green light. Here's my card. Call me if you run into anything else."

"Don't you want to see his body?" Rocky asked.

Robertson glanced toward the tow truck. "I'll get a report once the M.E. has had time with him." He handed over his card, turned and got into his car and left.

Clearly, he assumed his word would be Giorgio's command. *He assumed wrong*, Giorgio thought.

As Robertson pulled back onto the highway under a cloud of dust, Rocky asked, "Why didn't you tell him about the flash drive we found?"

"Because it's *our* evidence, and I may need something to trade later."

"Are we going to back off?"

"Hell, no. Give Swan a call and see if he's seen what's on that flash drive yet."

Rocky pulled out his phone and dialed the big cop. Meanwhile, Giorgio walked over to where the sheriff stood guard over the extraction of the car. They had just brought it over the lip of the ravine and were about to settle it onto solid ground.

When they finished, the tow truck driver jumped out to disengage the winch. Officers stepped in to check the car, all wearing blue nitrile gloves.

Giorgio leaned in the driver's side window to view the battered body of young Dave Baker. He was still strapped in by the seat belt but slumped toward the passenger seat. Blood ran down his face, as well as the back of his neck. Giorgio peered closer and noticed an open wound on the back of his head.

He pointed to the head wound. "I have a feeling the ME will conclude he was killed somewhere else and put into the car before it went off the road."

The sheriff nodded. "Looks that way."

"Okay, keep us in the loop," Giorgio said, handing his card to the sheriff. He started back towards Rocky.

Rocky was just hanging up from speaking with Swan. "Chuck says he just opened the flash drive this morning and will meet us at the station."

Giorgio turned back to glance at the Malibu. "This case is beginning to feel like an octopus, with tentacles going everywhere. I'm not sure which tentacle Baker fits onto. But he became a liability to someone." The image of the man with the white hair and ponytail at the Cave flashed through Giorgio's mind. "You know, there was a guy at that club the other night who was staring at us when we were talking with Baker."

"Any idea who he was?" Rocky asked, getting into the car.

Giorgio slipped into the driver's seat. "Maybe."

CHAPTER TWENTY-SIX

Swan was at his computer when Giorgio and Rocky returned to the station. He waved them over, a large bruise still visible on his forehead.

"You'll want to see this," he said.

"How are you feeling?" Giorgio asked.

"Okay," he said, looking up.

They moved in behind him. He had inserted the flash drive and began to flip through a series of grainy pictures as Rocky and Giorgio looked over his shoulder.

"Sorry, I didn't get to these until this morning. But it appears that most of these are from the dogfighting ring. I assume it was Baker who took them. He got a lot of close-ups of people, especially three or four guys who appear over and over. My guess is they're the organizers."

The bulk of the photos were of a group of twenty or thirty people crowded around a ring created by a low wire fence. The grainy pictures had all been taken at night, outside, in a grove of trees. The center of the ring was lit by battery-operated scoop lights set on tall stands around the perimeter of the fence. Only the two dogs mauling each other in the center of the ring were lit well. One dog was a large black and tan Rottweiler, which seemed to have the advantage over a mixed-breed shepherd. It was clear the shepherd would lose this fight, and Giorgio felt a pang of regret knowing the dog would die a horrible, senseless death. *This is what Shadow escaped*, he thought.

"So, who can we ID?" he asked.

"It's hard to ID them in the group photos. Let me show you the close-ups."

Swan scrolled forward and enlarged one with four men standing right under one of the scoop lights.

"That's Cordova, the guy in the red Camaro," Rocky said, pointing to a heavy-set, bald guy with a meaty nose and pock-marked cheeks.

"Look at this one," Swan said as he scrolled to the next shot.

"That's Jackson Cook," Giorgio said, referring to a tall, dark-haired man in his early thirties. He had thick, wavy hair and was standing next to a Jeep, one hand resting on the hood, facing the camera with a dour expression. "Look at his face."

"He's looking directly at the camera," Rocky said.

"Right. I wonder if he sees that Baker is taking his picture."

"Well, that would be the kiss of death," Rocky said.

"There's something familiar about him," Giorgio murmured, staring hard at the image.

"Yeah, well, you've seen him a couple of times now," Rocky said.

Giorgio shook his head. "No, it's something else."

A variety of other men and a few women appeared in the photos that followed. Most of them were focused on the fight, cheering on the dogs in the ring. But it was Cook, Cordova, and two others who showed up over and over. In two pictures, Cordova was standing off to one side accepting money from someone.

"So, Cordova takes the bets," Giorgio said.

"Looks like," Swan said.

"I wonder who these two guys are," Giorgio said, pointing at two grungy men who appeared to be standing guard over the fight. One had a thick beard and long stringy hair. The other was of medium height, solidly built, and wore a heavy metal chain around his neck. Both had tattoos along both arms and on their necks. The guy with the beard even had one that extended up his cheek.

"I have a gut feeling that's the guy who took a baseball bat to your head," he said, pointing to the guy with the big necklace.

"And maybe the guy who broke into your house?" Rocky asked.

"Yeah," Giorgio replied in a low voice. "We can show these to Angie. See if she can ID him."

"There are a few more I want you to see," Swan said.

He scrolled to the last four photos on the file. These final shots had been taken in a garage or warehouse. Two clinical-looking metal tables had been set up in front of a set of shelves that held two rows of dog kennels. Above the kennels was a set of dirty windows and a banged-up metal sign for STP motor oil.

"I wonder where the hell this is," Giorgio said.

The four shots were a series of photos of the guy with the metal chain taking a small black dog from a kennel and putting it onto one of the tables.

"Here's where it gets ugly," Swan said.

He switched the photo to video and suddenly they were watching the guy with the beard put something over the dog's face. The dog struggled and then went limp. The men talked in low voices, so it was difficult to catch what they said. But Giorgio heard someone say, "Hurry up, Mateo."

The guy with the chain necklace picked up a scalpel and sliced open the dog's stomach. Blood gushed out, flooding the table. He ignored the mess and shoved a gloved hand into the dog's midsection. He felt around and grabbed onto the stomach. In another swift movement, he opened the stomach. Dropping the scalpel, he reached in and removed several small plastic bags covered in blood and bodily fluids. He held it up to Jackson Cook, who looked at it with a shameless grin.

"Pay dirt," Cook said.

"Get on with it, Jackson," a voice said.

"Shit," Giorgio murmured. "Wait a minute! Stop the video. Who's that in the background?"

He pointed to the far right of the photo, where the blurry image of someone watching from the shadows appeared. All that was visible was the man's hand wearing a large gold gem-encrusted ring.

"Probably their mob boss," Swan said.

"That's who Robertson wants," Giorgio said. "I'd bet my life on it."

Giorgio inhaled, feeling a depression settle over him like a heavy mist. "Okay, I'm sure this is what got Baker killed. We will have to turn it over to the FBI. But first let's make copies of everything. Monday, I want to see if the Sheriff's office will help us with some facial recognition so we can at least ID the two guys with Cordova and Cook."

"So, when do we give what's-his-name the flash drive?" Rocky asked.

"Tomorrow. But first, I want to talk to Cook before the FBI rounds him up."

"The timing's going to be a little dicey," Rocky said. "They're going to want to know why we didn't give them this today."

"Right. But, you know what? My house was broken into yesterday, scaring the bejesus out of my wife, and I'm a little tied up getting a handle on that," Giorgio said with a shrug.

"I get it," Rocky said. "Hard to compartmentalize when you're emotionally involved."

"Exactly."

"Okay," Swan said, "I'll just make a copy and then take off."

"And you and I have a date tonight," Giorgio said to his brother. "That's our priority right now. We are too damned close. We need to know who this Maestro guy is and how all of this is connected to Lindsey Nagel. And…I want to know who that Mateo guy is. Get a still of him and send it to me. I want to see if Angie recognizes him," he said to Swan. "And now, once again, I have to figure out what the heck someone wears to a gig like this."

"Maybe you could borrow that Dracula cape from the theater," Rocky quipped.

"Funny. But first, let's go see Jackson Cook. Then I need to get something from evidence."

"Why?" Rocky asked.

"I want something of Baker's to give to Flame."

Rocky's eyebrows arched in recognition. "Right. To get a read on his death."

CHAPTER TWENTY-SEVEN

Jackson Cook owned an expensive condo in Arcadia. Rocky looked up at the modern structure made of plaster, steel, and lots of tinted glass.

"This guy has some money," he said, getting out of the car.

"Yeah," Giorgio said, coming around the car. "Too much glass for me, but I guess dogfighting and drugs pay well."

The sliding glass front doors opened onto a slick marble floor, accented with leafy plants located around the perimeter. The elevators were on their left. A curved staircase wound up to the second and third floors from the center of the building.

They went to the elevators and punched the button for the third floor.

"What if he's not there?" Rocky asked.

"Something tells me he'll be there."

Rocky smiled. "You and your hunches."

They stepped off the elevator onto a rich, gray carpet. Number 315 was at the end of the hallway. Giorgio paused as he lifted his hand to ring the doorbell. From inside, they could hear the soft sound of a piano playing in the background.

"That's Rachmaninov's Piano Concerto No.2.," Rocky said. When Giorgio gave him a quizzical look, he replied, "What? Rachel was into classical music."

"Yeah, well, remember what Flame said about classical music?" Giorgio rang the bell.

The door was unlatched a moment later, and Jackson Cook stood before them dressed in loose-fitting sweatpants. No shirt. No shoes.

Giorgio took notice of his physique. He was Rocky's height, but broader in the shoulders and more muscular. He clearly had a close relationship with body-building equipment. Whether that was out of vanity or a sense of preservation because he was running drugs, Giorgio didn't know.

"Jackson Cook?" Giorgio asked, showing his badge.

The man's deep brown eyes narrowed. "Yes?"

"We're with the Sierra Madre Police Department. We'd appreciate a few minutes of your time."

"What's this about?"

"May we come in?"

He shifted his gaze to Rocky, seemed to size him up and then stepped back.

"I only have a few minutes," he said. "I'm supposed to meet my father."

The officers moved into an elaborately appointed living room. High-end black leather furniture complemented several colorful modern pieces of artwork that hung around the room. A floor to ceiling cherry wood bookcase stood against one wall. It was filled with books and small, expensive-looking sculptures and glass pieces.

While Giorgio and Rocky glanced around the room, Cook disappeared into the bedroom and came back buttoning up a deep blue silk shirt. He moved to the marble-topped bar that separated the room from the small galley-style kitchen and perched one hip on a black, leather stool.

"What can I do for you?"

Giorgio turned to him. "You recognize us, I presume."

Cook held Giorgio's gaze for a moment. "You were in my dad's office the other day."

"Then I assume you know about the woman who was found dead up in Bailey Canyon."

He shrugged his shoulders. "Yeah. So what? She worked for my dad. I didn't know her."

"Are you familiar with Bailey Canyon?"

Again, he paused. He got up and went to a Keurig machine on the back counter, picked a small container of coffee and stuck it into the machine. While he placed a mug into the slot and turned it on, he said, "I know where it is. I've never been up there, though."

"Where were you last Saturday night?"

He turned to Giorgio as the coffee began to stream into the cup. "Saturday?" He shrugged his shoulders again. "I was here most of the night."

Giorgio chuckled. "A young, single guy? You stayed home alone on a Saturday night."

A self-satisfied smile played across his lips. "I didn't say I was alone."

"Who was with you?" Rocky asked.

"Just a friend. We're thinking of going into business together. We were discussing some ideas." He turned to grab the mug of coffee.

His casual attitude intrigued Giorgio. He was lying, but he was completely comfortable with it.

"I'll need the name of your friend," Giorgio said.

And then it happened. The first tic of nervousness. Cook inhaled and covered a long pause by leaning into his mug of steaming coffee. His eyes fluttered a couple of times as he considered his answer.

"Um…sure," he said, swallowing. "Blaine Cross. He's my broker. He works at Empire Investments. He's out-of-town now, though."

Giorgio smiled. He was smart enough to give himself some space by saying his friend was out-of-town. "No problem," Giorgio replied. "You said you were here most of the evening. Where were you the rest of the evening?"

Again, he paused. Then, he got irritated. "Why all the questions? I told you, I didn't know the woman who died."

"Right, but you did know Dave Baker."

He froze.

A second later, he said, "Who the hell is Dave Baker?"

Now it was Giorgio's turn to appear casual. He began to wander around the room, fingering books, and collectibles. "He worked at Radio Shack. But I think you know that."

Giorgio paused at a small, framed photo. The picture was of three men with their arms around each other. The man in the middle was the elder Dr. Cook. And on each side were his sons. Giorgio got so lost in the photo that Rocky took up the slack.

"You deny knowing Baker?" Rocky asked.

"I don't know who the hell you're talking about."

Giorgio turned. "Young kid. Collected dogs for you."

Cook scoffed, "Do I look like I have a dog?" he asked, gesturing around the room.

"You own several as a matter of fact. Dozens I would assume. Fighting dogs."

Cook grew quiet. Then, he strode towards the door. "I think it's time you left."

Both brothers remained where they were.

Rocky turned to his brother. "Funny, how whenever we're interviewing someone and get a little too close to the crime they're committing, they suddenly want you to leave."

"I agree--funny," Giorgio said. He reached for a CD from among several that sat on one of the bookshelves.

"I said, leave!" Cook demanded, opening the front door.

Giorgio's hand paused mid-air. He stopped and turned.

"Whatever you say, Mr. Cook."

"Doctor Cook!" he responded.

Giorgio smiled. He and Rocky moved toward the door. As Giorgio passed Cook, he paused and looked up at him.

"I wouldn't leave town if I were you."

Cook slammed the door on Giorgio's heel.

A few feet from the door, Rocky said, "Well, he was lying through his ass."

"Yeah. And now we need to go see his brother."

"Why are we going to talk to his brother?"

Giorgio turned to Rocky. "Because it turns out Jackson Cook has a twin."

CHAPTER TWENTY-EIGHT

After some research, they found the name of Cook's twin; it was Jeffrey. He was a hedge fund manager who worked from home. But he wasn't in when they called, putting a halt for the day to that line of questioning.

"Okay," Giorgio said. "I need to stop by the evidence locker, and then I have to go home and check on Angie. I'll pick you up around six-thirty," he said to Rocky.

When he arrived home, Angie was less than enthusiastic that he would be gone for the evening, but he assured her there would be a squad car out front.

"Listen," he said. "Take a look at this." He pulled up the photo of the man named Mateo on his phone and showed it to her. "Recognize him?"

Her eyes flared, but she took the phone from him and studied the photo.

"I'm not sure. I'm trying to picture him in a hoodie. But, yes, I think that's the man."

"Okay, we're trying to find out who he is. As soon as we do, we'll pick him up. No one in their right mind would attempt another break-in with the police so visible outside, so you'll be safe. Besides," he said. "You have the best defender right there," he said, pointing to Shadow.

The dog seemed to know they were talking about her. She stood up and wagged her tail.

"I know. I'm keeping her next to me tonight. By the way, Grosvenor is going outside by himself now. He gets tired easily, but he's on the mend."

"Well, that's the best news I've heard all day."

"Joe," she said, placing her hand on his arm. "I've been thinking. About Shadow. Maybe we could keep her. She adores Grosvenor, and the kids have grown fond of her."

He watched his wife's expression. Although she had been initially terrified of this dog, she now seemed afraid to live without her.

He kissed her forehead. "We'll talk about it later."

÷

The line of partygoers looked like an assortment of characters from a Halloween party. It included Goths and vampires, with a smattering of folks who looked normal.

They were in South Pasadena at a warehouse surrounded by other warehouses and stacks of shipping containers. McCready had checked the area out in advance and found most of the buildings were in use by legitimate companies. This one, however, had been empty for over six months.

As they eyed the partygoers, Giorgio's gaze landed on a familiar face—Flame. She had chosen to come with her aunt. They were chatting with two other women dressed in long, black dresses with fitted bodices.

"I hope we made the right decision by splitting up," Giorgio said to Rocky. "I wonder why she brought her aunt."

"She wanted someone to talk to. Plus, I suppose two psychic minds are better than one," Rocky said, glancing around. "Once again, however, I think we're underdressed."

"Did you talk to her this afternoon and let her know what we want?"

"Yeah. Her goal will be to seek out whoever this Maestro guy is and see if she can get a read on him."

"Okay, then let's skip this part," Giorgio said.

He stepped out of line and marched past thirty or forty people, including Flame, without acknowledging any of them. Once he made it to the head of the line, he showed his badge to the hulk of a man at the door taking tickets.

"We're off duty and have been hired by the Society for extra security," he lied.

The man nodded and stepped aside, allowing the two officers inside.

"Guess the captain didn't want to pay the $250 to get us in," Rocky said with a laugh.

"I only asked for Flame and her aunt," Giorgio replied.

Inside, the warehouse was bare except for what the Society had brought in for the party. They stood on a concrete floor with a vaulted ceiling and windows high above them. A bar occupied each corner of the room, while the central area was filled with a throng of writhing bodies moving to the beat of a band playing on a stage at the far end.

"How many people do you think are in here?" Giorgio yelled over his shoulder. "Maybe 300?"

"At least," Rocky yelled back.

"That's good money." Giorgio began scanning the crowd. "Plus, they probably get a cut on the booze."

Giorgio glanced at the bars, where each bartender was dressed like a vampire: white face paint with blood stains at the mouth, white ruffled shirts, and black pants.

Along the left side of the room were four roped-off spaces made to look like rooms from a Victorian mansion. The closest one to them included a Queen Anne sofa and working Tiffany lamps. A sign read, "The Sitting Room."

"What the heck is this supposed to be?" Rocky said, nodding toward the area.

"Must be part of the murder mystery."

Small square tables and chairs lined one side of the room in rows of three. Most were occupied, but Giorgio found an empty one by the wall and turned the chair so that he faced the room.

"Do you think this is just a big party?" he asked his brother.

"Dunno," Rocky said from across the table. His eyes scanned the room. "The flyer said something about following clues."

They ordered club sodas from a young man and bided their time until they saw Flame and her aunt come through the front door. Their eyes met, and Giorgio acknowledged Flame with a slight nod. She and her aunt disappeared into the crowd.

"By the way," Giorgio began, "we were so busy today, I forgot to ask how it went with the brunette last night."

"Uneventful," Rocky replied. He gave Giorgio a rueful smile. "Just not my type."

Giorgio laughed. "I've never met a woman who wasn't your type."

"Not this time. She was a racist and belittled everyone she talked about."

"Too bad. And no new information?"

"Maybe. She mentioned Mimi. That blond. She said they went out for drinks one night, and Mimi got hammered. They got to talking about Dr. Cook, Sr. because Lynette, that's the brunette, thought he was hot. And Mimi warned her off."

"Why?"

"She told Lynette to think of Dr. Cook, Sr. as a mob boss. Someone you don't want to fool with."

"Hmmm," Giorgio murmured. "I wonder if that means Cook, Sr. is head of the drug operation."

"Dunno. We ought to see if we can get that video cleaned up so we could identify the man in the background."

"Agreed."

They watched the crowd until a high-pitched alarm began to pulse, and the band stopped. Instead of running for the exits, the party guests paused and looked at their phones.

"What's going on?" Giorgio asked.

"They got some kind of message," Rocky said, shifting his glance from one person to another.

As they watched, people broke away from one another and began roaming the room. They appeared to be looking for something or someone. One by one, people began to separate into groups of four. Eventually, the band started up again.

"They're dividing up," Giorgio said. "It looks like blondes have found other blondes, and brunettes have found other brunettes. Okay, now I feel like I'm in some sort of sci-fi movie. This is *really* weird."

As the band played in the background, about a third of the room continued to dance. A group of three young women and one man, all redheads, approached the table next to them and sat down. They huddled over their phones.

"Excuse me," Rocky said, leaning into one of the redheads. "We were invited by some friends and got in free, so we don't know what's going on. What are you all looking at?"

The thin woman with red curls piled atop her head gave him a broad smile. "It's an app. When the alarm goes off, we get instructions. We follow them, and by the end of the evening we'll have enough clues to try and solve the murder."

"What do you get if you win?"

"Twenty-five hundred dollars."

"Wow. That's good money. But how did you know to get the app?"

"When you paid for a ticket. The instructions were on the ticket."

"And when that alarm goes off…"

"It tells us we're getting instructions or a clue. This was our first one," she said. "We had to find three people with the same color hair. We'll work together now as a team."

"Thanks," Rocky said. "By the way, who got killed?"

"Here," she said. She scooched her chair toward Rocky and leaned in closer than necessary to show him her phone. "This is the body."

Rocky glanced down. "You mind?" He took the phone and showed it to his brother, who studied it.

A man dressed in fatigues, a heavy vest and combat boots lay sprawled on the floor. Next to him was a wooden spike tipped with blood.

"Thanks," Giorgio said,

Rocky handed the phone back. He rewarded the young woman with a brilliant smile before turning back to his brother. "Recognize him?" he asked Giorgio in a lowered voice.

"No. But he's either been drained of his blood or at least made to look like it. Notice the two holes in his neck?"

Rocky turned back to the redhead. "So, was this guy killed by a vampire?"

"Of course," she said, laughing. She gave Rocky a seductive smile. "This guy is Mr. X," she said, pointing at the picture. "See here? It says he was a vampire hunter."

"Why is it a murder mystery then, if you already know the vampire killed him?" Rocky said.

"But which vampire?" she said, leaning in to whisper into his ear. "We're all vampires tonight." She licked Rocky's neck, making him jump.

In the background, Giorgio just shook his head in bewilderment.

They were interrupted by the arrival of Flame and her aunt. The redhead looked at Flame and frowned.

"You look like the only two people with dark brown hair that haven't paired up yet," Flame said. "Mind if we sit down?"

"Please." Giorgio pulled out a chair for Flame's aunt.

When Flame sat next to Rocky, the redhead turned away and scooted her chair back to her own table. The four conspirators leaned in to gain some privacy.

"You don't have your phones out," Flame commented.

"We didn't pay to get in," Rocky replied.

"So, you didn't get the app."

"Right. But our friend explained how some of it works," Rocky said gesturing to the redhead sitting behind him.

Flame glanced over his shoulder at the woman and then put her phone on the table. "Okay. Here's the deal. We got divided up according to hair color. Red. Brunette. Blond. Black. And gray. Each team was given a code. For instance, redheads are Code G. Don't ask me why. We're Code Z. Anyway, they message each set of teams with instructions or clues, and we're supposed to respond."

"By teams?" Giorgio said.

"Yes."

"But I thought just one person could win," Rocky said.

Flame glanced at him her dark eyes gleaming in the low light. "Technically. But I suppose it organizes the room better if we're in groups of four."

Both her aunt's and her phone beeped.

"What is it?" Giorgio asked.

The women studied their phones.

"All redheads are supposed to go to the library and watch a video. Blonds are supposed to go to the office."

They all looked up and watched several groups of people move toward the first and fourth roped off areas.

"There are probably more redheads here than anything," Rocky commented. "They've all dyed their hair."

"Right," Flame's aunt said. "Very few blonds. And there are a few groups of people who have colored their hair blue, green or purple." She chuckled. "Not sure what their code is."

Flame's brown eyes were peering through the crowd and then turned to Giorgio. "We've walked past all four roped off areas. The library has a wingback leather chair and an ottoman. On the ottoman is an open book and a pair of spectacles. The book is Bram Stoker's *Dracula*. The office has a working safe in it."

"And the other two rooms?" Giorgio asked.

"A sitting room and a butler's pantry, complete with a stocked liquor cabinet."

"But the body was found in the library," Flame's aunt said. "You can tell, because there is a chalk outline on the floor."

Giorgio laughed. "I wonder if they know we don't do that."

The women's phones beeped again, and they both looked down.

"What is it?" Rocky asked.

"We're supposed to go to the sitting room," Flame responded. She stood. "Are you coming with us?"

"No," Giorgio said. "We're not here to play the game. But we should be moving around." He stood as well. "Let's split up again. Rocky and I can play ignorance when we talk to people. And you guys can work within the context of the game. We need to know who this Maestro guy is, but also anything you can find out about Dave Baker."

"Who's he?" Flame's aunt asked.

"He was a friend of our victim and a member of the vampire group she joined just before she died. But now, he's dead, too. Found in the victim's car down a ravine with his head bashed in."

"Sounds like someone is trying to frame him," Flame said.

"That's what I think." He reached into his pocket. "I picked this up from evidence today," he said pulling out Baker's metal necklace with the peace symbol pendant. He handed it to Flame. "It's been broken. I think it might have been pulled off him by his killer. Any chance you can read it?"

She wrapped her fingers around it, closed her eyes a moment and then opened them. "Yes," she said, gazing around the room. "And whoever killed him is here tonight."

CHAPTER TWENTY-NINE

Giorgio and Rocky went to the bar to get drinks, while Flame and her aunt left to find the sitting room to get their first clue.

For the next hour, Giorgio and Rocky mingled at the bar, talking mostly to women. They conferred with each other a couple of times but didn't learn much until a tall brunette finally told Giorgio the man known as The Maestro wouldn't appear until someone had won the game. Then, she said, he would present that person with a $2,500 check and an invitation to join the exclusive Essence of Life Society.

"Are you part of the club?" Giorgio asked her.

She was a good three inches taller than he was and gazed down on him with a look of disdain.

"It's not a 'club'. It's a society of people who believe in the concept of vampirism and the transfer of the body's reliance on the soul to other forms of energy."

"The what?" he asked with a more sarcastic edge than he had intended.

She frowned. "You're not a believer, I take it?"

"No, it's not that," he replied, trying to regain his footing. "I…I'm just new at this." He spun his glass on the bar a couple of times, thinking.

"You're a cop."

His head came up with a jerk. "What makes you say that?"

"It's practically written across your forehead."

He smiled feeling the color come to his cheeks. "My wife often says that. Sorry. I'm not here to arrest anyone. We're just here as added security," he said, gesturing to the room. "I am interested though."

Her eyes wandered over the crowd. "Well, most of these people aren't members of the society, nor are they true believers. They just come for the fun of it. Like a Halloween dress-up party."

Her voice had a sadness to it, which prompted Giorgio to ask, "I take it you are a believer."

She shifted her deep brown, heavily made-up eyes to him. Unlike many of the women in the crowd, she seemed under-dressed. She wore slim black pants with black high heels, a long-sleeved, black V-neck sweater and a bejeweled black choker accented with a dangling, ruby red tear drop.

"I believe in all sorts of other-worldly things. Who's to say that vampires or werewolves or any other aberration don't exist?"

A short chill rippled through Giorgio. "Like ghosts?"

"Yes, like ghosts. Or UFOs or Bigfoot. I believe in the possibility," she stressed. "Because no one's ever proved they *don't* exist. So, what is it that you're hoping to learn here?"

Giorgio caught Rocky's eye. He was talking to a petite blond right behind the brunette. Rocky took the hint and excused himself to join Giorgio.

"This is my brother, Rocky."

The brunette's restrained countenance relaxed. Rocky had that effect on women. She reached out a graceful hand, which Rocky clasped. She was almost as tall as he was.

"Rocky," she repeated his name. "Charmed," she murmured. "I'm Renalda. Two Rs. There's good chemistry in that."

Rocky flashed her a winning smile. "I'm sure there is." He glanced around the room. "You know, I find this whole thing fascinating. One thing's for sure, this Essence Society attracts the best-looking women."

Renalda's eyes twinkled. Inwardly, Giorgio groaned.

"Renalda was just going to explain more about the society. I thought you'd like to hear it," Giorgio said.

"I've learned a little," Rocky said. "Doesn't membership in the society cost like a thousand dollars?"

"Yes. Normally. But if you win the game tonight then the fee is waived."

"And you think most of the people here would like to join," he said.

A small smile flickered across her lips. "You haven't met The Maestro. He can be quite compelling."

"Where does the group...sorry, society meet?" Giorgio asked.

A cloud veiled her face. "We don't give out details to humans."

"Humans?" Giorgio said with a short chuckle.

"People who don't belong. You must be initiated first."

"Does the initiation include drinking someone's blood?" Rocky asked, leaning into her.

She turned to him, a hungry look in her eyes. "Let's put it this way…if you were to join," she said, reaching up and cupping her long fingers under his chin, "I'd fight to the death to be your initiator." She brushed her lips against his and then disappeared into the crowd.

"Shit," Giorgio exclaimed, watching her tall figure melt into a group that crowded the bar. He glanced back at his brother. "How do you do that? Did it feel different?"

"What?" Rocky asked, touching his lips with the tips of his fingers.

"The kiss. Was it electrifying? I mean, if she's a vampire, it should have felt…different."

"Jesus, you're an idiot. She's just an attractive woman."

"Who's obviously attracted to *you*."

"Can I help it?" Rocky asked. "I'm like a magnet."

"Now, who's the idiot?"

Giorgio's phone pinged. It was a text from Flame.

"Flame wants us. They're over at the library."

The brothers pushed their way through the mingling crowd to the other side of the cavernous space. They met Flame and her aunt at the vignette labelled The Library.

"What is it?" Giorgio asked Flame.

She was standing next to a red rope that divided the library setting from the rest of the room. Flame pointed to a fireplace that stood close to them. Inside were fake logs that burned with a rotating red light made to look like flames. A group of black-and-white vintage photos stretched across the mantle, with a heavy, brass candlestick anchoring each end.

She pointed to the candlestick closest to them. "See the blood on the bottom of that candlestick?"

Giorgio zeroed in on a dark smear across the candlestick's base.

"Yes," he said. "There also seems to be drops of blood on the mantle itself. So, what's wrong? Isn't that part of the game?"

"That's real blood," she replied.

"Well, they deal in real blood," he said. "They could have gotten it anywhere."

"No," Cora spoke up. "You showed us his picture. That blood belongs to Dave Baker."

"What?" Giorgio leaned over the rope to study the candlestick. "How do you know that? I thought you couldn't get a good connection to Baker."

"You forget. We touched that necklace you said he wore around his neck. It had his blood on it, and we've touched this blood," Flame said.

"You touched it?" Rocky asked.

"Cora did."

Cora shrugged. "I just wanted to know if it was real."

Giorgio looked at her with appreciation. "And you're sure it's Baker's blood?"

"I was immediately connected to the man who owned the necklace. So, I presume it's his blood."

Giorgio sighed. "He had a big gash in the back of his head." He glanced back at the candlestick. "It could have been made by the base of a candlestick."

"It's evidence. But how do we get it?" Rocky asked. "At least without giving away why we want it?"

"Leave that up to me," Cora said, patting the large satchel she carried over her arm.

"You're going to steal it?" Rocky asked.

"It's not valuable," she quipped. "At least not in monetary terms."

Rocky looked unconvinced. "It could be dangerous though, if it's the murder weapon."

"They can't be too worried about it," Flame quipped. "After all, they've left it in plain sight."

"A little like they're thumbing their nose at the idea of killing someone," Giorgio added. "But we need to find a way to maintain the chain of custody."

"The what?" Cora asked.

"It won't be accepted in court if you just steal it. You aren't law enforcement. And putting it in your bag could contaminate the blood."

Cora frowned. "Then what do we do?"

"Just stay here and guard it. I'll be back in a minute."

He left them and went to the bar near the front door. Leaning over to talk to the bartender, he said, "Say, listen, do you have a clean plastic bag? Someone is feeling sick."

The young man grimaced. "Sure. Hold on."

He bent down behind the bar and came back with a folded, black plastic bag. "Here you go."

"Thanks."

Giorgio returned to the others. "Okay, do you have a tissue or something?"

"Um, yeah," she replied. She reached into her big bag, rummaged around, and came out with an old-fashioned handkerchief. "Will this do?"

"Yeah. Pick it up with that. You don't want your fingerprints on it. And then drop it into this." He handed her the black trash bag. "Got it?"

"Yes. I can do that." She took the bag, folded it even smaller and dropped it into her purse.

"By the way, how close are people to solving the game?" Rocky asked.

"We've received all the clues," Flame said. "And I've already submitted my answer."

He smiled at her. "Boy, remind me never to keep a secret from you."

"You couldn't if you tried," she said with a twinkle in her eye.

He leaned into her shoulder and murmured, "Care to give it a try?"

"Anytime," she said with a grin.

Giorgio was amused at the obvious flirting, but not surprised. He had always suspected Rocky was attracted to the young psychic. But for the first time, watching Flame's reaction, he thought that perhaps she returned the feelings.

"How did you submit your answer?" Giorgio asked.

"Online," Cora replied. "We both came up with the same answer, but Flame submitted hers first."

"What difference does that make?" Rocky asked.

"The first correct answer wins," Cora said.

An unwanted chill rippled through Giorgio. He had no doubt that Flame's answer would be correct. But would she be the first correct answer submitted?

He hoped not.

A familiar face in the crowd caught his eye, and he turned to focus on it. He nudged his brother.

"That's Cordova," he said, nodding to his right.

Moving through the crowd was the bald, heavy-set man. He seemed to be headed toward the bar at the far corner.

"I wonder if Cook is here."

Giorgio's gaze followed Cordova as he was swallowed up by the crowd. He turned back to Cora. "You said earlier that death was present here. If you touched the man who killed Baker, would you know it?"

"Of course."

He reached out and grabbed her hand. "Come with me. You stay with Flame," he said to his brother.

He guided Flame's aunt through the crowd, following in the same direction he had seen Cordova go. It took a minute or two to make it to the other side of the room, where he stopped.

"Who are we looking for?" she asked.

"A man in a blue sports coat. He's a big, bald guy," he replied.

They searched the faces nearest them. Giorgio said, "There he is."

Cordova was standing at the front corner of the room at the bar. He held a glass in his hand and seemed to be studying the stage.

"Think you can find a way to touch him without bringing attention to yourself?"

"Well, I'll probably bring attention to myself, but it won't matter. I'll be fine."

She weaved her way to where Cordova stood. The little woman moved up to the bar right next to him and ordered a drink. Cordova paid no attention to her. He seemed to be waiting for something to happen on stage.

The bartender handed her the drink, which she paid for. Then, she spun around and bumped into Cordova, spilling his drink.

He came to attention, arching away from her, his hands in the air. With lightning speed, she grabbed one of his hands, expressing what Giorgio assumed were her apologies.

The entire exchange was over in a moment. Cordova was irritated but seemed to dismiss the incident. He pulled away from her, put his empty glass on the bar and grabbed a napkin to dry his hand.

Cora smiled up at Cordova, paid for his second drink and found her way back to Giorgio.

"Nice job," he said with appreciation.

She gave him a cat with a canary smile. "Easy-peasy. And, before you ask—yes, he's your killer."

CHAPTER THIRTY

The sound of a gong reverberated through the room, and everyone lapsed into silence. While Cora and Giorgio returned to where Rocky stood, the band grew silent. Like lemmings, one by one, everyone in the crowd turned towards the stage.

Heavy red drapes were drawn across the back of the room. The band was positioned on one end of the stage, while a large ornate golden cymbal hung from a frame at the other. Standing next to the gong was a tall African American man with a shaved head. He was dressed in a blue, Victorian waistcoat, complete with a ruffled collar and black cravat. A single gold hoop earring hung from his left ear.

"Jeez, I wonder if he has a cheesy accent, too," Rocky quipped.

The big man waited for the murmurs to subside. As complete silence overtook the room, he lifted a bulky wooden mallet and hit the gong again.

"Hear ye, hear ye," he called out. "Tonight, you have come to delve into the realm of mystic fantasies. As mortals, you crave the light, while vampires crave the darkness. There is a bridge, however, between the darkness and the light. And, as mortal hybrids, members of the Essence of Life Society cross that bridge to experience the pleasure and pain of virtual vampirism as they continue to walk among humans. Tonight, one of you shall win the exalted opportunity to join this elite group."

Murmurs of excitement rolled through the crowd, as a rising level of anticipation permeated the room. People began to close ranks, pushing toward the stage. Flame stepped away and was swallowed up by the crowd in front of them.

"Where'd she go?" Giorgio asked in alarm.

"Don't worry about her," Flame's aunt said. "She knows what she's doing."

"I see her," Rocky said, scanning the crowd. "She's moving toward the stage."

The gong sounded again. People stopped moving and strained to see the stage.

"Please bow your heads," the man said, "in reverence for…The Maestro."

Giorgio stared in disbelief as most people in the room bowed their heads. The overhead lights dimmed, and a spotlight lit up center stage. A moment later, the curtains parted and a tall man with a bone-white hair pulled back into a ponytail stepped into the light. He was dressed in a black tight-waisted coat, white shirt, and crimson cravat, with black pants tucked into black leather riding boots. He brandished a shiny black cane with a brass skull's head.

It was the man Giorgio had seen at the bar the night he and Rocky had gone to the Cave to talk with the tattoo artist. The Maestro stared at the crowd through black eyes that appeared to be either dilated from drugs or enlarged through some sort of contact lenses. Either way, his pallid complexion was achieved through stage makeup, giving him the appearance of a hollow other-worldly being. The Maestro lifted a hand to signal quiet; the sharpened tips of his long, red fingernails further added to the image of a fantastical predator.

"My friends," he said in a deep baritone voice. "I welcome you."

Giorgio noticed speakers set into the corners above the stage and assumed The Maestro was wearing a body mic to contextualize his voice, making him sound even more ethereal than he looked. The effect on the audience, especially the women, was mesmerizing.

"He's quite the character," Giorgio mumbled to Rocky.

Rocky didn't respond. He stared at the man with an intensity that surprised Giorgio.

"We hope you've enjoyed the *Essence of Murder* tonight, staged just for you," The Maestro said.

Applause erupted, along with some shouts of acclaim.

The Maestro smiled as if he had just swallowed a glass of the most expensive wine. "I'm so pleased," he said. "Our small group worked very hard to make this a night of extreme anticipation and pleasure."

"I'd give up my soul for a night of extreme pleasure with him," an attractive woman next to Giorgio said. She and her friend giggled as they fanned their faces in fake heat flashes.

"Now, for the announcement you've all been waiting for," he continued. "The winner of tonight's murder mystery and the opportunity to join the Essence of Life Society."

Giorgio straightened up. "Can you see Flame?" he asked Rocky.

"I think she's close to the stage."

"She's over by the bar," Cora said. "Stop worrying. She's prepared."

"Prepared for what?" Giorgio asked with alarm.

Another gong stopped all conversation. The room fell silent again, and The Maestro tapped the stage with his cane to get everyone's attention.

"First, we shall reveal the murderer of Mr. X." He paused again, allowing the anticipation to rise. "As you know, Mr. X was a lethal vampire hunter who killed many of our brethren. So, I'm pleased to announce that it was none other than Juniper Ravenstalk, vampire of the Southern District, who successfully brought our nemesis down."

A few cheers went up, while others looked downcast and murmured groans because they had guessed incorrectly.

"So, in this group, murder is a good thing," Rocky mumbled.

"At least when they've killed a vampire hunter," Giorgio agreed.

"I'm pleased and a little surprised to announce our winner tonight," The Maestro went on. "Surprised because this individual submitted her answer a full half hour before anyone else."

Murmurs rolled through the room again. Giorgio glanced at Cora and caught her smiling. As if she sensed Giorgio's gaze upon her, she turned to him.

"You'll have to admit, she's talented. Much more so than me."

"Would Rose Marie Glendive please come to the stage."

"It's not her," Giorgio said with a sigh of relief.

"She didn't win?" Rocky asked in surprise.

But it was Flame who stepped onto the stage.

"What?" Giorgio blurted, catching glimpses of her as she crossed the stage.

Cora chuckled. "You didn't think her mother named her Flame, did you? Her Christian name is Rose Marie."

"Shit!" Giorgio wasn't happy, and a heavy feeling settled in the pit of his stomach as he watched the attractive petite woman glide toward The Maestro. The room burst into another round of applause, and several people let out whoops of support.

The Maestro raised a hand again to ask for silence. When Flame reached his side, he turned to her.

"Congratulations, Rose Marie. That's a beautiful name." From inside his coat, he pulled out two gold envelopes. "I have here a check for $2,500 with your name on it."

He reached out to hand her the first envelope. As she took it from him, she wrapped her hand around his outstretched fingers. For a moment, he seemed to go still, even teetering slightly. He pulled away and used his cane to steady himself. Although his face was covered in white makeup, Giorgio could have sworn he blanched.

"What will you do with all that money?" he asked, his voice faltering.

She lifted her chin and looked into his eyes. "I plan to give it to a dog rescue group."

Flame didn't say or do anything without a reason; Giorgio knew her answer was calculated. He was sure that it was also meant to provoke a response. And it did.

The slick grin on The Maestro's face disappeared, and he seemed to suck in a small breath. The two remained locked in eye contact for a moment, and then he held out the second envelope, this time keeping his fingers away from her touch.

"And here's your invitation to join our little group," he said more quietly, giving her a slight bow.

Flame smiled and took the envelope.

"I'd be proud to join the society," she crooned. "I've heard so much about it…and you."

"Let's hear it for the beautiful Rose Marie," he said, turning to the crowd.

The room erupted in a final round of applause as The Maestro spun on his heel and retreated through the curtains.

Flame watched him go, the corners of her mouth turned up in a half smile.

CHAPTER THIRTY-ONE

After the event, the four sleuths met at the closest coffee shop to share information. Once they'd settled into a booth, Rocky ordered French fries and a Coke. Giorgio asked for a cup of coffee.

When the waitress left to place their orders, Giorgio turned to Flame, who had opened one of the envelopes and was perusing a sheet of gold-leafed paper.

"What does it say?"

She finished reading and then handed it to him. "It's a rather antiquated way of inviting me to join the Society. Once I do, I pledge fealty and complete confidentiality to The Maestro and the group."

Giorgio scanned the paper. "You have to go through a ritual." He gave her a questioning look.

"Right," she said, as the waitress slid a cup of tea in front of her.

"Are you going to do it?" Rocky asked with a hint of concern.

He was tapping his fingers on the table. She watched him a moment and then sighed.

"Isn't that what you want? Someone to get inside the group and find out if they murdered the woman you found in the canyon?"

Rocky stopped tapping. "Not if it puts you in danger."

Her gaze softened. "I'll be fine."

"What happened on stage tonight?" Giorgio asked. "When you touched him."

She shifted her eyes to her aunt, who dropped her chin and focused on her own beverage.

"What's going on?" Giorgio asked with a sharp edge to his voice. He looked back and forth between the two women. "You know something."

Flame sighed. "I purposely grabbed his hand. I needed to read him if I could. I thought that's what you wanted."

"And?" Giorgio asked.

She let the moment draw out as she took a sip of tea. "It wasn't what I thought," she said. "I figured if he was this deep, dark soul who recruited young women for the wrong reasons and then killed them, I'd find blackness there."

"But you didn't?" Rocky said.

"No. He is remarkably free of any darkness."

"But he responded to you," her aunt prodded her.

"Yes. I think I shocked him. Maybe, literally."

"What does that mean?" Rocky asked.

Cora turned to him. "When we attempt to read someone by physical contact, there is a transfer of energy. Some people feel it as a small electrical charge. Did you notice how he pulled away when she touched him?"

"Yeah," Giorgio said. "He looked…"

"Surprised," Rocky said, finishing his sentence.

"He felt it, and it scared him. That's why he left immediately," Cora said.

"So, now what?" Rocky asked.

The waitress arrived with Rocky's fries and the men's drinks. Giorgio glanced back at the letter.

"It says here that Flame has to attend an Essence Society council meeting to take the oath and then sign it in blood. Then, they expect her to participate in the blood ritual to 'confirm the bonds of community,' whatever that means." Giorgio looked at Flame. "Are you sure you want to do this? We can find other ways to get information."

"Where is this ritual supposed to take place?" Rocky asked.

"Someplace they call the sacred space," Giorgio said glancing at the letter.

"You think that's the glen up in the canyon?"

Giorgio shrugged. "I don't know." He looked over at Flame again. "So?"

"I'm not afraid. I don't believe in vampires. This is all a big game to these people."

"But what if they drug you?" Cora asked.

It was natural for her aunt to worry, and frankly, Giorgio was pleased that she might share his concern.

"People have already died, and it's a real possibility they use drugs in the ceremony. Remember what we found in Lindsey Nagel's system," he said.

"Look," Flame began. "I'm supposed to sign something at the council meeting first. That ought to tell me whether I should go through with the ritual."

"When's the council meeting?" Cora asked.

"Monday night," she replied.

Rocky had just taken a sip of Coke. He put it down. "Where?"

"It doesn't say," Giorgio said, scanning the letter again. "It says she will be picked up at eleven o'clock."

"At her house?" Rocky's alarm was palpable.

"No." Giorgio looked over at his brother. "At the corner of 3rd and Kohl in Arcadia."

The group went silent as the two brothers stared at each other.

"Isn't that where that auto parts store is?" Rocky asked.

"Yeah," Giorgio said. He swiveled his head to stare at Flame. "That's why you told him you were going to give the $2,500 to a dog rescue. Because you suspect he's connected to the dogfighting."

She smiled coyly. "You know me so well."

"Now you need to catch me up to speed," Cora said.

"The dogs," Flame replied. "Didn't you see it? Dave Baker was involved with picking up and delivering dogs to someone. I figured it had something to do with the society or The Maestro. I think his reaction said it all."

"Don't forget this," Cora said. She reached into her big satchel and pulled out the black trash bag that held the blood-stained candlestick. "The young man who died from this deserves justice, too."

Giorgio took the bag and then looked at his brother. "Tomorrow we visit Jeffrey Cook. Then, perhaps Cook, Sr. Seems the entire family is wrapped up in this."

"What do you mean?" Rocky asked.

"Because, while Jackson Cook oversees the dogfighting ring, Lindsey Nagel was killed as part of the Essence Society. So, who is this Maestro guy and how does he connect the two groups?"

"You know, don't you?" Rocky asked him.

"Let's say I have a hunch."

CHAPTER THIRTY-TWO

Jeffrey Cook lived in a large Craftsman-style home near the Rose Bowl in Pasadena. As they pulled into the long driveway the next day, Giorgio scanned the exterior, taking in the home's wide, overhanging eaves, low-pitched covered front porch, river rock chimney, and thick wooden pillars framing the entry steps.

"The Cook boys have done well for themselves," he commented.

"Yeah," Rocky agreed, climbing out of the sedan.

Giorgio stepped out of the car and slammed the door. A moment later, he was knocking on a beautifully carved, oak door. Several seconds went by before an image flitted past the beveled side window as someone approached the door. When the door opened, a tall, muscular black man with a shaved head greeted them.

"You were at the event Saturday night," Giorgio said without introduction.

The man's espresso eyes flared, and then a smile etched its way across his full lips.

"And you're the two police officers who faked their way in as hired security," he said with a deep baritone voice.

Giorgio smiled. "Your people are good. Why did you allow us to stay?"

He shrugged his muscled shoulders and flinched his head to one side. "We weren't doing anything illegal."

Giorgio pulled his coat aside to show his badge. "I'm Detective Giorgio Salvatori with the Sierra Madre police. This is Rocky Salvatori, also a detective," he said. "We'd like to speak to Mr. Cook if we could."

"May I tell him what this is about?"

"A murder investigation."

Giorgio was done playing games with the Cooks. He needed answers.

"Please come in. I'll see if Jeffrey is available."

The man opened the door wide and then disappeared down a long hallway into the back of the house, leaving Rocky to close the door behind them.

If Giorgio was impressed with the home from the street view, the inside made him salivate. Like most Craftsman bungalows, wood was everywhere; hardwood floors, open-beamed ceiling, paneled walls, and built-in shelving and window seats set off by beveled glass cupboards. His own Spanish-style home had been built in the 1930s and had much of the original wood, plaster, and hardware. But this home had been completely restored, and the wood gleamed.

Voices from the back of the house brought him to attention. A moment later, Jeffrey Cook appeared through a doorway at the end of the hall.

He looked almost identical to his brother: tall, broad-shouldered, with thick dark hair. But there was something different about him— something vulnerable. His muscles weren't hardened like Jackson's, and those broad shoulders were slightly stooped.

He also walked with a cane. But it wasn't part of any mythical image; he used the cane because he needed it.

"I'm Jeffrey Cook," he said.

"We're Detectives Giorgio and Rocky Salvatori. We need to talk to you about Lindsey Nagel."

"How can I help you?"

The piercing blue eyes that Jackson Cook used to intimidate his adversaries were softer in his twin. Not only were they rimmed by pale shadows, this young man had a placid expression that made him approachable.

"We're investigating her death," Giorgio said. "We have a few questions."

A cloud passed over Cook's face, but he gestured to his left. "Please, come in. Samuel is getting us something to drink."

They preceded him into the living room, where a huge antique rug covered the center of the hardwood floor in front of a river rock fireplace that rose to the ceiling. An enormous porch window flooded the room with morning light, bathing the mixture of antique and modern furniture in a soft glow.

The brothers sat at opposite ends of a rich gray sofa in front of the window, while Cook took an upholstered armchair facing them.

As Giorgio watched Cook lower himself into the chair, he said, "The cane isn't just a prop then?"

Once he was settled Cook smiled, holding the cane out to one side. "No. Not anymore. I have MS. I was diagnosed two years ago, and it's beginning to take its toll."

"I'm sorry," Giorgio said.

"No need to be. I've accepted it. I'm young, but I've had a good life. *Have* a good life," he said with emphasis.

Giorgio's mind was whirring. *How would someone so debilitated hike into the glen to conduct the rituals?*

"I know about Lindsey Nagel," Cook continued. "But only what I read in the paper. I understand her body was found up in Bailey Canyon."

They were interrupted when Samuel appeared with a tray of iced tea. "I considered alcohol," he said, placing the tray on a teak coffee table in front of the officers. "But I know you're on duty."

He straightened up and then disappeared again.

"So, he works for you?"

"Yes. I manage a hedge fund. He has assisted me with that for many years, and now that I…well, my health is failing, he's agreed to help me out here at home. I realize that at some point I'll have to hire a caretaker, but for now, Samuel has been a lifesaver."

"And he participates in the Essence of Life Society," Rocky said.

Cook's gaze shifted to Rocky. "Yes. That's how I met him. He was one of our earliest acolytes."

"So, *you're* The Maestro?" Rocky asked.

"That is my role," he said.

"What about Lindsey Nagel? How did she get involved?" Giorgio asked.

Cook took a deep breath and lowered his eyes. "She was referred by one of our members. She came to a council meeting and was accepted into the society."

"Who referred her?" Giorgio asked.

"I believe it was Mimi Watkins."

"And she agreed to the ritual," Rocky said, a touch of disgust in his voice.

Cook looked up. "Yes. She was to be initiated last weekend. But I am sure you know that, or you wouldn't be here."

"We need the details," Giorgio demanded. "And not what you read in the paper."

Cook sighed. "I only know what I was told."

"I don't understand." Giorgio said.

"I wasn't there that night."

Giorgio's heart skipped a beat and his eyebrows arched. "Your brother took your place."

A small smile played at the corner of Cook's mouth. "Yes. He used to do it only occasionally, but lately he's had to do it more often." He glanced down at his legs. "I just can't...can't..."

"Navigate the hillsides," Rocky said, finishing the sentence.

"We've talked about changing locations, especially after Ms. Nagel's death. That was an unfortunate accident."

"Accident?" Giorgio asked. "How do you know that?"

Cook's brows clenched. "Of course, it was an accident. Either that or she died of natural causes."

"Let me settle that for you," Giorgio said. "It was neither. It was murder."

The air seemed to go still in the room as the expression on Cook's face froze. Giorgio remained silent, allowing the man to process the information.

"Murder?" he said, shaking his head. "No. You're wrong. I was told she just stopped breathing."

"Who told you that?"

He shifted his weight. "My brother."

"So, he told you she died," Rocky interjected, his voice inflected with anger. "And then someone called 911."

Cook flinched and dropped his chin. "No. I was told they buried her."

"Tell us exactly what you were told," Giorgio said.

He inhaled, held his breath a moment and then exhaled. "Jackson said she was on the altar, ready to be pierced. And then she just stopped breathing. No one knew what to do. But Jackson was afraid of the publicity and so decided to bury her."

"Afraid of the publicity?" Giorgio asked.

There was another pause before he said, "He was afraid for the entire family, really. The reason he would protect my father is obvious. And it's obvious why he would protect himself. Doctors rely on their good reputations. But as a hedge fund manager, I also depend solely on my reputation. My clients are in the million-dollar plus category. They would leave me in droves if they found out their money manager dabbled in vampirism."

"Except now you're on the hook for obstruction of justice," Rocky said.

Cook shifted his gaze to Rocky. "I know. I said as much to Jackson. He seemed to think it wasn't that much of a threat. But I also thought about Lindsey's family and the fact that they would never know what happened to her. Unfortunately, Jackson can be quite convincing and was sure no one in the group would say anything." He dropped his chin again. "I'm so sorry. She was a nice young woman."

"And you did nothing?" Rocky said with disgust.

Cook sighed. "In my current state, I…well, I just didn't have the strength to fight Jackson on it."

"What else were you told about Ms. Nagel's death?" Giorgio asked.

Cook leaned forward and grabbed a glass of iced tea. "Please," he said, nodding toward the other two glasses. "It's Samuel's special blend of sweet tea."

Both Rocky and Giorgio ignored the refreshments.

"Mr. Cook, we need to know exactly what happened in the glen," Giorgio pressed.

Cook sipped his tea and then sat back. "I just know that she was prepared for the initiation at the Fortress, as always. Then transported by two Centurions and my brother to the glen."

"Where is this fortress?" Rocky asked.

Cook glanced at Rocky and seemed to weigh whether to answer the question or not. Finally, he said, "My father owns some property in the foothills. It has an old city maintenance building on it. That's what we use."

"Was Nagel drugged that night?" Giorgio asked.

"No. We don't use drugs. We encourage initiates to be fully *present* at the initiation…to experience their own sense of euphoria."

"Nagel was drugged," Giorgio stated flatly. "With GHB."

"No. That can't be. No one in the Society would have given her something like that. She must have taken it herself."

"No, because she'd already taken Xanax. She was what they call polyphobic. Afraid of everything. Especially sharp objects."

"But the essence device…"

"The what?" Rocky asked.

Cook seemed confused for a moment and then set his tea down and stood unsteadily. He went to a bookcase that flanked the stone fireplace and pulled a wooden box off the shelf and brought it to the coffee table. The box was carved with a large triangle inset with a circle that looked like an eye.

"Here," he said, flipping open the lid. "This is the essence device. It's what we use to draw blood during the initiation ritual."

Nestled inside the box, in a green velvet cushion, was a metal device shaped something like a fortune cookie. It had a half-circle trough where a person would place his teeth. On the opposite side, where your incisor teeth would be, were two sharp, steel prongs.

Giorgio reached in and lifted it up. He turned it over and found a tiny hole at the end of each prong.

"So," Giorgio began, turning it over again, "you can suck blood through this?"

Cook smiled. "Sounds disgusting to you, doesn't it?"

Giorgio handed it to Rocky, who studied it briefly.

"But not to you, I take it?" he asked.

"I can't begin to explain the concept of vampirism to a non-believer."

Rocky dropped the device back into the box. "This thing is now part of a murder investigation," he said.

"I understand," Cook said. "But that's not the one that was used on Ms. Nagel. My brother would have that one."

"We'll be visiting him again, then. Does Samuel go to the initiations?" Giorgio asked.

"Yes."

"Call him in here, please."

"He won't know any more about that night than I do. He was here with me."

"I'd still like to talk with him," Giorgio said.

"Of course." Cook reached into the pocket of his vest and removed a small, silver bell. He rang it. A moment later, Samuel appeared.

"What is it?" the big man asked.

Giorgio stood up. "Where were you last Saturday night?"

Samuel glanced at his employer as if looking for permission to speak. Cook gave him an affirmative nod.

"Uh…we were here. Jeffrey wasn't feeling well."

"You didn't go to the glen?"

"No."

"As I said, detectives, Jackson conducted the ceremony that night," Cook said.

"But someone dug her up," Giorgio said, staring at Samuel. "Someone strong enough to carry her down the trail and leave her at the creek."

The big man straightened up, stiffening his muscles. "It wasn't me. We…uh…talked about going in to retrieve her the next day…but with Jeffrey's disability we couldn't."

"You didn't go alone?"

"No. Well, not before she was discovered. We decided that I *should* go in alone. So, I hiked in on Sunday night, but the grave was empty. And I didn't know where she had been taken."

"So, you just kept quiet about it?" Rocky said, also standing.

Cook lifted himself out of his chair again and leaned on his cane. "Yes. We kept quiet. We honestly didn't know what was going on. I contacted my brother when Samuel found the grave empty, but he knew nothing about it, either. I assure you, none of us wished Ms. Nagel any harm."

"How well do you know Dave Baker?" Giorgio asked him.

"Dave?" Cook asked. "He's been part of the group for some time. Why?"

"When was the last time you saw him?"

Cook paused. "Um…I'm not sure. Why?"

"Were you at The Cave a few nights ago?"

"No," he replied, shaking his head. "My brother often goes there, however."

A lightbulb went off in Giorgio's head. "So, he dresses up as The Maestro at other times. Not just for Society business."

"Um…yes. I believe he does. He doesn't ask my permission, though. Why are you asking about Dave Baker?"

"He was found dead this weekend. The back of his head bashed in. Then he was put into Ms. Nagel's car before it was pushed into a deep canyon."

"What?" Cook teetered and then fell back into his chair. "But that's awful. Why would anyone do that?"

"What do you know about Baker?"

Cook shook his head. "Not much. Other than he liked to write. He was kind of shy. Why would someone kill him?"

Giorgio wondered how much he should tell about Baker and the little he knew about Jackson Cook and the dogfighting.

"Did you ever see other groups up in the glen or near the glen when you were there?"

"I'm not sure what you mean," Cook said.

"We found what was left of a dogfighting ring up there. It looked like it had been shut down a month or so before we found it."

Both Samuel and Cook tensed.

"We had nothing to do with that," Cook said.

"But you knew it was there."

Cook took a deep breath. "I was aware of it. We'd hear them occasionally."

"But you don't know who ran it?"

When Cook didn't reply, Giorgio continued. "Mr. Cook, you're already on the hook for obstruction of justice. I don't think you want to add to that."

Cook gave a deep sigh. He dropped his head. "My brother. I urged him to stop. Or at least to move it. I was afraid for him, and I was afraid it would bring harm to the Society. Anyway, he finally agreed to move it about two months ago. But I don't know where."

"We believe Baker was involved somehow," Giorgio said. "We saw him passing off a dog to a large, bald man who drives a red Camaro."

"Arthur?" Cook said, glancing up.

"Who is Arthur?" Rocky asked.

"Arthur Cordova. He's my brother's body man."

"He needs a body man?" Rocky asked.

"I call him that," Cook said. "He follows Jackson around. Always by his side. I've never liked him. But Jackson trusts him implicitly."

Giorgio's phone rang. He pulled it from his pocket and noted that the call was from McCready. "Excuse me." He stepped into the entryway to answer it.

"We got the DNA back on that tuft of hair you guys found stuck in a tree," McCready said. "It belongs to Craig Velchy, Nagel's ex-husband."

"Is it an exact match?" Giorgio asked McCready.

"As close as you can get. His DNA is in the system because of a DUI last year."

"Okay, where's Swan? Did he go interview him?"

"Velchy wasn't there."

"Then, let's get a search warrant for his place. If he didn't kill her, he must have been the one who carried her out."

"But, Joe, we also found Phillips and the girlfriend. We brought them in."

"Excellent. Grab Swan and interview them. As soon as we have the search warrant, we'll go see Velchy again."

Giorgio hung up and returned to the living room. Giorgio decided not to say anything about the drug business, knowing that he'd blow the FBI's investigation.

"Mr. Cook, you realize that dogfighting is a felony. Your brother is looking at a big fine and up to three years in jail."

"I...I..." he stuttered, stopping. He shook his head again, as if trying to dislodge cobwebs in his brain. "Jackson isn't a bad person. He is a good doctor and a good partner for my father. He got involved in dogfighting as a spectator many years ago and then kind of inherited it from one of the guys he befriended. He's just a bit of an adrenalin junkie."

"We think he's more than that," Giorgio said. "It was you at the Essence of Murder last night. Is that right? Not your brother." Giorgio asked.

"Yes," Cook said, shaken. "The event was my idea. We spent months putting it together."

"When the young woman who won the game mentioned she would give her money to a dog rescue group, you tried to pull away. Why?"

He dropped his head. "Because I knew about the dogfighting ring. I knew that Jackson sometimes gets dogs off Craigslist and from rescue groups by pretending to adopt them."

"One last question," Giorgio said. "How much do you know about what your brother and father are doing at the clinic?"

This time, Cook's head snapped up, and his eyes grew wide. "What?"

"We believe Lindsey Nagel discovered something illegal at the clinic that got her killed."

"No, that can't be true. My father is an exceptionally good surgeon. He would never jeopardize his practice."

Giorgio paused a moment, staring at him, trying to judge his veracity. Finally, he said, "Okay, we're done here. But let me remind you that this is a murder investigation. Neither one of you is to say anything to your brother or your father about what we've discussed, or I will throw the book at you. And with your disability, you could die in jail."

Jeffrey Cook nodded without saying anything, and the two officers left.

CHAPTER THIRTY-THREE

They picked up Swan, and then the three men headed for Craig Velchy's apartment. In the car, Giorgio's phone pinged. It was McCready.

"I checked a forestry map and that road you told me about is a forest service road. It's supposed to be blocked off by a metal gate, but I had Mulhaney drive up there. There's a chain on it, but the lock has been broken, so anyone could drive through it."

"Thanks. That's what I figured. I doubt it's used very much."

"Well, Mulhaney said the lock had been put back on so that from a distance, it looked like it was locked."

"Got it. We're on our way to Velchy's."

Ten minutes later they were at his front door facing Velchy dressed in sweatpants and a sloppy t-shirt.

"What d'you want?" he said in a gruff voice. "I told you everything I know."

Giorgio pulled out the search warrant. "We have a warrant to search your apartment. Step aside."

Velchy's eyes narrowed as he glanced at the paper. He stepped back and pulled the door open. "Have at it. I got nothing to hide."

Giorgio nodded and led the group inside. Swan closed the door and stood in front of it.

"Where were you forty-five minutes ago?"

Velchy frowned. "I went out to grab a latte and some donuts." He pointed to the kitchen counter where a white paper bag sat.

"Okay, take a seat," Giorgio said. He noticed Velchy staring at Swan, blocking his exit. "Don't even think about it. He was an All-American wrestler."

Velchy fell back and took a chair close to the window, his arms crossed, his face set like stone.

"What are you looking for? I told you, I didn't hurt Lindsey."

While Rocky searched through cupboards and closets, Giorgio stood in front of Velchy.

"Maybe not. But your DNA matches DNA we found near the crime scene."

Velchy didn't say anything. He just turned and looked out the window.

"What were you doing up there?"

Velchy took a long pause before saying, "Like I said. I followed her that night."

"To the restaurant, you said. What about after that?" When Velchy didn't answer, Giorgio said, "Look. We think we have enough to charge you with obstruction of justice. So, unless you want to spend the night in jail, talk to us."

He took a deep breath. "After dinner, she went to some old brick building behind the power station. There were several cars out front. She was in there for, I don't know, about thirty minutes. And then they got into a big SUV and drove out to a parking lot above the canyon. There were about ten other cars already there. Some bald dude helped her out of the car. A blond woman joined her and then they all hiked into the woods. I followed, but at a distance."

"What do you mean, helped her out of the car? Did she look drugged?"

"No, not exactly. But Lindsey takes a lot of Xanax for her phobias, so she just seemed pliable, if you know what I mean. Not all there."

"And you followed them?"

"Yeah."

"What happened when you got to the glen?"

He brought his hands together in his lap. "I watched from a distance. They gathered around and recited something, and then Lindsey climbed up onto this table thing."

"Who was leading the group?"

"Some big guy with white hair pulled back in a ponytail. He looked like Brad Pitt from that vampire movie."

"Lestat," Giorgio said.

"Yeah."

"And she was already in the nightdress?"

"Yeah. She must've changed back at the brick building. I didn't see her carrying anything with her."

"Giorgio," Rocky said from behind.

Giorgio turned to find Rocky holding up a pair of Velchy's boots. "They're a match."

"Good. Bag 'em." He turned back to Velchy. "Keep going."

"That's about it. The dude dressed like Lestat placed something against her neck and then sort of climbed onto the table and leaned into her for a moment. It looked like he was going to drink her blood or something. I almost came out of my hiding place because I knew she'd freak out if he punctured her neck with something sharp." He stopped and gazed out the window a moment. "But then she seemed to go limp." Velchy stopped. Swallowed. And then took a deep breath. "Anyway, then all hell broke loose. Lestat climbed off her. People started flitting around her, slapping her face, putting their fingers on her neck. I couldn't hear what they were saying, but it was pretty clear something was wrong." He dropped his head.

"She was dead."

"I guess so. A couple of the women started crying, and everyone stepped back from her like she had the plague."

"What happened next?"

"Lestat huddled up with the bald guy, and I guess that's when they decided to bury her."

"And you watched all of that without doing anything?"

He pulled himself out of the chair and gazed out the window. "I was numb. I could barely breathe. I didn't know what to do. I thought about rushing down there, but she had a restraining order against me. And I have a record. I was afraid if I got involved, they could just blame it on me." He turned to Giorgio. "Look, I admit I abused Lindsey. I'm a control freak. But I would never have killed her. All I could think about was that if I showed myself, I was going to jail."

"Okay, so you watched them bury her."

His fists clenched, and the muscles in his jaw tightened. "Yeah."

"When did you dig her up?"

His eyes flared. "How'd you know it was me?"

"Because we're good at our jobs."

He let out a deflated breath. "After they left, I sat for a while pretty much in shock. Then I decided that I couldn't just leave her there. No one would even know she was gone. So, I dug her up and took her down to the creek."

"You wanted someone to find her?"

"Yeah. Hardest thing I have ever done. But I couldn't let her death go unnoticed. She deserved better than that," he said, his voice catching.

"Nothing else here," Rocky said coming out of the bedroom.

"Okay, I have just a couple more questions," Giorgio said over his shoulder.

Just then Giorgio's phone rang. He put up a finger to ask Velchy to wait a moment and turned away.

"Yeah," he said into the phone.

It was McCready.

"Just got a call that Adira Karim is in the hospital. She was run off the road down in Long Beach last night."

"How bad was it?"

"She's pretty banged up. Her chest was partially crushed, so she's already been in and out of surgery, and she's not breathing too well."

"How did they know to call us?"

"I guess she asked for you as soon as she was brought in. She told a nurse that someone tried to kill her."

Giorgio paused a moment to consider his options. He could send Swan or Rocky down to Long Beach. But hearing that Nagel's friend had been run off the road meant she was probably right and that it had been done on purpose.

"Okay, I'm going to head down there." He hung up and turned to Velchy. "Listen, I'm sorry about your wife, but don't go anywhere. We still need your help. But one more question before we go. Did you see anyone give anything to Lindsey that night? A bottle of water. Something to eat. Anything."

The big man's eyes turned inward as he thought back to the night in the canyon. "Um…no. I…don't think so."

"Okay, thanks. And sit tight. You still may be on the hook for obstruction of justice, but the fact you're cooperating will go in your favor."

Rocky and Giorgio headed for the door when Velchy called out, "Wait! Yes. I did see something."

They turned back. "When Lindsey got out of the SUV in the parking lot, the blond woman handed her a can of soda or something. Then they headed off onto the trail."

Bingo, Giorgio thought.

"Thanks. We'll be in touch."

Velchy nodded and the three officers left the apartment with Velchy's boots in a plastic bag.

"What was the phone call?" Rocky asked once they were in the hallway.

"That friend of Nagel's, Adira Karim? She was run off the road down in Long Beach. My guess is that she was leaving town after she talked to me."

"Is she dead?"

"No. But she's already been in surgery. I'm going down there to see what she knows. Call McCready and have him track down a blond woman who works at the clinic named Mimi Watkins. And I want you guys to hike back into the area where we think the dogfighting ring is. We need some proof beyond what's on that flash drive. Just don't get caught. Or killed," he said, almost as an afterthought.

Giorgio's phone rang again.

"Yeah," he barked, hitting the elevator button.

"Joe, more bad news," McCready said. "Lindsey's mother just called. She's pretty freaked out. Someone broke into her house."

"Shit," Giorgio growled. "I'll send Rocky down there. He's met her. Call Mulhaney and see if he can come in. If not, call Renfrew and see if she's free. I want someone to go with Swan back to the Angeles National Forest to see if we can get photos of that dogfighting ring. And since I have you, I need you to bring a blond named Mimi Watkins in for questioning. She works at the clinic. We believe she's the one who brought Nagel into the Society and was with her when they brought her to the glen that night. Got all that?"

"Yep."

"Good. I'm on my way to Long Beach."

CHAPTER THIRTY-FOUR

Even in Sunday traffic, the drive to Long Beach took over forty-five minutes. It was just before noon by the time Giorgio pulled into the large parking structure at Long Beach Medical Center. He showed his badge to the volunteer at the front desk and was directed to the intensive care unit on the third floor.

A tiny nurse with short, black hair intercepted him at the ICU reception desk.

"I'm Rachel Miller," she said with a brief handshake. "I'm an ER nurse. I'm the one who spoke to Ms. Karim. I told them to page me when you arrived downstairs." She gestured to a small waiting room to one side, and they moved over to talk in private.

"How's she doing?"

"Not well, I'm afraid. The doctors are cautiously optimistic, but one lung was punctured. Her leg was broken as well as several ribs, and she has a concussion. But she's a strong young woman and determined to see you."

"I'll be very careful with her."

"She's intubated, so she can't talk," the nurse said. "But she can write. You will have only a minute or so. Let me tell you first what she told me before she went into surgery, so she doesn't have to repeat it. She said she was on her way to her mother's house here in Long Beach, when a black SUV pulled alongside her. They were the only two cars on the road, and she said the SUV suddenly swerved right into her, pushing her over the curb and into a light post."

"Did she see who was driving?"

"No. Just a big man, she said, and that she was sure he was trying to kill her. That's when she told me to call you. She could hardly breathe, so that's all she could get out before she was rushed into surgery."

Giorgio thanked her, and the two pushed through double doors into the Intensive Care Unit. They passed four patients with curtains drawn before stopping at the last bed.

Adira Karim was in her early thirties, olive-skinned, with medium-length dark hair. A two-inch tube, which kept her airway open, was hooked up to a breathing apparatus that sucked air in and out like a pair of bellows.

Nurse Miller touched the back of the woman's hand and said her name. The woman's eyelids fluttered open. It took a moment for her rich brown eyes to focus, but when she saw Giorgio, she attempted a smile.

"Adira, this is Detective Salvatori. I've already told him what you told me, and I have a pad of paper here," she said. She pulled out a small pad and a retractable pencil. The young woman nodded. "I can hold it, while you write. Are you right or left-handed?"

She lifted her right hand, so Nurse Miller moved around to the other side of the bed. Then she glanced at Giorgio. "Go ahead."

Giorgio stepped up to the bed and rested his hand on her forearm. "I'll only stay as long as you're able," he said. "Let's just do some yes or no questions first so all you have to do is blink. Let's say once for yes. Twice for no." She blinked once. "Okay. Good. You said he was a big man. Do you mean tall?"

She blinked twice.

"Big, as in heavy set."

She blinked once, yes.

"Had you ever seen him before?"

No.

"Would you recognize him if you saw him again?"

No.

"But you're sure he was heavy?"

Yes.

"Bald?"

Her eyes opened wide, and she blinked once. Yes.

"Did you see the license plate?"

No.

"Did he ever pull in front of you?"

Yes.

"Was there anything else about the car that was memorable? Stickers? Or something hanging from the rearview mirror?"

She thought a moment, and then her eyes grew wide again. She blinked once and looked over to Nurse Miller. She reached out with her right hand and grasped the pencil. While the nurse supported the pad of paper, she slowly wrote four letters.

Nurse Miller read it and looked over at Giorgio, holding up the pad. All that was written was LACC in shaky handwriting.

"I don't know what that is," he said.

"I do," Nurse Miller said. "It stands for Los Angeles City College. My brother went there." She looked at Ms. Karim. "Was it a sticker? On the back of the car?"

Yes.

"Okay, that's good," he encouraged her. "And you're sure that he drove right into you, unprovoked?"

Yes.

"Were there any witnesses?"

She thought a moment and then hunched her shoulders.

"You don't know."

No.

Ms. Karim's eyes closed for a moment, and Nurse Miller straightened up.

"I'm afraid that will have to be all for now," she said.

She pulled back, but the young woman reached out and grabbed her hand. Her eyes were open and glaring at her as she shook her head no. She pointed at the pad of paper, and the nurse held it out again.

With faltering strokes, Karim pressed the pencil to the pad and wrote for several seconds. The pencil slipped a few times, but she persevered and then indicated that Nurse Miller should give it to Giorgio.

Giorgio moved around the bed and took the pad. On it were multiple slash marks meant to look like letters. He studied it for a moment and then tried to sound out the letters.

"Med-something. And then it looks like fraud."

She shook her head no and then reached up and grabbed strands of her hair, pulling them out straight.

"Hair?" he said. "Is that what you mean?'

Yes.

"Okay, Med-i-cal…"

She stopped him with a raised hand.

He tried again. "Not medical. Med-i-hair?"

She nodded yes, her eyes alight with enthusiasm.

"No," Nurse Miller stopped him. "She means Medi-*care*."

Adira Karim touched her nose and then pointed at Nurse Miller.

"Medicare fraud," he said. "Dr. Cook?"

She touched her nose again and then pulled her arms up against her chest as if she were cradling a baby. He squinted at her, trying to understand. And then it hit him.

"Dr. Edward Cook…and his son!"

Yes.

"They're both committing Medicare fraud?"

Yes.

"And Dr. Morro?"

She hunched her shoulders.

"You're not sure. How do you know this?"

She reached out for the pad again and drew something. When Nurse Miller turned it toward Giorgio, what he saw made him furrow his brow.

"It's an arrow. I don't know what that means."

She paused a moment and grimaced in frustration. Then, her eyelids drooped and closed.

"Okay," he said, realizing that she was fading. "Listen, you said earlier that Lindsey put something about the Medicare fraud in her book."

Ms. Karim nodded slowly; her eyes still closed.

"But we have her computer and didn't find anything like that in the book."

She opened her eyes and shook her head. Nurse Miller reached out and quieted her by placing a hand on her shoulder.

"Slow down, Adira. Here. Write it down."

The young woman reached out to write again. She was exhausted by now and had real trouble this time in forming her letters. When she was done, her hand fell back onto the bed.

Nurse Miller turned the pad so Giorgio could see it. He read from the very shaky lettering.

"Not computer."

Giorgio inhaled when he realized what she meant. "The insurance forms we found in the box in her apartment?"

She nodded again, her head drooping to one side.

"Okay, one last thing. Kent Bledsoe. Did you know him?"

She gave him a single nod; her energy was spent.

"Mrs. Simpson told us he left suddenly and went back home to Michigan to see his parents. That's why Lindsey took over his job."

She shook her head and reached out for the pad again. She wrote slowly, concentrating to keep her hand steady. When she was done, the nurse handed the pad to Giorgio.

On it, she had written, "No. Maine. Parents dead."

CHAPTER THIRTY-FIVE

Giorgio was halfway back from the hospital when McCready called.

"Listen, that blond woman you asked me to find is one of the eye technicians at the clinic and lives here in Sierra Madre."

"Did you pick her up?"

"Yeah, she's here and not too happy."

"Okay, we need to find out everything we can about Kent Bledsoe. He worked in the billing department at the clinic before Lindsey. Her supervisor told us he left to go back to Michigan to see his parents. That's why Lindsey took his place. But Karim just told me Kent's parents are dead and that he came from Maine."

"You think he's another victim?"

"Well, something's not right. Let's see if we can find him."

"Okay. I'll do a background and see if I can get a photo off social media. Also, we interviewed Phillips and his girlfriend. Nothing there. I'll fill you in later."

÷

It was just after two o'clock when Giorgio got back to the station. Mulhaney was waiting for him at the front counter.

"Have you heard from Rocky or Swan?"

"Yeah. Rocky is still with Mrs. Nagel. She's pretty upset. Someone broke in while she was at church. I guess they trashed her house."

"Probably looking for that flash drive. She didn't see anything?"

"No. They were gone when she got back."

"Okay, tell Rocky to head back here. What about Swan?"

"He's on his way back from the forest."

"All right, tell McCready I want him to join me when I talk to Watkins."

Mulhaney nodded and went in search of the young redhead. Meanwhile, Giorgio stopped at the vending machine and grabbed lunch, which consisted of a Snickers bar and a Coke.

He had just wolfed down the candy bar and popped the tab on the soda when McCready appeared at his elbow.

"Find out anything about Bledsoe?" Giorgio asked.

"Yeah. He did move here from Maine. About eight years ago. His parents were killed when he was in high school, so he lived with an aunt until he graduated. Then he came out here for college and stayed."

Giorgio contemplated the information. "Is the aunt still alive?"

"Yes, but she hasn't seen him in two years. In fact, she didn't know he was missing," McCready answered.

"Okay, we need to find his car registration and track him down."

"I'm already on it."

"Alright, grab the recorder. We're going to interview Mimi Watkins," Giorgio said.

McCready hurried to his desk and pulled a hand-held recorder from the drawer. He then joined Giorgio as they entered the interview room.

Mimi Watkins had medium-length yellow-blond hair, drawn-on skinny eyebrows, large brown eyes, and generous lips. She sat with her hands clasped together on the table. An officer stood in the corner behind her.

Giorgio nodded to the officer, who left. He took the seat opposite Watkins, while McCready sat at the end of the table, placing the recorder in front of him.

"Why am I here?" she snapped.

Giorgio indicated to McCready that he should start the recorder. He stated his name, McCready's name, the date, and the fact they were interviewing a woman named Mimi Watkins.

"Ms. Watkins, we brought you in to discuss the death of Lindsey Nagel and will be recording the interview."

"I didn't have anything to do with her death."

"I didn't say you did. We just need some information."

"Don't I need a lawyer?"

He sighed. "You can ask for one. But this shouldn't take long. And then we can get you out of here."

Her eyes shifted to McCready and then she crossed her arms. "Okay. I'll talk to you."

"How long have you worked at Southwest Eye Clinic?" he asked her.

"Five years."

"And you're a technician? Do you work for Dr. Edward Cook or Jackson Cook?"

"Jackson. He's an ophthalmologist."

"And what does a technician do?" Giorgio asked.

She paused before replying. "We take all sorts of measurements on the eyes. Dilate them if we have to and record what we find on the computer."

"And then the doctor comes in and does what?"

"Reviews the data we put into the computer, does some other tests, like have them read the eye chart. All of that data also gets put into the computer."

"And the data you put into the computer is what determines whether they are a candidate for something like cataract surgery. Right?"

"Um…that's right."

Giorgio leaned forward. "And Jackson's father does the surgery."

"That's right."

"Never Dr. Morro?"

Her eyes narrowed. "Not usually. Jackson's patients go to his father."

"How close are Jackson and his father?"

She shrugged. "Pretty close. I mean, they're not best buds or anything, but I've never seen them at odds with each other."

"And how did Lindsey fit in at the clinic?"

"Lindsey? Well, most of the time she was there she was in accounting. But when Kent left, she was moved temporarily into the billing department."

"And where did Kent go when he left?"

"I was told he went back to Michigan to help his parents out."

As Giorgio watched her, he noted how careful she was being with her answers. "So, what did
Lindsey do in billing?"

She paused before answering, making Giorgio think she might lie.

"She would use the paperwork generated by us to bill the insurance companies, including Medicare and Medicaid."

"I don't know much about billing," he said, "but I assume each procedure has a code. Is that right?"

"Yes."

"Who assigns those?"

She paused again, this time tightening her lips. "The doctors do."

"Based on the assessment of the patient's eyes?"

She grew still for a moment, staring at him. "That's right."

"So, what would happen, I mean, what would the procedure be if Lindsey had found something wrong, say a discrepancy in the billing? What would she have done?"

Her shoulders stiffened. "I'm not sure where you're going with this. But there were no discrepancies with the billing."

"That's okay, Ms. Watkins. We are just trying to understand what everyone's role is in the company. So, in a case like that, where there *might* be a problem, who would she talk to?"

She took a deep breath and leaned back in her chair. "I would assume Mrs. Simpson. She's the supervisor."

"Not Jackson or his father?"

Again, she shrugged, but her shoulders were tense. "I guess she could have gone to either one of them. But, like I said, Mrs. Simpson was her immediate supervisor."

"You were the one who invited Lindsey to join the vampire group. Is that right?"

The question took her by surprise, and she paused. Then, she let out a scoffing laugh. "Vampire group. I don't know what you mean."

"You know that her death wasn't an accident?"

This time, her face grew pale.

"I had nothing to do with that."

"But you were there when she died. We have a witness."

She paused, dropping her hands into her lap. Giorgio waited while she attempted to control her breathing.

Finally, she said, "Yes. I was there that night." A note of defeat had edged its way into her voice.

"And you're the one who invited her to join the Society."

"Yes."

"How long have you been a member?"

"Two years," she replied. "But I don't go that often. I just thought…Lindsey was so tense all the time. So afraid of everything. I thought it would be good for her."

"How close are you to Jeffrey Cook?"

"Jackson's brother? I hardly know him."

"So, you go to the rituals when Jackson is playing the Maestro."

"I'm telling you Lindsey's death was an accident."

"How do you know that?"

240

She paused and took a deep breath. "Because no one did anything to her. One minute she was fine, and the next minute she wasn't. She just stopped breathing."

"You knew she'd taken Xanax that night?" Giorgio pressed her.

Her chin came up in defiance. "How would I know that?"

"Because you two were close friends. We have been told she took Xanax for everything. For instance, when she got the tattoo. You were there for that."

She stared at him. "Yes. Lindsey was scared of…well, everything. Needles. Crowds. The large group that night would have freaked her out. Then there was the essence device. It's very sharp."

"In order to pierce her neck?"

"Yes. It's very sharp," she confirmed. "So, yes, I assumed she took something to calm herself down that night."

"Then why give her GHB?"

Her head came up with a jerk. "What?"

"They found Xanax *and* GHB in her system. A healthy dose of it. It was the combination that killed her." He paused, staring at her. "And you gave her the GHB."

Her mouth opened and closed. "No…no, I didn't."

"You're lying."

"No. I…I really don't know who would have done that."

"You handed her the can of Sprite, though."

She sucked in a pocket of air. "How did you…?" She stopped, staring at him. "Yes. When we got out of the car."

"Why?"

Her eyes shifted toward the recorder and then back again.

"Arthur told me to give it to her," she said quickly, dropping her head.

"Did she ask for a drink?"

"Not that I know of. But she took it, and I saw her take sips as we hiked into the glen."

"Did you see Arthur open the can or put anything into it?"

Her breath had begun to speed up, and her eyes kept flitting over to the recorder.

"No. I…he just handed the can to me. Is that where they found the GHB?"

"Who drove the car that night to the glen?"

"Jackson. Arthur rode in the front with him. I rode in the back with Lindsey."

241

"Did you see them pass anything between them?"

"No," she said, shaking her head.

Giorgio narrowed his eyes as he watched her. Then he leaned forward. "Ms. Watkins, what do you know about what's going on at the clinic?"

This time, there was a long pause as she seemed to stare right through him.

"I think I need a lawyer."

CHAPTER THIRTY-SIX

By the time they were finished with the Watkins interview, Rocky and Swan were both back. The four men huddled up in the squad room.

"Are we going to hold Watkins?" McCready asked.

"Yeah. We've got 72 hours, and her attorney is on his way. I'm not done with her yet." He turned to the white board. "So, it was Arthur Cordova, Jackson Cook's body man, who wanted Lindsey Nagel to have a can of soda," Giorgio said, standing in front of the white board. "He handed the can to Watkins, and she gave it to Nagel."

"Either Cordova put the GHB into the Sprite or Watkins did," Swan said.

"How about Cook?" Rocky asked.

"He was driving," Giorgio said. "He could have ordered it, but it was probably Cordova who spiked the drink."

"How do we prove it?" Rocky asked.

Giorgio sighed. "I don't know. Yet. But we also know that it was Jackson who pretended to be The Maestro that night and not Jeffrey." He wrote on the board as he talked. "This makes it less likely that Jeffrey Cook is a suspect."

He looked around to see the other three men nod in agreement.

"And Velchy has admitted to digging her up and moving her," Rocky said. "So, I don't think he killed her."

"Right," Giorgio said. "I think he's clear of murder charges."

McCready was leaning against the doorjamb. "That leaves three possibilities for who gave her the GHB...Jackson Cook, Arthur Cordova, and Mimi Watkins. All connected to the clinic, all connected to the Society."

Giorgio stood back, staring at the board. "Yeah. I don't see anyone else. I doubt Cordova does much of anything without orders from his boss." He turned to the others. "According to Adira Karim, it was a big, bald dude in a black SUV who ran her off the road. So, he's not afraid to take someone out if he has to. And according to Flame's aunt, he's the one who killed Dave Baker." He turned back to stare at the board. "But I'm also not convinced Mimi Watkins didn't do Lindsey in, or at least know about it. I just don't think she's an unwitting partner in all of this."

"Maybe they're all in on it," McCready said.

"Possibly. I think it all hinges on who Lindsey talked to at the clinic about the Medicare fraud." He whirled around to McCready. "I almost forgot. Where are those three pages we found in the box that had Nagel's book in it?"

"Sorry. Evidence locker," McCready replied.

"Have we found anyone who can help us understand them?"

McCready glanced at the floor. "No. Sorry. With everything else, I forgot about it."

"That's okay. But Karim just told us those sheets are evidence of the fraud, so we need to figure out what they mean."

"Got it," McCready said and left.

"Listen," Swan said. "Don't you think if Nagel were going to tell someone about the fraud, she'd tell her friend Mimi first? And then Mimi told Jackson?"

"Maybe," Giorgio said, thinking. "It's hard to tell. Mimi has been at the clinic a couple of years. And she works for Jackson. Lindsey might have been suspicious of that relationship and gone to someone else first."

"Are you thinking Watkins and Jackson are having an affair?" Rocky asked.

"It's a possibility. If they are, Nagel probably wouldn't have confided in Watkins or Jackson. Maybe Mrs. Simpson. Or the big kahuna himself, Edward Cook. But it's suspicious that just about the time Lindsey started in the billing department, Mimi invited her to join the vampire society. After all, Lindsey would've been the last person anyone would think of to invite to a group like that."

"You think there was an ulterior motive for inviting her to join?" Swan asked.

"Yeah. I do."

"But Watkins said she wasn't close to Jeffrey," Rocky added.

"That's what I mean. Mimi would be in it to protect Jackson, not Jeffrey," Giorgio said.

McCready appeared at the door with the box containing Lindsey Nagel's book and put it onto Giorgio's desk. Giorgio opened the box, reached in, and pulled out the three insurance forms.

"Okay, it looks like these are Medicare bills," he said, scanning them. "They're all for someone named Martin Hogarth. He's 85 and lives at the Aero Dementia Care Facility."

"Shit!" McCready exclaimed. "That's where my gran lives."

"Damn," Giorgio mumbled. "Aero Dementia Care Facility." He looked around at his comrades. "I need to call the Long Beach Hospital."

"Why?" Rocky asked.

"Because Karim drew an arrow on the notepad when I was there, but she was too weak to tell me what it meant." he said, circling his desk.

Giorgio dialed the hospital and asked for Nurse Miller. He was told she was off duty and wouldn't return until the next day.

"Damn," he said. "Look," he said into the phone, "this is a police investigation. Any chance I can get her home phone number?"

"You'd have to talk to HR," the voice on the other end said. "And they won't be in until tomorrow."

"Thanks." He hung up. "She's not back until tomorrow. God, I hate weekends."

"Don't you think the likelihood that you're right is high?" Rocky asked.

"Yeah. Drew, didn't the facility just take your gran to the eye clinic?" Giorgio asked.

"Yeah."

"Do you know who the doctor was?"

"No. But I can find out."

"But she *was* told she needed cataract surgery, and you don't think she does."

"Right," McCready said.

Giorgio's heart rate was now in overdrive. "Let's assume she saw Cook. Any chance you can get her in to see another ophthalmologist? Someone we can trust. Don't tell whoever it is that she's been diagnosed by Jackson Cook. See what they say first. We need a second opinion on the cataract surgery."

"Um…yeah. Sure."

McCready went to his desk. Giorgio turned to Rocky.

"As soon as Drew is done, I want you to call and tell them that you're a friend of Adira Karim. You're trying to get a message to her, and someone told you that she volunteered there."

"Did she?"

"I don't know. But it's the only explanation I can think of as to why she would know about the Medicare fraud. She must have some connection to the Aero Care facility. Hopefully, they'll recognize her name."

"Got it," Rocky said.

McCready reappeared at the doorway. "I got an emergency appointment for my gran tomorrow morning with my mom's doctor. She then arranged to take my gran out for the day, which shouldn't raise any suspicions."

"Good job. This may be the proof we need."

Giorgio turned to Rocky and nodded. Rocky picked up the phone. While he was dialing, Giorgio started to close the box that contained the loose pages to Nagel's book. The box flew off the desk, scattering much of the contents across the coffee-stained linoleum floor.

"Whoa, good job," Swan said, stepping forward to pick them up.

Giorgio's heart rate skyrocketed. He glanced around the room. McCready was already leaning down to help scoop up loose papers, while Rocky was on the phone. No one else had been close to the box, and he was positive he hadn't hit it by mistake.

His skin tingled; he knew the boy had to be in the room. *But where?*

Giorgio leaned down to help, feeling his pulse thump in his ears.

"What the…?" Swan murmured, standing up with a stack of sheets in his hand. He was scanning the top page.

"What is it?" Giorgio asked.

With a crinkled brow, Swan glanced at his partner before reading from the sheet. "Beginning of Chapter Sixteen," he said. "'People who thought they might have cataracts came to the clinic because of symptoms such as light sensitivity, nearsightedness, and cloudy vision. In many cases, the filmy look to their eye was evident without special equipment. But the woman in the chair didn't have any of those symptoms. She was a patient at a memory care facility and sat like a stone, unaware of her very presence in the room as the doctor ran the standard tests on her.'"

"That's from the book?" Giorgio asked, alarmed.

"Yeah. It goes on… 'I watched as the doctor went to the computer and tapped away at the keys. He then shared with the woman's caregiver that she had severe cataracts in both eyes and would require surgery. But I knew from my preliminary tests, that that wasn't true. When I checked the computer later, the information I had put into the woman's record had been changed to support the doctor's diagnosis. This was a clear case of Medicare fraud. The problem was that I didn't know what to do.'"

"Shit," Giorgio murmured. As the hairs on the back of his neck prickled, he swiveled his head to the far corner of the room. A mist hung in the air next to the whiteboard, causing a cold chill to envelop his entire body. He looked around to see if anyone else was aware of the boy's presence, but all three men had huddled up, attempting to read the page in Swan's hand.

When Giorgio turned back, the mist was gone, and he swallowed a mouthful of sour spit. It took him a moment to collect himself.

"Okay," he said, swallowing. "I think we have a good picture of what Lindsey Nagel discovered. Now, we need to prove it. What did you find out about the dogfighting ring?" he asked Swan, shifting gears.

Swan returned to his chair, while Rocky perched on the edge of his desk.

"We used a telephoto lens and got photos," Swan said. "There were two guys watching the place. Same two guys on the flash drive. Six dogs chained to the ground with a makeshift fighting ring." He paused, dropping his head, and taking a deep sigh.

"What?" Giorgio asked.

"They put a Rottweiler into the ring with a small, mixed breed dog. Let's just say it was hard to watch."

Giorgio's stomach turned at the thought of the small dog being ripped to pieces. He took a breath.

"Did you get photos of that?"

"Yeah," Swan said. "But I don't ever want to have to look at them again."

"Copy that. All right. Print them out and let's see if we can get a judge to give us a search warrant to raid that trailer. Since it's in La Canada, we'll need to work through the department over there." He turned to Rocky. "Any luck with the care facility?"

"Yeah. And you and I need to go to the track and place some bets."

"What do you mean?"

"Adira Karim was a volunteer there. Every Saturday, like clockwork."

CHAPTER THIRTY-SEVEN

Monday morning, Giorgio rolled out of bed at 6:30 a.m., stretched, and hit the shower. He was in the kitchen before Angie made it out of bed. Shadow came over with her head down and tail wagging, while Grosvenor slowly and painfully pulled himself up from his pillow to lumber over and get his share of attention.

"Hey, Bud," Giorgio said, cupping his hand around Grosvenor's snout. With his other hand he patted Shadow on the head. "C'mon, let's take you guys outside."

The dogs followed him to the door and to the back gate, stepping gingerly into the backyard, prancing at the cold dampness on the grass. Giorgio watched while Shadow trotted over to a tree to squat. Grosvenor squatted where he was.

Giorgio waited for them to finish, glancing at the big oak tree tucked into the corner by the garage. He wondered if the boy was near. The tree seemed to be one of his favorite spots to appear and disappear, and it made Giorgio wonder how often, and how close the boy was at all times.

When the dogs were done with their morning routine, they all went back inside, and Giorgio fed them. He was in the middle of scrambling some eggs when Angie appeared in a silk robe and slippers.

"You're up early."

He turned. "Yeah. I've got a lot to do today. You want some eggs?"

"No. You finish up, and I'll make the kids' breakfast when you're done."

He used a spatula to deliver the eggs onto the top of a piece of buttered toast and then dropped the pan into the sink.

"I'll do dishes tonight," he said. "I want to get going."

Angie stepped to the sink to rinse out the pan. "No problem. By the way, we're overdo to take Grosvenor back to the vet to have them change his dressings."

"Shit. That's right."

"I can do it," she offered. Angie glanced over to where Grosvenor had plopped back down on his pillow and Shadow now lay beside him. "They're like two peas in a pod," she said with affection.

"Can you handle both of them?" he asked.

She lifted her gaze to meet his. "It won't be easy. Grosvenor isn't stable on his feet yet. I will have a lot to handle just with him. And the kids will be in school."

"Okay, I'll take Shadow to work with me." Giorgio sat down and looked over to where the dogs lay together. "You still thinking of keeping her?"

Angie snuck a glance at him. "Tony wants to. And she fits the family well."

He swallowed a bit of toast and egg. "She's a good dog. But I understand that having two dogs may be a bit too much for us."

Angie moved over to kiss the top of his head. "I think we can manage. Be careful out there today."

÷

It was just shy of eight o'clock when Giorgio stopped at McCready's desk on his way to his office. He had Shadow on a leash.

"You're in early," McCready said.

"Yes, but why is it that I never beat you?"

The young redhead smiled. "'Cuz I'm a kissass."

Giorgio chuckled. "Well, it's working."

McCready eyed the dog. "You know, I can't watch her today. I have my grandmother's eye appointment this morning."

"I remember. No problem. What time is the appointment?"

"Eleven o'clock."

"Okay. Have you found out anything on Kent Bledsoe?"

"Yeah." McCready pulled up some notes on his computer screen. "He drove a 2002 Toyota Camry. I got the VIN number and started checking accident and police reports of abandoned vehicles. When I didn't find anything there, I checked salvage yards. Turns out, someone delivered his car to a yard in Marina del Rey about a week ago."

Giorgio's antenna went up. "Do we know who?"

"Not yet. I sent Officer Renfrew and her partner down there with a photo of Bledsoe to see if they still had the car."

"Okay. I need to call the hospital in Long Beach to talk with Karim's nurse. Let me know if you hear anything."

Once inside the office, Giorgio released the dog's leash and grabbed the phone before he was even in his chair. He called the hospital and asked for Nurse Miller. When she came on the line, he identified himself and asked, "How is Adira doing?"

"Better," the nurse replied. "Her breathing tube has been removed."

"That's great. Any chance she could answer a couple of quick questions?"

"I'll have to check with the ICU nurse. I'll call you right back."

While he waited, he found a ceramic bowl in the cupboard and filled it with water and placed it on the floor next to his desk for Shadow. When Nurse Miller called back, there was relief in her voice.

"Yes," Nurse Miller said. "She is doing well enough that I was told I could switch the call up there. Hold on."

It was a few seconds before a second voice said, "Detective?"

"Yes. Who is this?"

"I'm Nurse Ventris. I'm going to hold the phone to Ms. Karim's ear. Just a minute."

There was a shuffling noise and then a weak voice said, "Hello?"

"Hello, Ms. Karim. This is Detective Salvatori again. I just have a couple of questions. I won't be long. I need to know if one of the technicians at the clinic, a woman named Mimi Watkins, is involved romantically with anyone there. Do you know?"

"Yes," came the weak reply. "It was rumored she was having an affair with Dr. Cook."

"That's what I thought," he replied. "Okay, last question. Did the arrow you drew when I was there the other day refer to the Aero Memory Care Facility? It's spelled Aero. And, if so, what connection do you have with it?"

"Yes," she said in a raspy voice. "It's in Arcadia. I volunteered there."

"Are you the one that alerted Lindsey to the fact that the clinic was ordering unnecessary procedures on patients?"

There was a deep sigh on the other end of the phone. "Yes. There were at least three patients that had cataract surgery. But I knew them all well and was sure they didn't need it. I talked to Lindsey about it and asked her to check it out." Her voice caught, and she had to pause a moment. "I'm afraid I'm the one who got her killed."

"It's not your fault," he assured her. "And we'll be calling the Long Beach police to have them post a guard at your door. We want you safe and healthy."

"Thank you," she said weakly. "I'm so sorry."

"No. Thank you so much. I'll keep good thoughts for your recovery."

"Good luck, Detective."

They hung up and Giorgio went to the whiteboard to add the new information. As he was filling it in, Rocky and Swan walked in.

"I see you brought Shadow," Rocky said, walking over and crouching down to pet the dog.

"Angie is taking Grosvenor to the vet to get his bandages changed."

"So, what's new?" his brother asked.

"I just talked with the nurse down in Long Beach," Giorgio said as he finished writing. "Not only did Karim volunteer at the Aero Memory Care facility—she's the one who alerted Lindsey to the possible fraud."

"That makes sense. According to those sheets we found on the cataract patient Martin Hogarth, he lived there," Swan said, going to his desk. "She probably knew him."

McCready appeared at the door. "Joe, I just heard from Officer Renfrew. They found Kent Bledsoe's body."

÷

Rocky agreed to watch Shadow while Giorgio and Swan left for Marina del Rey. Officer Renfrew had already called the local police department, who would meet them there.

It was almost nine o'clock by the time they pulled into the Kohler Bros. Salvage Yard. Like most salvage yards, it was in an industrial area on the outskirts of town. Two local police cruisers were parked just inside the entrance.

It promised to be a warm day, and the sun beat down on the abundance of metal in the yard, ratcheting up the heat in the surrounding area. Giorgio parked in front of an old white trailer that served as the office. Around them were piles of recycled auto parts and cars sandwiched one on top of the other. A rangy dog with spikey hair wandered up to their car as they pushed open the doors.

"Places like this always make me feel like I'm living in the middle of the apocalypse," Swan said, glancing around.

"Well, just don't ever chase a perp into a place like this," Giorgio said. "Too many places to hide."

"Sounds like you speak from experience," Swan said as they closed the car doors.

"Yep. And it did not go well," Giorgio replied.

They headed towards a group of emergency personnel about thirty yards in front of them. The junkyard dog followed them as they walked to the group huddled in front of what was left of a tan Toyota Camry. Not a big car to begin with, it now looked as flat as a large skateboard.

"Detective Salvatori," a voice said.

Giorgio turned to find Officer Renfrew with her dark eyes creased in concern.

Where's the body?" he asked.

"You mean what's left of the body," she said with an arched brow. "Over here."

She took him to the rear of the car where the trunk lid had been removed. What lay inside the trunk, along with the raw odor of blood and rotting flesh, almost turned his stomach. He lifted the back of his hand to his mouth.

"How do we know it's Bledsoe?" he asked, staring down at the bloodied mess of bones, organs, and flesh.

"We found his wallet and license," she said. "But forensics will confirm it."

"Do we know how he died?"

"No. He could have been drunk or drugged when they put him into the car. Or, he could have been dead already."

Someone appeared at Giorgio's shoulder, making him turn.

"This is Detective Reed from Marina del Rey PD," Renfrew said, introducing him to a tall, thin man standing next to him.

The two men shook hands.

"This is Detective Swan," Giorgio said.

The big detective nodded to Reed. "So, what do we have here?" Reed asked.

Giorgio glanced back into the trunk of the car. "This guy is connected to the death of a woman in Sierra Madre. We've been looking for him." Giorgio sighed. "We'll need to talk to the owner of the yard. Care to join me?"

Reed nodded. "Sure. We've called for the technicians and the medical examiner. I assume you'll want access to the car and any of the forensics."

"Yeah. Thanks." Giorgio turned to Renfrew. "Listen, we need to know if they have any CCTV footage," he said, glancing up and around him.

"They don't," she said. "I already asked. Nothing here valuable enough to protect, I was told."

"Has anyone gotten a description of whoever it was who dropped off the car?"

"Yes. Big bald guy," Reed replied.

"Shit. One more player in this game."

"You know him?" Reed asked.

"Haven't had the pleasure. But we know who he is. Okay, where's the owner?"

"Over there," Reed said, pointing to a disheveled man in a long-sleeved, dirty red shirt and overalls.

"Alright. I know your people will document everything, but mind if we back you up?"

"Not at all."

Giorgio turned to Swan. "Can you stay here and help get photos of everything. Renfrew, can you hang around until their forensics people get here. They'll take the car, but we'll want to go over it later."

She nodded and turned away. Giorgio and Reed went to talk with the owner.

"You the owner?" Giorgio asked, approaching him.

The man in the overalls turned to him. He was an inch or so taller than Giorgio, medium weight, with graying hair that curled behind his ears.

"Yeah. Jerry Kohler."

He extended a hand, sleeve rolled up to the elbow. Giorgio shook it.

"I'm Detective Salvatori, Sierra Madre Police. The guy in the trunk was someone of interest in a murder case."

Kohler rolled back on his heels. "I wondered," he murmured. "We don't usually get dead bodies in the cars that are dropped off." He attempted a weak smile but came up short. "So, what can I do to help?"

"Did the big bald guy who dropped off the car give you a name?"

"Naw. He just showed up around a couple of weeks ago and dropped it off. Said he didn't need it anymore. My nephew dealt with him."

"Was the man alone?" Giorgio asked.

Kohler had to think a minute. "No. There was a car waiting for him."

"Do you remember what it looked like?"

"Yeah. Black SUV. I couldn't see the driver, though. Like I said, my nephew did the paperwork. I was busy with other things."

"What about the Camry? Why did you crush it?"

"It had been in a bad accident. I don't know how the guy drove it in here. He told us the insurance company had determined it was a total loss. We took a few parts off it, but that's all."

"And you never opened the trunk?"

He hunched his shoulders. "No. My nephew said the bald guy had completely cleaned it out. It wasn't supposed to be crushed until last weekend. But it had already been done when I got in the next day."

Giorgio's antenna went up. "What day was that?"

"Um…Thursday of that week. I'd have to check the exact date."

"Who does the crushing?" Reed asked.

"My nephew. He said he was going out of town with some friends on Friday, so he came in early on Thursday to get the cars out of the way."

"Is your nephew here today?"

"No. He has classes on Mondays."

"Where?"

"PCC."

"What's his name?" Giorgio asked him.

Kohler paused and stuck his hands in his pockets. "Has he done anything wrong?"

"We just need to talk to him."

"Um…okay. His name is Raymond Pietro. He lives with his mother in Pasadena."

"Okay, we'll need a number," Giorgio said. Kohler recited the number from memory, and Giorgio wrote it down. "Anything else you can think of that might be of help?"

Kohler shook his head. "No. I offered the guy $150 for the car, but he said he didn't care about the money. Oh, yeah," he said. "He signed our scrap metal sheet, and I noticed he wore a large ring on his right hand. Looked like a class ring. You know the type. I didn't see where it was from, though."

"That's good," Giorgio said, making a note. "Thanks. Listen, can you get us that sheet?"

"Sure. Give me a minute. Ray would have filed it."

While Kohler went into the office, Giorgio turned to Reed. "Here's my card. Let me know where they take the car. And maybe you could send over the forensics report when it's finished?"

Reed smiled. "No problem. How important was this guy to your case?"

"Not sure. He disappeared a few weeks ago, we think, because he found something irregular at a local medical clinic. The body of the woman who replaced him was found up in Bailey Canyon. It's her death we're investigating."

"Looks like you're investigating two murders now."

"More like three," Giorgio replied with a sigh. "There was another guy found in her car with his head bashed in."

"Shit," Reed said.

Kohler returned with the paper. "Here you go," he said, handing it to Giorgio.

"Thanks. We may be back if we have more questions." He gestured to Detective Reed. "The Marina del Ray police will take the car, but you'll get a receipt." Giorgio handed his card to Kohler. "Let me know if you remember anything else."

"Okay," Kohler said.

"By the way," Giorgio began, "what does your nephew look like?"

"Tall. Thin. Stringy blond hair."

"Thanks again," Giorgio said. He glanced at the signature on the scrap metal sheet but didn't recognize it. No surprise there.

Giorgio thanked Detective Reed and returned to the Camry, where Swan was snapping pictures of everything. Giorgio stared at the goopy mess and shivered in disgust.

"Listen, on the way back, we need to re-interview Bledsoe's boss, Mrs. Simpson, to find out who came up with the idea that Bledsoe returned to Michigan and not Maine," he said to Swan.

"What if she doesn't know?"

Giorgio shrugged. "Someone had to have come up with the story. We need to find out who."

CHAPTER THIRTY-EIGHT

It was just before noon by the time Giorgio and Swan got to the clinic. They went to the basement to find Mrs. Simpson. She was in a budget meeting, so they were forced to wait near the coffee bar. A few minutes into their wait, Ted Freemont, the IT guy, wandered by.

"Hey, Detective," he said, stopping in front of them. "How's your investigation going?"

Giorgio perked up. "Good. We're here to talk with Mrs. Simpson again. Listen, Ted, did you know Kent Bledsoe very well?"

"Not too well. We had a beer once after work not too long ago. He was into a bunch of weird stuff like Dungeons and Dragons and horror movies. That's not my thing."

"How long ago was that?"

Young Freemont had to think. "Oh, I don't know. About six weeks ago, I guess."

"Who suggested the drink?"

"Uh…he did. He stopped by my office that afternoon."

"Did he mention anything to you that raised a red flag?"

"Like what?"

"I don't know. Anything odd."

"Um…let me think. We didn't talk that much about work that night," he said, dropping his head. "But wait a minute. He did ask me who could change billing codes once they were in the computer."

"What prompted the question?"

"Nothing. It came out of the blue."

"And what was your answer?"

"I told him that anyone who has access to the file can change them."

"And it's the doctors who assign the codes, right?"

"Right. Then everything is sent to the billing department."

"And the billing people can change the codes."

"Yes, technically."

"Did Kent say why he was asking?"

"No."

"Detective Salvatori," a stern voice said.

The three men turned to find Mrs. Simpson standing at the hallway entrance, dressed in a navy-blue pants suit. "Still talking about Doogie Howser?"

Giorgio turned back to Freemont. "Thanks." He got up and stepped over to Mrs. Simpson. "This is a murder investigation, Mrs. Simpson. We'll talk to whoever might have the information we need."

She maintained eye contact with him but flinched at his rebuke. "Fine. Let's go to my office."

She led them back down the hallway. Once inside her office, Giorgio introduced Swan, and they sat down facing her.

"What can I do for you, Detective?" she asked, her lips pulled tight.

"We need to know who told you that Kent Bledsoe went back to Michigan when he left," Giorgio asked.

Her eyes shifted to Swan and then back again. "Why does that matter?"

"Bledsoe reported to you, didn't he?"

"Yes."

"When he quit, did he tell you himself that he was leaving for Michigan?"

She gave a slight shake of her head. "No. As I told you."

"Who told you?"

She inhaled, contemplating her answer. In situations like this, Giorgio often found that someone like Simpson would worry about implicating someone above her and would hesitate, weighing the implications of their answer.

"Mimi Watkins told me."

"What did she say?" he asked.

The woman began to wring her hands as they rested on the desk. "When Kent didn't show up for work, we called his apartment, but no one answered."

"What day was that?"

"Oh, dear, let me see." She turned to her computer. "I had to generate a final paycheck," she said, as she typed. "Um…it was, oh yes, here it is. It was the 14th when I ordered the check. So, it would have been the day before when he left." She returned her attention to them.

"So, what did Mimi tell you?"

"I was in the cafeteria when I ran into her. I asked her if she'd seen him that day. And she told me that Kent had quit to go back to Michigan to help his parents."

"Did she say how she knew that?"

"I asked her that. I mean, she's a technician, and I didn't think they knew each other that well. But she said Dr. Cook had told her."

"Jackson Cook?"

"Yes."

"But why would Bledsoe tell Dr. Cook he was quitting and not you?" Swan asked her.

She turned to him with a frown. "Exactly what I wanted to know. I went to Jackson's office later that day and asked him. I was a little miffed, to be honest with you. Even though Jackson works just three days a week, you'd think he owns the place and not his father. He flashes that big gold ring of his around to let everyone know he's second-in-command."

"What do you mean?"

"Oh. He and his father have matching rings. Or almost matching. Jackson's is inlaid with a blue sapphire. His father's is inlaid with a ruby. Jackson always makes sure you see it. It's a symbol he can't resist. Anyway, while he played with his ring, he told me that he happened to see Kent on the way into the building that morning. When he asked Kent why he was here so early, Kent said he was cleaning out his desk and leaving to go back to Michigan to help his parents. He told Jackson he was in a hurry to leave town and so asked Jackson to let me know. I'm not sure why Jackson told Mimi. But he told me he'd just forgotten about it until I came to his office."

"Where did you send his final check?"

"His apartment. I assumed it would get forwarded." She paused and sat back in her chair.

Giorgio watched her and then said, "What?"

"It came back. The check. I...I just got it back yesterday. I was going to review his personnel file to see if he had given us his parents' address."

"Mrs. Simpson, Kent Bledsoe's body was found this morning. He's dead. We can get a subpoena, but we need to see that personnel file."

Her face blanched. "Of course." She got up and went to a lateral file cabinet against the wall, opened a drawer and found Bledsoe's file folder. "Here," she said, handing it to Giorgio.

"Thank you. Is Jackson here today?" Giorgio asked.

"No. He works Tuesdays, Wednesdays, and Thursdays."

"All right. Thank you, again. We'll find our way out."

"Um…how did he die? Kent."

"We're not at liberty to say."

In the elevator, Swan asked, "What about Dr. Edward Cook? Shouldn't we go see him?"

"Rocky and I talked with him last week. He didn't have much to say. And until we can get more information about the fraud, I don't want to tip my hand to him. But I think we just identified the ringleader of the drug operation, so to speak."

"What do you mean?" Swan asked.

"The man standing in the shadows of that video was wearing a gold ruby ring."

Swan released a breath. "Damn. The feds will want to know that. But how are we going to get more information on the medical fraud?"

"I'm hoping we'll know more after McCready's grandmother has that second eye appointment. Depending on the results, we'll ask for a subpoena for both the clinic's records and the memory care facility records. Meanwhile, I'm going to take another run at Mimi Watkins. And I want you to study Bledsoe's personnel file. See if there's anything in there we can use."

÷

After leaving Mrs. Simpson, Giorgio and Swan grabbed a quick bite before returning to the station. By the time they ambled down the hallway toward their office, McCready was back at his desk.

"How'd it go with your grandmother?" Giorgio asked him.

McCready looked up with a sly grin. "I think we've got 'em. Dr. Bartholomew, that's my mom's eye doctor, said my grandmother doesn't have cataracts. When I asked if there was any way another doctor could have made a mistake, he said not a chance." McCready pulled out a sheet of paper and handed it to Giorgio. "And he gave me the results of her tests."

Giorgio scanned the sheet filled with numbers and percentages. "I have no idea what I'm looking at. I'll take your word for it. Let's book this into evidence. Would he be willing to testify?"

"I didn't ask. But he was angry when I told him another doctor had diagnosed her with cataracts. And he wasn't surprised to hear it was Jackson Cook."

"And you're sure it was Cook?"

"Yeah. I had my mom ask the care facility."

"What else did her doctor say?"

"Just that he's had suspicions about Cook for a while. He knew that their clinic worked a lot with vulnerable populations, and that my gran was the third patient of Dr. Cook's he'd been asked to give a second opinion on in six months. He said he'd thought about reporting it before, and now said that he would."

"I don't suppose he told you who the first two people were?"

"No. But once we get a subpoena, we can ask him."

"Right. Okay, I need to talk to Mimi Watkins again. Call her lawyer and get her out of the holding cell."

Twenty minutes later, Giorgio and McCready stepped into the interview room. Mimi Watkins looked disheveled after her night in jail and more than a little pissed. When her lawyer, a young hard-edged looking woman arrived, she joined them.

"I have nothing more to say," Watkins said with a snarl. "I want to go home."

"You will soon. I just have a few more questions about Kent Bledsoe."

She gave him a sullen stare and then nodded. "Fine."

"We found his body this morning," he told her, watching her flinch at the news. "He'd been put into the back of his car and dropped off at a salvage yard where it was crushed…with him inside. Do you know anything about that?"

Her eyes registered her surprise at the news, and she glanced at her attorney, who turned cold eyes on Giorgio.

"What are you suggesting?" she asked.

"Nothing yet," he replied. "But we have it on good authority that your client was the one who told Bledsoe's boss that he had left town to take care of his parents in Michigan." He turned to Watkins. "Is that right? We just need to know who told you that."

She swallowed hard. "Jackson told me that," she replied, her throat constricting so that she had to take a deep breath. "He said Kent had cleaned out his desk first thing that morning and left for Michigan."

"Except his parents don't live in Michigan. He's from Maine. And his parents are both dead."

A pall fell over the room. Watkins gulped a few times and seemed to have trouble breathing.

"I…I didn't know," she said. She glanced down to the table and shook her head as if to dispel the cobwebs. "I…that's what Jackson told me." She shook her head before mumbling, "God, how did I get myself into this mess?"

"I guess it gets back to the company you keep," he replied. "For instance, who do you know who works at Kohler Salvage Yard?"

Her eyes met his. "No one."

"Maybe someone in the Essence Society?"

She shook her head again. "I don't know. I don't think so."

"Does the name Raymond Pietro mean anything to you?"

"There is a Ray in the Society, but I don't know his last name."

"What does he look like?"

She thought a moment. "Kind of scrawny. Maybe five-eleven with blond hair."

"Okay. How can we get a list of Society members?"

"Um…Jeffrey would have that. They have all new members sign something they call the Book of the Dead."

"Where does he keep this Book of the Dead?"

"At the Fortress. They have an office there." She took a breath and then leaned forward on the bench. "I didn't know about Kent, Detective. Really. I liked him."

"Okay. We'll be releasing you soon. But when we do, don't leave the area."

She nodded; her eyes filled with tears. He went back to his office. On his way past McCready's desk, he instructed him to release Watkins.

"I think she's given us everything she knows. I have to call Flame," he said.

At his desk, he dialed the psychic's number. When she answered, he asked, "Isn't your orientation meeting for the Essence Society tonight?"

"Hello, detective," she said when he didn't introduce himself.

"Sorry," he mumbled. "I uh…when I get on a case I…"

"No apologies necessary," Flame said, cutting him off. "Yes. The orientation meeting is at eight o'clock tonight."

"Okay, if you have a minute, I wanted to stop by."

"I have a client coming in."

"I'll wait 'til you're free." He hung up and grabbed his coat.

"Going to see Flame?" Rocky asked from across the room.

Giorgio glanced at his brother. "Yeah. I want her to wear a wire, and I assume she'll resist."

"Well, don't be a bully. Not everyone sees the world the way you do. Try to be polite about it."

"I don't have time to be polite. We already have three dead bodies. I'll take Shadow with me and drop her off to Angie on my way back. In the meantime, make yourself useful and call Jeffrey Cook and see if Raymond Pietro is a member of the Society."

CHAPTER THIRTY-NINE

Giorgio left the pit bull in the car when he got to Mirabelle's and waited in the reception area until a young balding man emerged through a side door. Flame appeared in the doorway behind him, dressed in baggy black pants and a white muslin top. The man thanked her and left.

She turned to Giorgio. "So, what's up?"

"Your meeting is eight o'clock. Rocky and I will be at your house by 7:15."

"Okay, but why?"

"I want you to wear a wire."

She expelled a scoffing breath. "Really, detective. I'll be okay."

"It's not a request," he said. 'It's for your own protection."

"Why?"

"Twin brothers play-act as The Maestro. Jeffrey Cook was the one at the murder game. The one who gave you the two envelopes. It's his brother Jackson Cook I'm worried about. He was the one in the canyon the night Lindsey Nagel was killed. He also runs a dogfighting ring and a drug operation. We warned Jeffrey not to say anything to Jackson about you, but…," he paused and shrugged his shoulders. "They're family. Anyway, it was clear Jeffrey recognized something about you when he handed the envelope to you."

"Do you know which one will be there tonight?" she asked.

"No. We didn't want to tip our hand by asking."

"Okay. I understand. I'll wear the wire. I'll walk you out," she said, moving toward the door.

They left the small building and walked to the car. As they approached, Shadow stuck her head out the open window.

"Who's this?" Flame asked, reaching out a hand.

"My son named her Shadow. She chased off a mountain lion the other day when we were up in the canyon searching for clues. We think she escaped a dogfighting ring up there."

Flame cupped the dog's heavy head in her hand. She narrowed her eyes again, concentrating, while Shadow attempted to lick her hand. Finally, Flame released her.

"Yes, she's a fighting dog," she said. "But she's also connected to the boy."

Giorgio's head snapped around. "What?"

"The boy who follows you around. There's a connection between them. I can't tell you how, though."

Giorgio was silent for a moment, a jumble of thoughts in his head. He reached into his pocket and extracted the battered dog tag.

"What does this tell you?"

She took it from him and rubbed her fingers across the word Sombra. "Hmmm," she muttered. "Yes, it belongs to the dog. What does Sombra mean?"

"Shadow."

Her gaze eyes shifted toward him as a small smile played across her lips. "The boy has a sense of humor. But he is in your corner. You know that, right?"

"I believe that. But I never quite know how to translate what he's trying to tell me. He's the one who gave me the dog tag. Someday, you're going to have to tell me how he does that."

She laughed out loud. "I have no idea. It's not like there is a book you can buy online that tells you everything you want to know about the other side. In fact, I only know the bare minimum of how I can read people and speak to the dead. Beyond that, it's a crap shoot. How did he give this to you?" she asked, holding up the dog tag.

"He appeared in my house for the first time and threw it at me. To be honest, it freaked me out."

"Hmmm." She studied the dog tag again. "I've only heard of something like that once before. I mean, the idea of something corporeal like this being transferred from the possession of a spirit to a living being. I don't know how it works. But like I said before, the entire universe is made up of energy. It can't be created or destroyed. It's a constant. Some people believe that we are merely transformed into a new form of energy when we die."

Giorgio pictured Christian in his head. "So, the boy is just a new form of energy?"

She chuckled. "I guess. I don't know for sure. No one does."

"He just freaks me out," Giorgio said. "I never get used to seeing him."

"Trust me, my abilities freaked me out when I was little. The first time I let anyone know what I could do was when I was at a friend's house and her dead grandfather appeared next to her bed. He told me that she needed to avoid eating the chicken at dinner that night. I told her and she told her mom. I was never invited to their house again."

"Did the girl eat the chicken at dinner?"

Once again, Flame laughed. "Yes, and she choked on a bone and had to be taken to the hospital."

Shadow had put her paws on the open window and swiped the back of Flame's hand with her tongue. Flame giggled as she pushed the dog back.

"Did you know that animals can sense ghosts?" She nodded toward Shadow.

"Already happened," he said. "Christian appeared in our backyard the other night. Shadow stared right at him, and then he pointed at her. It gave me the chills."

"I think the boy is trying to tell you something about Shadow." She handed the dog tag back. "Keep her close."

"Listen. I assume it will be Jeffrey at the initiation tonight. But I don't want to take chances. That's why I want you to wear a wire."

"I've got it. But I'll know that, too," she said. "I mean, I'll know which brother it is. I've touched Jeffrey. So, even if they are identical twins, their energies will be completely different."

"Here," he said, handing the dog tag back. "I think you should keep this. I have a hunch you're supposed to carry it with you."

She studied him for a moment. "You're a sensitive, whether you know it or not. You should develop that skill."

"I don't think so. It's enough just being a cop."

Flame turned the tag over in her hands. "Well, I'm glad to know you listen to your hunches. Since the boy is connected to this tag, perhaps what you're feeling is that it's the boy who is supposed to be with me." She rubbed her thumb over the surface of the dog tag and then stuffed the tag into the pocket of her jeans. "I'll keep it with me."

÷

At home that night, Angie reported that one of Grosvenor's wounds had gotten infected and so the vet had kept him overnight. The kids had finished dinner early and were doing homework, while Giorgio moved the chicken fettuccine around on his plate, uninterested. Angie sat across from him.

"Joe," she said. When he didn't look up, she repeated, "Joe."

He stopped twirling a noodle and glanced at her. "What?"

"I know you have a lot on your mind, but I hope you remember that the kids have a science fair at school tonight."

"Um…no. Sorry, I forgot. I won't be able to go."

She reached out and placed her hand over his. "I know. But the kids and I will be gone for most of the evening. Is there any chance you can take Shadow with you tonight? Maybe someone at the station could watch her."

He glanced over to Grosvenor's bed where the pit bull laid watching them. Shadow seemed lost without Grosvenor. He remembered what Flame had said. Apparently, there was work yet for her to do.

"Yeah. I'll take her," he said. "She might be of help."

"You're worried, aren't you?" she said.

"Yeah. Flame volunteered for this, but there are too many variables, and that makes me uncomfortable."

"She's a strong young woman," Angie said. "And if what you've told me about her is true, she also has strong intuitions. I think she'll know if she's in danger."

"But she's not invincible. Sometimes these things happen fast." He pushed his plate away. "Sorry. I'm just not hungry."

She grabbed the plate and took it to the counter. "I'll save it for later." She turned to him. "I know you're worried about Flame. But something tells me that you need to be careful, too, tonight."

CHAPTER FORTY

At 7:15, Giorgio and Rocky left Shadow in the car and arrived on the doorstep of the little white bungalow. Rocky bristled with nervous energy, shifting his weight from one foot to the other and flexing the fingers on both hands. Giorgio, on the other hand, stood as if he were made of stone, struggling with a deep feeling of dread.

"Now that we know Raymond Pietro is part of the Society, do we still want to go through with this?" Rocky asked.

"I'm not sure he adds any risk," Giorgio replied. "Although I assume he knew the body was in the trunk of the car when he smashed it. Did you get a sense whether Jeffrey Cook will be the one running the meeting tonight?"

"Yes. I asked him if there were any upcoming Society meetings, because we wanted to talk with Pietro."

"What'd he say?"

"He said there was a council meeting tonight but that he didn't expect Pietro to be there. But if he showed up, he said he'd call me."

"Okay. That gives me a little less heartburn."

He knocked on the door and then waited. The surrounding neighborhood was eerily quiet, increasing the foreboding he had in the pit of his stomach. When Flame's aunt answered the door, her face pinched with concern, he almost turned around and left. But he couldn't. He knew Flame would go through with the initiation one way or the other. All he could do was to keep her as safe as possible.

"She's in the kitchen," Cora said.

She led them through the small dining room into the kitchen where Flame was throwing on a light jean jacket.

"We need to hide a listening device on you," Rocky said, holding the bug in his hand. "We're afraid they might make you…uh…change into something else for the initiation."

Rocky was tapping his left hand against his thigh. The fact that he held a black belt in Krav Maga and yet was nervous around the woman he had a crush on was endearing, even to Giorgio. But as adept as Rocky was at martial arts, this little woman had more power over him right now than any man ever could.

Flame smiled. "In other words, take my clothes off," she said.

"Yes," Rocky said.

Rocky towered over Flame, staring into her eyes for a moment before reaching for her ear. She flinched away, and he pulled back his hand.

"You need to remove one of your earrings," he said, gesturing to her earlobe.

Flame paused a moment and then reached up and removed one of the four studs in her left ear. Rocky reached out and positioned the bug through the hole and affixed the backing. The bug was shaped like a tiny cupcake, and he used his index finger and thumb to doublecheck it to make sure it was secure. The entire thing played out in less than thirty seconds, and yet Giorgio felt he was intruding on an intimate moment between the two.

"The top has a microphone in it," Rocky explained, pulling his hand away.

"I'll be fine," she stressed, staring up at him.

Rocky held her gaze and then stepped back.

Giorgio glanced at Flame's aunt. "You're sure you're okay with this?"

Cora crossed her arms over her chest and shifted her weight. "No. Frankly, I'm not. But I learned a long time ago that she will do what she will do," she said, glancing at Flame.

Flame reached out and grabbed her aunt's hand. "It will all be okay, Auntie. You'll see."

"Okay, then let's test it," Giorgio said. "Stay here."

He retreated to the front room, closing the door behind him. He placed a wireless ear bud in his ear and then called out to Flame, "Okay, say something in a quiet voice."

"I'm here with my aunt and the very handsome Officer Salvatori," she whispered.

Giorgio smiled, knowing that Rocky was squirming now, or at least, blushing. He returned to the kitchen. "We're good to go. Listen," he began. "Look around when you get there. Take note of the room and everyone in it. We'll debrief you later. We've been told it will be Jeffrey tonight and not his brother, so I'm less worried than I was before. But first and foremost, pay attention to your instincts."

"I always do," she said and turned to leave the kitchen.

"Flame," her aunt said, stopping her. Cora stepped forward and pulled Flame into an embrace. "Be careful, honey. This isn't a game."

"I know," Flamed mumbled.

Flame left the small bungalow and climbed into her black-and-white Mini Cooper. Giorgio and Rocky remained for a moment on the front step with her aunt.

"Bring her home safely," Cora said, grasping Giorgio's forearm. "I can't see the future, but I don't have to. I know this isn't going to be safe. She sometimes has more confidence in her abilities than she should, and it makes her reckless."

"We'll do everything humanly possible to keep her safe," Giorgio said with more self-assurance then he felt.

They followed Flame at a distance to the auto parts store, where she pulled into the rear parking lot as she had been instructed. The big black SUV was parked nearby. Swan and McCready had arrived earlier and were stationed around the corner of the store, where they waited in the dark.

"I don't like this," Rocky said as Giorgio pulled up across the street and parked. "She's too vulnerable."

"Look, I know you like her. But she's stronger than you think," Giorgio said, ignoring the queasiness in his stomach.

They watched from the darkened interior of their car as Flame got out and stood beside the Mini Cooper, never once glancing in their direction. A moment later, the back door to the store opened, and Arthur Cordova and Mateo emerged.

"Shit," Rocky murmured. "That's Cordova and his guard. I really don't like this."

"Hang tight," Giorgio said.

The two men greeted Flame, and the three of them got into the SUV and pulled out of the lot. The officers allowed the SUV to get to the end of the block before Giorgio directed Swan and McCready to follow. Their procedure was to have the two police vehicles rotate off and on to minimize the chance they were spotted, keeping in close radio contact with each other.

"Where are we going?" Flame asked, her voice coming through the receiver on Giorgio's dash.

"We don't give out that information in advance," a gruff voice replied.

Giorgio assumed it was Cordova talking.

"Okay. No problem," Flame responded. "Will I get to meet The Maestro?"

"You ask a lot of questions," Cordova said.

"Shit!" Rocky exclaimed. "She needs to just shut up and play along."

"Again. Give her a chance."

Rocky turned to look at Giorgio in the shadowed car interior. "She's only going to *have* one chance at this, Joe. These people are killers."

"I know," Giorgio replied. "But remember that it will be Jeffrey tonight. I don't see him as a killer."

Giorgio knew that fueling Rocky's nervousness was the memory of his fiancée's murder just before their wedding back in New York a few years earlier. His brother was too familiar with losing someone he cared about.

"We'll be right there if she needs us," Giorgio reassured Rocky. "We won't let her down."

As if she'd been listening, Flame remained silent for the rest of the drive. Less than ten minutes later, the big car pulled onto a dirt road that wound into a wooded area northwest of Sierra Madre. Giorgio was a block or so behind them and cut his front beams, pulling to the side of the road as the taillights of the SUV disappeared into the trees.

"Aren't we going to follow?" Rocky asked.

"Yeah. I just want to give them a head start. Tell Swan to stay back here."

He waited a few seconds and then pulled onto the dirt road, leaving his lights off. The moon was in its third quarter, so not bright enough to lend much assistance under the canopy of trees. The road twisted and turned. Although he could follow the red taillights, they didn't illuminate the road enough to avoid ruts and ditches.

"Help me keep an eye out so we don't hit anything," he said to Rocky.

"Will do."

Less than a minute later, they caught sight of an old brick building, and Giorgio rolled to a stop.

"What the heck is that?" Rocky mumbled, leaning forward to stare at the dilapidated structure.

Giorgio was peering through the front windshield. "Remember? Jeffrey said it was an old city maintenance building."

"So, this is the Fortress?"

"Must be," Giorgio replied. "Let's see what they do. By the way, notice the sticker on the back of the SUV?" Giorgio said, nodding toward the back of the big black car, where the white letters LACC were visible. "That's the car that ran Adira Karim off the road."

While he spoke, Flame and Cordova exited the car and went inside the building. The driver pulled the SUV around to the back of the building.

"I wonder what he's doing," Rocky mumbled.

Once the SUV was out of sight, Giorgio pulled his car under a tree that sat off to the side of the building and killed the engine. Meanwhile, Flame's voice came through the receiver.

"Is this the Fortress?"

"Just wait here," Cordova said gruffly.

"Fine," Flame said. "I don't have to change clothes or anything, do I?"

"Just stay here. I'll be back in a minute."

The listening device picked up muted voices in the background.

"This place looks right out of Disneyland," Flame murmured. "Complete with rustic candlesticks, an altar, and hanging banners with Celtic symbols."

"She needs to be careful," Rocky said.

He leaned forward, tapping his fingers on the dash of the car.

"Give her some space," Giorgio replied. "She's smart."

Flame grew quiet, while they heard some shuffling sounds and more voices in the background. A voice erupted close to Flame.

"Welcome to the Fortress," the voice said. "Please, follow me."

"Who was that?" Rocky asked.

"Don't know," Giorgio replied. "A woman, though."

"Where am I going?" Flame asked.

"To prepare to meet The Maestro," the voice replied.

"I wonder where they're taking her," Rocky said.

"In here," the voice said. "My name is Renalda."

"Renalda?" Rocky blurted, turning to Giorgio. "That's the woman from the murder mystery."

"Well, we knew she was a member," Giorgio said.

"Take off all your clothes, even your underclothes," Renalda said. "Then, put this on."

"I thought I wouldn't have to change," Flame said.

"We're all dressed like this. When we're at the Fortress, we stand before The Maestro in our barest and most vulnerable form. When you have changed, stand in front of the altar. Do not say anything until you're spoken to. The Maestro will meet you there."

"What do I have to do?" Flame asked.

"Just follow his instructions. It's quite simple, really. But don't take too long. Everyone is waiting."

There was the sound of a door opening and closing and then silence.

"Shit," Rocky exclaimed. "Can't we get up close enough to watch the ceremony?"

"Too risky," Giorgio replied. "We can hear what's going on. Be patient."

As the seconds passed, there were more shuffling sounds as Flame removed her clothes and dressed in the initiation clothes.

"Okay, I'm in my initiation dress," Flame said. "Don't know what's going to happen next. I can feel The Maestro, though. The one I met at the mystery game. He's close. But there is an evil presence here, too."

"The evil presence she feels could be Jackson," Rocky said.

"Wait, someone is coming," Flame whispered.

A door opened somewhere, and a man's voice cut in. "Come with me."

"Renalda told me to go out to the altar," Flame said.

"You need to come with me."

"Is this the way to the altar?"

"Quiet!"

There were footsteps and then a soft rustling noise followed by a woman's groan.

"Hurry up and grab her feet," the voice said.

Giorgio and Rocky were out of the car in an instant, running for the entrance. They burst into a long room shrouded in darkness. A group of ten or twelve people, all dressed in white robes, milled about in front of a richly carved wooden table. There was red and white fabric draped everywhere. The light in the room came from four large wax candles that sat on tall wooden candlesticks that flanked the table. A small podium holding a large book sat in the middle of the table.

"Sierra Madre Police!" Giorgio shouted, holding out his badge. "Where is she?"

The group turned with looks of surprise. In the middle was the statuesque figure of Renalda.

"Officers. What's going on?" she asked. Her eyes sought out Rocky. "Who are you looking for? This is a private affair."

"We want the young woman who just came in here," Giorgio replied, striding towards her.

Renalda nodded toward a side door. "She's getting ready. She'll be out in a minute."

Rocky had drawn his weapon and moved to the door indicated by Renalda. He opened it, ducked inside, and came right back out. "She's not in there. Where the hell is she?" he shouted, advancing on Renalda.

"I swear, I don't know," she said, stepping back. "She was supposed to come out as soon as she was dressed. The Maestro is almost ready."

"Is there a back door?" Giorgio demanded, grabbing her wrist.

"Back there," a tall man said, stepping forward and gesturing to his left.

"It's down the hallway," Renalda said, her face twisted in concern.

Giorgio released her wrist and skirted the table. Rocky joined him as they jogged down the short hallway to a back door. Rocky slammed through the door, and they emerged into a dark space between the brick building and a large wooden shed. Rocky quickly checked the shed.

"Damn it! There's no one in there," he said, coming back out. "And the SUV is gone!"

"What are we going to do with her?" a voice sounded in Giorgio's earpiece.

Giorgio held out his hand to stop Rocky. He reached up to the receiver in his ear. Rocky stopped and listened.

"We'll meet up with Jackson," Cordova said. "He has a plan."

"C'mon," Giorgio commanded.

They hurried back inside just as Jeffrey Cook stepped out of a room dressed in black pants and a ruffled, white shirt. He hadn't yet donned the white wig. But his eyes opened wide at the sight of the two police officers.

"Detectives, what are you doing here?"

"What happened to Flame?" Rocky demanded as he shoved Cook up against the wall.

Samuel had followed Jeffrey into the hallway and stepped to his side. "Officer. You had better have a good reason for manhandling Mr. Cook." Rocky let go of Cook, and the big black man stepped in between Rocky and his employer.

"Where's the young woman you were about to initiate?" Rocky barked at him.

Both men looked at each other and then over to where Renalda stood with the others.

"She's disappeared," Renalda told them, rubbing her forearm. "I don't know where she went."

"Who brought her here?" Cook asked Renalda.

"Your brother's man," she replied. "The bald guy."

Cook inhaled sharply and turned to Giorgio. "I'm sorry. There's been some sort of mistake. I asked someone else to pick her up." He turned back to Renalda. "Where's Damien? He was supposed to get her."

The tall woman hunched her broad shoulders. "He never showed."

Cook seemed to teeter, and Samuel reached out to steady him.

"Where would your brother take her?" Giorgio demanded, pressing forward.

"I…I don't know," he said, shaking his head. "I'm not sure what's going on."

"Don't you? A young woman has just been kidnapped from *your* initiation ceremony," Rocky almost shouted at him.

"But I don't understand," Cook said. "Who is she? And why were you following her?"

"Because she was working with us," Giorgio said. "Now, where would your brother take her?"

"Honestly, I don't know. But I can't imagine he'd hurt her."

"Dammit!" Giorgio exclaimed. "He's had at least two people killed already. What's he's going to do with her?"

Cook just looked at Giorgio in silence, his face strained with an inner pain. Giorgio whirled around and started for the front door. "C'mon, Rocky. I have an idea where they might be taking her."

CHAPTER FORTY-ONE

The brothers scrambled into the car as the receiver on the dash burst to life.

"This is dangerous," a voice said.

"Don't worry. Jackson knows what he's doing. Just drive."

Giorgio roared down the dirt road, throwing up a cloud of dust and stones in his wake. He turned to his brother whose face was set in an angry stare.

"Listen, take Shadow and switch places with Swan when we get to the main road," Giorgio said to Rocky.

"Why?" Rocky almost growled.

"Because we're going into the canyon." Rocky glanced at him. "Jackson Cook didn't impress me as being too creative. I have a feeling they'll return to the scene of the last crime and use that to play this out."

"I hope you're right," Rocky mumbled.

"Listen, you keep saying that if you had a nickel for every one of my hunches," he said. "Trust me on this."

Giorgio bumped onto the two-lane paved road and screeched to a halt next to Swan's waiting sedan. As Rocky exited the car with Shadow on a leash, Giorgio rolled down his window.

"What's up, Joe?" Swan asked, leaning out his window.

"Jackson Cook has taken Flame."

"We didn't see anyone come out this way," Swan said.

"I'm sure there's another way in there. I think they're going into the canyon. I want you to switch places with Rocky and come with me."

Swan started to get out as Rocky waited to take his place. "Okay, but why? What are we doing?"

"Rocky will go with Drew to the lower canyon trail and hike up to the glen. You and I will go in from the top so we can box them in."

"But why the switch?" Swan asked, stepping aside for Rocky.

Rocky allowed Shadow to jump into the sedan next to McCready, who was on his phone before he slipped in behind the wheel.

"You don't know how to find the glen. Rocky does."

"Got it." Swan nodded and raced around the rear of the car to climb in next to Giorgio.

"Hey, Joe!" McCready called out. "Mulhaney just called. The DNA they got in Nagel's apartment on that broken glass belongs to a guy named Juan Mateo."

"Bingo!" A fire burned inside Giorgio's belly. He leaned towards his brother. "You'll have to hurry, Rocky. It's a longer trek in the way you're going."

"Copy that. Listen, Jo, keep listening to that receiver. We can't let her...," Rocky said, his face tense with worry.

"I know," Giorgio said. "We'll get to them in time."

Rocky nodded. "Okay. But what about Shadow?"

"Bring her with you. But keep her quiet."

A dubious expression etched its way across Rocky's face, but he nodded, gunned the engine, and took off.

Ten minutes later, Giorgio and Swan swung into the upper dirt parking lot above the glen, where the black SUV and one other car were parked.

"You were right," Swan said. "They're here."

"Yeah," was all Giorgio could muster. "Call for backup. But tell them to come in silent."

He got out and glanced up to the sliver of a moon that hung in the sky. There would be little light, especially once they got under the cover of the trees. A breeze tickled his neck as he leaned into the car to grab a flashlight from the glove compartment.

"You know, I've been up that creek bed, and it's slow going," Swan said.

"I know," Giorgio said, starting off on the well-worn path that would lead them to the glen. "We'll be playing this by ear. Hopefully, whatever Cook has in mind will take them awhile. But as you'll see, coming in from the top not only makes us sitting ducks because there's just one way in, it would allow them to take off down the canyon. That's why I have Rocky coming up the other way."

They grew quiet after that, communicating in whispers as they moved along the trail. The forest was still except for the occasional sound of rustling leaves as the breeze shifted through the trees above them. And since the small flashlight cut a narrow swathe of light through the darkness, they were forced to move slowly.

When they passed the cut off to the now abandoned dogfighting ring, Giorgio glanced that way, wondering again about Shadow and the role she was supposed to play. The thought of the gray pit bull brought a heaviness to his gut he couldn't explain. And the fact his hunches were usually right made it worse.

They pushed forward until the old house and small family graveyard loomed dark and ominous in the pale moonlight. Giorgio held out his hand to stop Swan and drew his weapon. Swan did the same. With a nod, Giorgio crept toward the old structure.

He stopped when they were close enough to peek through one of the cracked and weathered window frames. No sounds emanated from the dilapidated building, just the musty smell of dust motes, old piss, and rat droppings.

Muffled voices rose from the glen below.

Giorgio motioned Swan away from the building and to the edge of the hill overlooking the glen. They crouched down behind some bushes to view the activities below.

A lantern sat on one of the tree stumps bathing the surrounding area in a soft glow. Cordova approached the altar with Flame held in his arms. He was about to lay her down, face up. She was dressed in a long white gown, and her eyes were closed.

As Cordova placed her, Giorgio watched for movement. Her chest rose and fell, which meant she was still breathing. But she wasn't moving. *Had she been drugged?*

A few feet away stood Jackson Cook and Mateo. Mateo held a leash connected to a large black-and-tan Rottweiler who paced back and forth, staring off into the darkness.

"Shit," Giorgio murmured. "I don't know what they have planned but it doesn't look good."

"Is there a trail down there?" Swan whispered.

"Yeah, but we'll have to be careful not to be heard. Especially by that damned dog. The problem is that we can't just wait here. We're too far away to get a clean shot without rifles if it comes to that."

They left their hiding place and moved carefully back to the path, which switch-backed down the slope. Keeping the flashlight pointed to the ground, they descended the hill as quietly as possible, stopping every couple of minutes to listen for any reaction from the men below.

The Rottweiler barked a few times, which made them freeze. But the dog was shushed each time by the handler. When there was no further alarm, they continued until they were standing in between the two trees that marked the entrance to the path. It was the spot where the boy had hovered on the day Grosvenor was attacked by the mountain lion.

Giorgio took a deep breath and crept behind the boulders that flanked Nagel's now abandoned grave and gestured for Swan to follow. They were just a few feet from the altar where Flame lay unconscious.

"Why did we even bring her here?" Cordova asked. "Why not just kill her back at the Fortress?"

"I told you. I want it to look just like that other bitch's death," Cook responded.

"But won't that blow back on you? You're connected to the Society," Cordova countered.

"Right. But I'll have a solid alibi. My father. Jeffrey won't."

"You'd set up your own fucking brother?" the dog handler asked. "That's cold."

"Not him. His bodyguard. No one would believe Jeffrey could bring her here. But that black bastard? Absolutely."

"But one way or the other, Jeffrey will be implicated," Cordova said. "He's your own brother."

"Yes. But he doesn't have long to live anyway," Jackson said.

An unearthly screech cut through the night air, stilling the men's conversation. Giorgio's head swiveled toward the bluff as the Rottweiler began uncontrollable barking.

"Fucking shit! What the hell was that?" Mateo asked, his voice riddled with fear.

It was the cougar.

Giorgio turned to Swan. He made a gesture with his hand like the clawing motion of a cat. Swan nodded.

"Nothing. Ignore it," Cook finally replied. "Let's get this over with. Give her the second injection, and then I'll use this stupid contraption to puncture her neck and be done with it."

Giorgio's muscles clenched. They were out of time. It would be at least another five to ten minutes before Rocky and McCready would get there, which meant that he and Swan were alone against three men and a fighting dog.

He turned to Swan whose face was set in a grim mask. Giorgio gestured that he would circle around to the men's left flank and that he wanted Swan to go right.

Swan nodded and crept to his right, while Giorgio moved to the farthest boulder on his left. He crouched down and inched around the base of the big rock until he could see the three men illuminated by the glow of the lantern.

Cordova stood next to one of the logs that formed the seating area and was reaching into a leather bag. Cook had moved in next to Flame and was pulling something out of his pocket. Whatever it was, he pushed it into his mouth.

The essence device.

Mateo stood about ten feet to the right with the dog. The Rottweiler, however, continued to bark ferociously at the hillside, no doubt aware of the mountain lion's presence somewhere above them. Giorgio wondered what threat the cat posed. He doubted it would come anywhere near so many people, especially with the dog there. On the other hand, it had attacked Grosvenor for no reason. It could be injured or starving by now.

He watched the men, knowing that he had to wait until the last possible moment, giving Rocky and McCready enough time to get into position. But when Cordova took a syringe out of the leather bag and held up a small vial of what Giorgio assumed was the GHB, his time was up. Within seconds, Cordova had filled the syringe and dropped the vial back into the bag.

There was another almost plaintive yowl from the cat some distance away, which threw the Rottweiler into a frenzy.

Cook removed the essence device from his mouth. "Shit. What the hell is up there?" He stepped a few feet away from Flame and craned his neck to see to the top of the rise.

The men were all focused on that direction. The dog handler had even drawn a weapon and was struggling to hold the dog back as it lunged forward, yanking at the leash in his hand.

"Sounds like a big cat," Cordova said. "There are cougars up here. Bull wouldn't be reacting that way if it were human. He's after blood."

"Hold onto him," he said to the dog handler. "We need to finish up and get out of here."

Just then, the Rottweiler snapped the leash and broke free. He burst forward, scrambling up the hill in an instant, crashing into the underbrush at the top.

One down, Giorgio thought.

"You fucking idiot!" Cook yelled at Mateo. "Bull's our best dog. Damn it! Okay, hurry up!" he said to Cordova.

Cordova reached out to hand him the syringe. Giorgio blew out a nervous breath, straightened up and stepped out from behind the boulder with his weapon drawn.

"Stop. Or I'll drop you where you are," he said in a low voice.

Mateo whipped around, pointing his gun at Giorgio. Cordova quickly pulled one of his own.

"Careful, muchachos," Swan said, appearing at the other end of the boulders. "Guns down," he said, aiming his at the dog handler.

The four men were in a standoff, while Cook watched the situation play out with a smile on his face.

"Well, well, well," he said, eyeing Giorgio. "If it isn't the intrepid Sierra Madre police."

As he talked, he inched back towards Flame's head.

"Drop the syringe," Giorgio said to Cordova. "I won't say it again."

The big bald man lifted his hands in submission and dropped the syringe back into the bag.

"Now, back away from the bag." Cordova did as he was told. "Drop the guns and get on the ground, both of you."

An ear-splitting screech made everyone jerk in the direction of the hillside. A second later, a bullet clipped Giorgio's gun, sending it into the grass. Swan felled the dog handler with a bullet to the shoulder. Giorgio rounded on Cook, intent on retrieving his gun, but Cook had backed up next to Flame's head with a small knife held to her throat. He was staring at Swan.

"Put the gun down, Detective," Cook said in a chillingly calm voice. "I've gutted dozens of dogs with this knife and can end her life in an instant."

Swan's gaze shifted to Giorgio, who nodded for Swan to comply. Swan dropped the gun.

How quickly the tables could turn, Giorgio thought to himself, his fingers stinging from the impact of the bullet.

"Now, both of you over here," Cook said, gesturing to the fire pit.

As Giorgio and Swan moved cautiously with their hands up, Cordova stepped over and picked up Swan's gun and stuck it into his belt. He then picked up his own.

The two officers turned towards the firepit with their backs to the path that led up from the creek bed. The five men now formed a triangle of sorts. Cook stood next to Flame. At the apex were Giorgio and Swan. And at the farthest point were Cordova and Mateo, who was struggling to his feet, holding his shoulder. Even though,, Mateo picked up his gun and pointed it limply at Swan.

In the background, the snarling dog and screaming cat engaged in battle, raising the hairs on Giorgio's neck. Cook, however, seemed content to let that drama play itself out, while he orchestrated the one in front of him.

"You realize you'll all have to die, now," Cook said with a weird sense of calm. "The question is, who first?" He looked down at Flame and stroked her cheek. "Too bad about the girl. She's pretty."

A rage built inside Giorgio at the thought Flame might lose her life to this bastard. He glanced around and saw the butt of his gun buried in the tall grass hallway between him and Cook. Giorgio contemplated his situation. He would have one opportunity to go for the gun. But he needed to signal Swan, who would be faced with the other two men. Just then, the Rottweiler re-appeared on the scene, closing the opportunity.

The big dog was limping, and blood slipped out the side of his mouth. Blood also ran down one shoulder, and he had gashes in his side. But he was the victor. The cat had either disappeared or was lying dead somewhere in the forest.

"Bull, come here," Cook ordered, slapping his thigh.

The big dog limped over to its owner, its muscles glistening under a sheen of sweat and blood. Cook cupped the dog's rock-hard head in his big hand.

"Good boy, Bull. You never let me down." The dog lowered his head, leaning against Cook's leg, accepting the attention. Cook lifted his gaze to Giorgio and Swan. His eyes narrowed and an evil grin spread across his face as a thought went through his head. "You know, I think I've changed my mind. Shooting the two of you would raise too many questions. I have a better idea." He glanced down at the dog and then over to Cordova and Mateo. "Want some fun, boys?"

Cordova began to chuckle. "Mincemeat," he murmured.

A jolt of electricity streaked through Giorgio's body. Cook meant to sick the dog on them.

Where the hell was Rocky?

"There are others who know we're up here," Giorgio said to Cook. "You'll be caught."

"Not me," Cook said. "My brother will take the fall. For everything. You see, I have this." He pulled the red cravat worn by Samuel at the murder game out of his pocket. "The gong master will go down for this and take Jeffrey with him. Too bad, really. I don't dislike my brother, but he's a dead man walking, anyway. And we'll make it look like the cat got to the two of you."

"What about the drug smuggling? The Feds are onto you," Giorgio said, knowing he had to stall.

"Oh, we'll just move operations like we have in the past. In fact, that is what my father and I discussed at breakfast yesterday," he said with a smile. "You know when you visited me? We decided it was time to move the entire operation, medical practice and all."

"So, you're done fleecing vulnerable patients here, then?" Giorgio said, stalling again.

He chuckled. "So, you knew about that, too. Yes, poor Lindsey figured out about our little Medicare scheme. So did Kent, I'm afraid.. But we had been talking about pulling up stakes for a while now. It's not good to stay too long in one place when you're scamming the federal government. They tend to look unkindly on things like that."

"But why kill her? Couldn't you have just deflected her? Gotten her to focus on something else?"

Giorgio angled himself so that he could glance back towards the path that came up from the creek bed, hoping that Rocky might be out there somewhere.

"I suppose," Cook said, stroking Flame's cheek. "But Lindsey was smart. Too smart. Just like this one."

A light flickered in the canyon below, and Giorgio's heart raced. It had to be Rocky and McCready getting closer.

He turned to Cook, hoping to stall another couple of minutes. That's when a mist began to gather a few feet behind Cook. Giorgio watched, transfixed, knowing it wasn't the weather. It was the boy. *But how in the world could he help?* Christian might have thrown things before, but could he wield a knife or shoot a gun?

"You. Move over there," Cook said, bringing Giorgio's attention back.

Cook had gestured for Swan to separate himself from Giorgio. Swan glanced at Giorgio and then moved several steps away from him. Whether that meant Cook was setting Swan up for the dog or him, Giorgio didn't know. Right now, he was focused on the mist, hoping against hope the boy would cause a disruption long enough to allow Rocky to get there.

When Swan stopped moving though, Cook glanced at Giorgio and smiled. "Too bad for you, Detective. Bull. Attack!" he shouted, making a hand gesture toward Giorgio.

The Rottweiler spun around and leapt forward with a vicious growl; teeth barred. Giorgio threw himself backwards, tripping over the firepit and landing on his back. With horror, he watched the Rottweiler come at him just as a gray projectile emerged from the shadows to slam into the Rottweiler's side, sending the muscular dog into the grass.

Shadow!

The Rottweiler was on its feet in a second, and the two dogs raged at each other in a vicious fight to the death. Giorgio's lungs seemed incapable of drawing breath as he sat up and scuttled out of the way, watching helplessly as the dogs tore into each other.

"Shoot the bitch!" Cook screamed to Cordova.

Cordova leveled his gun at the dogs but hesitated as they rolled and twisted, ripping into each other's flesh. Giorgio glanced at Cook, who was fixated on the dog fight, giving him the opportunity to crab-walk sideways until his hand brushed against the butt of his gun.

He and Swan shared a cautious glance. Giorgio nodded, and Swan turned abruptly and felled Mateo with a single blow.

Cordova was taken by surprise and spun around to aim his gun at Swan, but Giorgio grabbed his weapon and shot Cordova in the hip, bringing the bald man to one knee.

"Stop!" Cook bellowed.

Everyone froze. Giorgio kept his gun pointed at Cordova from where he sat in the grass, but eyed Cook who held the knife at Flame's throat again. A trickle of blood had begun to slip behind her ear.

"I swear, I'll do it."

There was a sharp yelp, and heads snapped around. The dog fight was over. The Rottweiler lay motionless, as a pool of blood spread slowly across the grass beneath its throat.

"Fuck that dog!" Cook bellowed.

Shadow's sides heaved as she turned to face Cook, her muscles twitching, her normally placid eyes glittering. Blood covered half her face, and her front shoulder bled from an open wound. But she was focused on Cook as if he were a prized piece of meat.

Cook went still, staring back at the pit bull, the boy's mist hovering behind him. When the pit bull didn't move, Cook's muscles tensed, and real fear appeared in those once arrogant eyes. He knew that regardless of what he did to Flame, the pit bull would crush his throat.

Without warning, Shadow bolted.

Cook gasped and stepped back as the dog left the ground, her powerful jaws reaching for him. He held out the knife in a weak attempt to protect himself, but Shadow took him down behind the altar, her growls echoing across the glen.

Giorgio's heart raced. He turned to Cordova, but Cordova had already dropped his gun and was doubled over in pain. Giorgio had twisted an ankle when he fell and had trouble getting to a standing position. Once he was upright, he nodded to Swan, who had scooped up Cordova's gun and stood guard over the two wounded men.

Giorgio hobbled toward the altar, hoping to call Shadow off. When the dog yelped in pain, he froze, his heart faltering.

The glen went quiet.

Seconds ticked by.

And then, like something out of a horror movie, Jackson Cook appeared from behind the altar, streaks of blood smeared across his face and neck, one eye socket ripped open and bleeding profusely.

A lopsided grin appeared, and once again, he brought the knife up, now dripping with Shadow's blood, and placed it against Flame's throat. Cook erupted in a maniacal laugh as he pulled himself to a standing position, the boy's mist closing in behind him.

"Well, that's over. A life for a life, right, Detective?" he said, gesturing to Bull's lifeless body. As Cook's chest rose and fell, the mist wrapped around his shoulders, moving forward to hover over Flame. Cook seemed unaware of it and looked down at her. "It's time to finish this."

As the tip of the knifed touched her skin, Flame's eyes popped open, and she sucked in a huge intake of breath, pulling the mist deep into her lungs.

"What the…?" Cook erupted, pulling back in shock.

The petite brunette suddenly swung her legs around and sat up facing Cook. Her right hand swept out and grabbed Cook's wrist in a vise-like grip, her fingers digging into his flesh. His eyes opened wide, and he tried to pull away. But it was as if she had the strength of ten men.

A noise made Giorgio turn. Rocky and McCready appeared out of the darkness with their weapons drawn. Giorgio put up a hand, and the two men halted.

"It's over, Cook," Giorgio said, turning back.

But Jackson Cook couldn't hear him. Flame's eyes had him locked in a trance. Blood appeared from where her nails bit into his skin, and he began to gasp for air.

And then it happened.

Flame produced the dog tag in her left hand and lifted it up so that Cook could see it. His eyes tracked the metal disc as she reached over and slapped it against the back of his hand. The metal seared his flesh, as a curl of smoke drifted into the night air. He began to writhe and scream in pain.

Giorgio's stomach turned as Cook's dark eyes glazed over and then rolled up into his eye sockets. Slowly, his body began to shake, his muscles flexed, and his entire body went rigid.

Jackson Cook gulped a final, sickening breath before Flame released his wrist, and he slumped to the ground.

CHAPTER FORTY-TWO

The four police officers stared at the scene before them in stunned silence. Then, Giorgio snapped to attention and called to his brother.

"Help Flame."

Rocky swung into action, while Giorgio hobbled to where Shadow lay on the ground behind the altar, blood pulsing from an open wound in her neck. His throat closed around an anguished cry, as he knelt beside her.

He slapped his hand over her neck, hoping to stem the flow of blood, but he knew it was too late. Cook had hit the carotid artery, and the little dog had seconds to live.

He reached out and stroked her head, tears streaming down his cheek.

"I'm so sorry, Shadow," he whispered. "You're such a good dog."

Her small gray eyes blinked at him, and she tried to rise, panting heavily.

"No," he shushed her, holding her down. "No, your fight is over. And you won, Shadow. We're all safe because of you," he whispered, choking on a sob.

A light glimmered next to Giorgio. The image of Christian Maynard appeared inches away. Giorgio flinched back, having never been this close to the boy before. Christian was staring at the dog and reached out a nearly transparent hand to place it on top of Giorgio's where it rested on Shadow's head. Giorgio felt a cool rush of energy flow through his fingers.

He glanced down at Shadow, whose eyes were watching the boy now. She had stopped panting and just stared at Christian. Shadow blinked once, as if communicating with the boy. And then, her gray eyes closed, and she was gone.

A moment later, the image of Christian Maynard faded, and Giorgio was left alone with an overwhelming sense of grief.

÷

Six officers arrived on the scene a few minutes later, and Rocky took charge to have them cordon off the area and take custody of Cordova and Mateo. The ME was called to remove the body of Jackson Cook. And forensics was called to process everything.

Meanwhile, Giorgio sat on one of the logs through all of it feeling like a dead battery. He stared for some time at Shadow lying lifeless in the grass wondering if she had gone with the boy somehow. He liked to think so. He wanted to think of her living pain free wherever the boy existed.

When the medical examiner arrived, he also took charge of both dogs' bodies. After all, they were part of a crime scene. And Shadow had attacked Cook. But when the investigation was over, Giorgio would ask for Shadow to be cremated so that her ashes could be scattered in their backyard. He dreaded the conversation he would have to have this time with the kids. And as he stared at her scarred and battered body, he wondered if he had made the right decision to bring her. *Had this been another time when he could have done it alone?*

He would probably never know. What he did know was that she had shown the bravery and tenacity of a dog ten times her size. And it was her bravery that had saved both he and Flame.

÷

The medical examiner ruled Jackson Cook's death a heart attack caused by stress. No one commented on the fact that he had never reported a heart condition prior to that time. And there was no explanation for the oddly shaped burn mark on the back of his hand, partly because the dog tag was never found.

Flame had no lingering affect from the initial injection of GHB they had dosed her with at the Fortress, other than a headache.

No one, not even Cordova or the dog handler, mentioned anything about the mist. Giorgio wasn't even sure they had seen it. In fact, Flame had no memory of anything that happened to her after she was drugged that night.

So, in the end, everyone's story seemed to match–Jackson Cook held a knife to Flame's throat and when she awoke, she sat up and grasped his wrist. Since he had already been compromised by the fight with Shadow, the pressure of her grip seemed to cause him enough distress to trigger a heart attack.

Cordova and Mateo blamed everything that happened that night on Jackson and agreed to testify against his father, who was the kingpin of the drug smuggling ring.

Giorgio called Agent Robertson and turned over the flash drive. And the DA resisted charging Craig Velchy with obstruction since it was only because he had dug up the body and made it visible that anyone had even known she died.

÷

It was several days later that Giorgio and Rocky visited Lindsey Nagel's mother. Her sister, Carey, was also there.

There was no smell of freshly baked cookies this time. It seemed as if Mrs. Nagel had finally dealt with the death of her daughter, and things were back to a new normal.

She sat in the same chair she had when they had visited her the first time, but she looked older. And sadder.

"You say you caught whoever killed my Lindsey," she said.

"Yes, ma'am," Giorgio replied. "At first we thought it had something to do with a vampire cult she got involved with, but in the end, they only used that as a cover. It was because she was trying to do the right thing. She'd uncovered a case of Medicare fraud at the clinic where she worked, and she shared that knowledge with the wrong person."

Mrs. Nagel dropped her head, drawing out a tissue to wipe her nose. "That's my Lindsey," she murmured. "Honest to a fault."

"And the person who killed her is dead?" Carey asked.

"Well, the person who gave the order to kill her is dead," Giorgio clarified. "But the man who administered the drug that killed her will go to jail for a very long time. And that's not all. Because of the investigation into Lindsey's death, we were able to end both an illegal dogfighting ring and a drug smuggling operation."

"So, she didn't die in vain," Mrs. Nagel said, her eyes hopeful.

"No," Giorgio said. "You daughter was a hero, Mrs. Nagel. For all her fears and phobias, she showed real courage in the end. She gathered evidence to prove what she knew to be true. In fact, the entire clinic has been shut down until a full investigation can be done."

"You can be proud of your daughter," Rocky added. "And…just so you know, she wasn't in any pain when she died. She had taken Xanax to calm her nerves, which they knew she would do. Then, they administered a second drug. It was the combination of the drugs that killed her."

Mrs. Nagel nodded her head. "Thank you. For everything."

When they were finished, Carey walked them to their car, her hands stuffed into the pockets of her jeans.

"You know, I loved my sister," she said, tears filling the corners of her eyes. "But growing up gay in a world that catered to a sister with a multitude of phobias wasn't easy. I felt invisible. I never felt like my struggles were as important as hers. So, I just swallowed them. I won't deny that I felt a strange sense of relief when she died. I know that sounds awful because I really did love her. But I thought that now, just maybe, my mom would pay attention to me the way she did to Lindsey." She reached up to whisk away a tear.

"We all carry burdens," Giorgio said. "It sounds like you were there for your sister when she needed you. Don't forget that. Now, you'll need to be there for your mother."

CHAPTER FORTY-THREE

It was two weeks later when Giorgio stepped through his front door one night and was greeted by a small dog that looked like a cross between a Dachshund and a Chihuahua. The dog came to a sliding halt at his feet barkng at him, its short, little legs bouncing up and down on the hardwood floor.

"Who the heck are you?" he asked, stepping back.

"That's Ginger," Angie said. She had appeared from the hallway, an apron hugging her slim frame. "I happened to be checking Craig's List for a shelf unit for the bedroom and came across an ad giving her away for free."

"And so, you adopted her?"

"Well, no," she said.

He looked up. "What do you mean?"

Grosvenor lumbered into the entryway from the den, where the kids were probably studying. His wounds had healed, leaving ugly scars that Giorgio hoped would eventually be covered by fur. But the Basset hound dropped his head as he came in for a greeting, his tail thumping.

Giorgio leaned down and reached out with his right hand to pet Grosvenor, while he let the new dog sniff his left hand, its long body wiggling back and forth like an undulating snake.

"Well, yes, I did technically adopt her," Angie said. "But not really."

He straightened up. "What are you talking about, Angie?"

She gave him a quick half smile. "*We're* going to find her a home." And with that, she turned and went back into the kitchen.

He threw his coat onto the chair against the wall and followed her, the two dogs following him.

"Angie, what the heck are you talking about? What do you mean *we're* going to find her a home? Why'd you adopt her if you don't want to keep her?"

She turned to him as she approached the stove, where she had something cooking in a large pot. His nostrils filled with the tangy aroma of tomato sauce, garlic, and onions.

"What's for dinner?"

"One question at a time. Do you want to keep her?"

He glanced down at the little dog who was now sitting at his feet, a look of expectation on her black and brown face.

"Um…no. I don't think so. But I don't get it."

"You said it yourself. Those dogfighting rings look for small dogs that are offered for free on Craigslist to use them as bait dogs. I saw this little girl who was being offered for free and thought…no way." She turned around and began to stir the sauce. "And, we're having spaghetti."

"With meatballs?"

She sighed in exasperation. "Of course, with meatballs. Now, take her outside before we eat. And, then get the kids."

He did as he was told and took both dogs into the backyard. It was a clear night, and the air was crisp. As Grosvenor visited his favorite bushes and lifted his leg, Ginger trotted right behind him.

A heaviness settled in Giorgio's chest as he watched them, thinking about Shadow and the first time he had brought her into the yard. Back then, he questioned her temperament and whether he should even have her around the kids. And, yet, she had not only been a perfect house guest, she had proven her worth by saving both Grosvenor and Flame, and protected Angie from an intruder.

He swallowed hard, pushing down the emotion that caught him unaware at the memories. Stuffing his hands into the pockets of his slacks, he focused on Grosvenor, judging how he moved and if there were any lingering effects from his injuries.

As Grosvenor ambled over to the big oak tree, the glimmer that appeared under the tree made Giorgio step back.

It was the boy, dressed in the same dark knickers and white shirt and suspenders. But this time, something was different. A second image appeared next to him. Smaller. And less distinct. But recognizable.

Shadow!

"Oh, shit," Giorgio whispered to himself. He inhaled a deep breath to calm his insides.

Shadow's image flickered in the low light, much like the boy's did. She looked up at Giorgio, those gray eyes merely dark shadows now. But her tail wagged as it had before, swinging her rear end back and forth. She was happy to see him.

He dropped into a crouching position, his elbows resting on his knees, a feeling of light-headedness overtaking him. He took several cleansing breaths to help focus his mind. When he glanced up, the boy and the dog were only a few feet in front of him. He reached out a hand toward Shadow. The dog moved forward and leaned in, panting happily. He attempted to pet her, but he could only feel a cool sensation on his hand.

Giorgio looked up at the boy. Christian pointed to the dog and nodded once. Giorgio swallowed. He understood.

He stood up and nodded back. "Thank you," he whispered. "Take care of her. She's a good dog."

The boy seemed to smile, and then the two images faded, leaving just the brisk night air behind.

The sob that bubbled up in his throat erupted before he could quell it, and he stood for a moment taking shuddering breaths. They were gone. Whether that was to the netherworld or another dimension, he had no idea. All he knew was that Shadow was safe now, and happy. And that's all he cared about.

He allowed himself another minute to gain his composure and then called for Grosvenor and Ginger. They followed him into the kitchen, where the kids sat on opposite sides of the small Formica table.

Tony had been unusually quiet since Shadow's death. The only question he'd asked when Giorgio told him how brave the pit bull had been was, "Why couldn't we have found her a home first?"

There was no answer for that. All Giorgio could do was wrap his arms around his son and hold him while the boy cried.

Tonight, however, there was a new light in his son's eyes. The boy reached down to pet Ginger and said, "Did Mom tell you, Dad? We're going to help rescue abandoned dogs. I think it's cool."

As Giorgio rolled up his sleeves to wash his hands, he shot his wife an understanding look. *So, that's what she was doing.* He had tried to right the wrong when she lost their baby by setting the house up as a childcare center. Now, she was trying to do the same thing for him. It was her way of helping him heal.

She smiled at him from across the kitchen, her eyes glistening with tears as she brought the bowl of spaghetti to the table. He finished up at the sink and then turned to his family.

"So, who's Ginger sleeping with tonight?" he asked. "Cuz, she sure as hell ain't sleeping with me."

THE END

AUTHOR'S NOTES

I grew up in Sierra Madre, which is the setting for the Detective Giorgio Salvatori books. It is a charming community that sits at the base of the San Gabriel Mountains, flanked by the cities of Pasadena, Arcadia, and Monrovia. I have the fondest memories of hiking the grounds around the Mater Dolorosa Retreat Center near my home (the setting for "Mass Murder"), driving past the Pinney House, (the setting for "Murder In The Past Tense") and hiking in Bailey Canyon, the setting for this book. But there are many more landmarks in the area, such as the Wistaria Vine (one of the 7 horticultural wonders of the world according to Guinness Book of World Records), the statue of the Violin Spider in the community park, and downtown Sierra Madre (setting for the Invasion of the Body Snatchers, 1956), all of which may serve as the setting for upcoming books. Stay tuned.

About Dogfighting

As a dog lover and someone who helps to rescue dogs, this was a hard book for me to write. After all, I can't stand to see any animals hurt. But I decided in my Old Maids of Mercer Island books to use them as soft platforms to explore social issues that need attention. And I thought that perhaps I could do that with this book as well. Two things: pit bulls do get a bad rap. And for a longtime it was from me. I was deathly afraid of all pit bulls. That is, until I started watching videos from a dog rescue group in Southern California that often saves abandoned pit bulls. I fell in love with some of these dogs. One that especially touched my heart was a gray female that had obviously been in a lot of fights. She was lost and alone on the streets of Los Angeles and looking for even the tiniest bit of attention. I decided to use her as the role model for Shadow. The good news–she did find a good home.

The second, and more important point, is how dogfighting rings find and use unwanted dogs for their dogfighting operations. They really do troll Craigslist and other sites to find dogs being given up for free. The rescue group I work with purposely does the same thing. But they go in and rescue the dog, find it a foster home, and eventually find it a forever home. I am often that foster home. The message here is…don't EVER offer up an animal for free. You have no idea what that person who comes calling has in mind for that poor animal.

Thank you so very much for reading *The Essence of Murder*. If you enjoyed this book, I would be honored if you would go back to Amazon.com and leave an honest review. I do read them. We "indie" authors thrive on reviews and word-of-mouth advertising. This will help position the book so that more people might also enjoy it. Thank you so much!

About the Author

Ms. Bohart holds a master's degree in theater, has been published in Woman's World, and has a story in *Dead on Demand*, an anthology of ghost stories that remained on the Library Journal's best seller list for six months. She did a short stint writing for Patch.com, teaches writing through the Continuing Education Program at Green River College, and wrote a monthly column for the Renton Reporter. She is also a common speaker at nonprofit conferences and has presented writing workshops as part of the Seattle Film Summit. As a thirty-year nonprofit professional, she now owns her own freelance writing company, Lil Dog Communications, and writes for individuals and nonprofits all over the world. *The Essence of Murder* is the third book in her Detective Giorgio Salvatori mystery series. She is also the author of the popular Old Maids of Mercer Island mystery series. Her entire list of books can be found on Amazon.com.

Follow Ms. Bohart

Website: www.lynnbohart-author.com
Twitter: @lbohart
Facebook: Facebook @ L.Bohart/author

www.ingramcontent.com/pod-product-compliance
Lightning Source LLC
Chambersburg PA
CBHW071258170626
46809CB00001B/268